MAKING FRIENDS

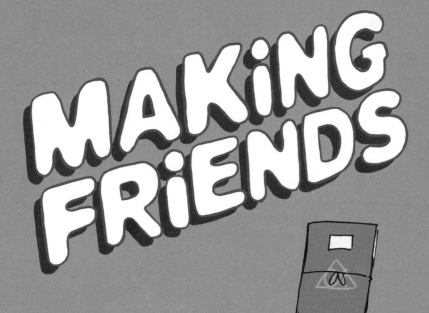

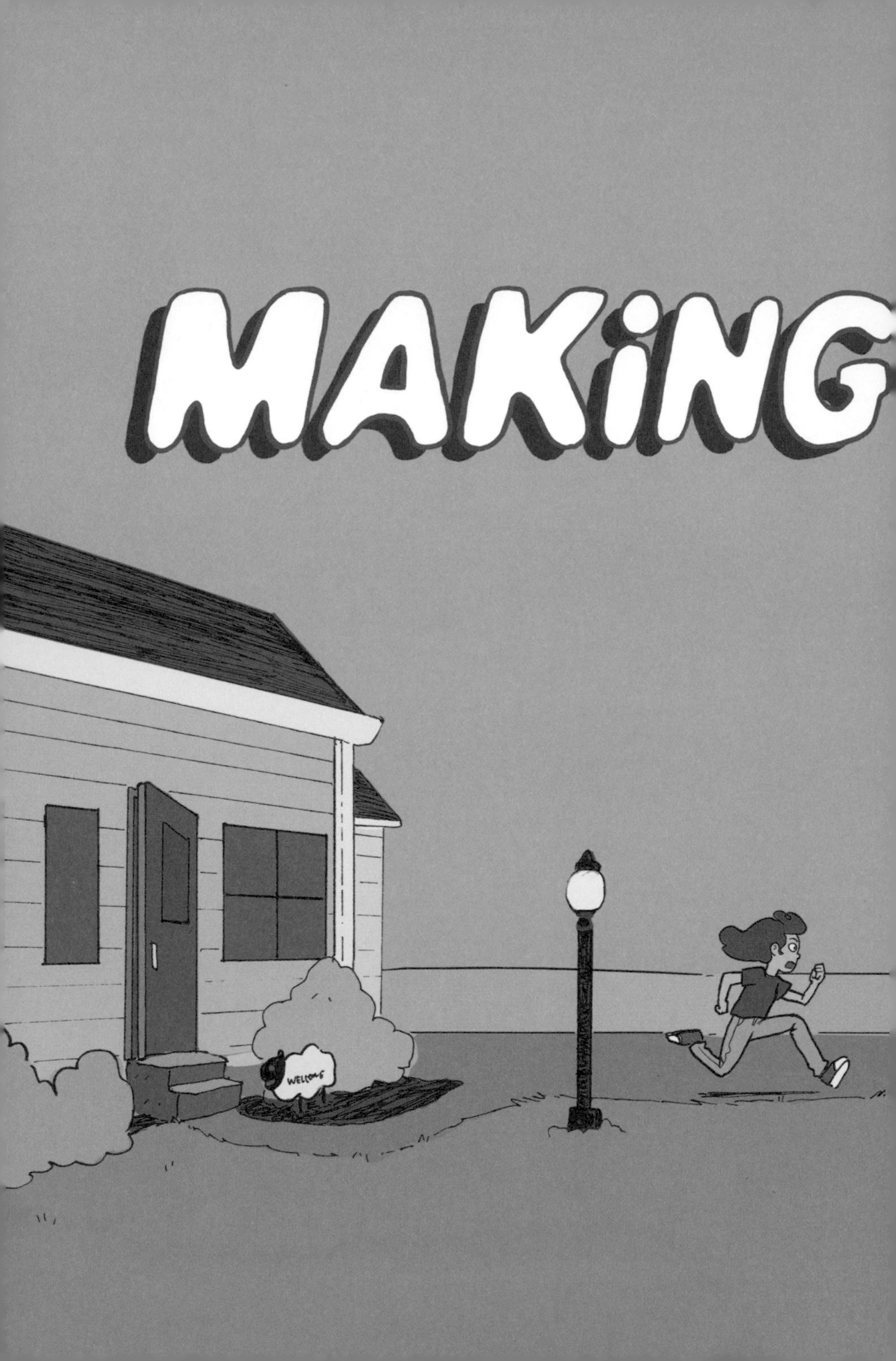
MAKiNG

FRiENDS

BY KRISTEN GUDSNUK

An Imprint of
SCHOLASTIC

Library of Congress Control Number: 2017953347

ISBN 978-1-338-13922-8 (hardcover)
ISBN 978-1-338-13921-1 (paperback)

10 9 8 7   20 21 22

Printed in China   62
First edition, August 2018
Edited by Adam Rau
Book design by Phil Falco
Creative Director: David Saylor

 To Penny.

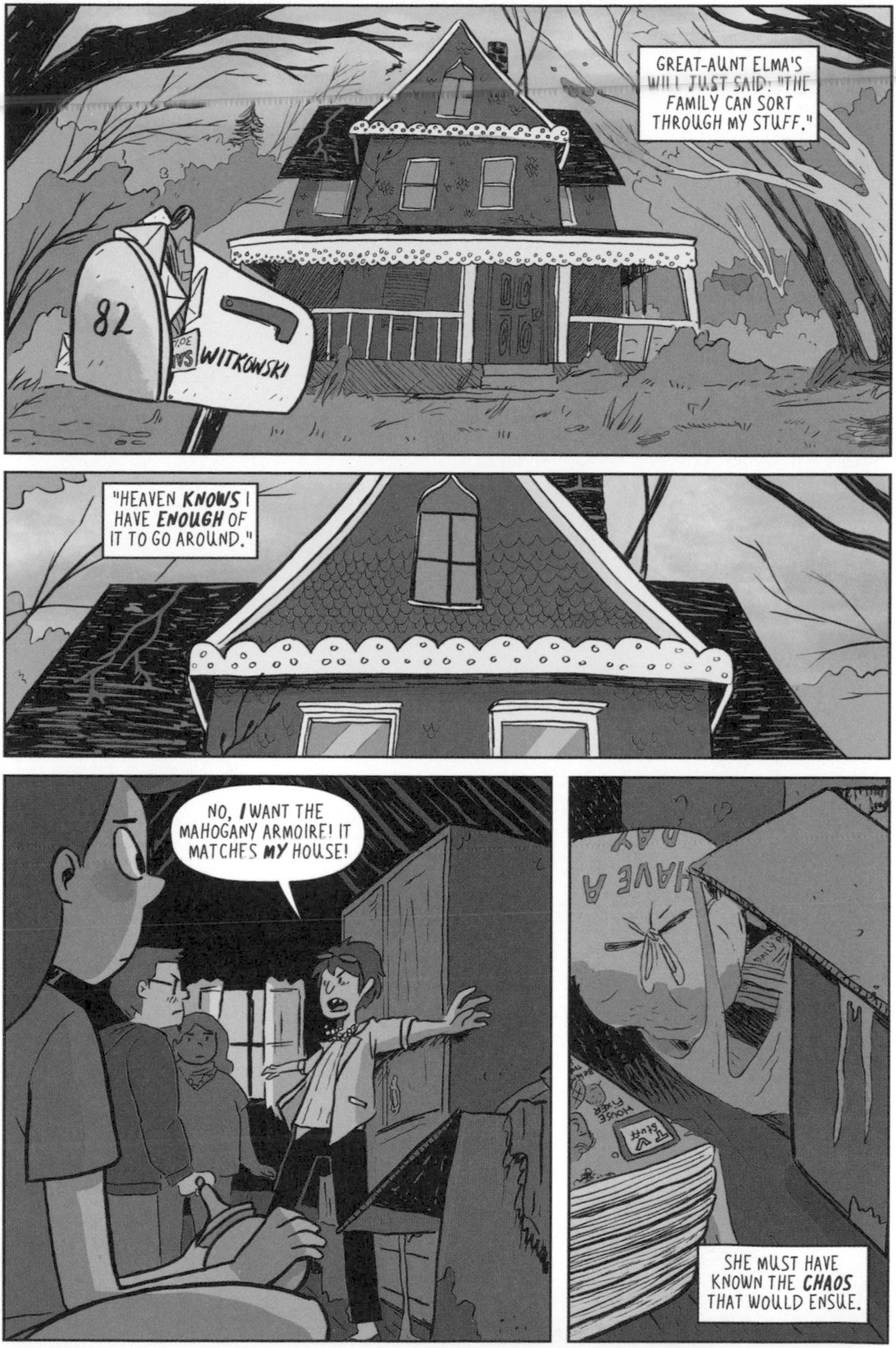
GREAT-AUNT ELMA'S WILL JUST SAID: "THE FAMILY CAN SORT THROUGH MY STUFF."
82
WITKOWSKI
"HEAVEN KNOWS I HAVE ENOUGH OF IT TO GO AROUND."
NO, I WANT THE MAHOGANY ARMOIRE! IT MATCHES MY HOUSE!
SHE MUST HAVE KNOWN THE CHAOS THAT WOULD ENSUE.

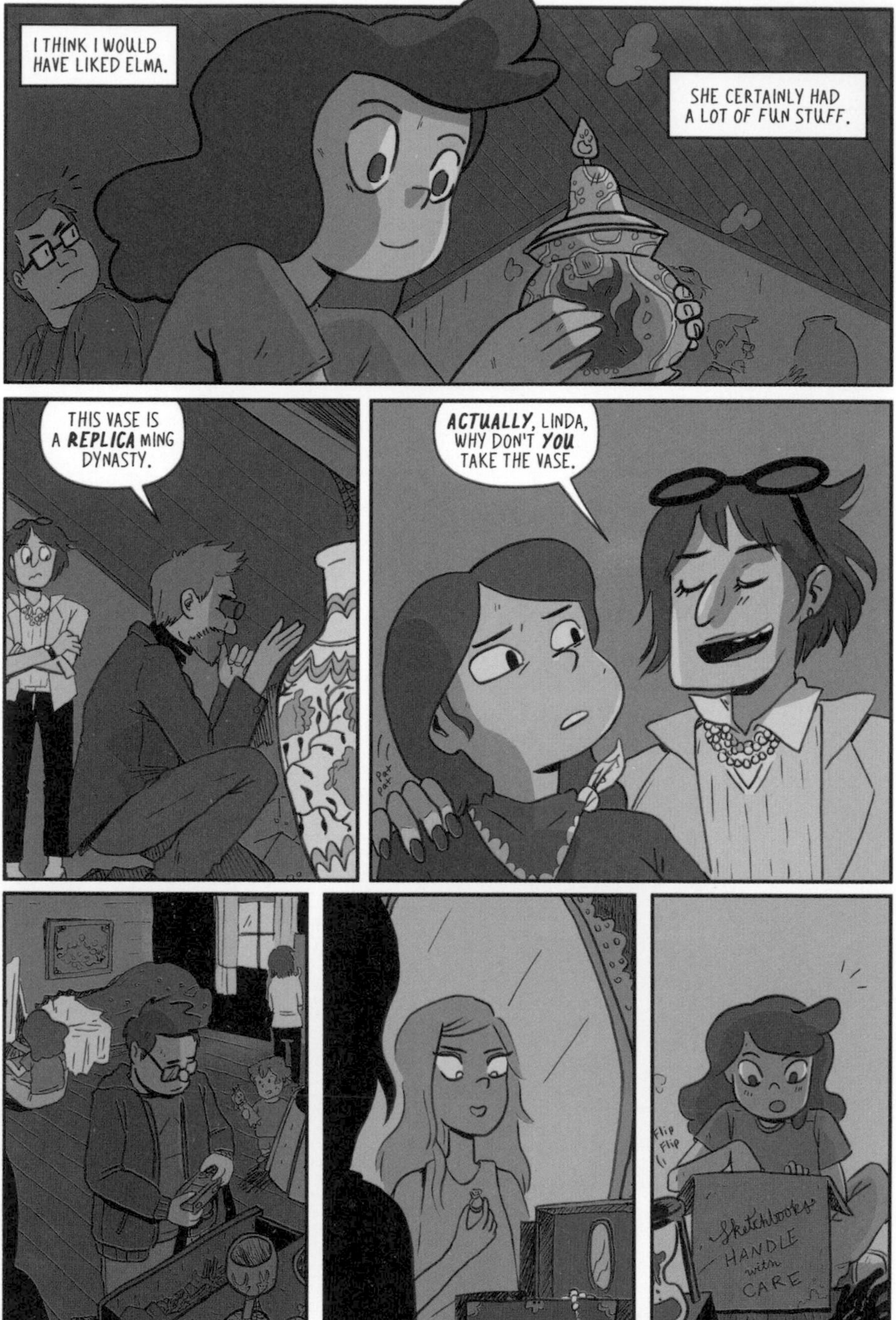
I THINK I WOULD HAVE LIKED ELMA.
SHE CERTAINLY HAD A LOT OF FUN STUFF.
THIS VASE IS A REPLICA MING DYNASTY.
ACTUALLY, LINDA, WHY DON'T YOU TAKE THE VASE.
Pat pat
Flip Flip
Sketchbooks HANDLE with CARE

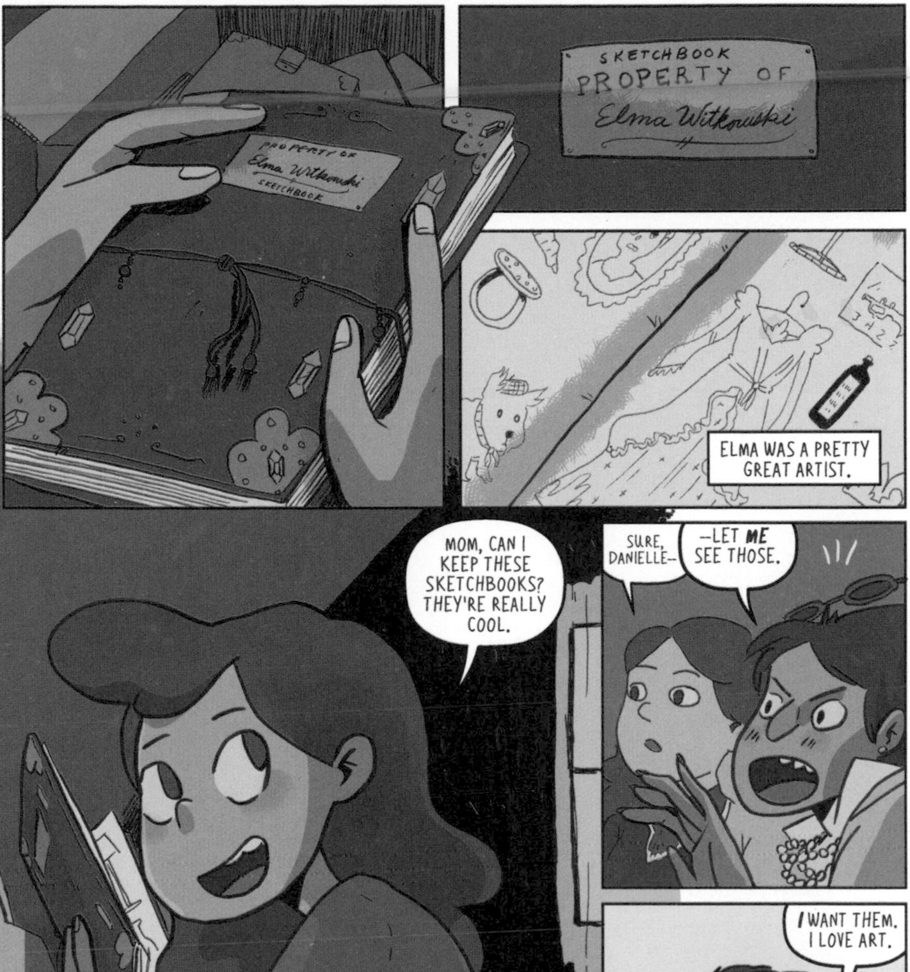
PROPERTY OF
Elma Witkowski
SKETCHBOOK
SKETCHBOOK
PROPERTY OF
Elma Witkowski
ELMA WAS A PRETTY GREAT ARTIST.
MOM, CAN I KEEP THESE SKETCHBOOKS? THEY'RE REALLY COOL.
SURE, DANIELLE--
--LET ME SEE THOSE.
I WANT THEM. I LOVE ART.

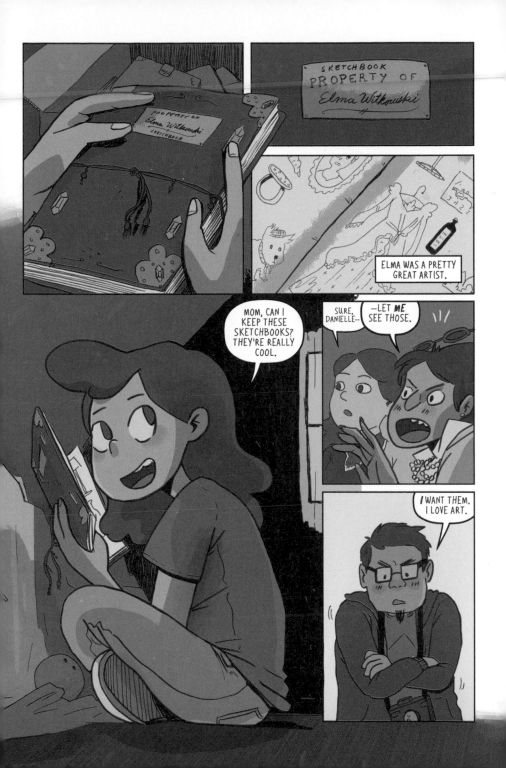

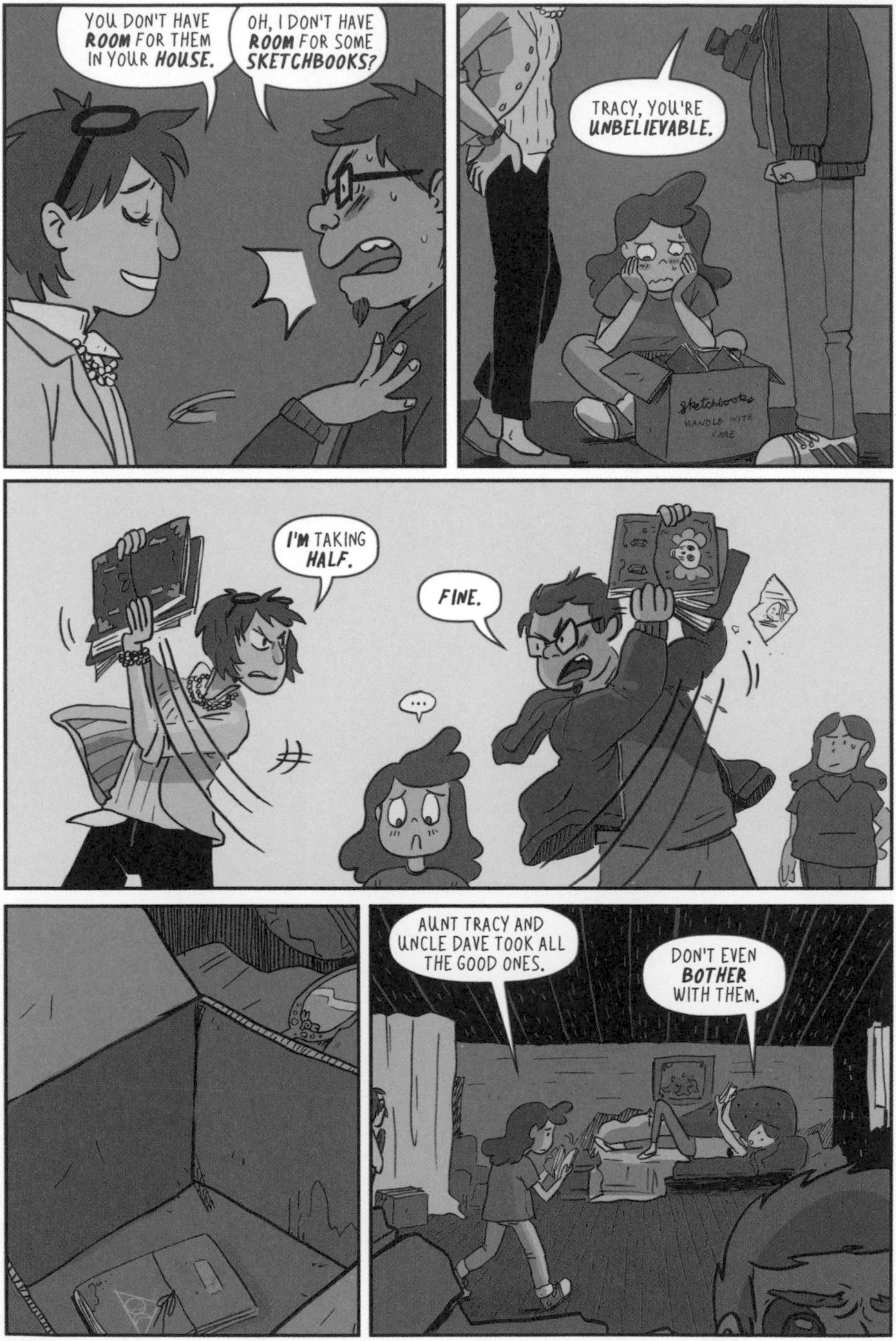

YOU DON'T HAVE **ROOM** FOR THEM IN YOUR **HOUSE.**
OH, I DON'T HAVE **ROOM** FOR SOME **SKETCHBOOKS?**
TRACY, YOU'RE **UNBELIEVABLE.**
SKETCHBOOKS HANDLE WITH CARE
I'M TAKING **HALF.**
FINE.
...
AUNT TRACY AND UNCLE DAVE TOOK ALL THE GOOD ONES.
DON'T EVEN **BOTHER** WITH THEM.

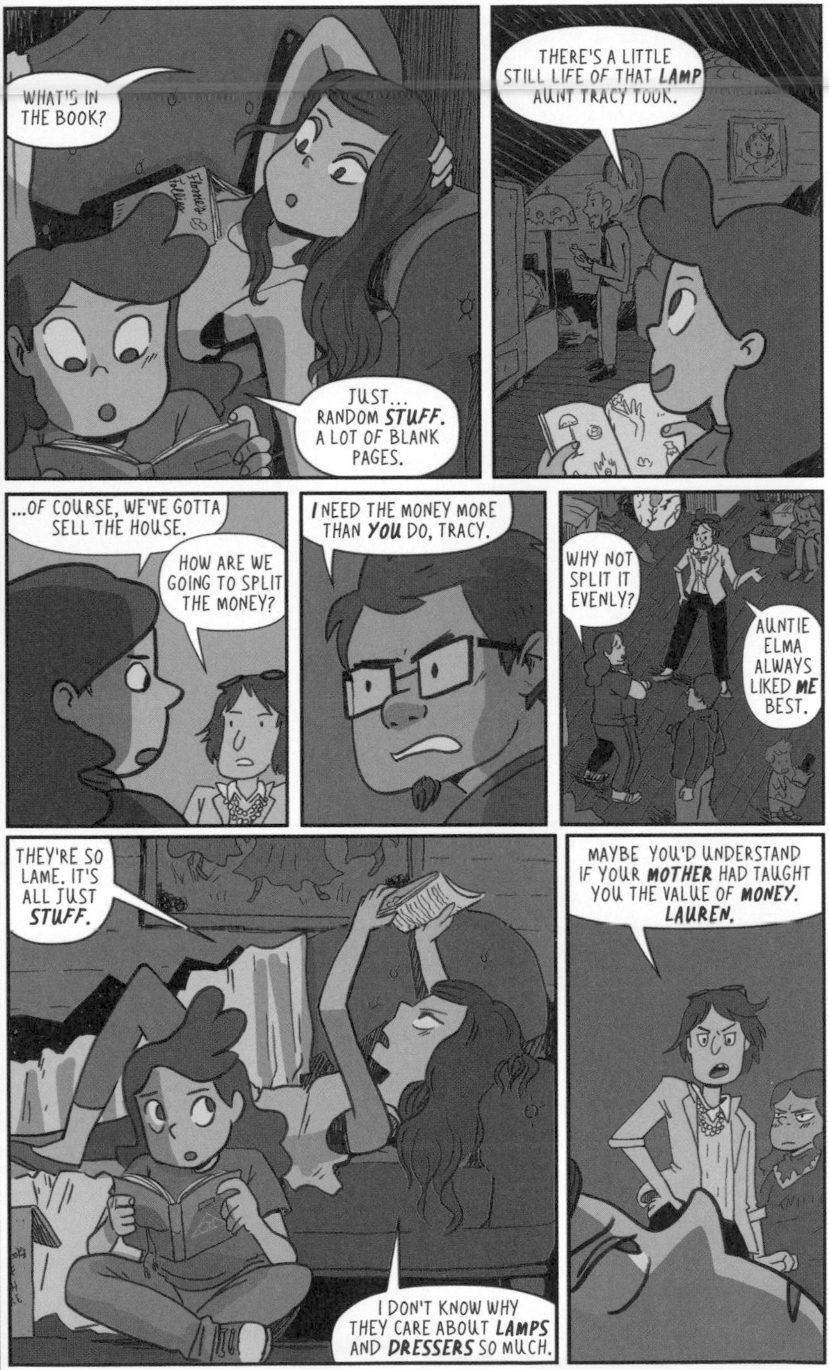
WHAT'S IN THE BOOK?
JUST... RANDOM STUFF. A LOT OF BLANK PAGES.
THERE'S A LITTLE STILL LIFE OF THAT LAMP AUNT TRACY TOOK.
...OF COURSE, WE'VE GOTTA SELL THE HOUSE.
HOW ARE WE GOING TO SPLIT THE MONEY?
I NEED THE MONEY MORE THAN YOU DO, TRACY.
WHY NOT SPLIT IT EVENLY?
AUNTIE ELMA ALWAYS LIKED ME BEST.
THEY'RE SO LAME. IT'S ALL JUST STUFF.
I DON'T KNOW WHY THEY CARE ABOUT LAMPS AND DRESSERS SO MUCH.
MAYBE YOU'D UNDERSTAND IF YOUR MOTHER HAD TAUGHT YOU THE VALUE OF MONEY, LAUREN.

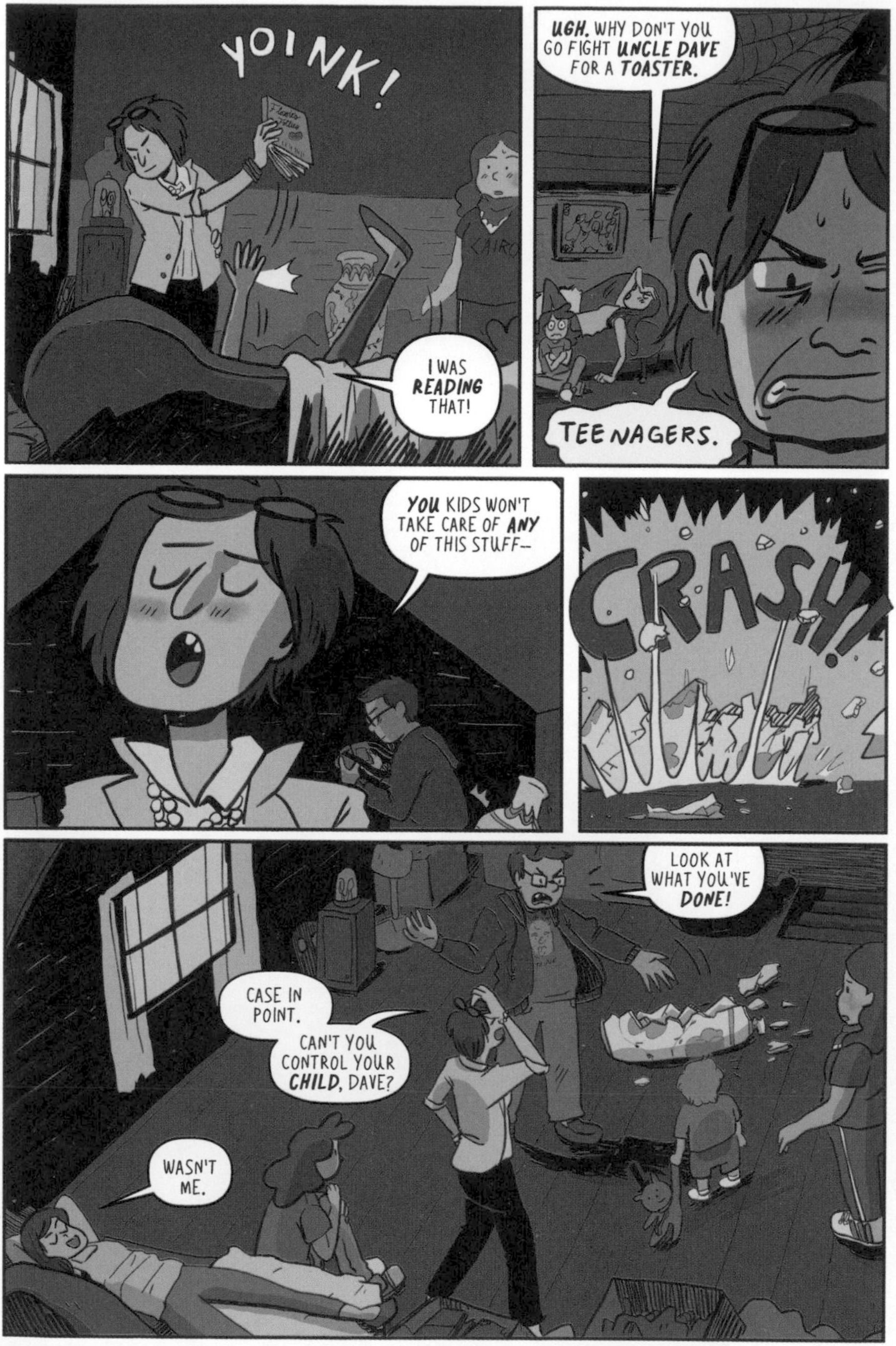
YOINK!
I WAS READING THAT!
UGH. WHY DON'T YOU GO FIGHT UNCLE DAVE FOR A TOASTER.
TEENAGERS.
YOU KIDS WON'T TAKE CARE OF ANY OF THIS STUFF--
CRASH!
LOOK AT WHAT YOU'VE DONE!
CASE IN POINT.
CAN'T YOU CONTROL YOUR CHILD, DAVE?
WASN'T ME.

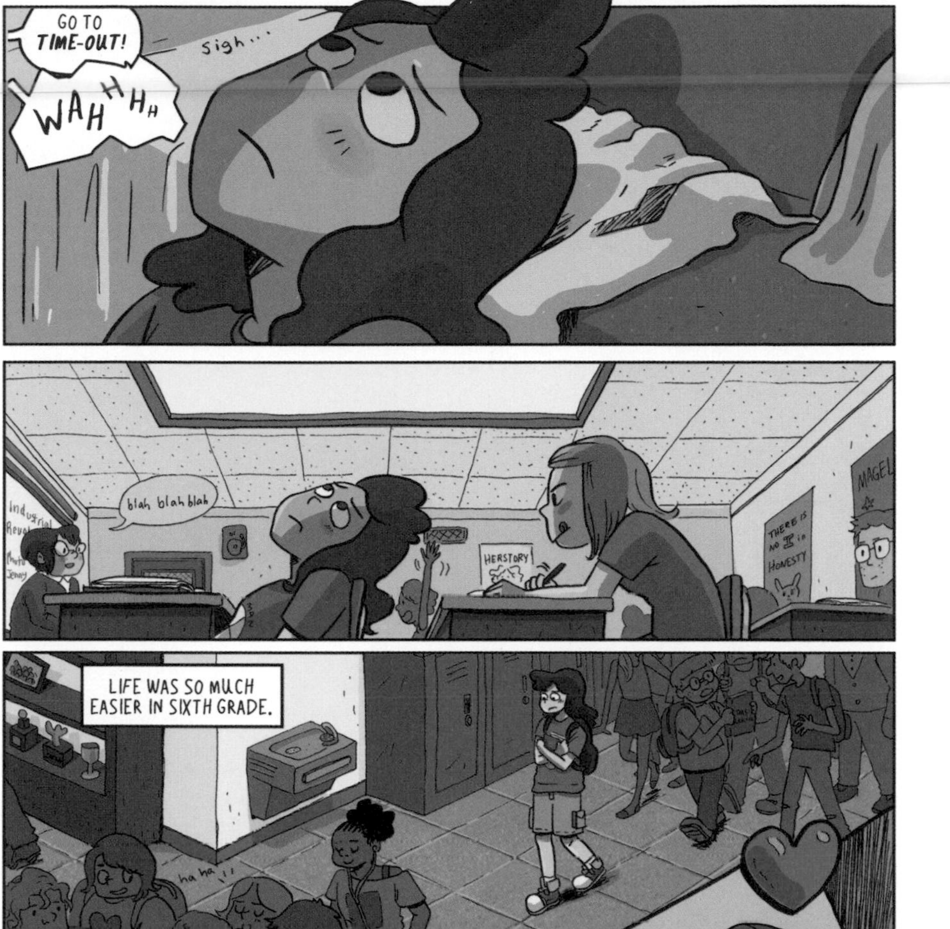
GO TO TIME-OUT!
Sigh...
WAHHHH
blah blah blah
HERSTORY
THERE IS NO I in HONESTY
LIFE WAS SO MUCH EASIER IN SIXTH GRADE.
ha ha
SOLAR SISTERS
I HAD JOAN AND LEAH.
SOLAR SISTERS
I KNEW WHERE I BELONGED.

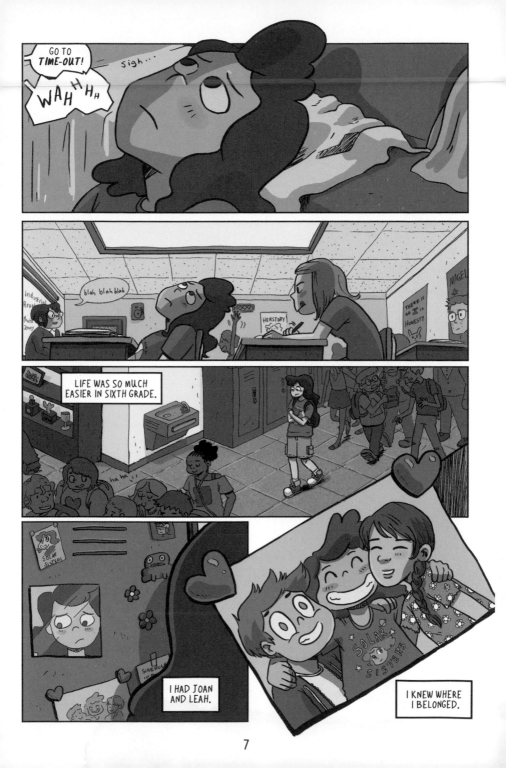

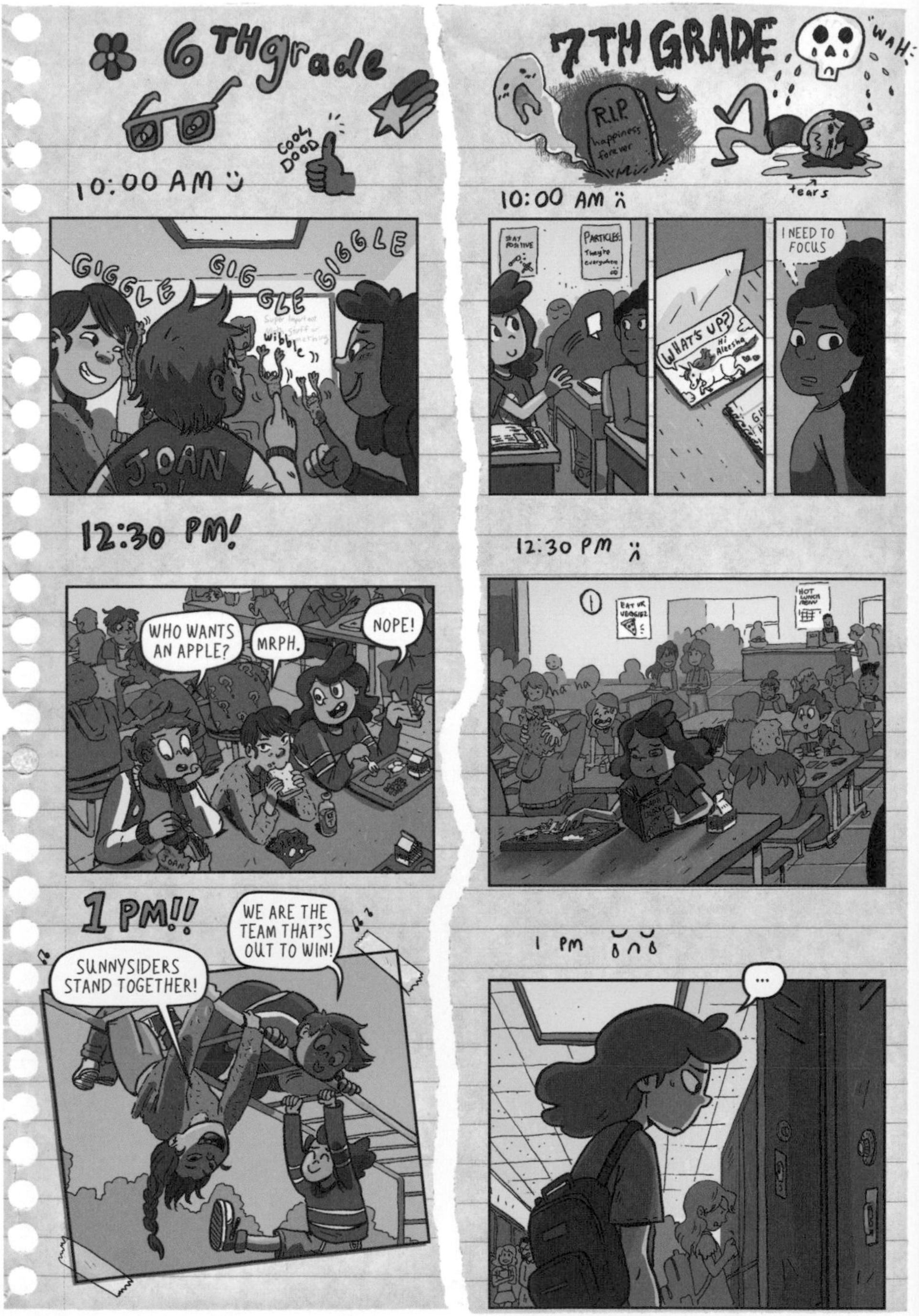
6THgrade
COOL DOOD
10:00 AM
GIGGLE
GIGGLE
GIGGLE
Wibble
JOAN
7TH GRADE
WAH!
R.I.P. happiness forever
tears
10:00 AM
STAY POSITIVE
PARTICLES: They're everywhere
WHAT'S UP?
Hi Aleesha
I NEED TO FOCUS
12:30 PM!
WHO WANTS AN APPLE?
MRPH.
NOPE!
12:30 PM
EAT UR VEGGIEZ
HOT LUNCH MENU
ha ha
1 PM!!
SUNNYSIDERS STAND TOGETHER!
WE ARE THE TEAM THAT'S OUT TO WIN!
1 PM
...

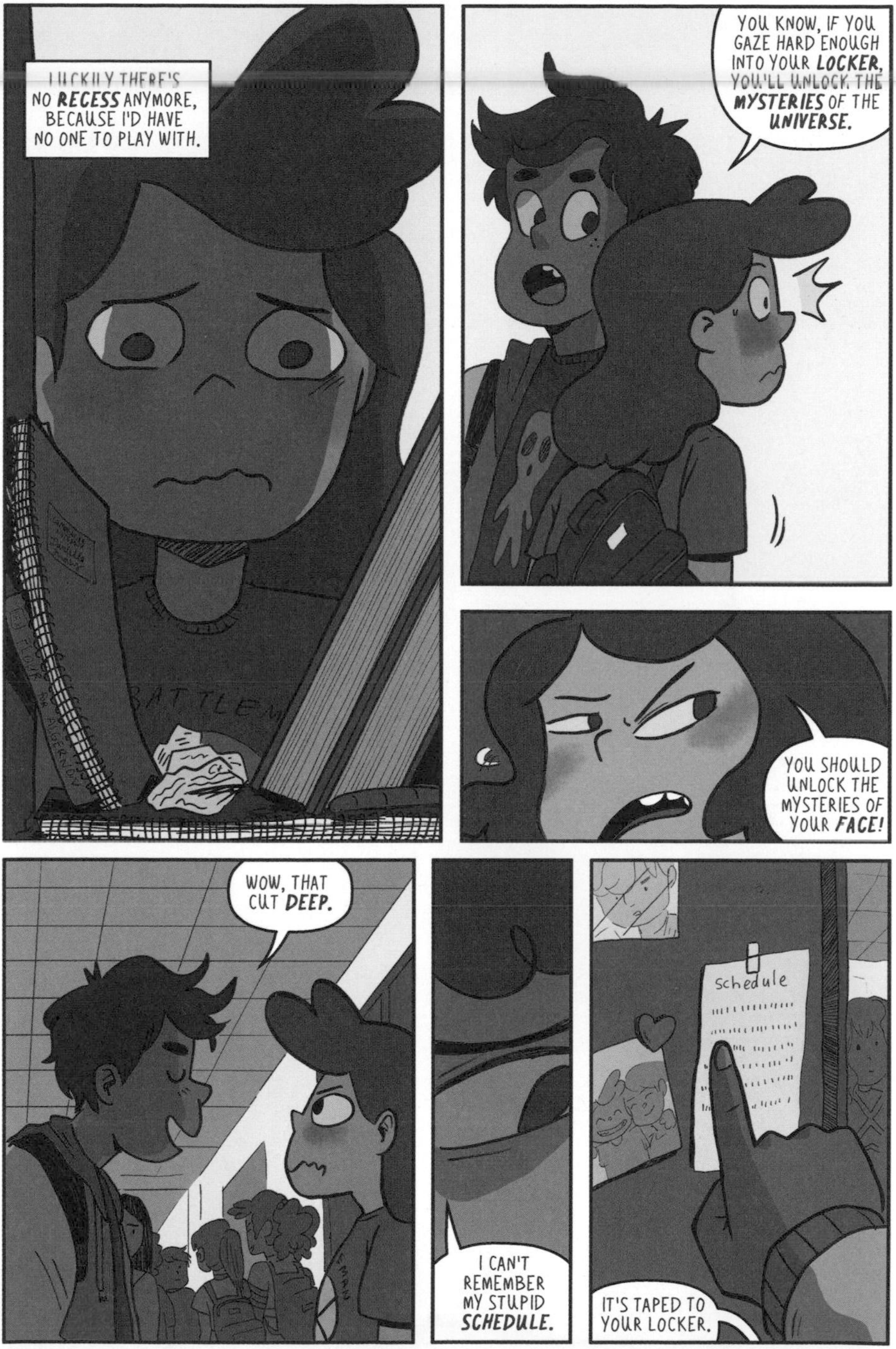
LUCKILY THERE'S NO RECESS ANYMORE, BECAUSE I'D HAVE NO ONE TO PLAY WITH.
YOU KNOW, IF YOU GAZE HARD ENOUGH INTO YOUR LOCKER, YOU'LL UNLOCK THE MYSTERIES OF THE UNIVERSE.
YOU SHOULD UNLOCK THE MYSTERIES OF YOUR FACE!
WOW, THAT CUT DEEP.
I CAN'T REMEMBER MY STUPID SCHEDULE.
Schedule
IT'S TAPED TO YOUR LOCKER.

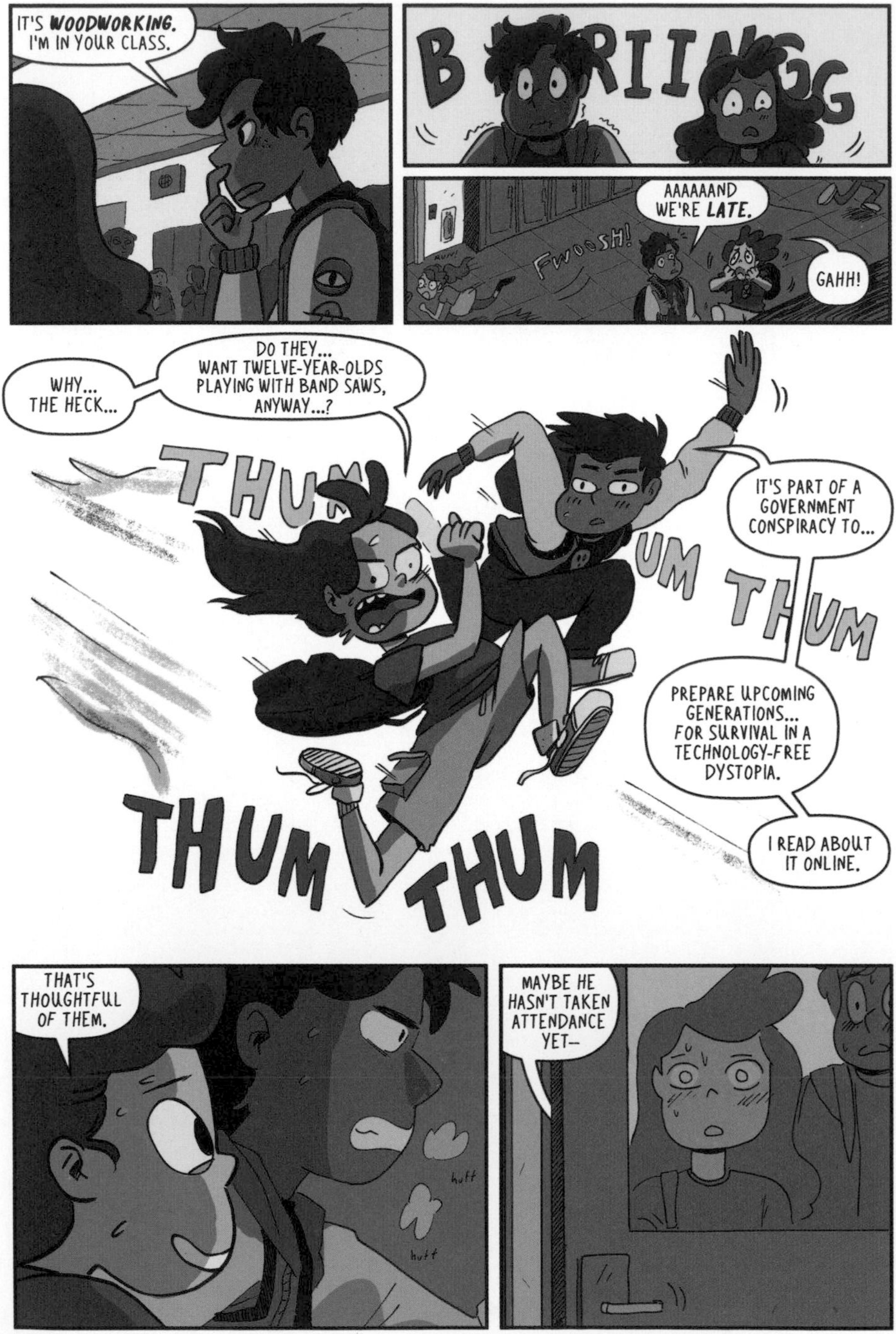
IT'S **WOODWORKING.** I'M IN YOUR CLASS.
AAAAAAND WE'RE **LATE.**
FWOOSH!
GAHH!
WHY... THE HECK...
DO THEY... WANT TWELVE-YEAR-OLDS PLAYING WITH BAND SAWS, ANYWAY...?
THUM
IT'S PART OF A GOVERNMENT CONSPIRACY TO...
UM THUM
PREPARE UPCOMING GENERATIONS... FOR SURVIVAL IN A TECHNOLOGY-FREE DYSTOPIA.
THUM THUM
I READ ABOUT IT ONLINE.
THAT'S THOUGHTFUL OF THEM.
huff
huff
MAYBE HE HASN'T TAKEN ATTENDANCE YET—

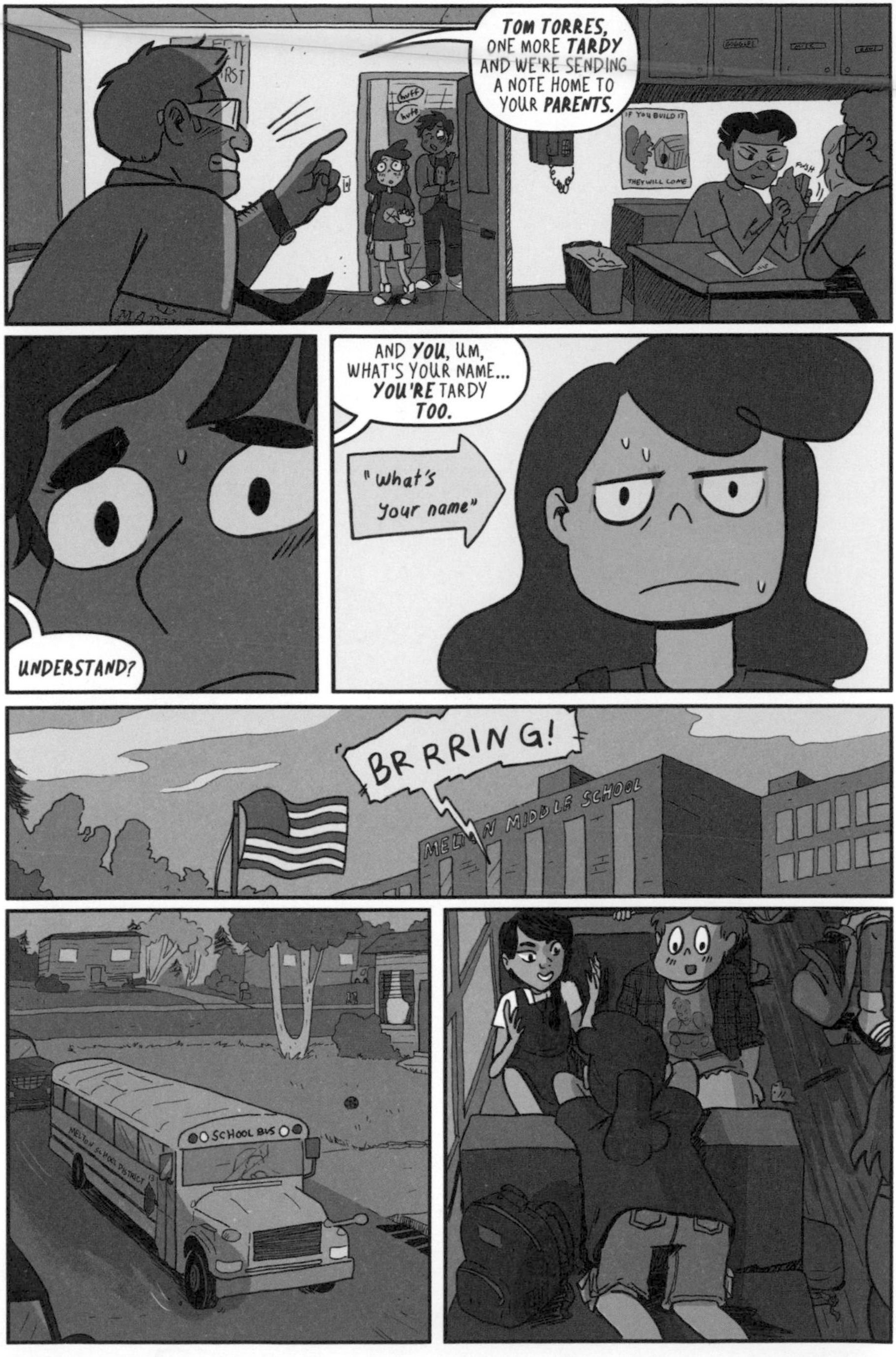
TOM TORRES, ONE MORE TARDY AND WE'RE SENDING A NOTE HOME TO YOUR PARENTS.
huff
huff
IF YOU BUILD IT
THEY WILL COME
UNDERSTAND?
AND YOU, UM, WHAT'S YOUR NAME... YOU'RE TARDY TOO.
"what's your name"
BRRRING!
MELTON MIDDLE SCHOOL
SCHOOL BUS
MELTON SCHOOL DISTRICT

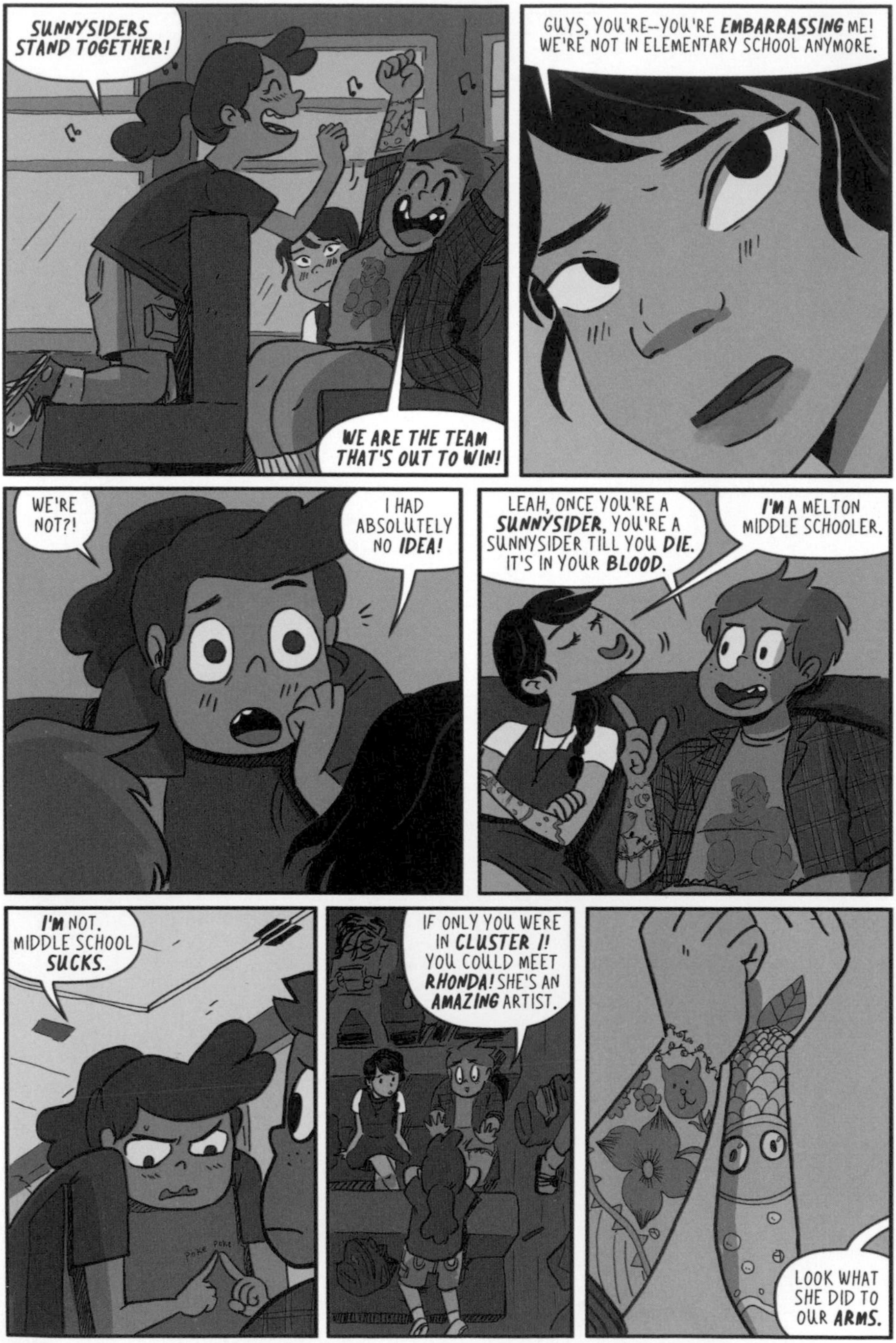
SUNNYSIDERS STAND TOGETHER!
WE ARE THE TEAM THAT'S OUT TO WIN!
GUYS, YOU'RE--YOU'RE EMBARRASSING ME! WE'RE NOT IN ELEMENTARY SCHOOL ANYMORE.
WE'RE NOT?!
I HAD ABSOLUTELY NO IDEA!
LEAH, ONCE YOU'RE A SUNNYSIDER, YOU'RE A SUNNYSIDER TILL YOU DIE. IT'S IN YOUR BLOOD.
I'M A MELTON MIDDLE SCHOOLER.
I'M NOT. MIDDLE SCHOOL SUCKS.
IF ONLY YOU WERE IN CLUSTER 1! YOU COULD MEET RHONDA! SHE'S AN AMAZING ARTIST.
LOOK WHAT SHE DID TO OUR ARMS.

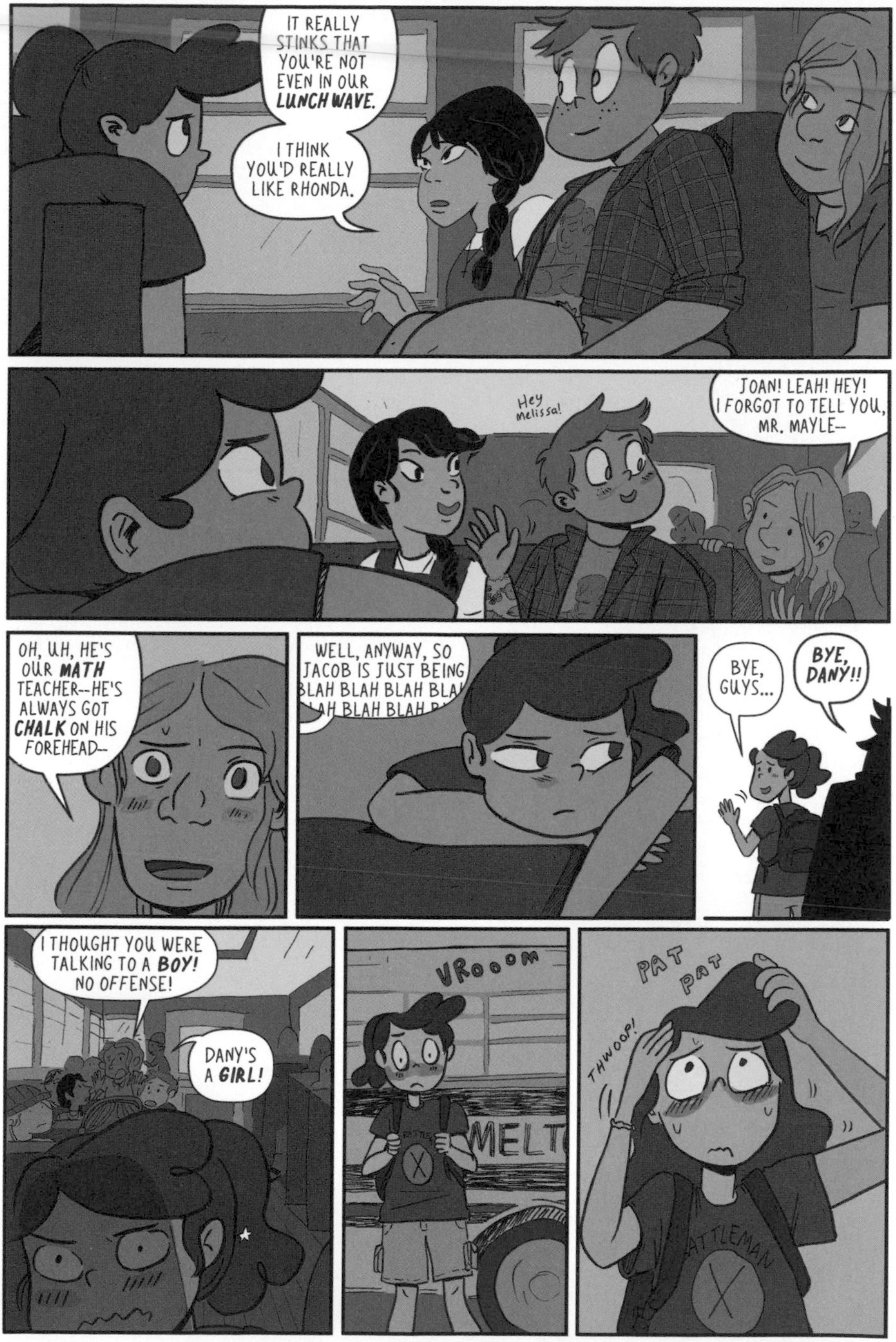
IT REALLY STINKS THAT YOU'RE NOT EVEN IN OUR **LUNCH WAVE.**
I THINK YOU'D REALLY LIKE RHONDA.
Hey melissa!
JOAN! LEAH! HEY! I FORGOT TO TELL YOU, MR. MAYLE--
OH, UH, HE'S OUR **MATH** TEACHER--HE'S ALWAYS GOT **CHALK** ON HIS FOREHEAD--
WELL, ANYWAY, SO JACOB IS JUST BEING BLAH BLAH BLAH BLAH BLAH BLAH BLAH
BYE, GUYS...
BYE, DANY!!
I THOUGHT YOU WERE TALKING TO A **BOY!** NO OFFENSE!
DANY'S A **GIRL!**
VROOOM
MELT
PAT PAT
THWOOP!

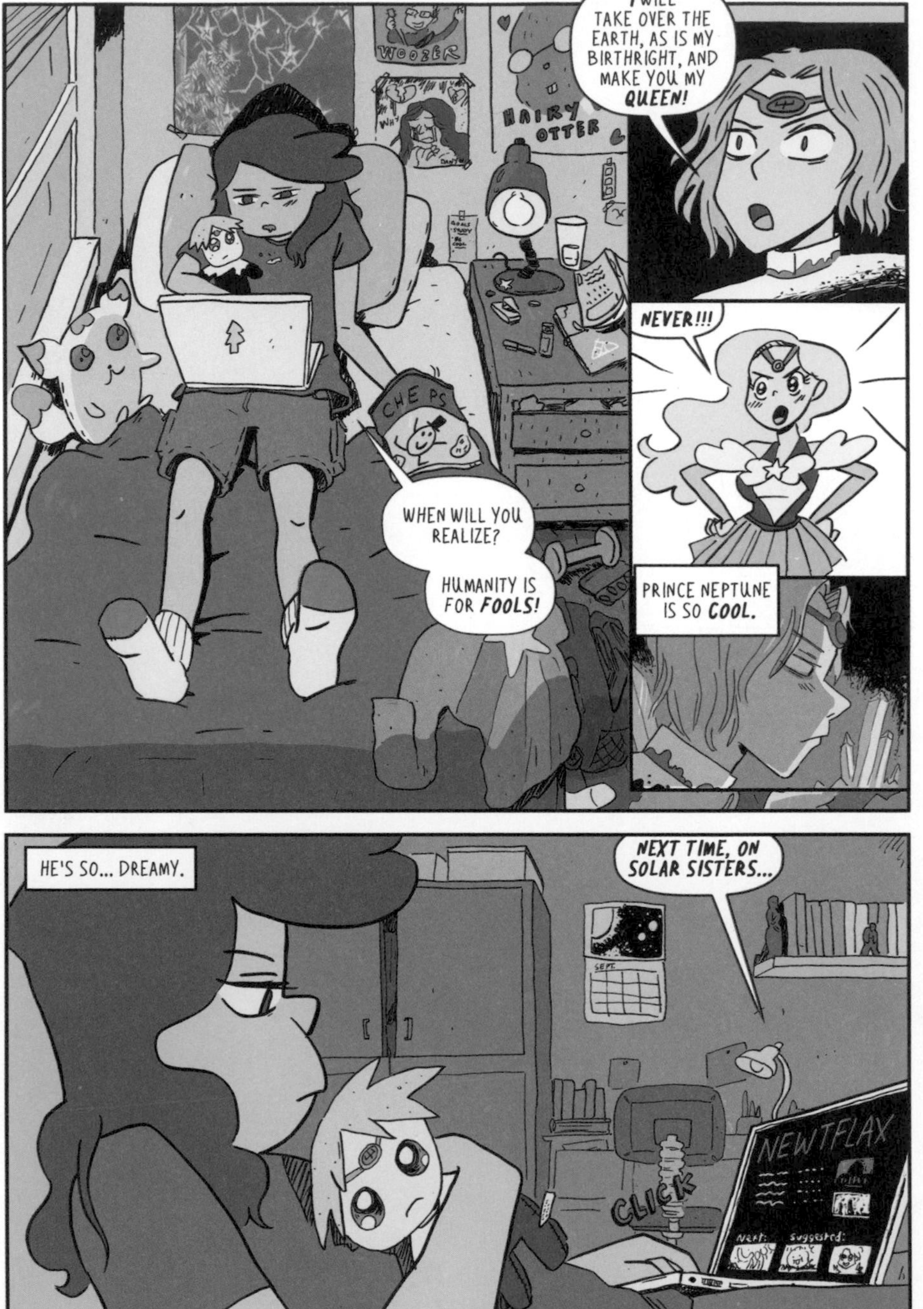
WOOZER
HAIRY OTTER
CHEPS
I WILL TAKE OVER THE EARTH, AS IS MY BIRTHRIGHT, AND MAKE YOU MY **QUEEN!**
NEVER!!!
WHEN WILL YOU REALIZE?
HUMANITY IS FOR **FOOLS!**
PRINCE NEPTUNE IS SO **COOL.**
HE'S SO... DREAMY.
NEXT TIME, ON SOLAR SISTERS...
CLICK
NEWTFLAX

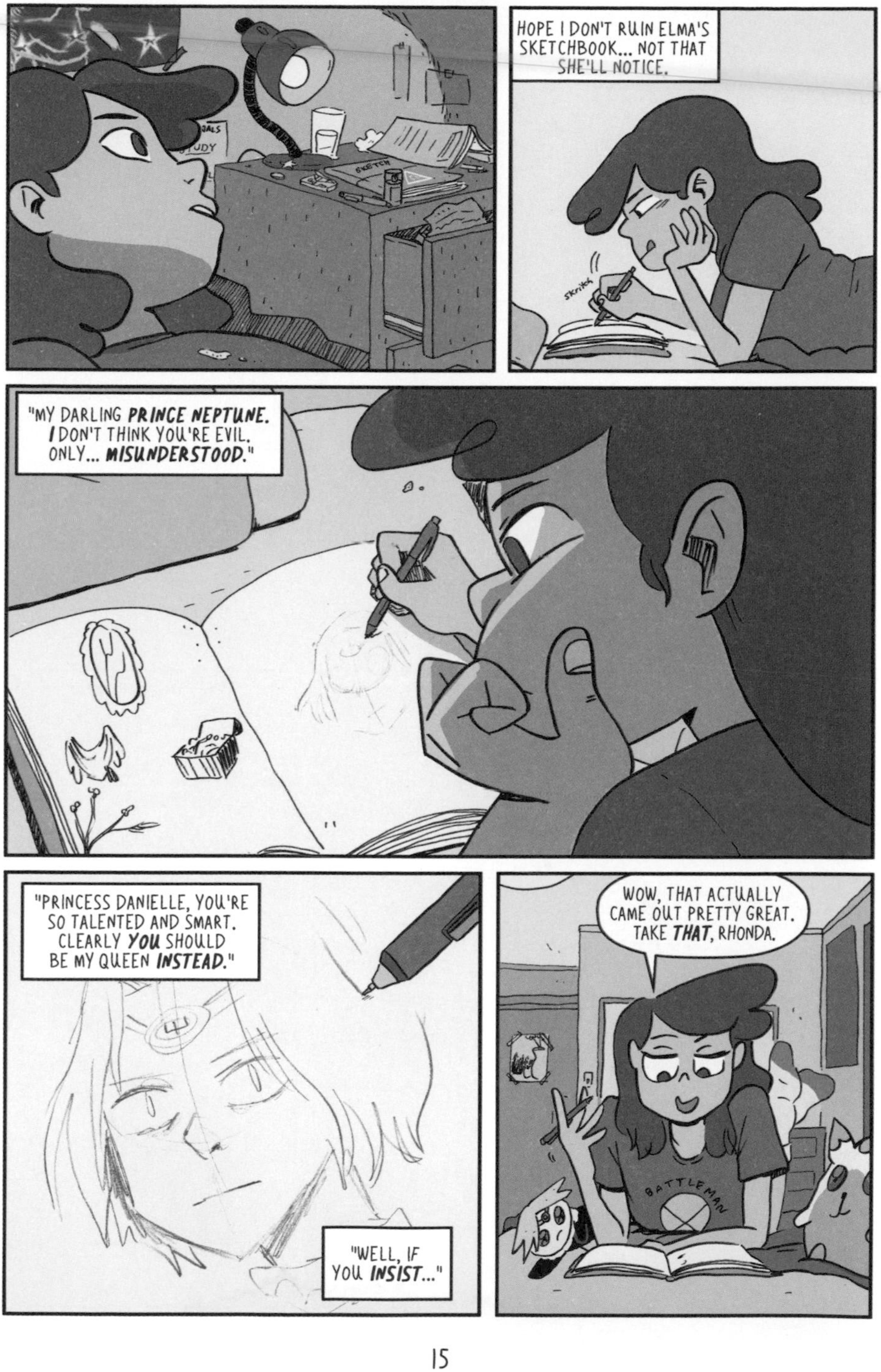
HOPE I DON'T RUIN ELMA'S SKETCHBOOK... NOT THAT SHE'LL NOTICE.
SKRITCH
"MY DARLING PRINCE NEPTUNE. I DON'T THINK YOU'RE EVIL. ONLY... MISUNDERSTOOD."
"PRINCESS DANIELLE, YOU'RE SO TALENTED AND SMART. CLEARLY YOU SHOULD BE MY QUEEN INSTEAD."
"WELL, IF YOU INSIST..."
WOW, THAT ACTUALLY CAME OUT PRETTY GREAT. TAKE THAT, RHONDA.
BATTLEMAN

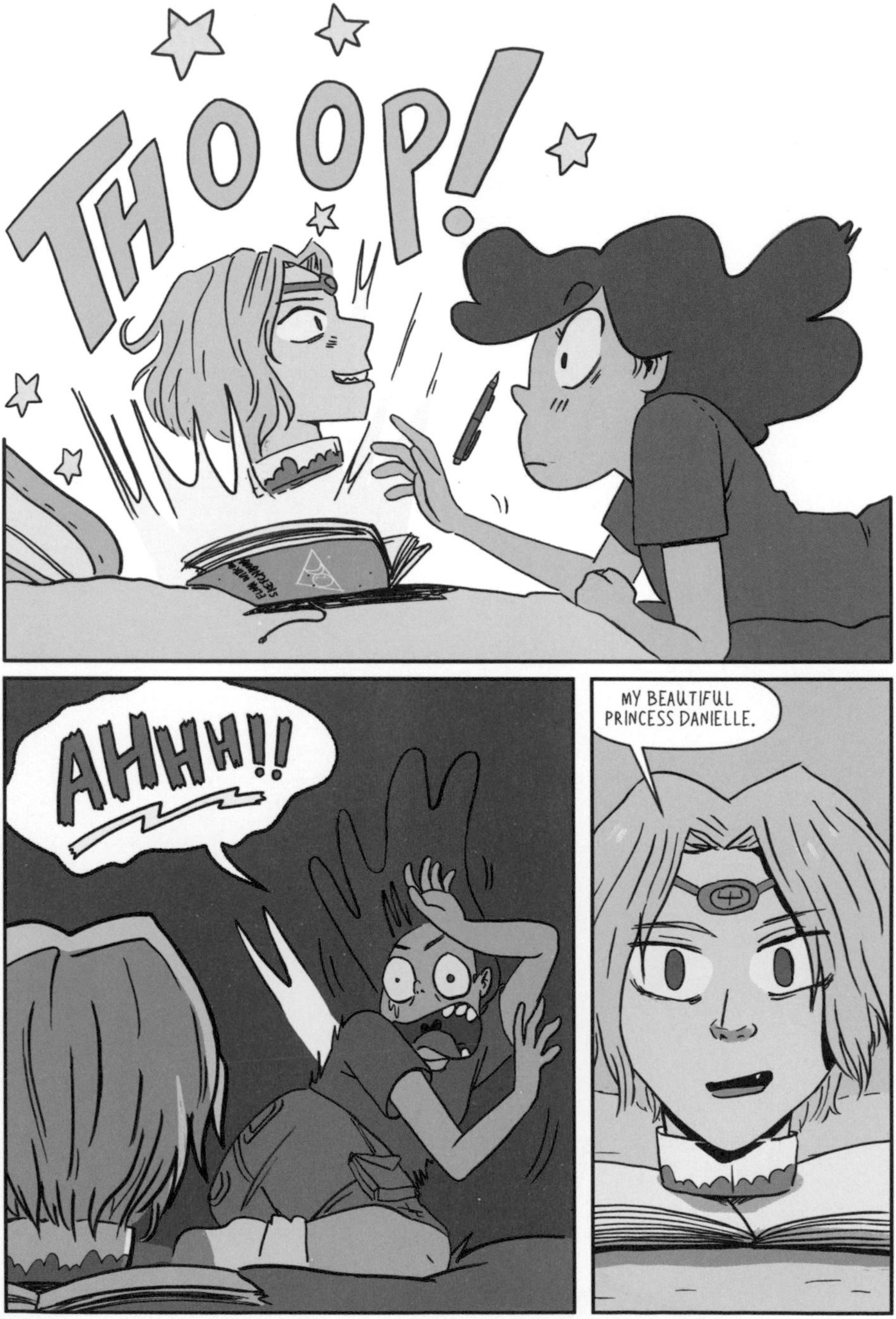
THOOP!
AHHH!!
MY BEAUTIFUL PRINCESS DANIELLE.

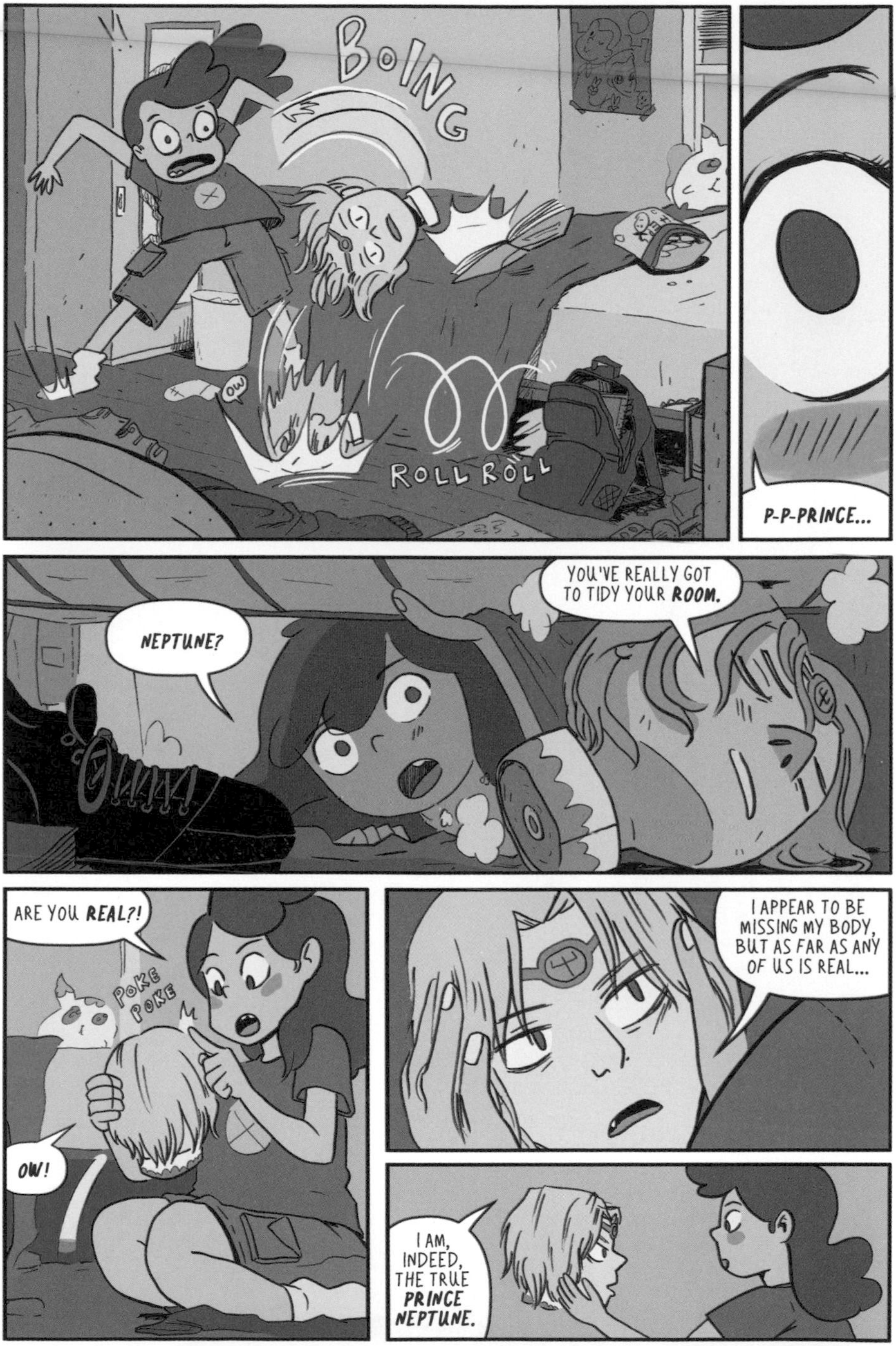

BOING
OW
ROLL ROLL
P-P-PRINCE...
NEPTUNE?
YOU'VE REALLY GOT TO TIDY YOUR **ROOM.**
ARE YOU **REAL?!**
POKE POKE
OW!
I APPEAR TO BE MISSING MY BODY, BUT AS FAR AS ANY OF US IS REAL...
I AM, INDEED, THE TRUE **PRINCE NEPTUNE.**

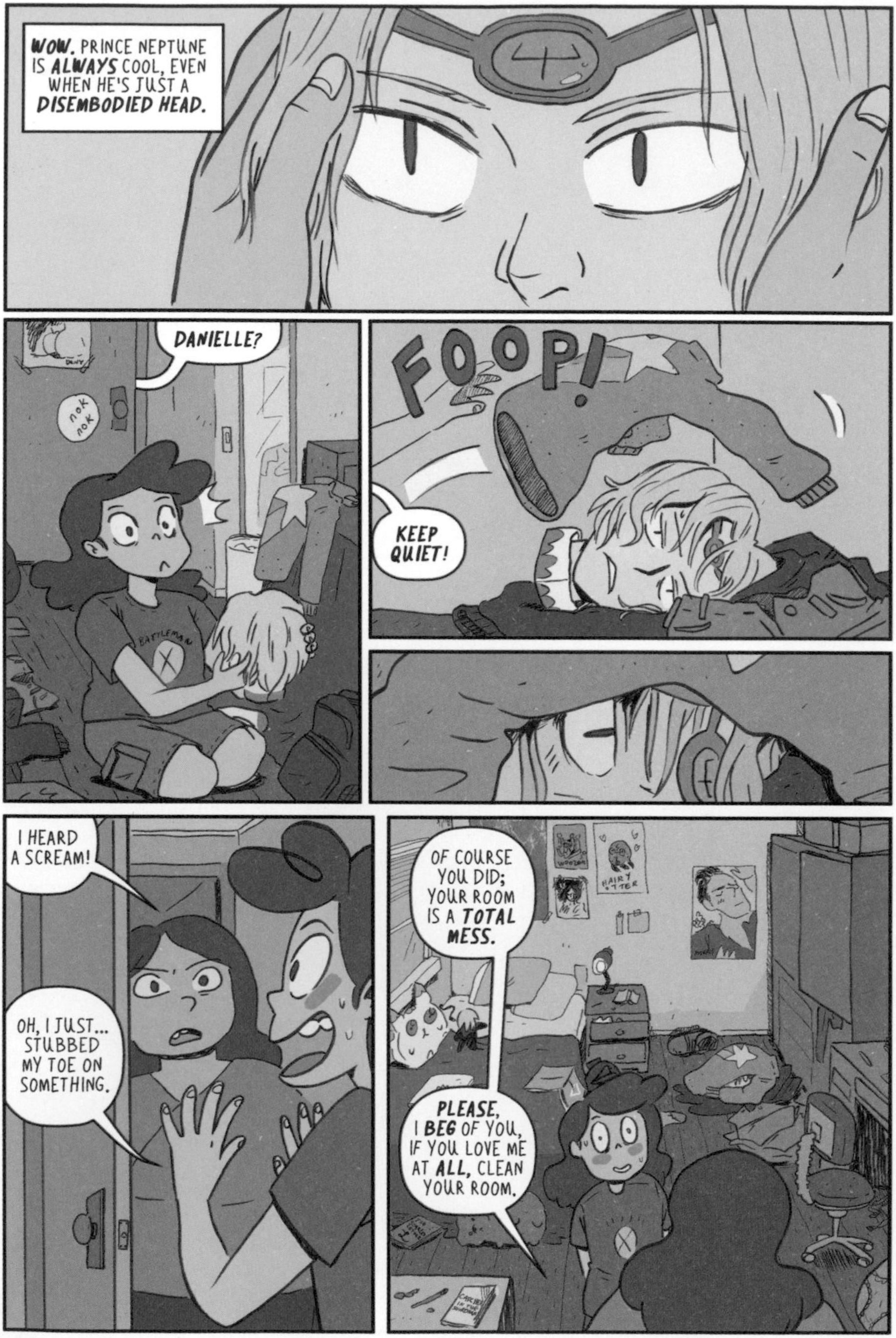
WOW. PRINCE NEPTUNE IS ALWAYS COOL, EVEN WHEN HE'S JUST A DISEMBODIED HEAD.
DANIELLE?
FOOP!
KEEP QUIET!
I HEARD A SCREAM!
OH, I JUST... STUBBED MY TOE ON SOMETHING.
OF COURSE YOU DID; YOUR ROOM IS A TOTAL MESS.
PLEASE, I BEG OF YOU, IF YOU LOVE ME AT ALL, CLEAN YOUR ROOM.

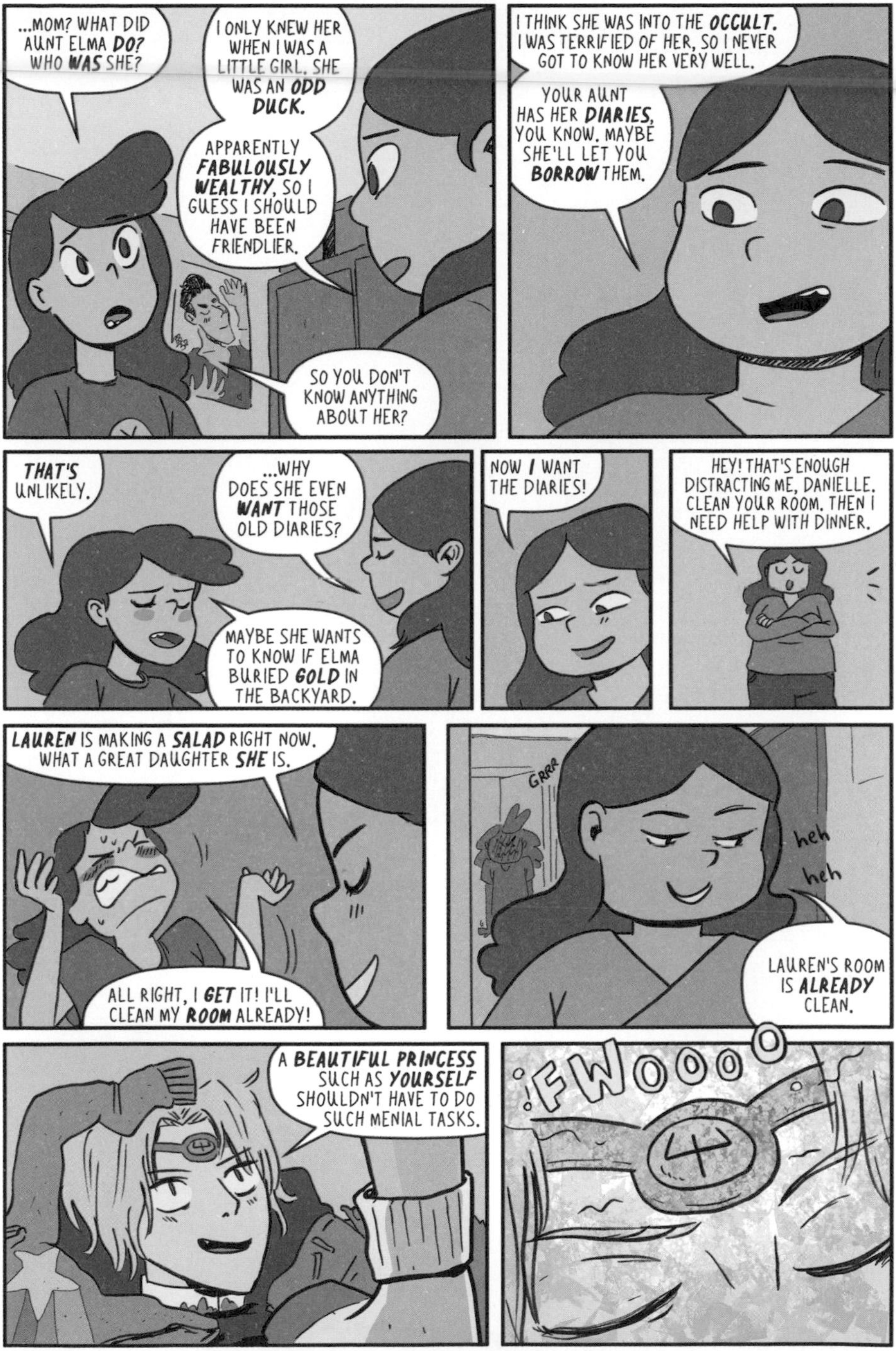

...MOM? WHAT DID AUNT ELMA DO? WHO WAS SHE?
I ONLY KNEW HER WHEN I WAS A LITTLE GIRL. SHE WAS AN ODD DUCK.
APPARENTLY FABULOUSLY WEALTHY, SO I GUESS I SHOULD HAVE BEEN FRIENDLIER.
SO YOU DON'T KNOW ANYTHING ABOUT HER?
I THINK SHE WAS INTO THE OCCULT. I WAS TERRIFIED OF HER, SO I NEVER GOT TO KNOW HER VERY WELL.
YOUR AUNT HAS HER DIARIES, YOU KNOW. MAYBE SHE'LL LET YOU BORROW THEM.
THAT'S UNLIKELY.
...WHY DOES SHE EVEN WANT THOSE OLD DIARIES?
MAYBE SHE WANTS TO KNOW IF ELMA BURIED GOLD IN THE BACKYARD.
NOW I WANT THE DIARIES!
HEY! THAT'S ENOUGH DISTRACTING ME, DANIELLE. CLEAN YOUR ROOM. THEN I NEED HELP WITH DINNER.
LAUREN IS MAKING A SALAD RIGHT NOW. WHAT A GREAT DAUGHTER SHE IS.
ALL RIGHT, I GET IT! I'LL CLEAN MY ROOM ALREADY!
GRRR
heh heh
LAUREN'S ROOM IS ALREADY CLEAN.
A BEAUTIFUL PRINCESS SUCH AS YOURSELF SHOULDN'T HAVE TO DO SUCH MENIAL TASKS.
FWOOOO

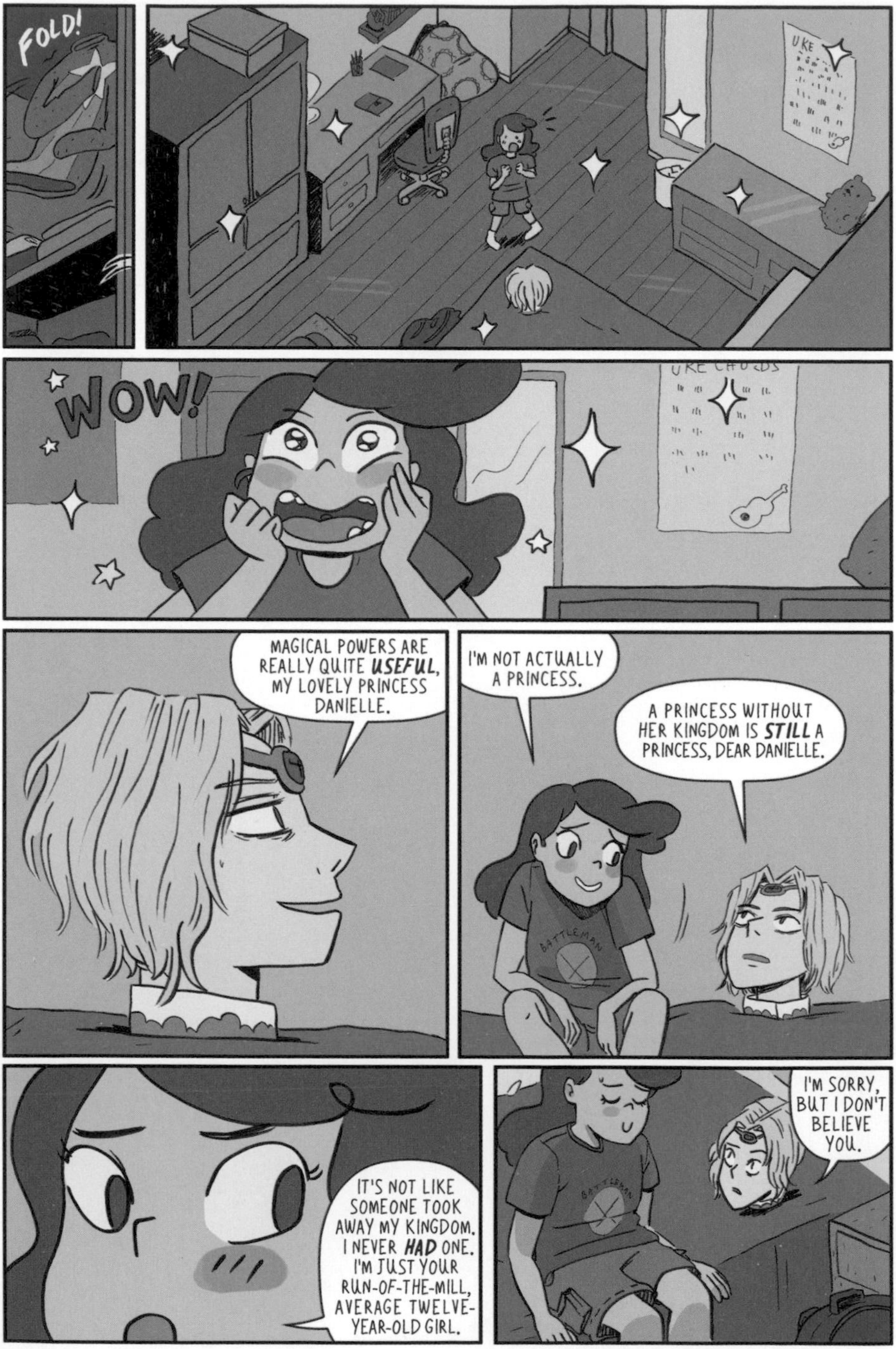
FOLD!
UKE
WOW!
UKE CHORDS
MAGICAL POWERS ARE REALLY QUITE **USEFUL**, MY LOVELY PRINCESS DANIELLE.
I'M NOT ACTUALLY A PRINCESS.
A PRINCESS WITHOUT HER KINGDOM IS **STILL** A PRINCESS, DEAR DANIELLE.
BATTLEMAN
IT'S NOT LIKE SOMEONE TOOK AWAY MY KINGDOM. I NEVER **HAD** ONE. I'M JUST YOUR RUN-OF-THE-MILL, AVERAGE TWELVE-YEAR-OLD GIRL.
I'M SORRY, BUT I DON'T BELIEVE YOU.

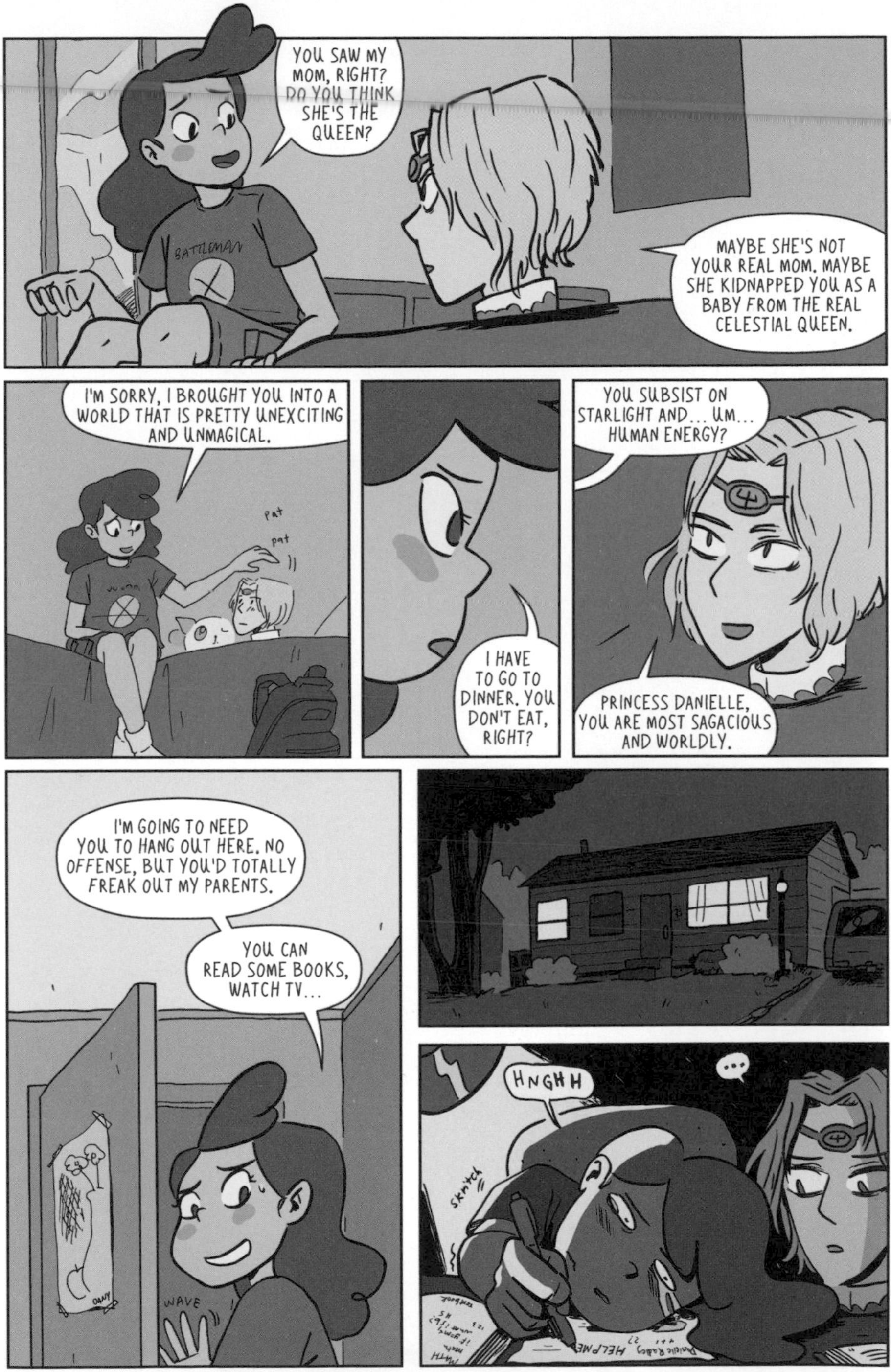

YOU SAW MY MOM, RIGHT? DO YOU THINK SHE'S THE QUEEN?
BATTLEMAN
MAYBE SHE'S NOT YOUR REAL MOM. MAYBE SHE KIDNAPPED YOU AS A BABY FROM THE REAL CELESTIAL QUEEN.
I'M SORRY, I BROUGHT YOU INTO A WORLD THAT IS PRETTY UNEXCITING AND UNMAGICAL.
pat
pat
YOU SUBSIST ON STARLIGHT AND... UM... HUMAN ENERGY?
I HAVE TO GO TO DINNER. YOU DON'T EAT, RIGHT?
PRINCESS DANIELLE, YOU ARE MOST SAGACIOUS AND WORLDLY.
I'M GOING TO NEED YOU TO HANG OUT HERE. NO OFFENSE, BUT YOU'D TOTALLY FREAK OUT MY PARENTS.
YOU CAN READ SOME BOOKS, WATCH TV...
WAVE
HNGHH
...
skritch
HELPME

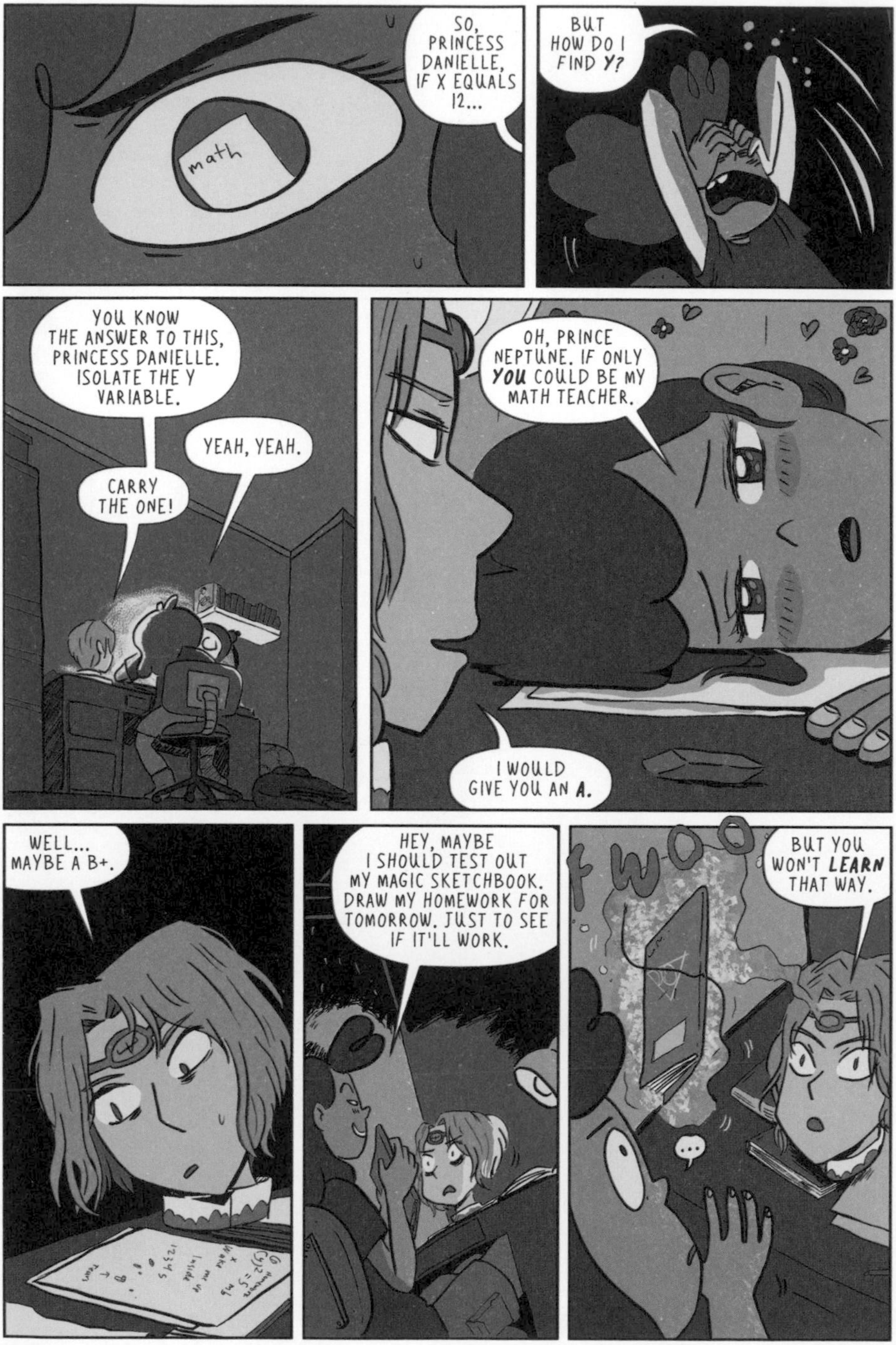
math
SO, PRINCESS DANIELLE, IF X EQUALS 12...
BUT HOW DO I FIND Y?
YOU KNOW THE ANSWER TO THIS, PRINCESS DANIELLE. ISOLATE THE Y VARIABLE.
YEAH, YEAH.
CARRY THE ONE!
OH, PRINCE NEPTUNE. IF ONLY YOU COULD BE MY MATH TEACHER.
I WOULD GIVE YOU AN A.
WELL... MAYBE A B+.
HEY, MAYBE I SHOULD TEST OUT MY MAGIC SKETCHBOOK. DRAW MY HOMEWORK FOR TOMORROW. JUST TO SEE IF IT'LL WORK.
FWOOO
BUT YOU WON'T LEARN THAT WAY.
...

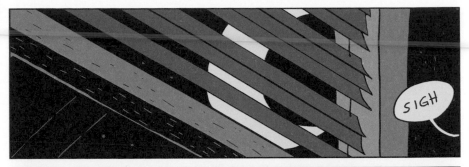

SIGH

WHAT AM I GOING TO *DO* WITH YOU?

YOU CAN'T GO OUT INTO THE WORLD.

YOU'RE A *BODILESS HEAD;* YOU'LL *SCARE* PEOPLE.

IF I COULD ACCOMPANY YOU ON YOUR JOURNEYS, PERHAPS IN A SATCHEL OF FINE SILK--

YOU MEAN MY BACKPACK? WON'T YOU BE BORED?

23

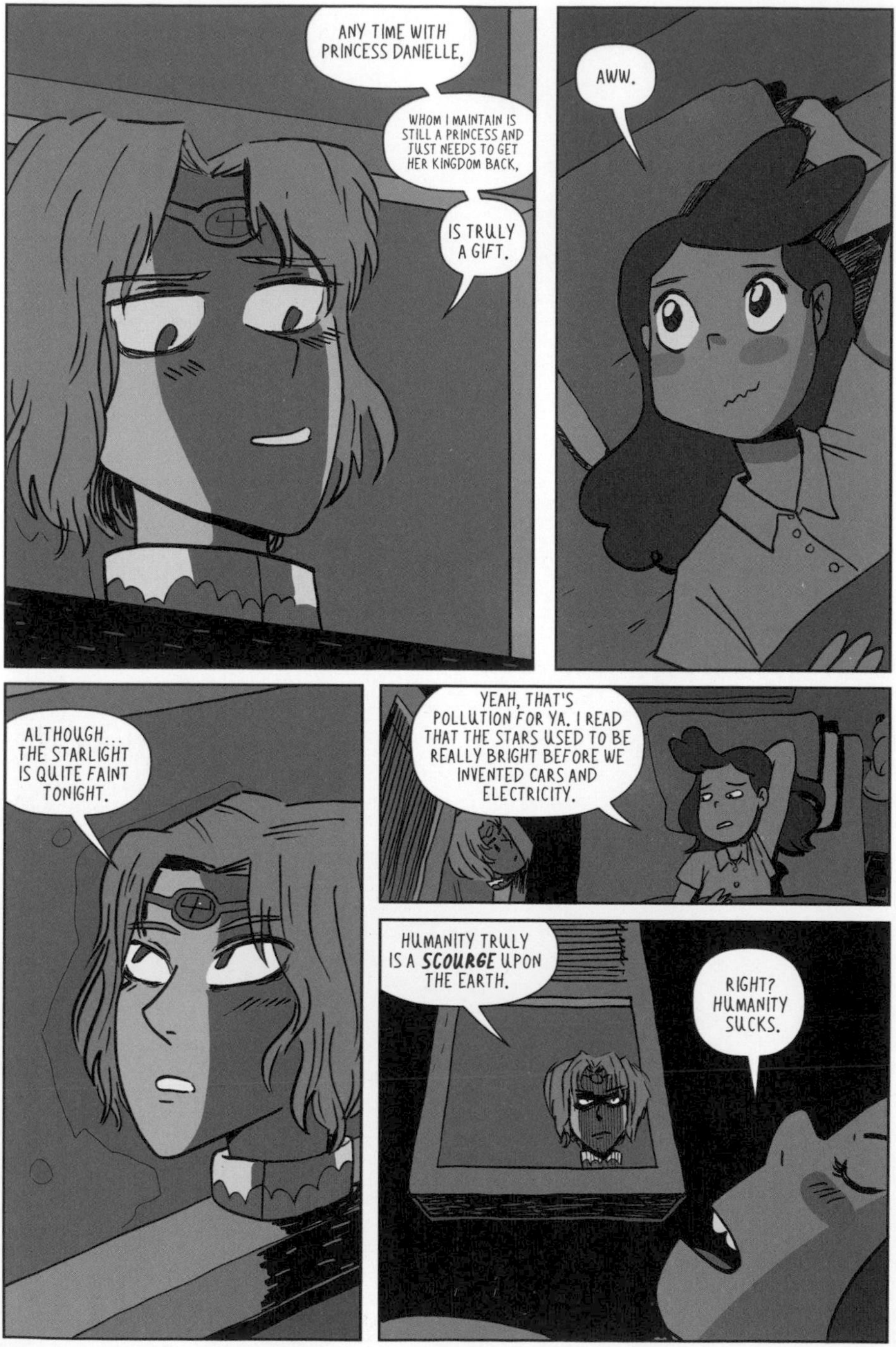
ANY TIME WITH PRINCESS DANIELLE,
WHOM I MAINTAIN IS STILL A PRINCESS AND JUST NEEDS TO GET HER KINGDOM BACK,
IS TRULY A GIFT.
AWW.
ALTHOUGH... THE STARLIGHT IS QUITE FAINT TONIGHT.
YEAH, THAT'S POLLUTION FOR YA. I READ THAT THE STARS USED TO BE REALLY BRIGHT BEFORE WE INVENTED CARS AND ELECTRICITY.
HUMANITY TRULY IS A SCOURGE UPON THE EARTH.
RIGHT? HUMANITY SUCKS.

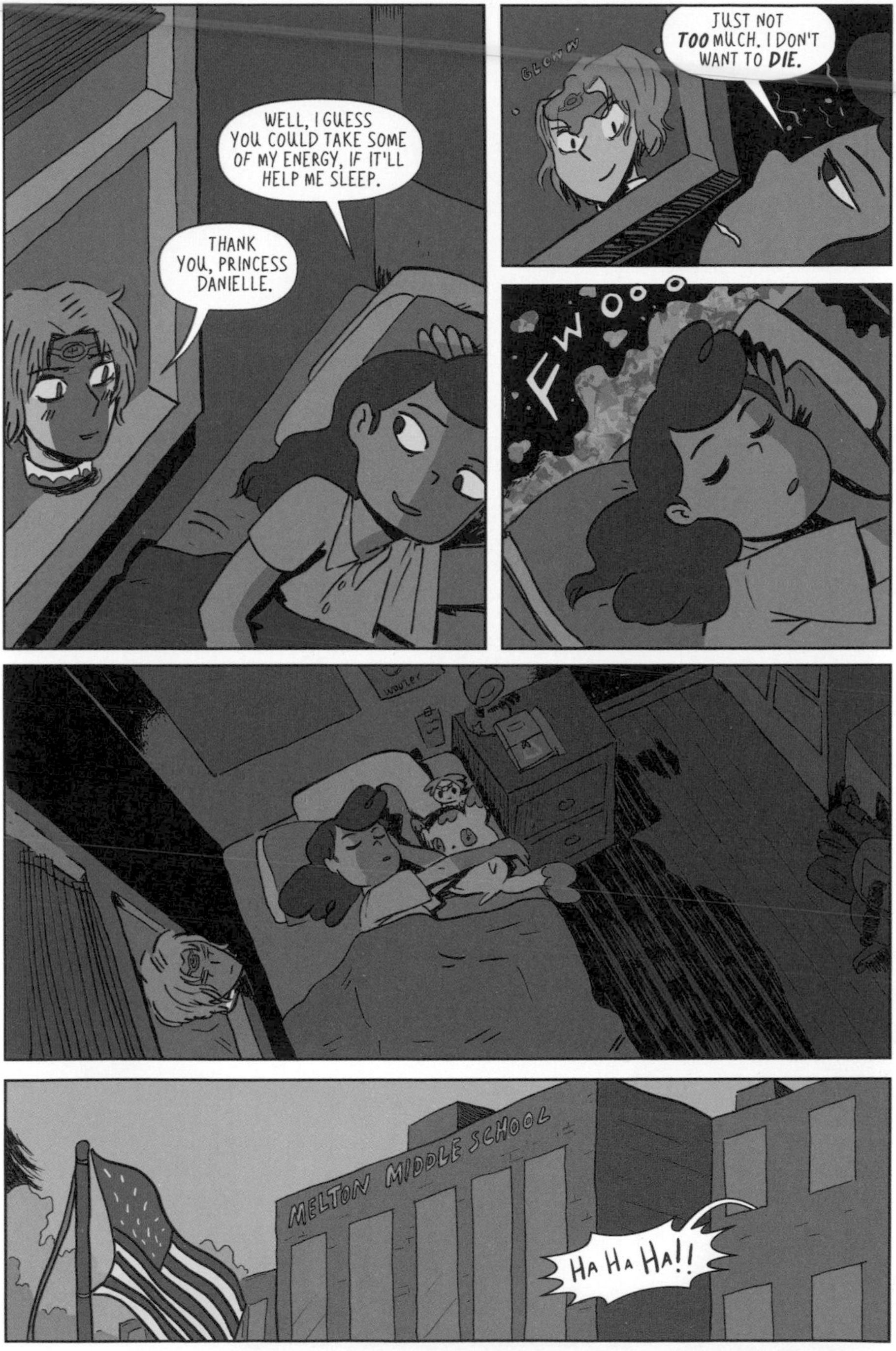
WELL, I GUESS YOU COULD TAKE SOME OF MY ENERGY, IF IT'LL HELP ME SLEEP.
THANK YOU, PRINCESS DANIELLE.
GLOWW
JUST NOT TOO MUCH. I DON'T WANT TO DIE.
FWOOO
MELTON MIDDLE SCHOOL
HA HA HA!!

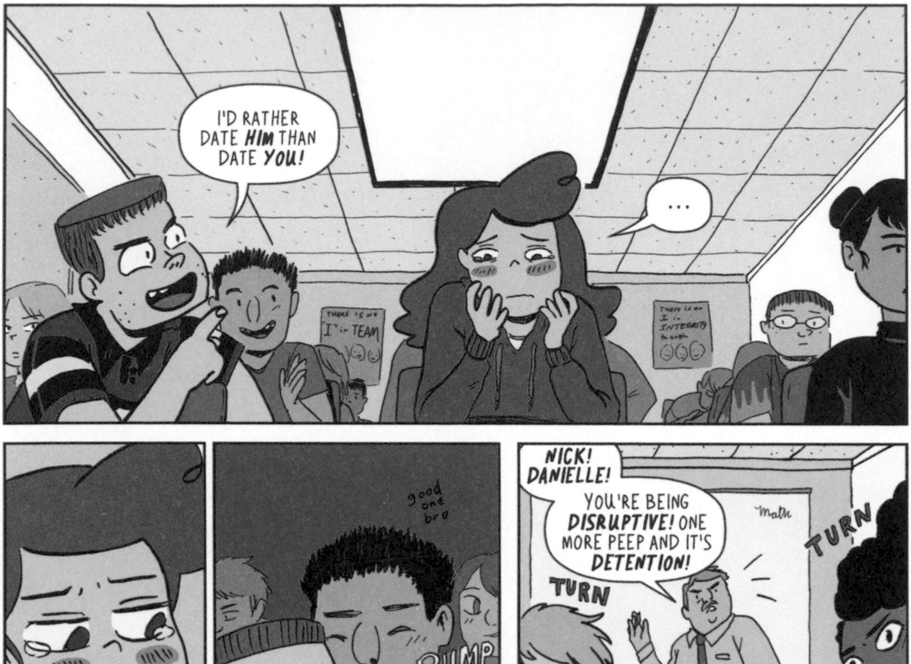
I'D RATHER DATE HIM THAN DATE YOU!
...
OKAY.
good one bro
BUMP
NICK! DANIELLE!
YOU'RE BEING DISRUPTIVE! ONE MORE PEEP AND IT'S DETENTION!
TURN
TURN
WAHHH
?
SLAM!

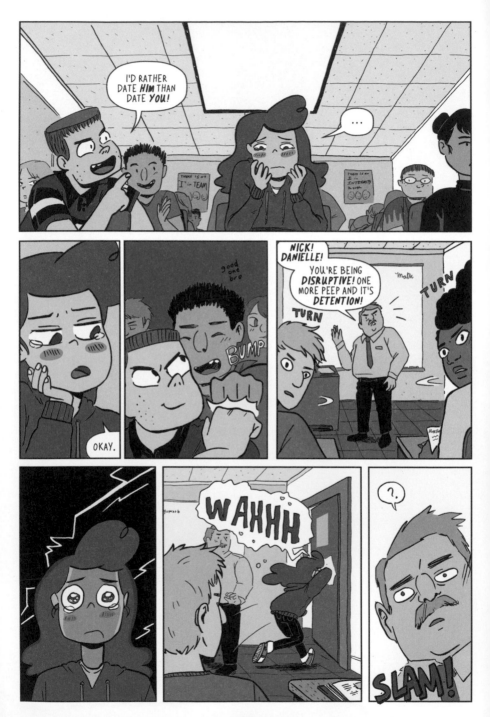

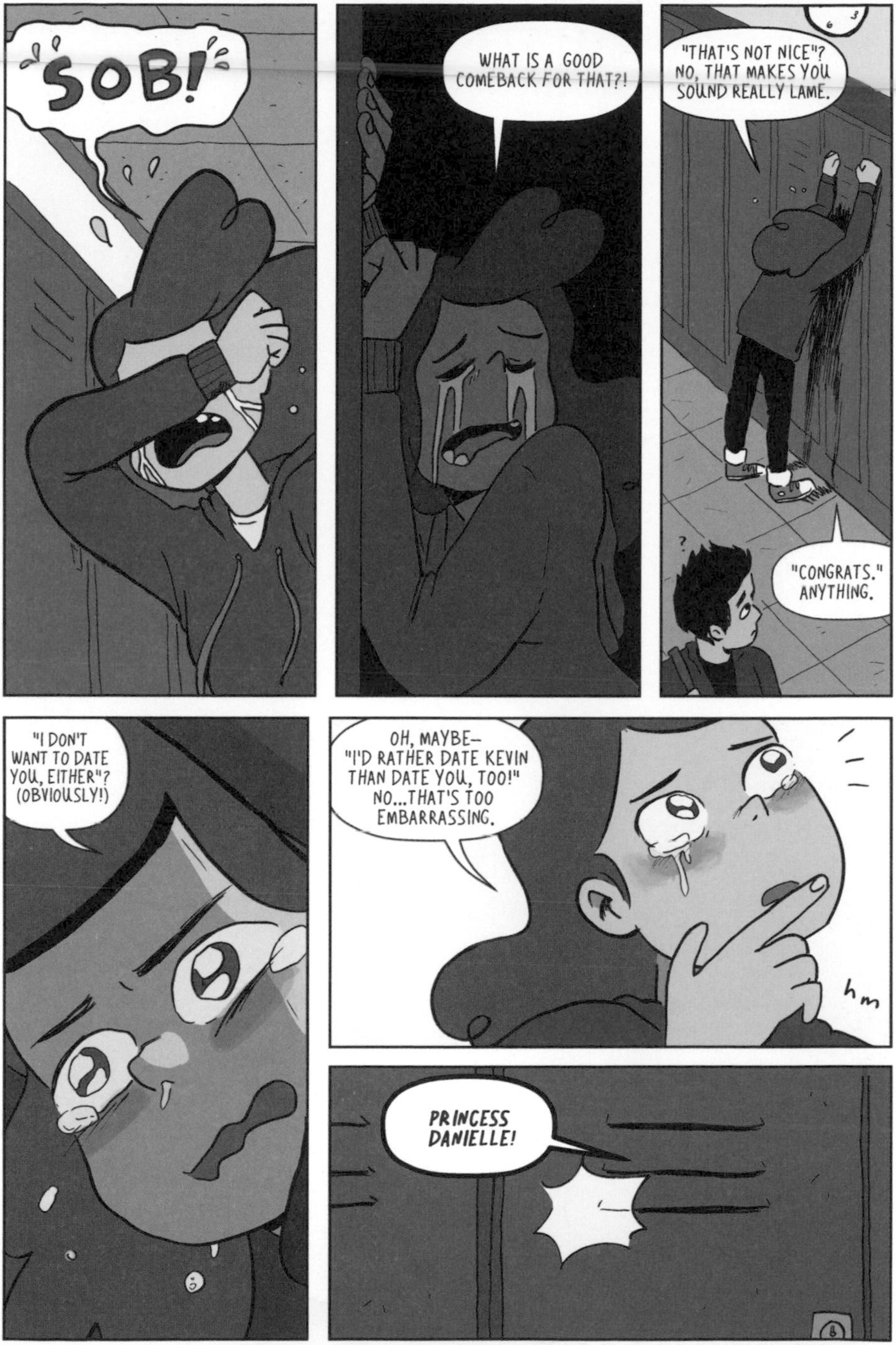
SOB!
WHAT IS A GOOD COMEBACK FOR THAT?!
"THAT'S NOT NICE"? NO, THAT MAKES YOU SOUND REALLY LAME.
?
"CONGRATS." ANYTHING.
"I DON'T WANT TO DATE YOU, EITHER"? (OBVIOUSLY!)
OH, MAYBE– "I'D RATHER DATE KEVIN THAN DATE YOU, TOO!" NO...THAT'S TOO EMBARRASSING.
hm
PRINCESS DANIELLE!

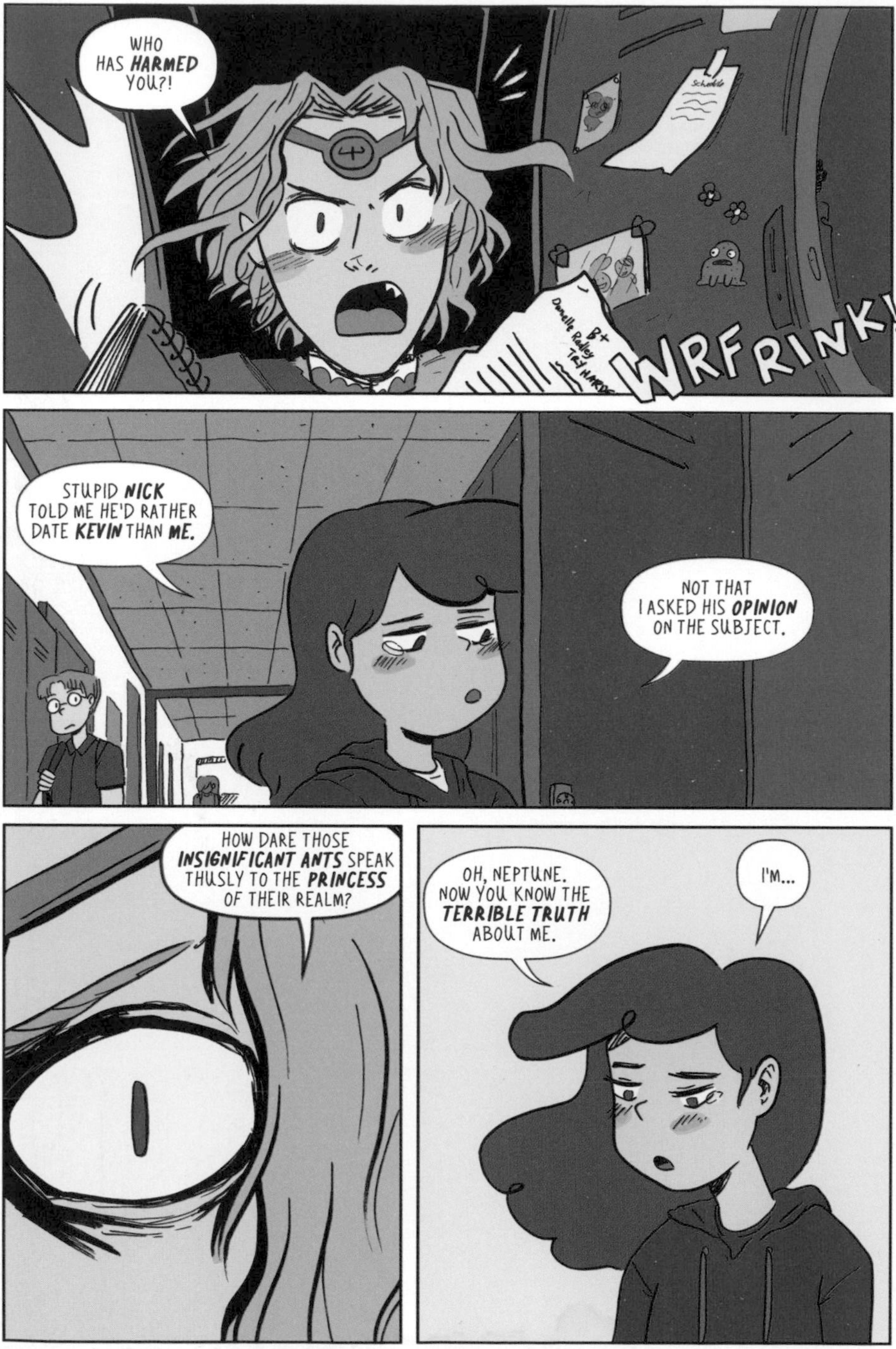
WHO HAS HARMED YOU?!
WRFRINK!
STUPID NICK TOLD ME HE'D RATHER DATE KEVIN THAN ME.
NOT THAT I ASKED HIS OPINION ON THE SUBJECT.
HOW DARE THOSE INSIGNIFICANT ANTS SPEAK THUSLY TO THE PRINCESS OF THEIR REALM?
OH, NEPTUNE. NOW YOU KNOW THE TERRIBLE TRUTH ABOUT ME.
I'M...

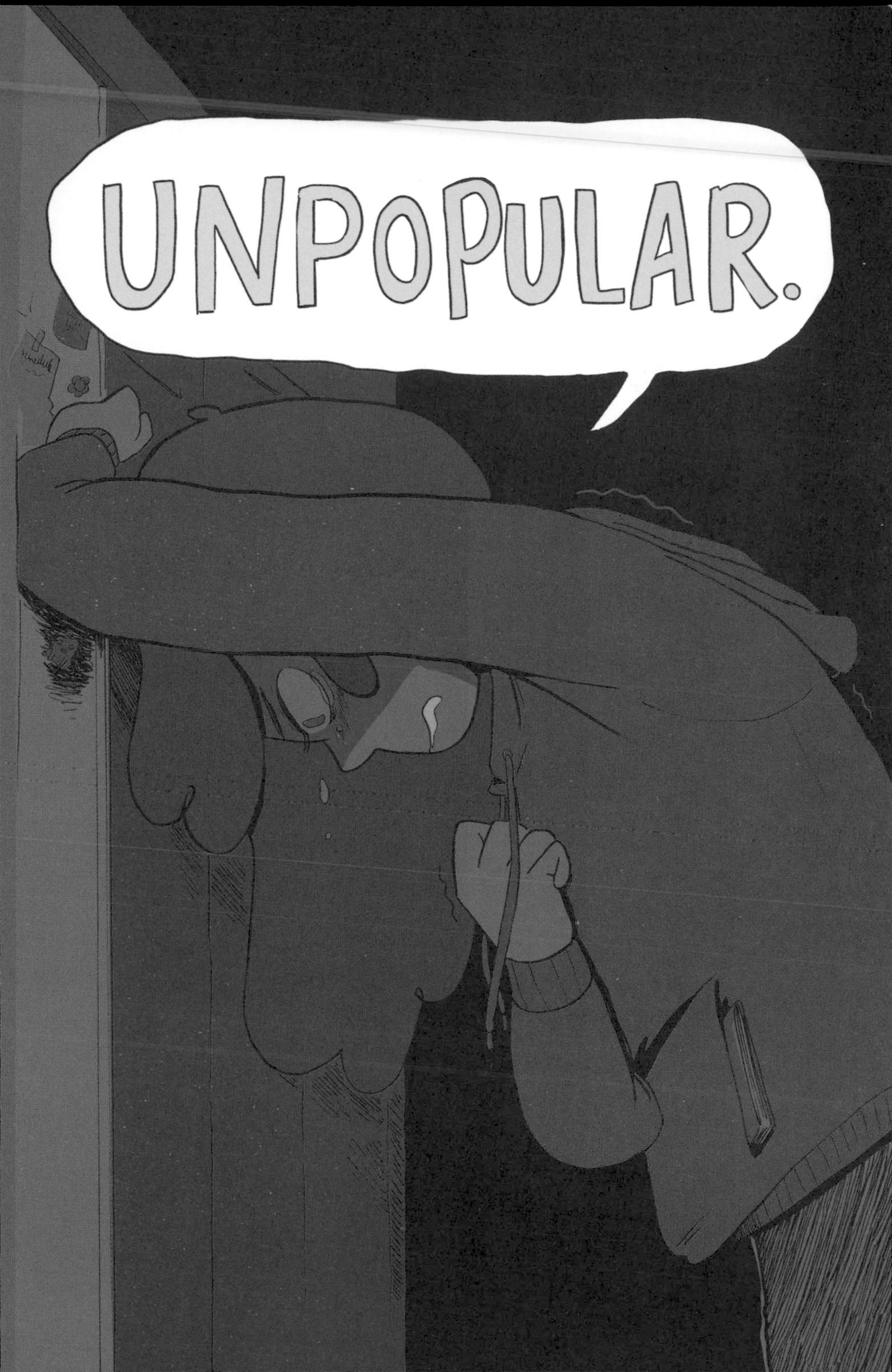
UNPOPULAR.

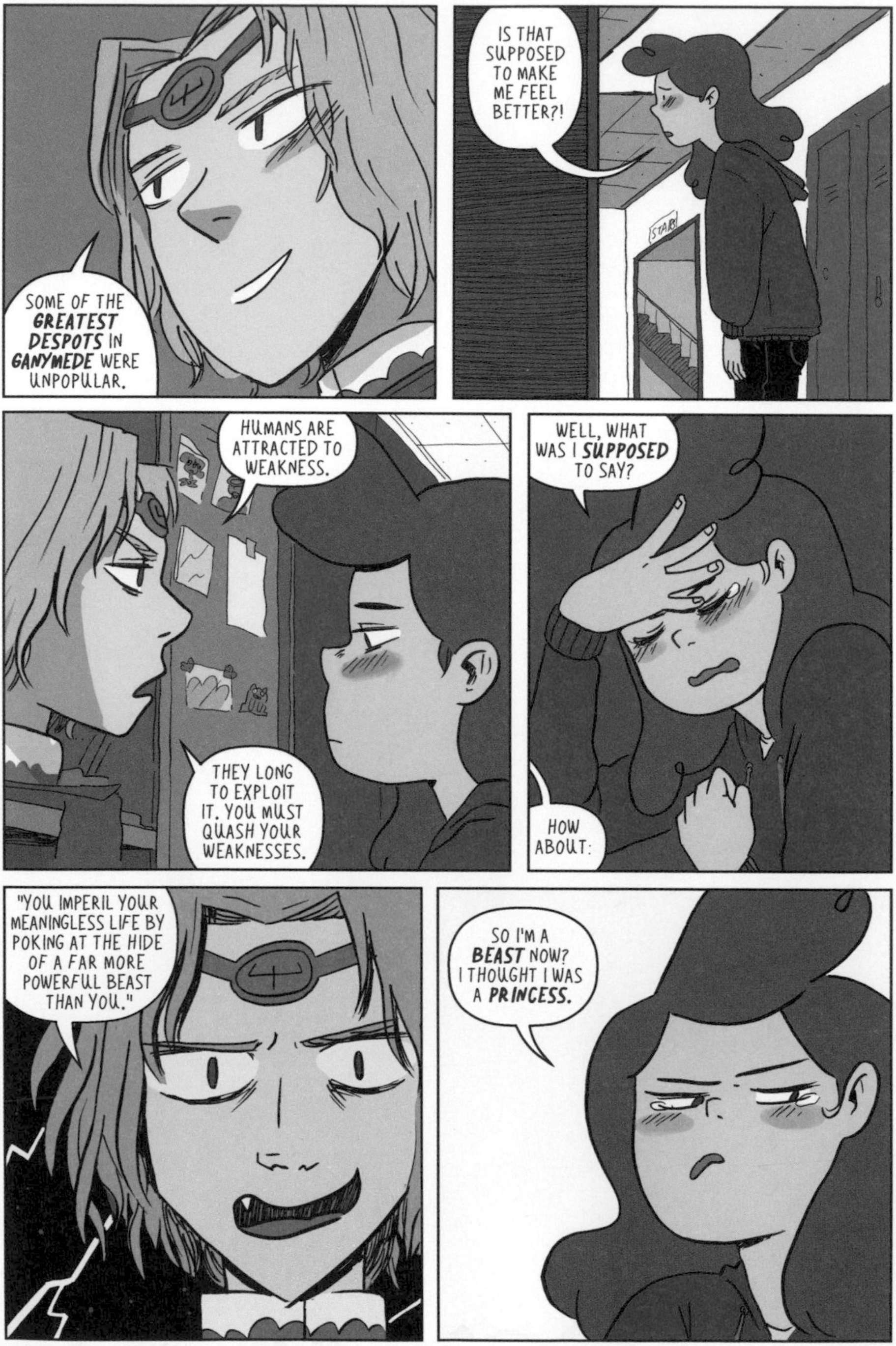
SOME OF THE **GREATEST DESPOTS** IN **GANYMEDE** WERE UNPOPULAR.
IS THAT SUPPOSED TO MAKE ME FEEL BETTER?!
STAIR
HUMANS ARE ATTRACTED TO WEAKNESS.
THEY LONG TO EXPLOIT IT. YOU MUST QUASH YOUR WEAKNESSES.
WELL, WHAT WAS I **SUPPOSED** TO SAY?
HOW ABOUT:
"YOU IMPERIL YOUR MEANINGLESS LIFE BY POKING AT THE HIDE OF A FAR MORE POWERFUL BEAST THAN YOU."
SO I'M A **BEAST** NOW? I THOUGHT I WAS A **PRINCESS.**

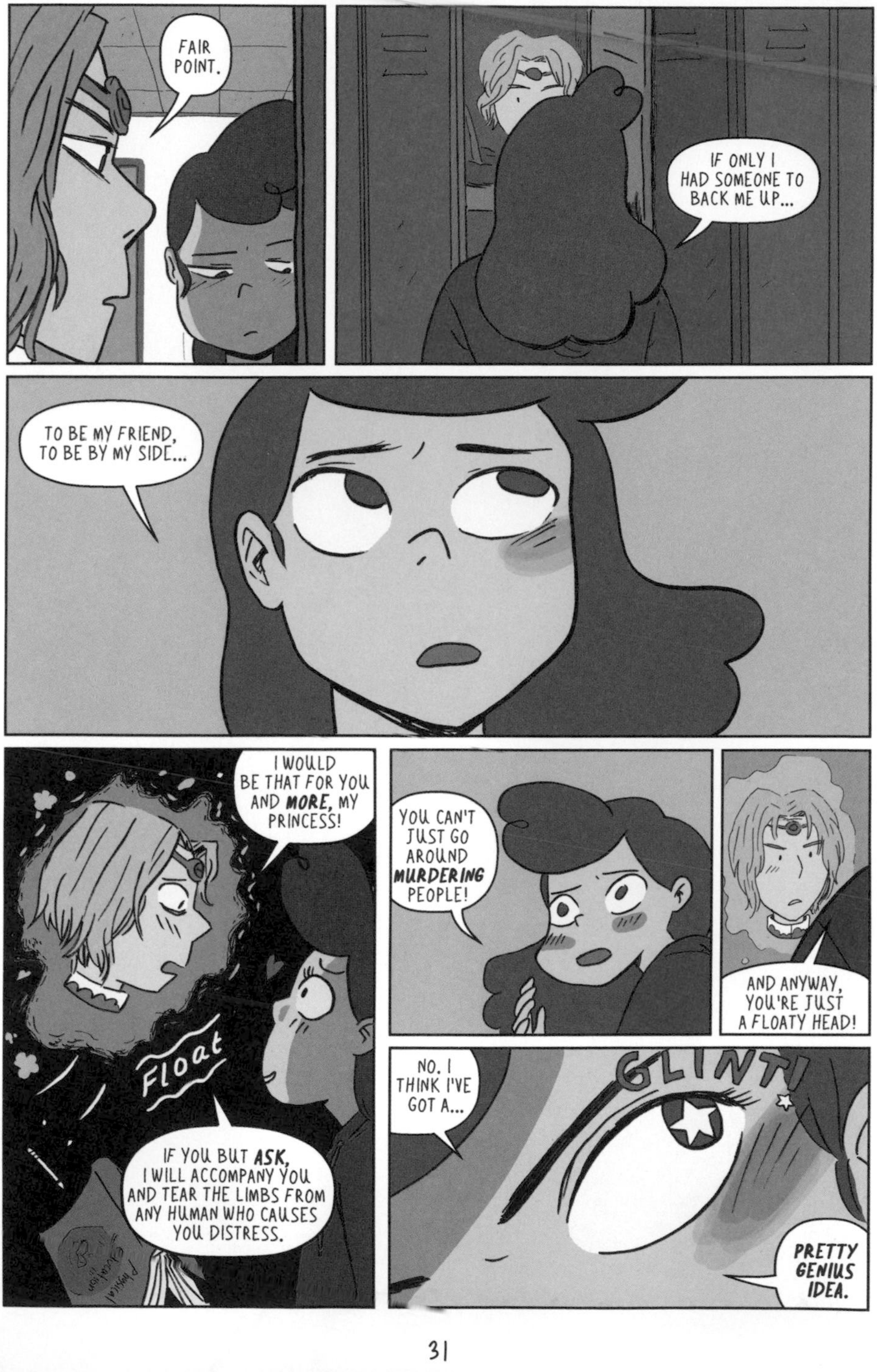
FAIR POINT.
IF ONLY I HAD SOMEONE TO BACK ME UP...
TO BE MY FRIEND, TO BE BY MY SIDE...
I WOULD BE THAT FOR YOU AND MORE, MY PRINCESS!
Float
IF YOU BUT ASK, I WILL ACCOMPANY YOU AND TEAR THE LIMBS FROM ANY HUMAN WHO CAUSES YOU DISTRESS.
YOU CAN'T JUST GO AROUND MURDERING PEOPLE!
AND ANYWAY, YOU'RE JUST A FLOATY HEAD!
NO. I THINK I'VE GOT A...
GLINT!
PRETTY GENIUS IDEA.

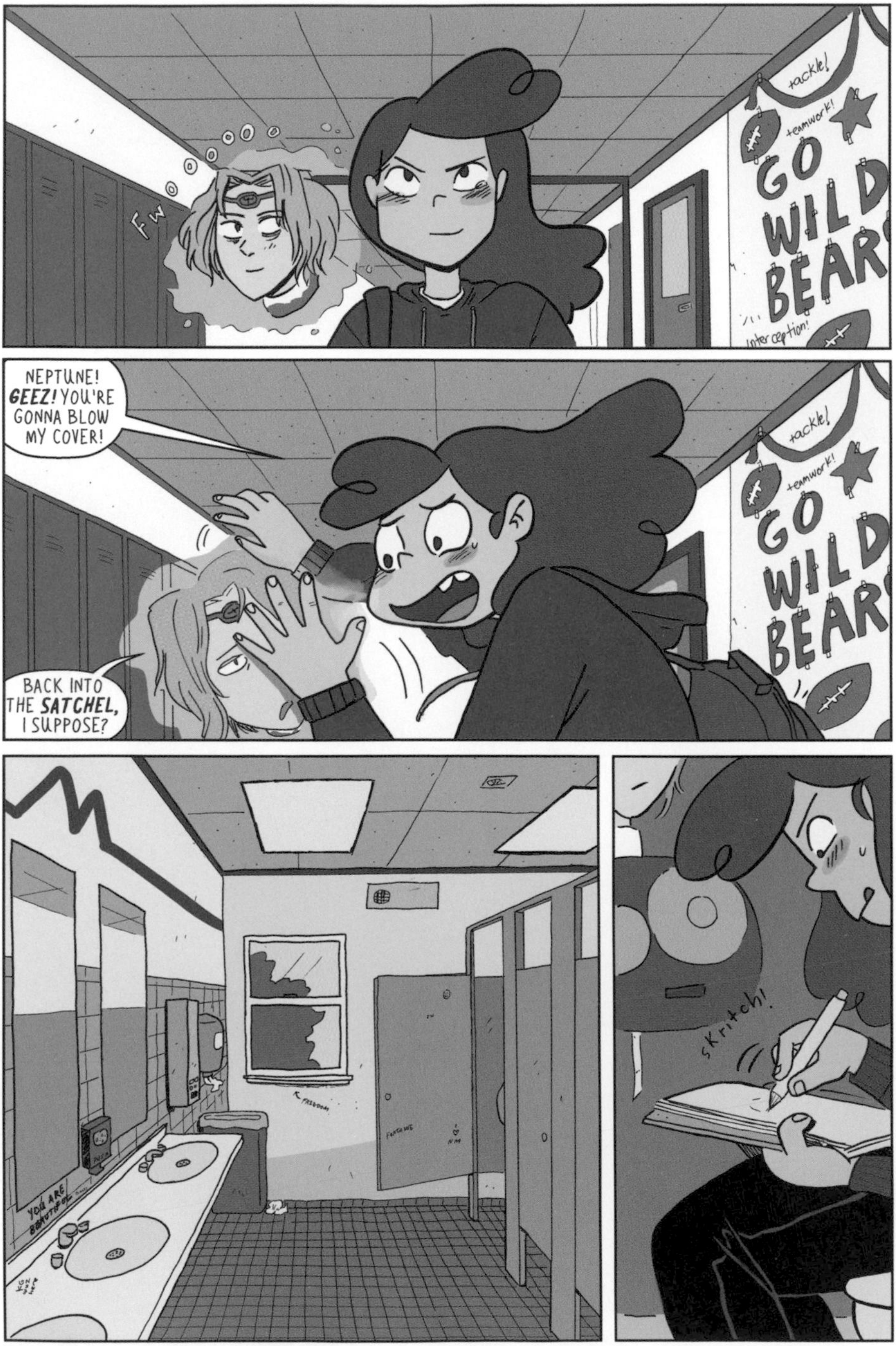
Fw
tackle!
teamwork!
GO WILD BEAR
interception!
NEPTUNE! GEEZ! YOU'RE GONNA BLOW MY COVER!
BACK INTO THE SATCHEL, I SUPPOSE?
tackle!
teamwork!
GO WILD BEAR
FREEDOM
YOU ARE BEAUTIFUL
sKritch!

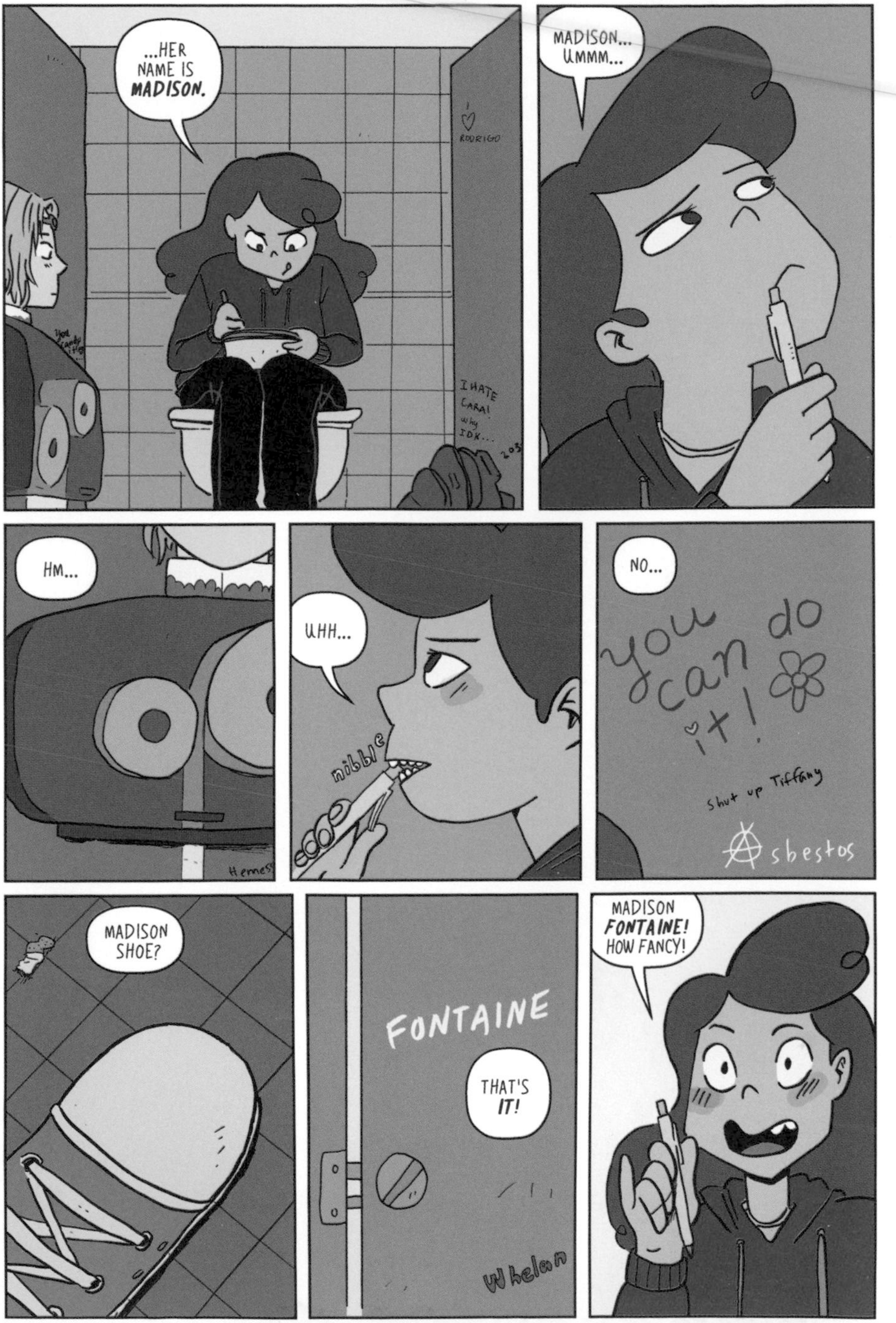
...HER NAME IS MADISON.
I ♡ RODRIGO
I HATE CARA! why IDK...
MADISON... UMMM...
HM...
UHH...
nibble
NO...
you can do it!
Shut up Tiffany
Asbestos
MADISON SHOE?
FONTAINE
THAT'S IT!
Whelan
MADISON FONTAINE! HOW FANCY!

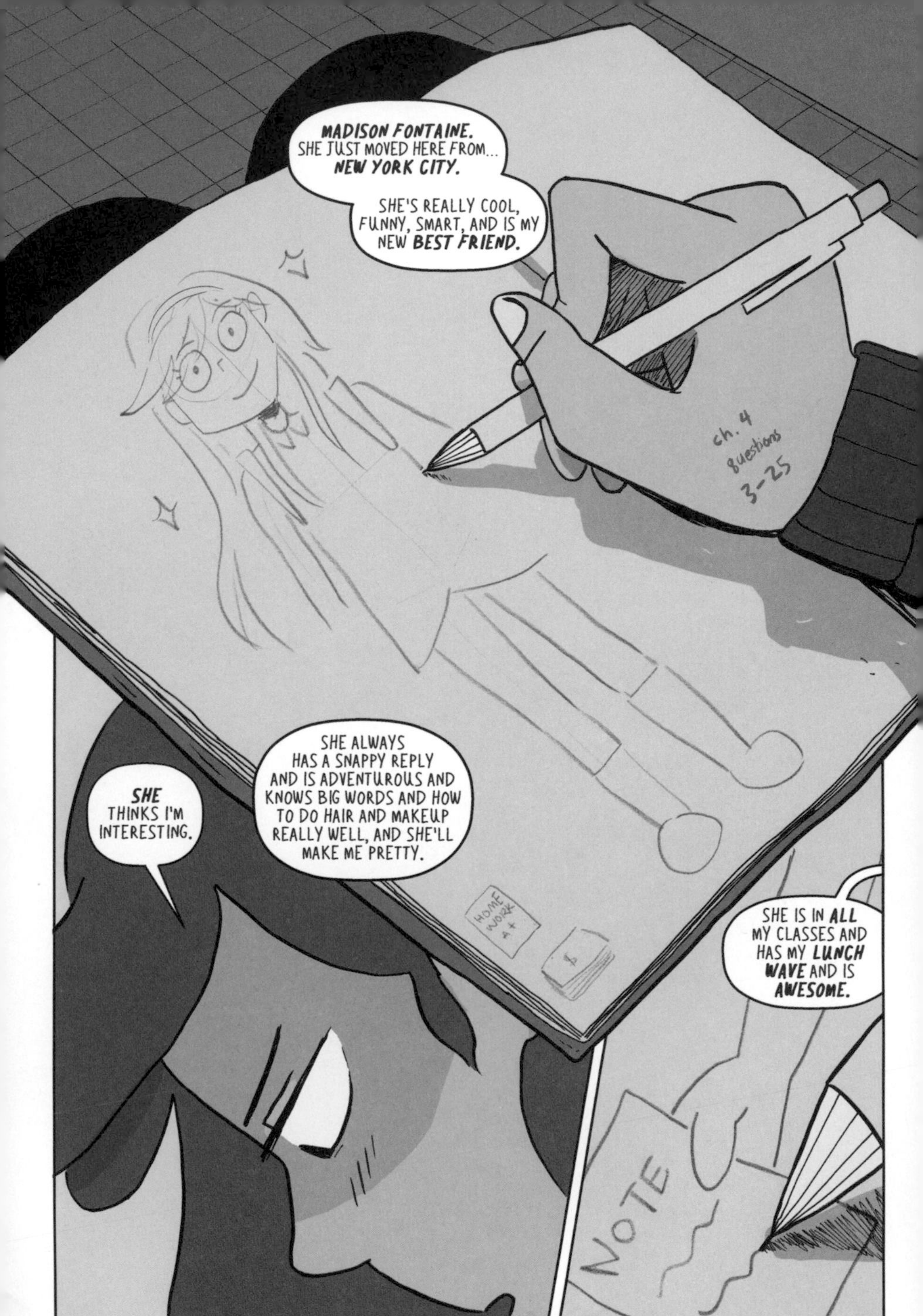
MADISON FONTAINE. SHE JUST MOVED HERE FROM... NEW YORK CITY.
SHE'S REALLY COOL, FUNNY, SMART, AND IS MY NEW BEST FRIEND.
ch. 4 questions 3-25
SHE THINKS I'M INTERESTING.
SHE ALWAYS HAS A SNAPPY REPLY AND IS ADVENTUROUS AND KNOWS BIG WORDS AND HOW TO DO HAIR AND MAKEUP REALLY WELL, AND SHE'LL MAKE ME PRETTY.
HOME WORK A+
SHE IS IN ALL MY CLASSES AND HAS MY LUNCH WAVE AND IS AWESOME.
NOTE

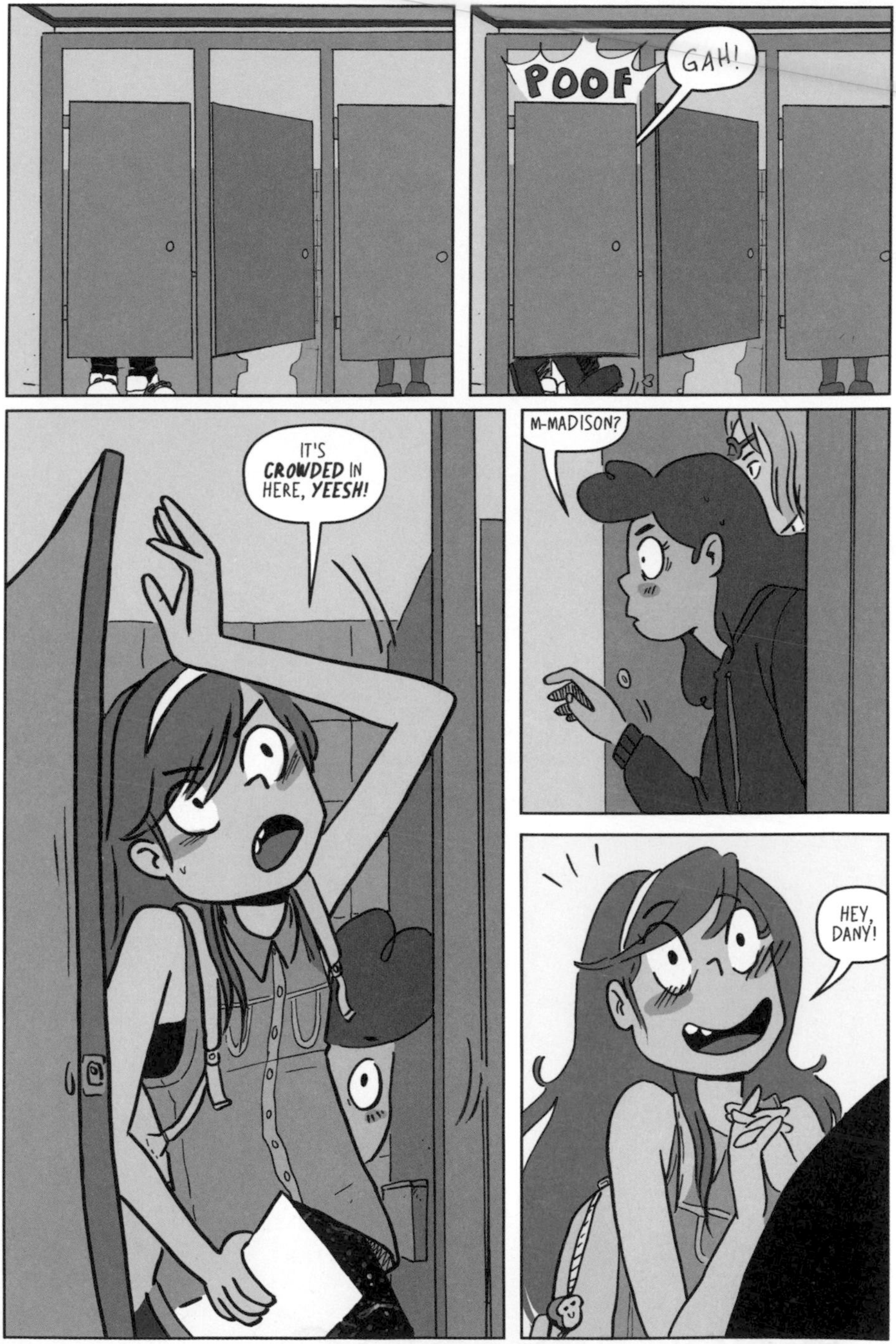
POOF
GAH!
IT'S CROWDED IN HERE, YEESH!
M-MADISON?
HEY, DANY!

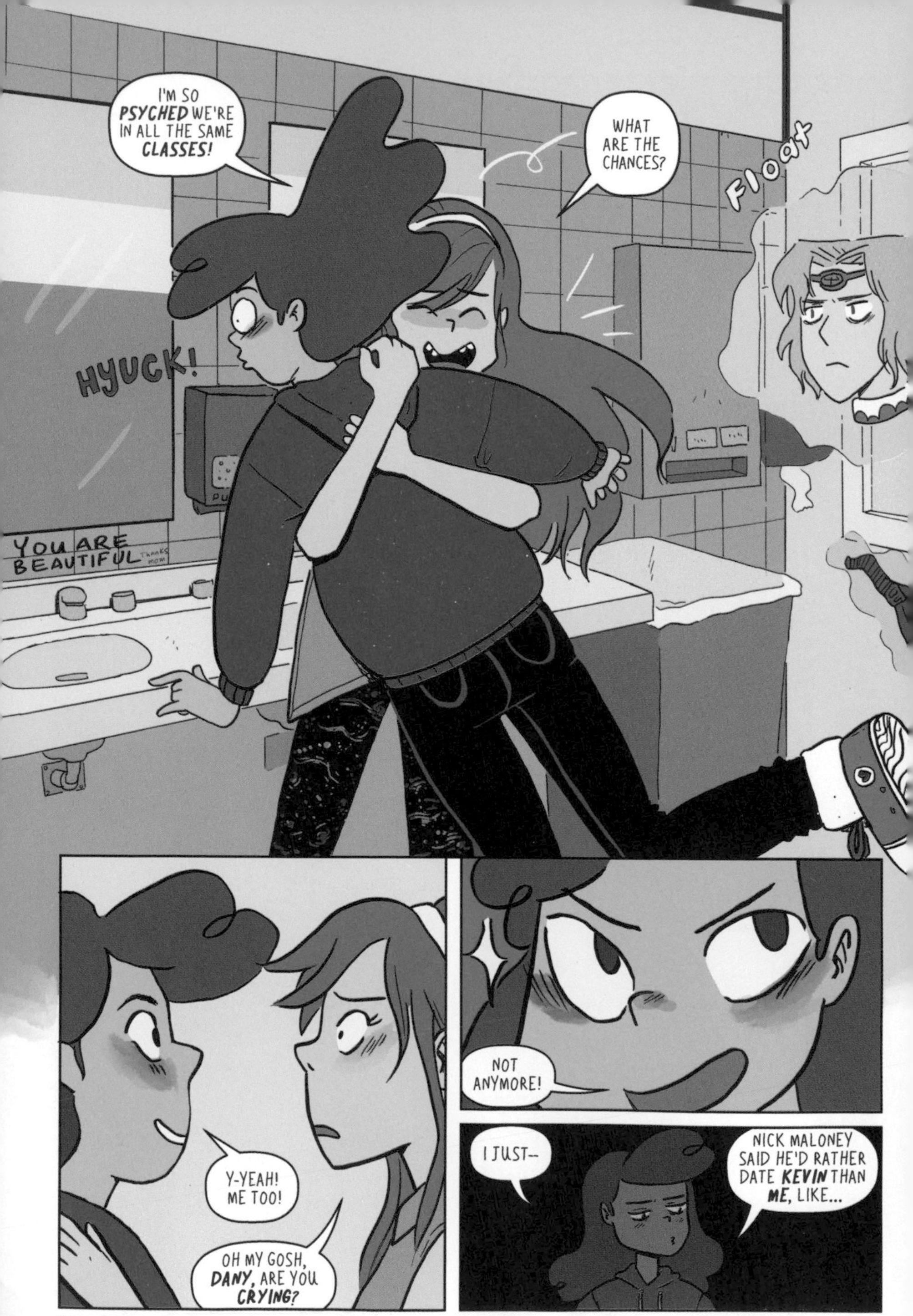

I'M SO PSYCHED WE'RE IN ALL THE SAME CLASSES!
WHAT ARE THE CHANCES?
Float
HYUCK!
YOU ARE BEAUTIFUL
Thanks mom
Y-YEAH! ME TOO!
OH MY GOSH, DANY, ARE YOU CRYING?
NOT ANYMORE!
I JUST--
NICK MALONEY SAID HE'D RATHER DATE KEVIN THAN ME, LIKE...

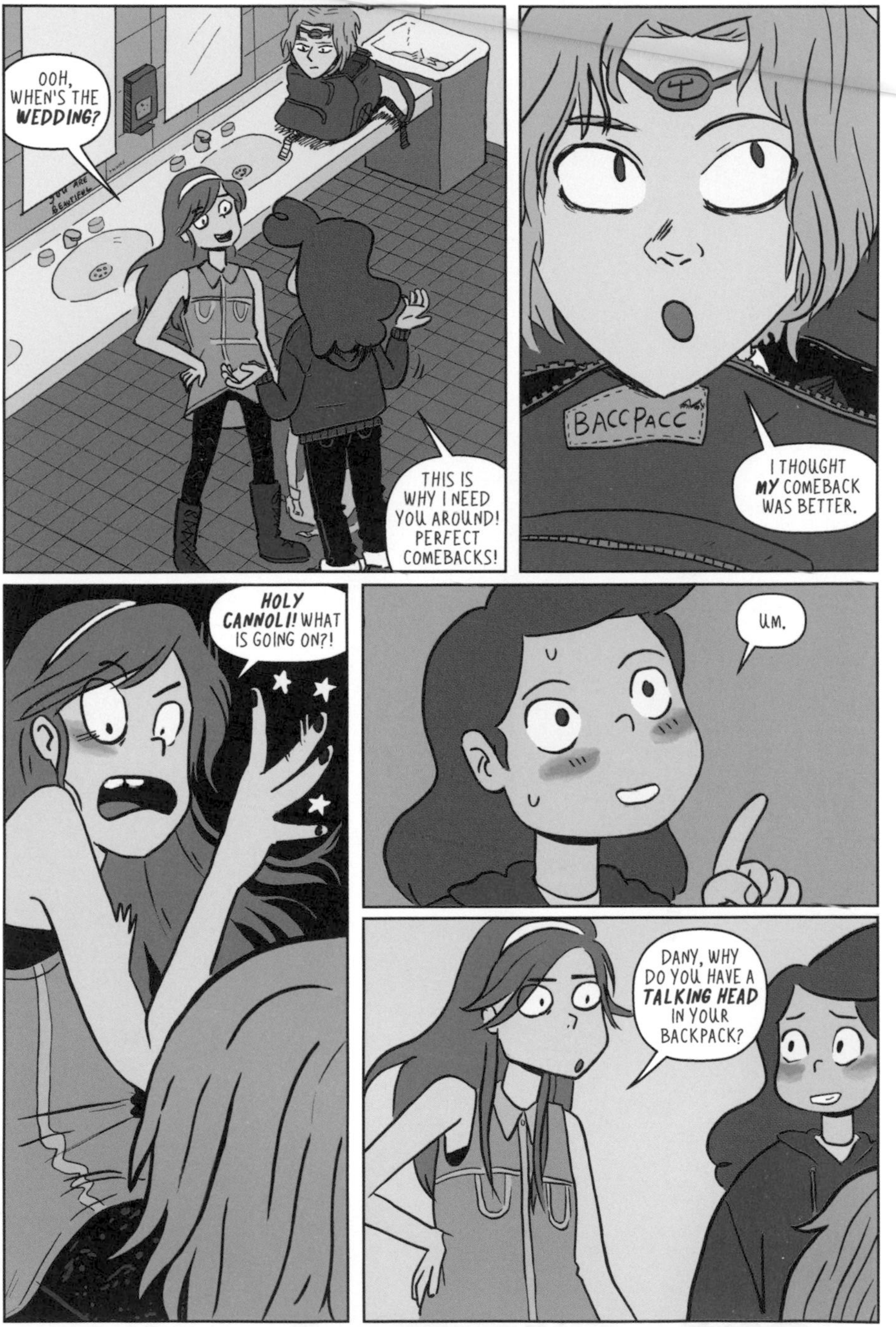
OOH, WHEN'S THE WEDDING?
YOU ARE BEAUTIFUL
THIS IS WHY I NEED YOU AROUND! PERFECT COMEBACKS!
BACCPACC
I THOUGHT MY COMEBACK WAS BETTER.
HOLY CANNOLI! WHAT IS GOING ON?!
UM.
DANY, WHY DO YOU HAVE A TALKING HEAD IN YOUR BACKPACK?

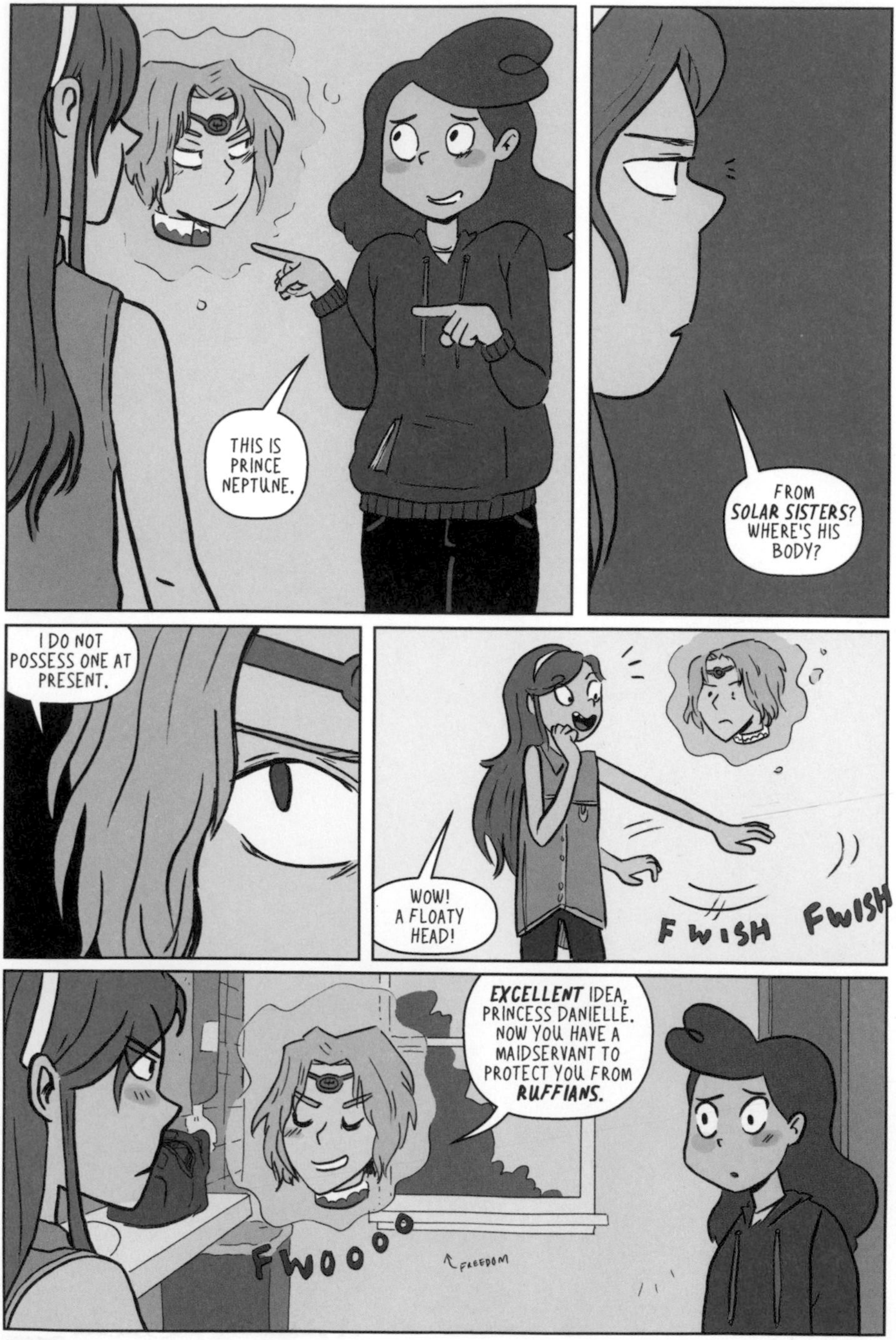
THIS IS PRINCE NEPTUNE.
FROM SOLAR SISTERS? WHERE'S HIS BODY?
I DO NOT POSSESS ONE AT PRESENT.
WOW! A FLOATY HEAD!
FWISH FWISH
EXCELLENT IDEA, PRINCESS DANIELLE. NOW YOU HAVE A MAIDSERVANT TO PROTECT YOU FROM RUFFIANS.
FWOOOO
FREEDOM

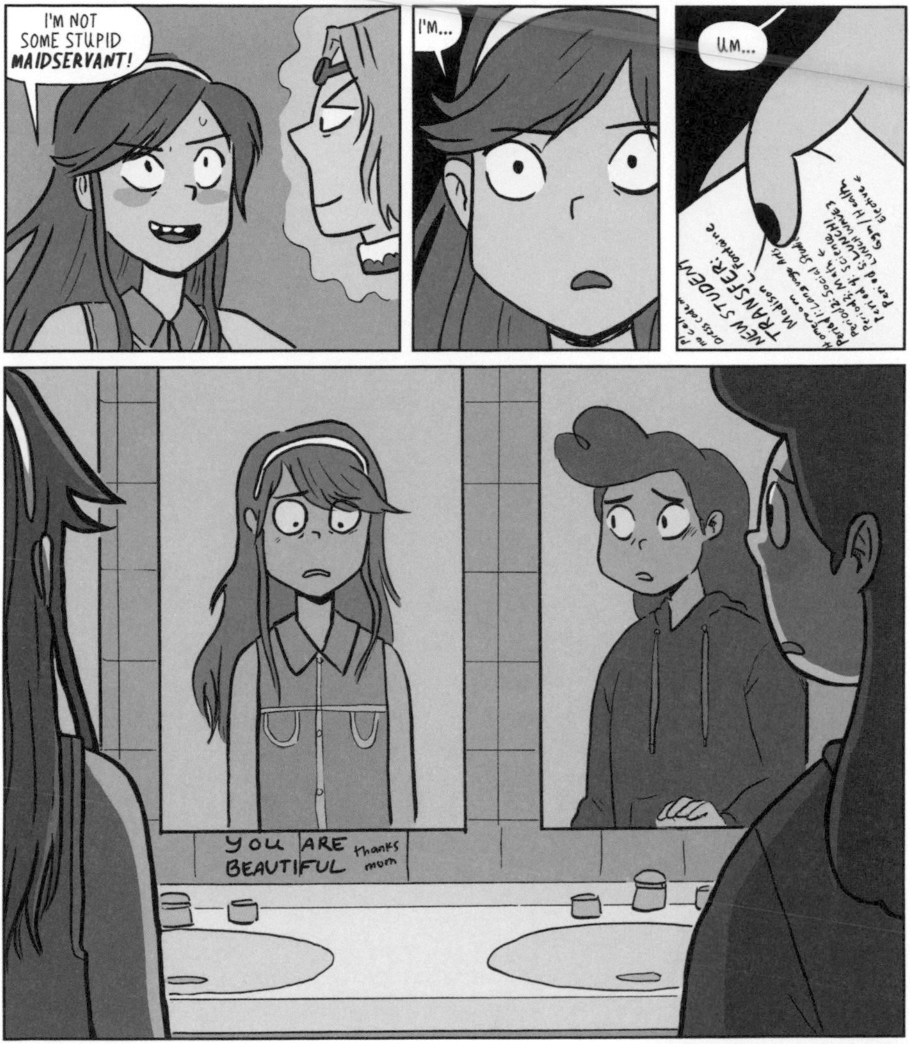
I'M NOT SOME STUPID **MAIDSERVANT!**
I'M...
UM...
NEW STUDENT
TRANSFER:
Madison L. Fontaine
YOU ARE BEAUTIFUL
thanks mom
...OH, DANY. LOOK AT YOU. I CAN'T LET YOU OUT THERE LOOKING LIKE YOU'RE SAD.

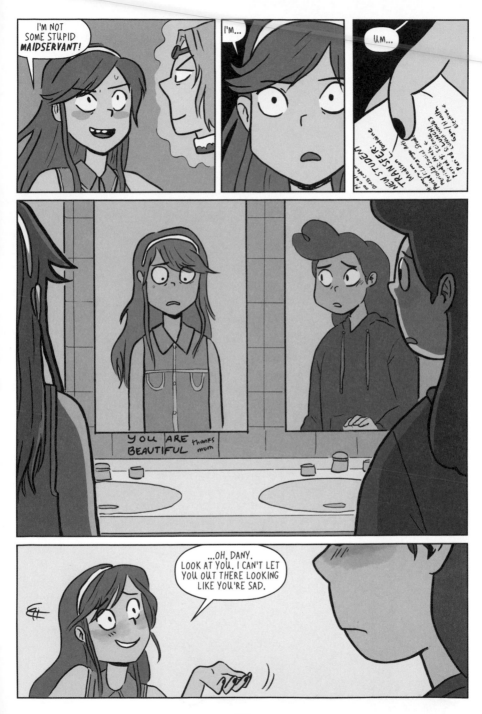

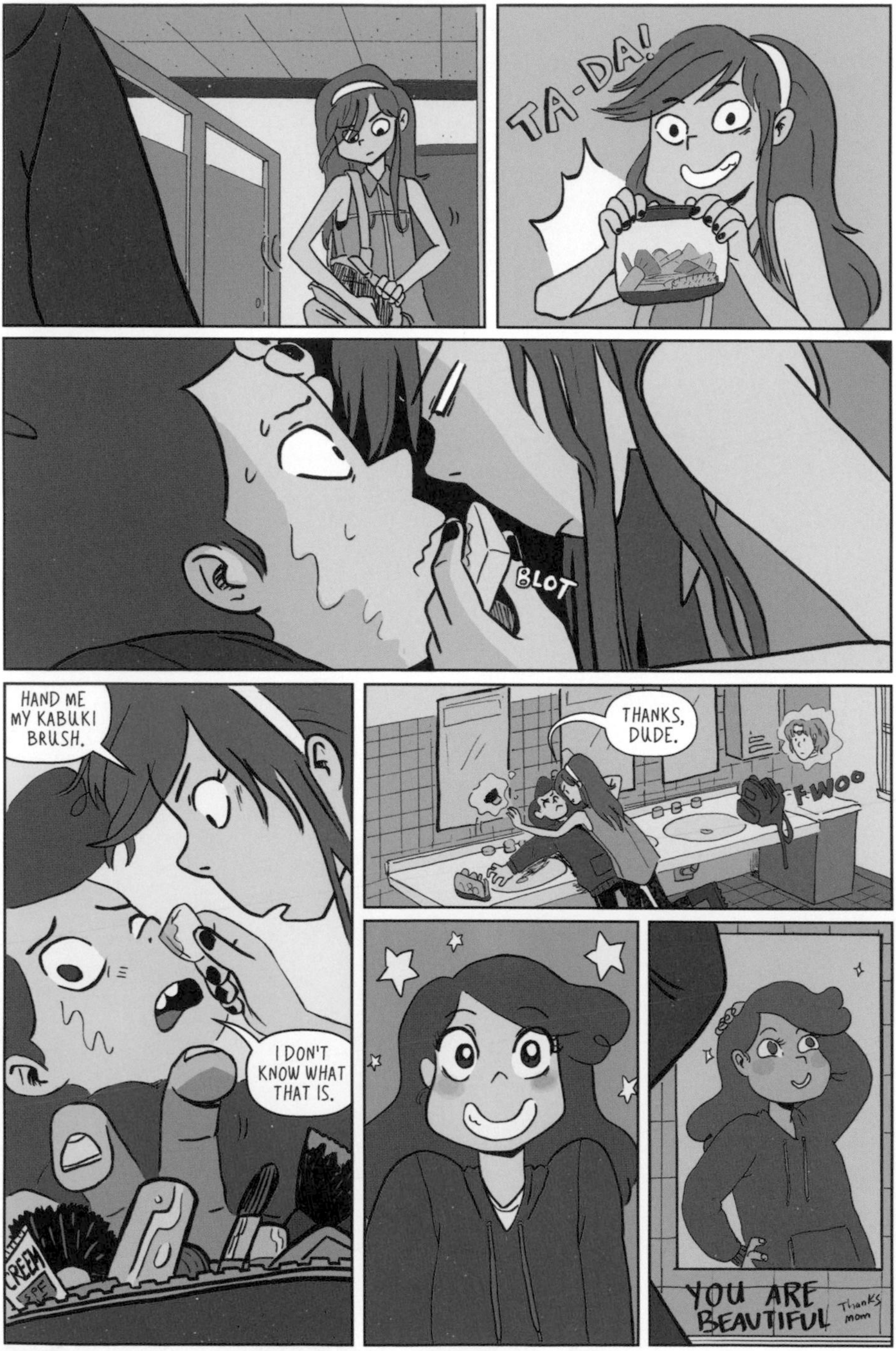
TA-DA!
BLOT
HAND ME MY KABUKI BRUSH.
I DON'T KNOW WHAT THAT IS.
THANKS, DUDE.
FWOO
CREEM
YOU ARE BEAUTIFUL
Thanks mom

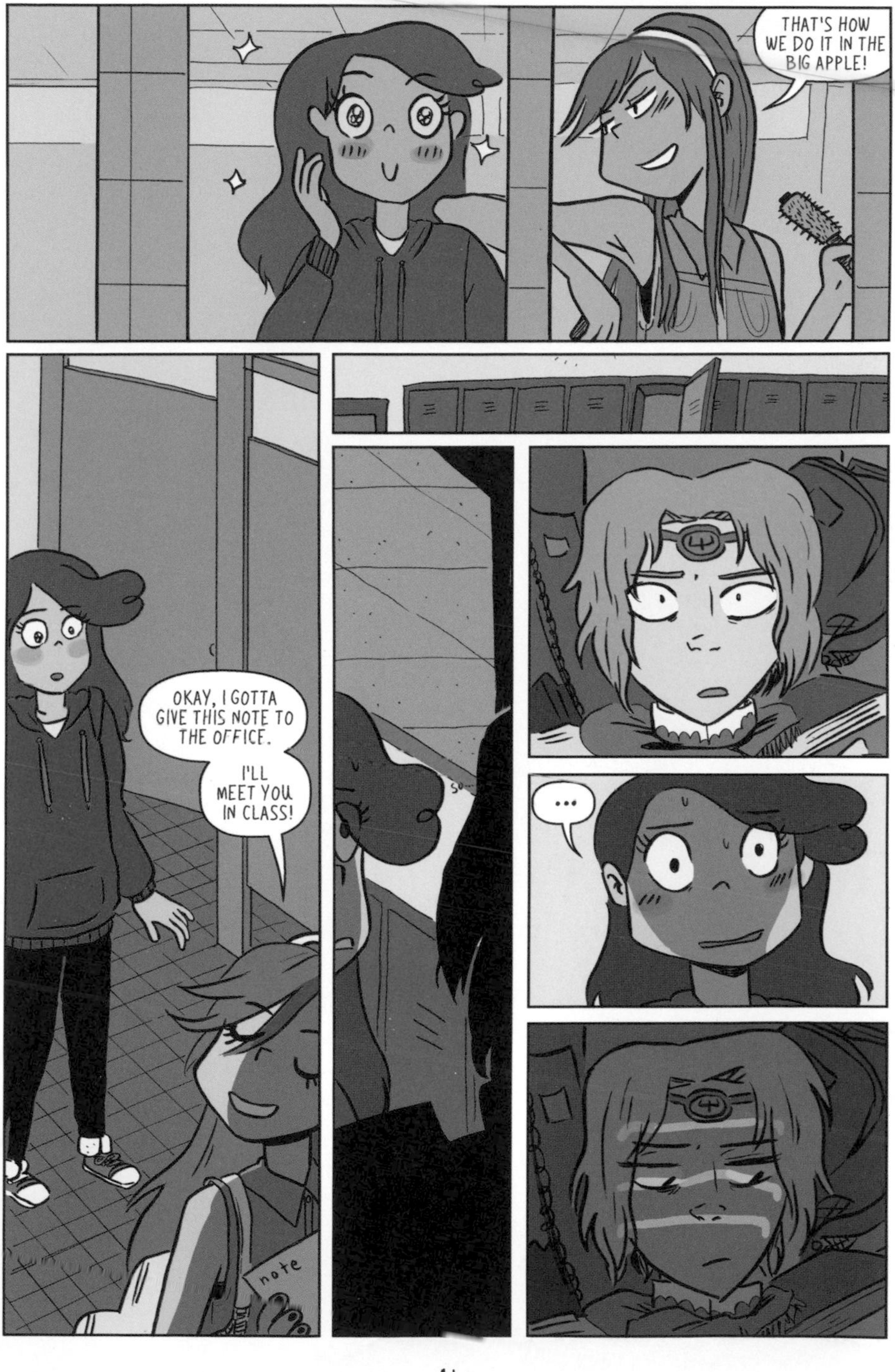
THAT'S HOW WE DO IT IN THE BIG APPLE!
OKAY, I GOTTA GIVE THIS NOTE TO THE OFFICE.
I'LL MEET YOU IN CLASS!
note
...

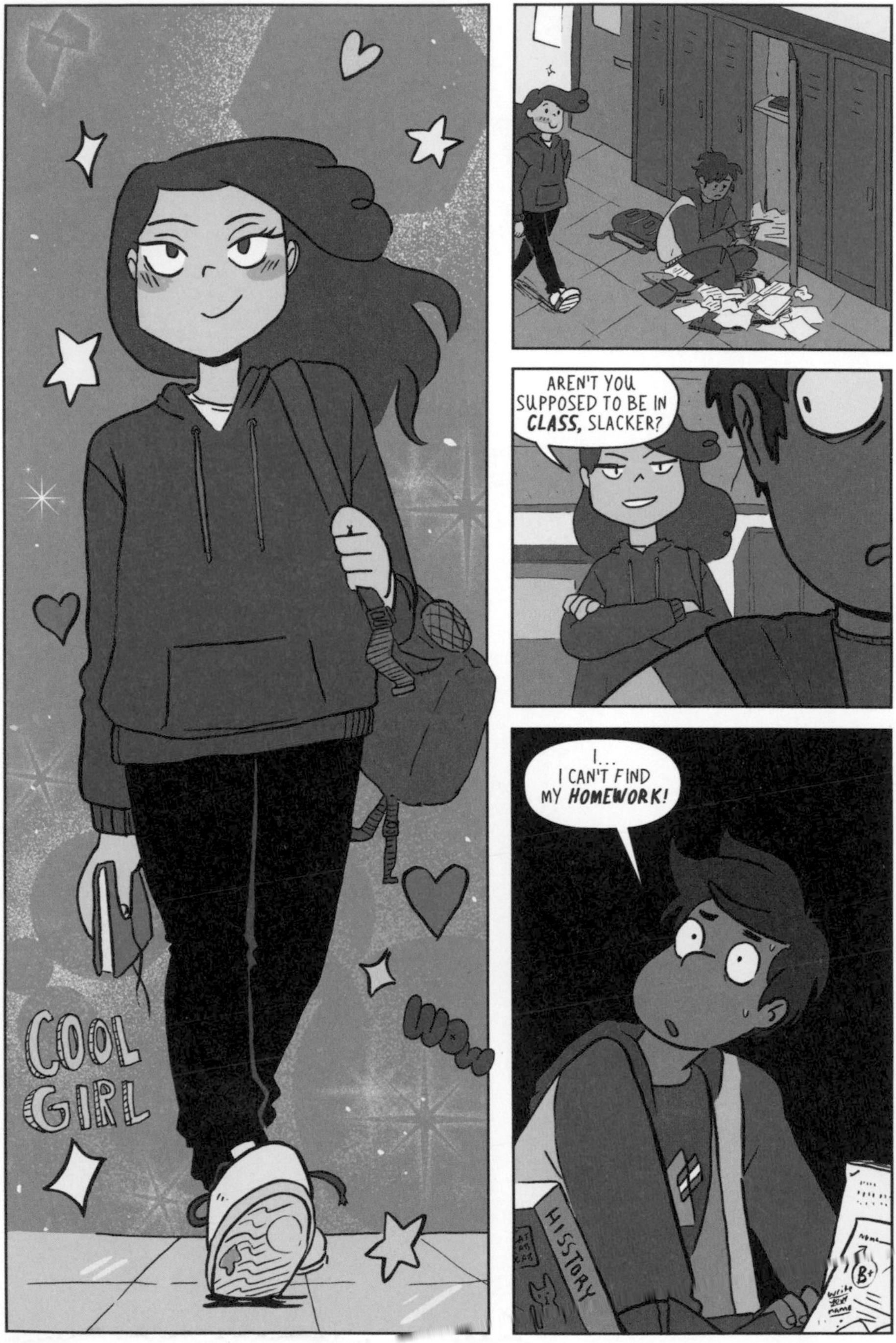
COOL GIRL
WOW
AREN'T YOU SUPPOSED TO BE IN CLASS, SLACKER?
I... I CAN'T FIND MY HOMEWORK!
HISSTORY
B+

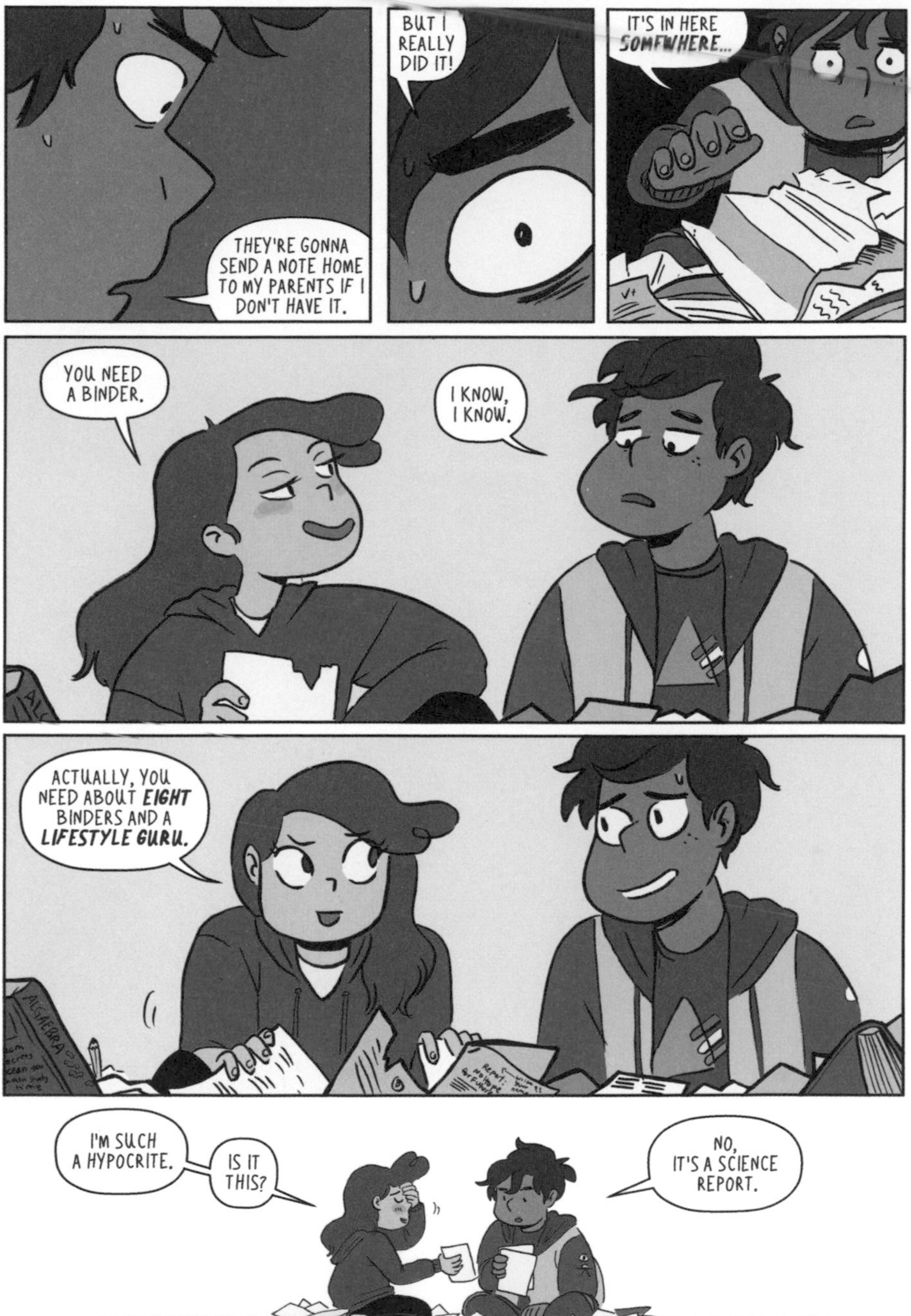
THEY'RE GONNA SEND A NOTE HOME TO MY PARENTS IF I DON'T HAVE IT.
BUT I REALLY DID IT!
IT'S IN HERE SOMEWHERE...
YOU NEED A BINDER.
I KNOW, I KNOW.
ACTUALLY, YOU NEED ABOUT EIGHT BINDERS AND A LIFESTYLE GURU.
ALGEBRA
I'M SUCH A HYPOCRITE.
IS IT THIS?
NO, IT'S A SCIENCE REPORT.

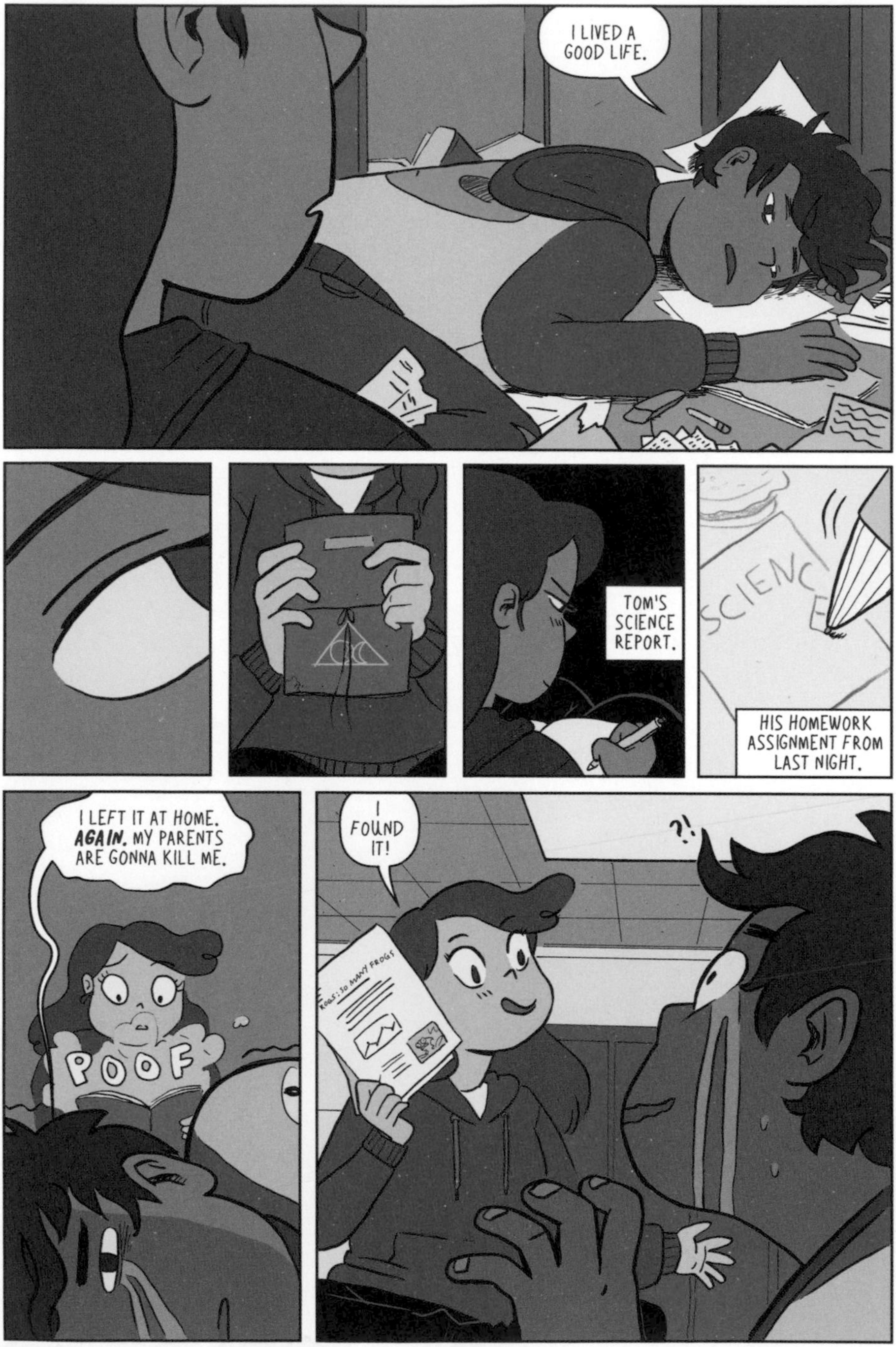

I LIVED A GOOD LIFE.
TOM'S SCIENCE REPORT.
SCIENCE
HIS HOMEWORK ASSIGNMENT FROM LAST NIGHT.
I LEFT IT AT HOME. **AGAIN.** MY PARENTS ARE GONNA KILL ME.
POOF
I FOUND IT!
FROGS: SO MANY FROGS
?!

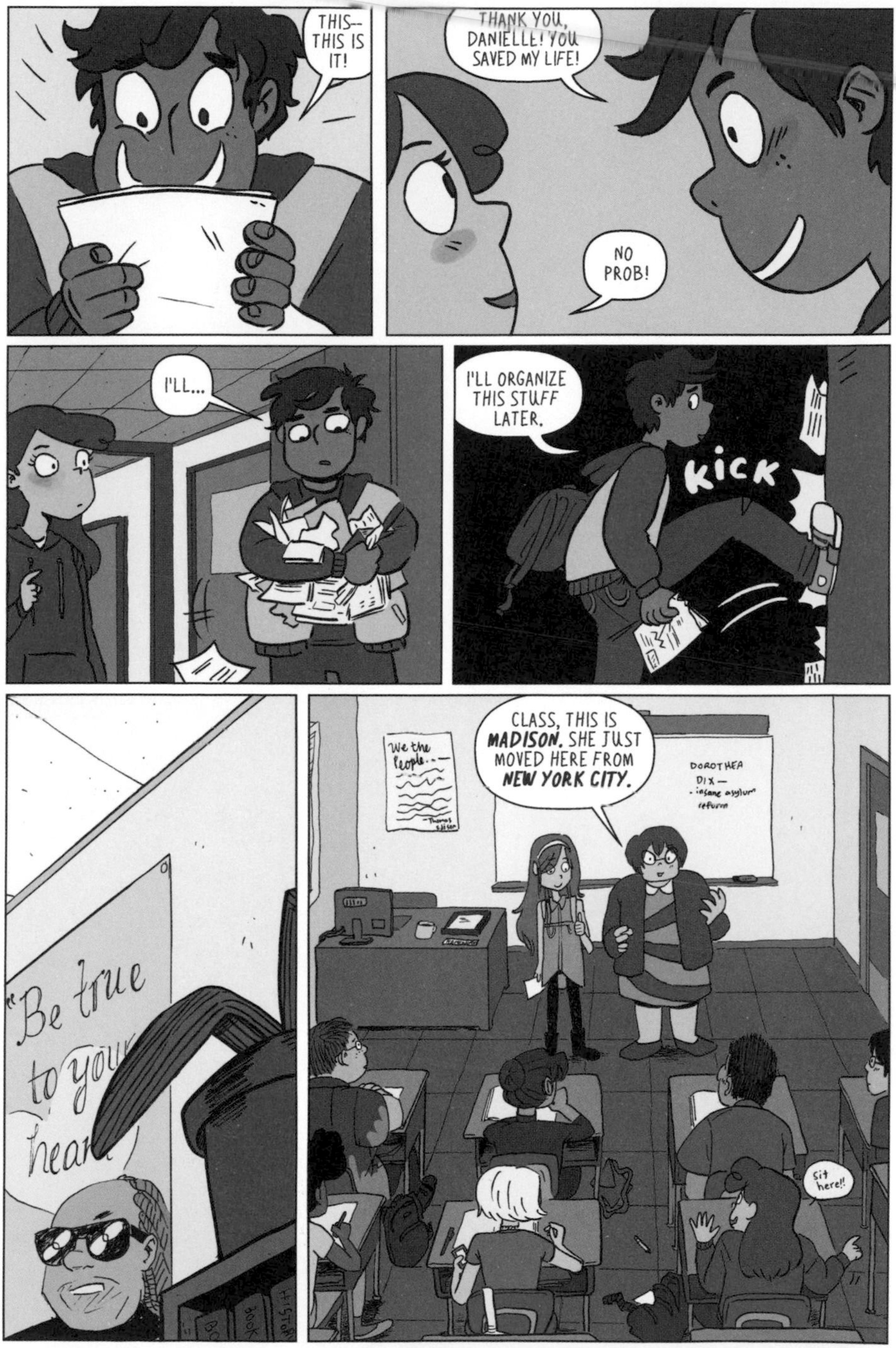
THIS-- THIS IS IT!
THANK YOU, DANIELLE! YOU SAVED MY LIFE!
NO PROB!
I'LL...
I'LL ORGANIZE THIS STUFF LATER.
KICK
"Be true to your heart"
We the People...
CLASS, THIS IS MADISON. SHE JUST MOVED HERE FROM NEW YORK CITY.
DOROTHEA DIX — - insane asylum reform
Sit here!!

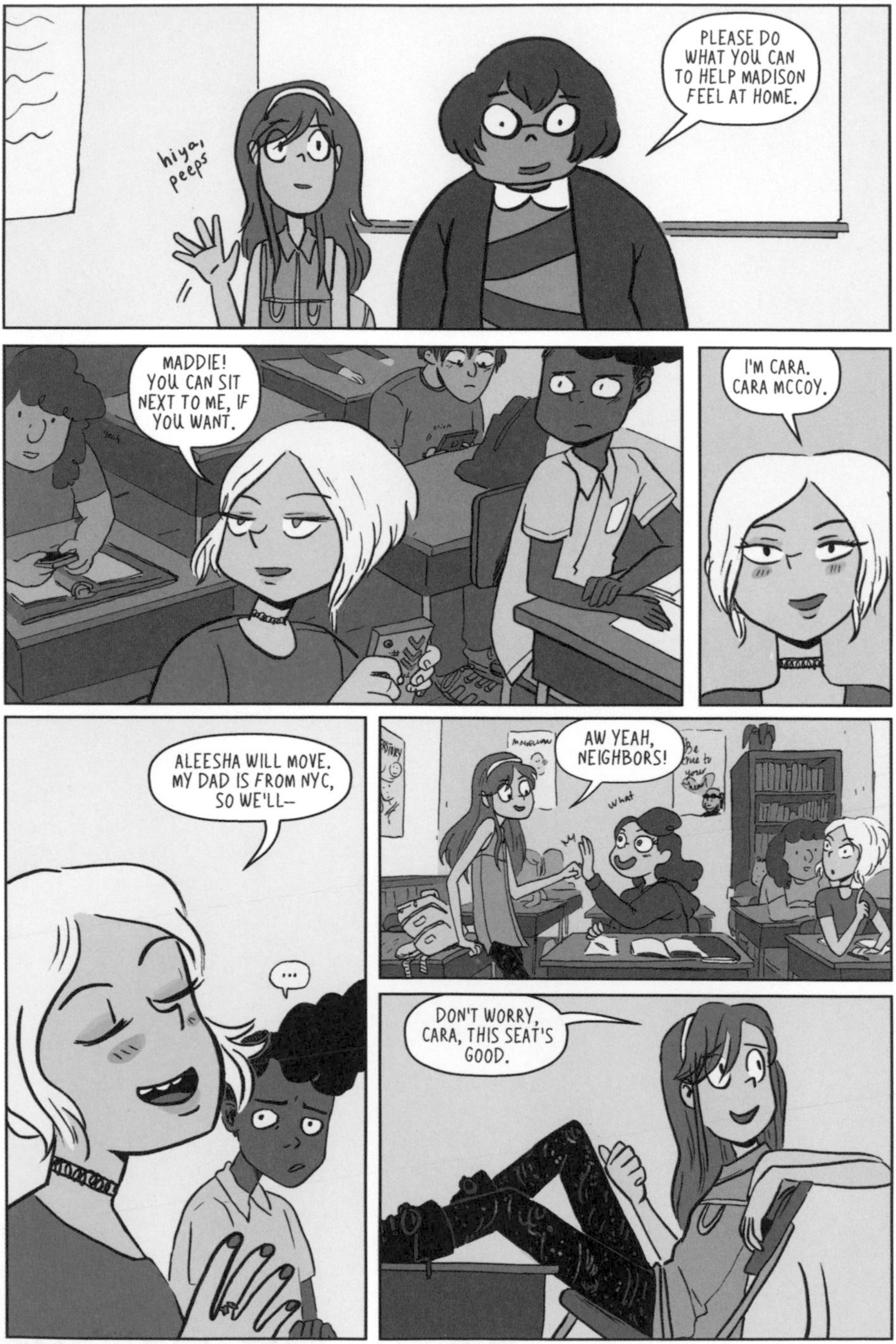
PLEASE DO WHAT YOU CAN TO HELP MADISON FEEL AT HOME.
hiya, peeps
MADDIE! YOU CAN SIT NEXT TO ME, IF YOU WANT.
I'M CARA. CARA MCCOY.
ALEESHA WILL MOVE. MY DAD IS FROM NYC, SO WE'LL--
...
AW YEAH, NEIGHBORS!
what
DON'T WORRY, CARA, THIS SEAT'S GOOD.

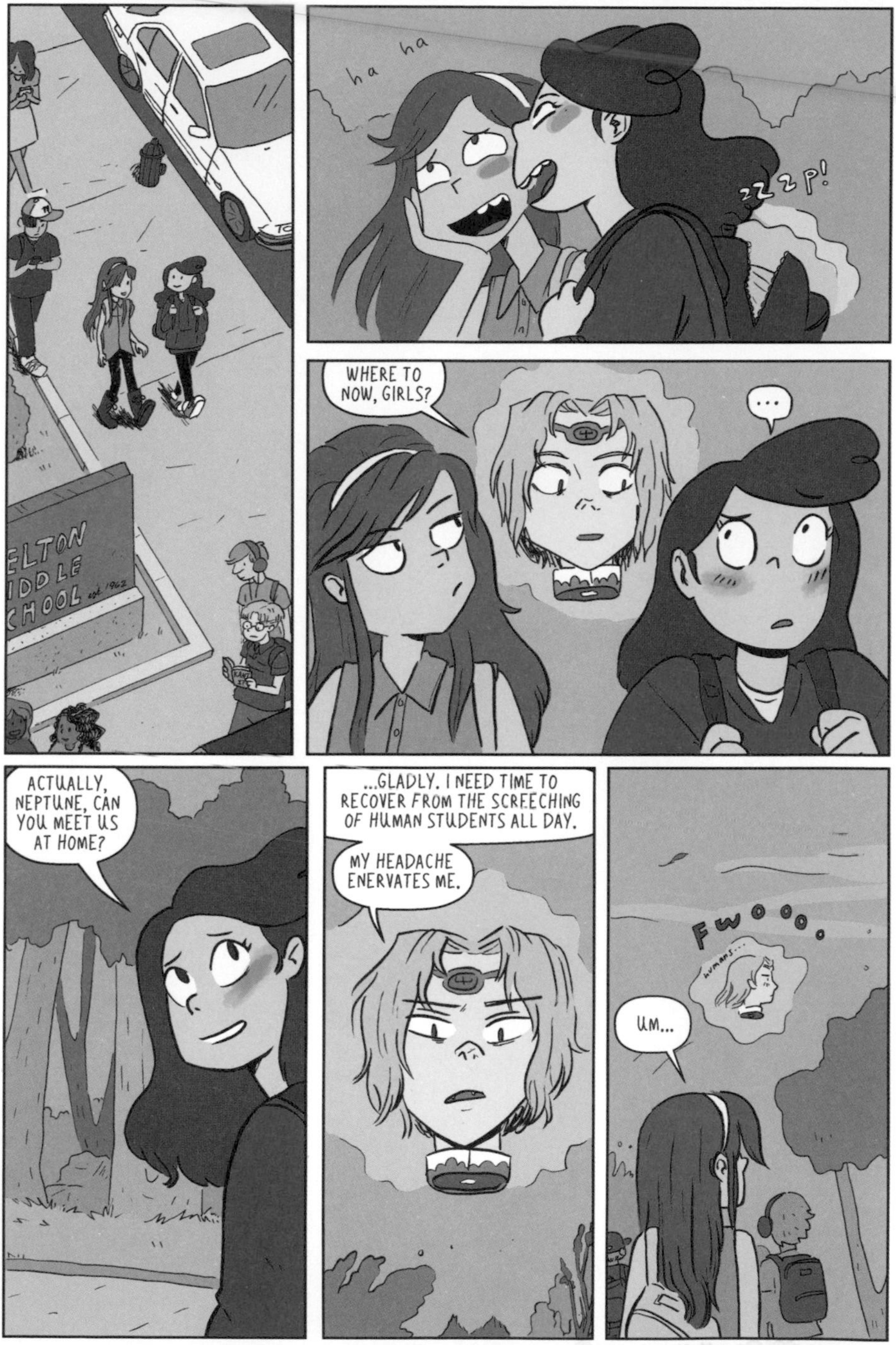
ELTON
IDDLE
SCHOOL est 1962
ha ha
ZZZP!
WHERE TO NOW, GIRLS?
...
ACTUALLY, NEPTUNE, CAN YOU MEET US AT HOME?
...GLADLY. I NEED TIME TO RECOVER FROM THE SCREECHING OF HUMAN STUDENTS ALL DAY.
MY HEADACHE ENERVATES ME.
FWOOOO
humans...
UM...

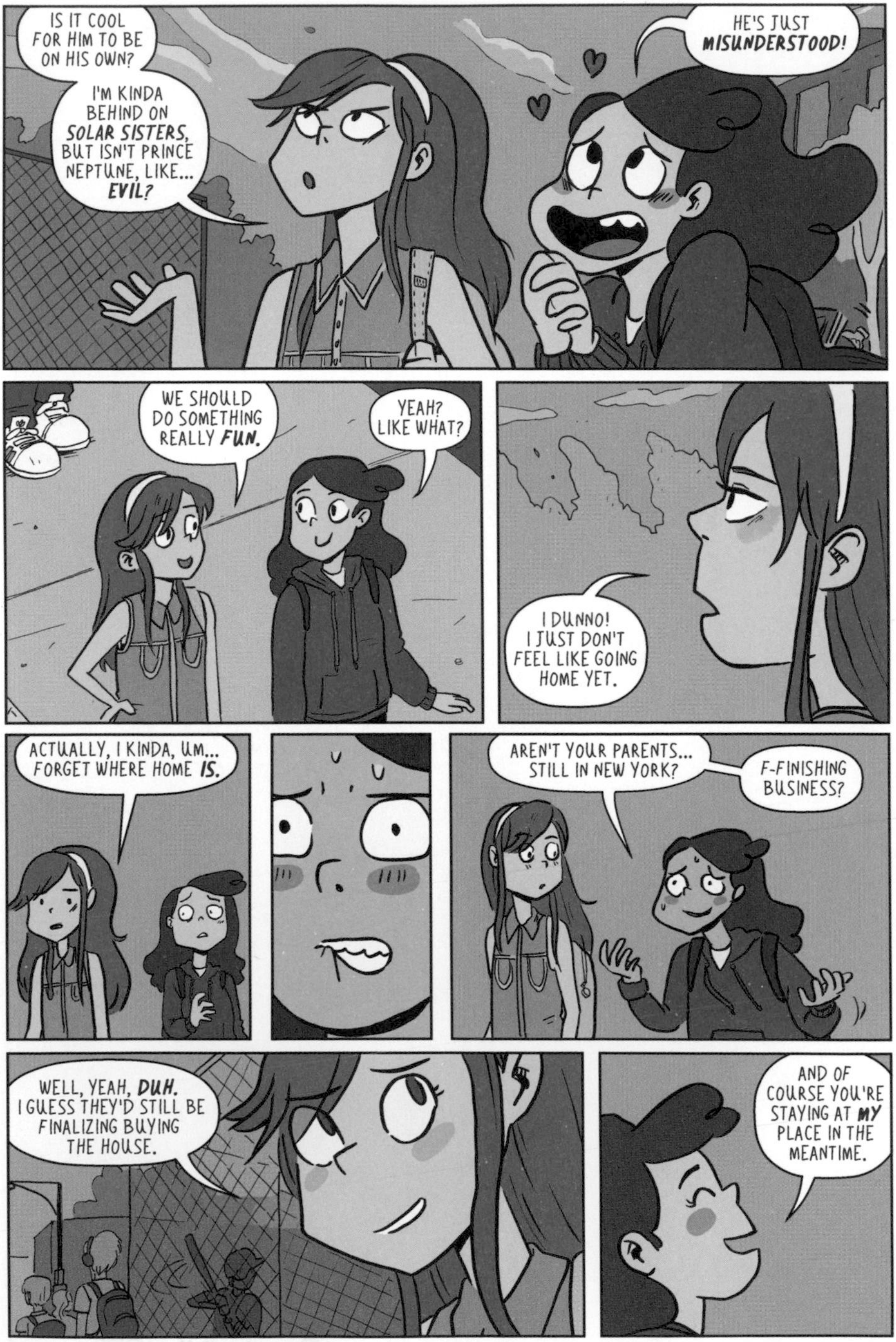

IS IT COOL FOR HIM TO BE ON HIS OWN?
I'M KINDA BEHIND ON SOLAR SISTERS, BUT ISN'T PRINCE NEPTUNE, LIKE... EVIL?
HE'S JUST MISUNDERSTOOD!
WE SHOULD DO SOMETHING REALLY FUN.
YEAH? LIKE WHAT?
I DUNNO! I JUST DON'T FEEL LIKE GOING HOME YET.
ACTUALLY, I KINDA, UM... FORGET WHERE HOME IS.
AREN'T YOUR PARENTS... STILL IN NEW YORK?
F-FINISHING BUSINESS?
WELL, YEAH, DUH. I GUESS THEY'D STILL BE FINALIZING BUYING THE HOUSE.
AND OF COURSE YOU'RE STAYING AT MY PLACE IN THE MEANTIME.

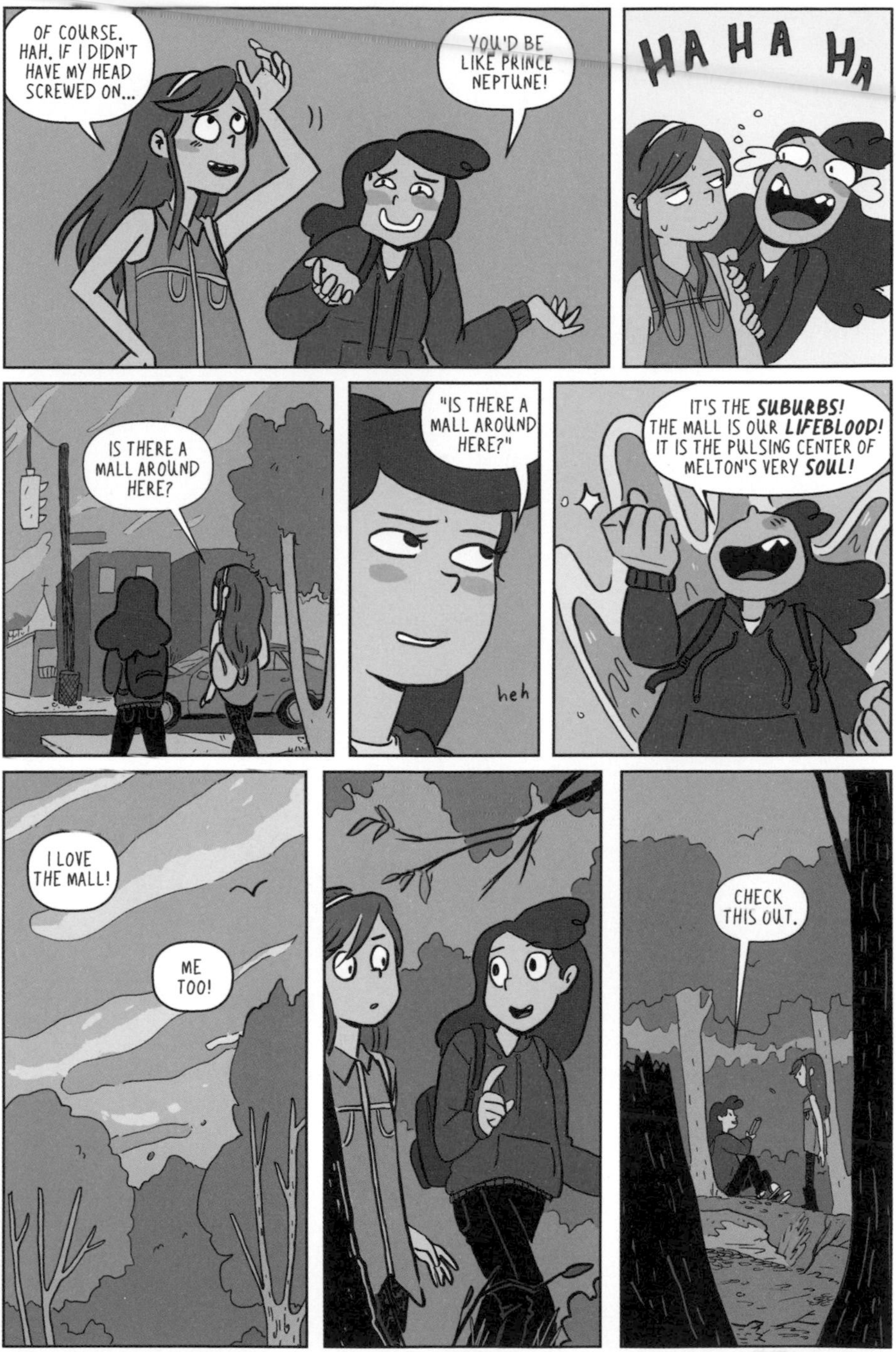
OF COURSE. HAH. IF I DIDN'T HAVE MY HEAD SCREWED ON...
YOU'D BE LIKE PRINCE NEPTUNE!
HA HA HA HA
IS THERE A MALL AROUND HERE?
"IS THERE A MALL AROUND HERE?"
heh
IT'S THE SUBURBS! THE MALL IS OUR LIFEBLOOD! IT IS THE PULSING CENTER OF MELTON'S VERY SOUL!
I LOVE THE MALL!
ME TOO!
CHECK THIS OUT.

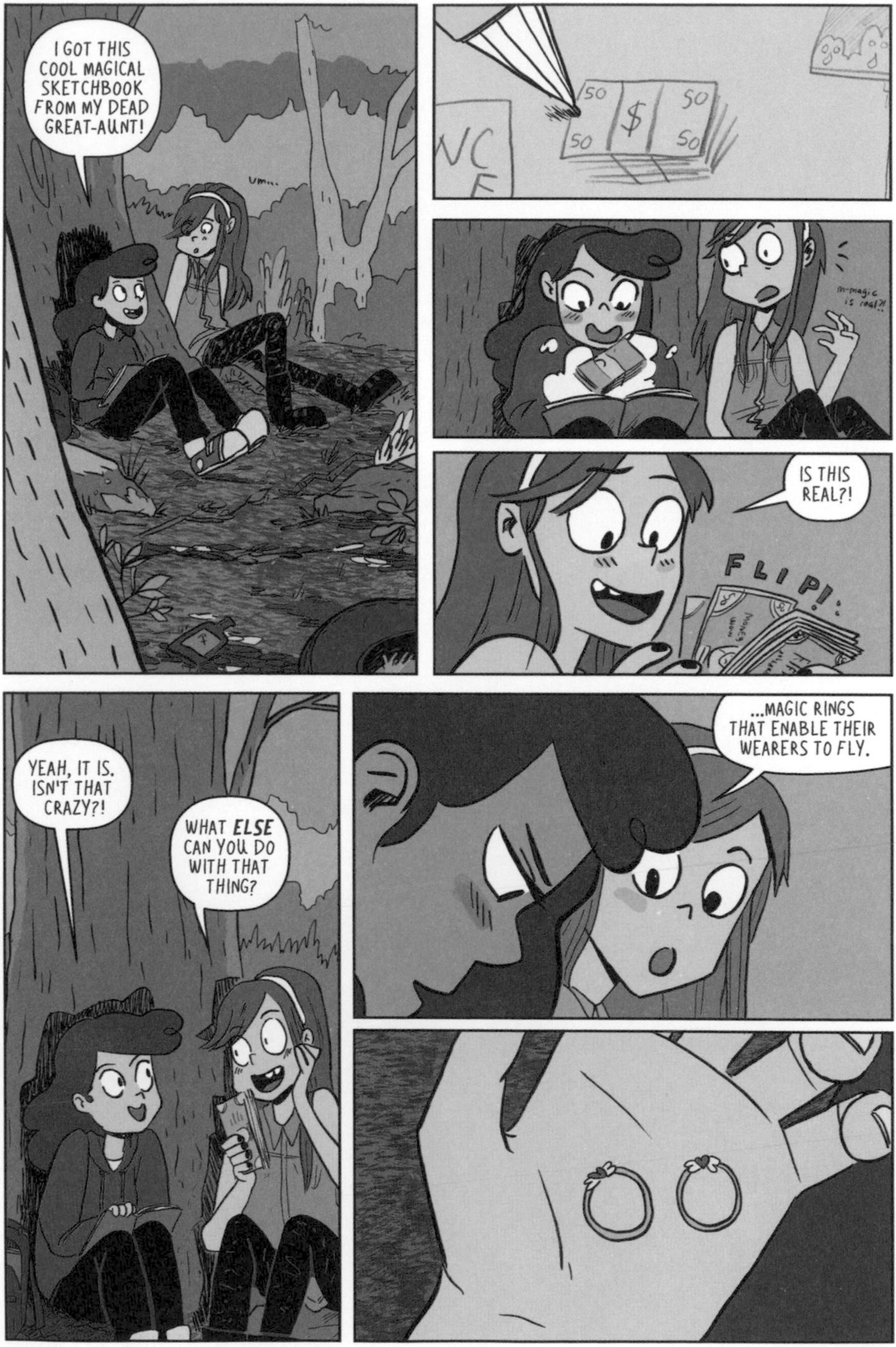
I GOT THIS COOL MAGICAL SKETCHBOOK FROM MY DEAD GREAT-AUNT!
um...
m-magic is real?!
IS THIS REAL?!
FLIP!
YEAH, IT IS. ISN'T THAT CRAZY?!
WHAT **ELSE** CAN YOU DO WITH THAT THING?
...MAGIC RINGS THAT ENABLE THEIR WEARERS TO FLY.

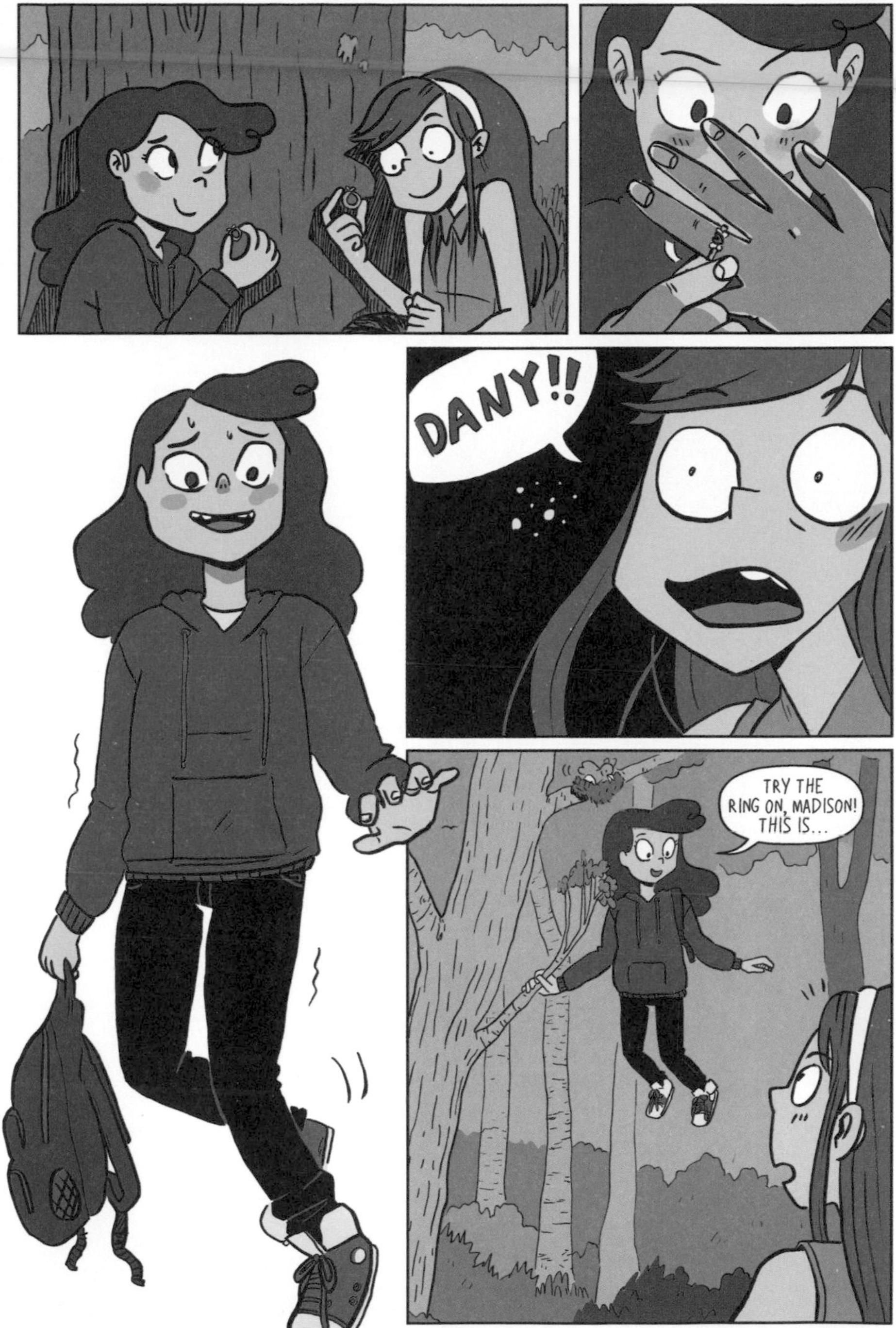
DANY!!
TRY THE RING ON, MADISON! THIS IS...

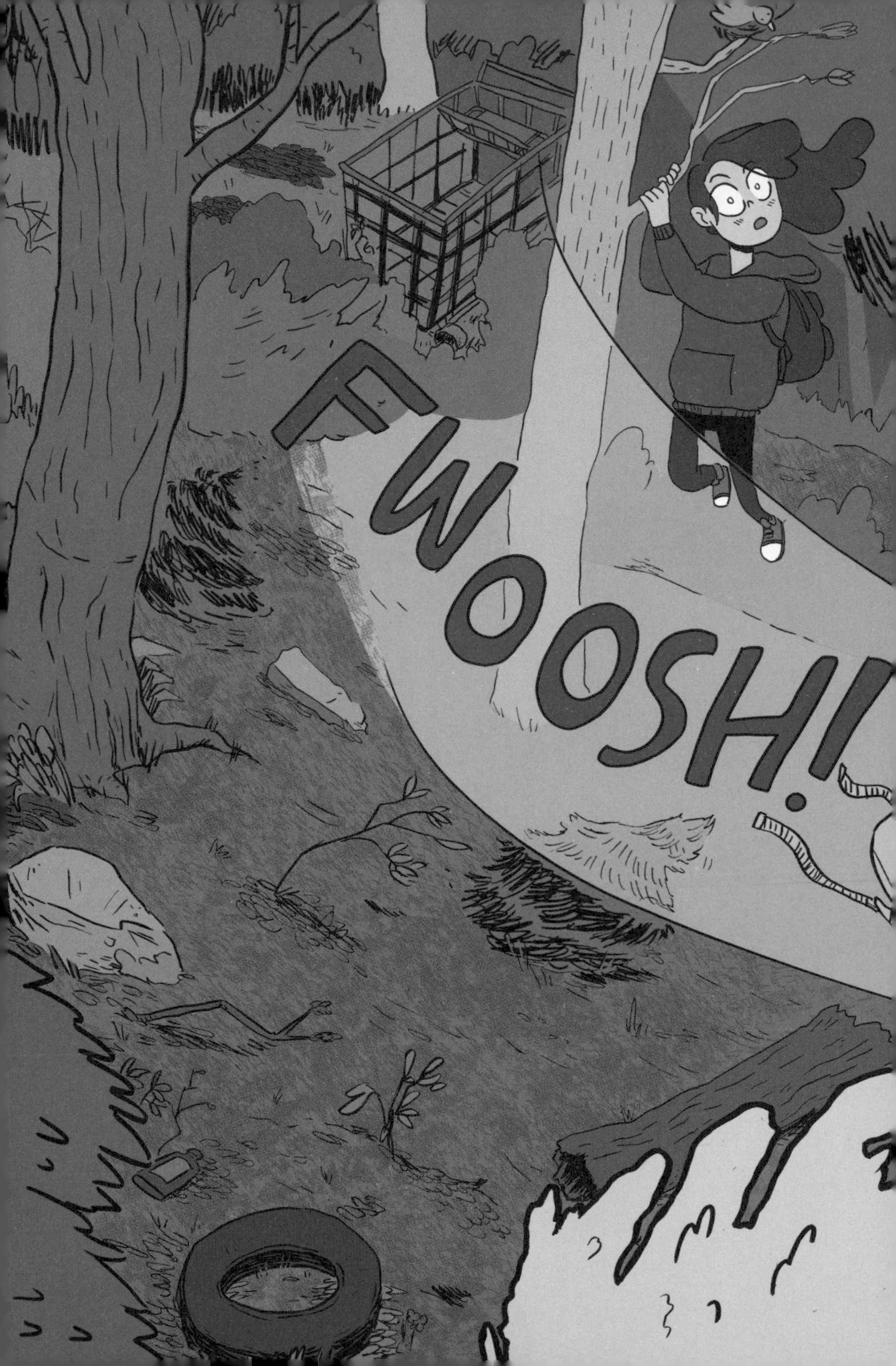
FWOOSH!

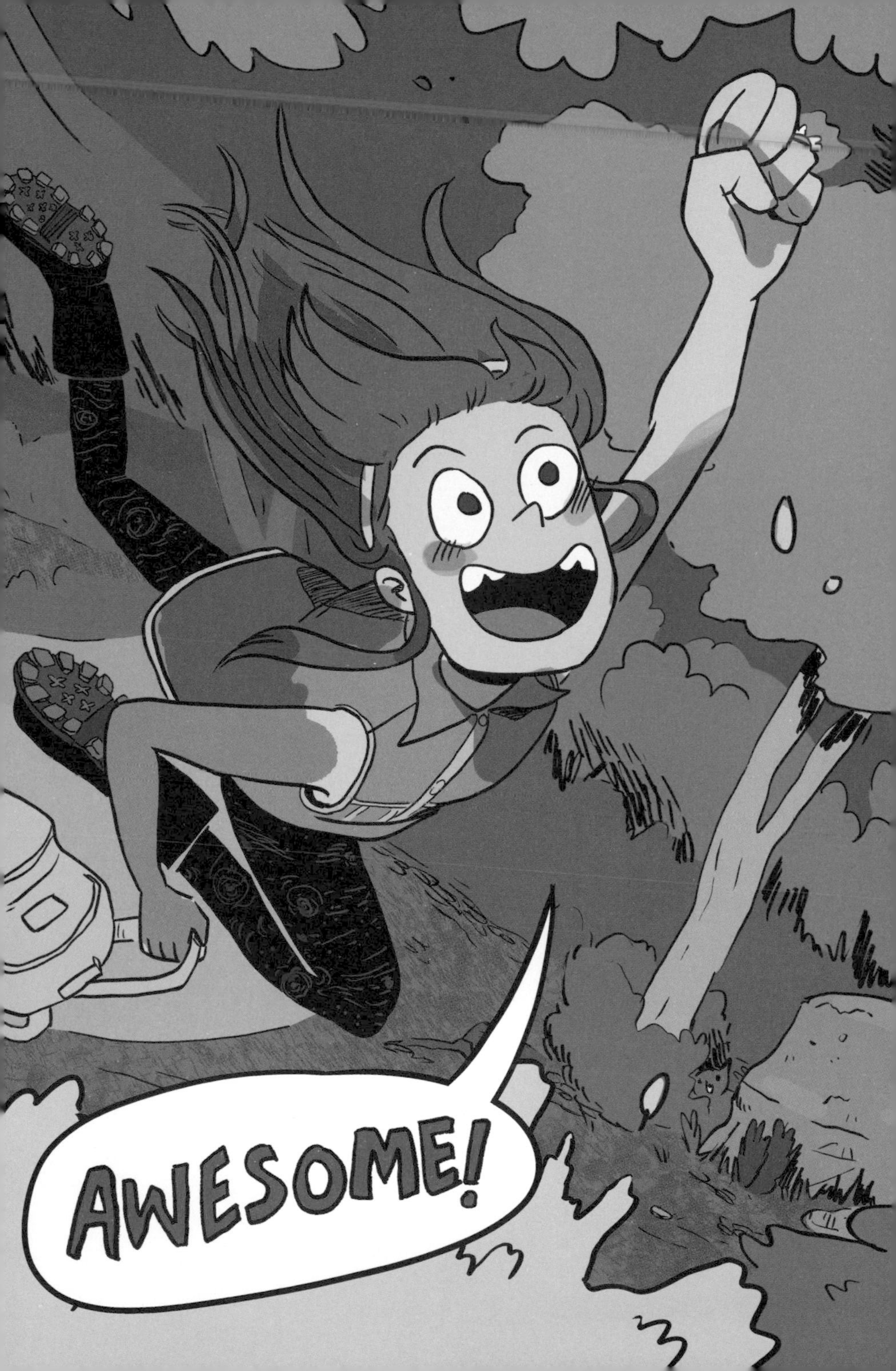
AWESOME!

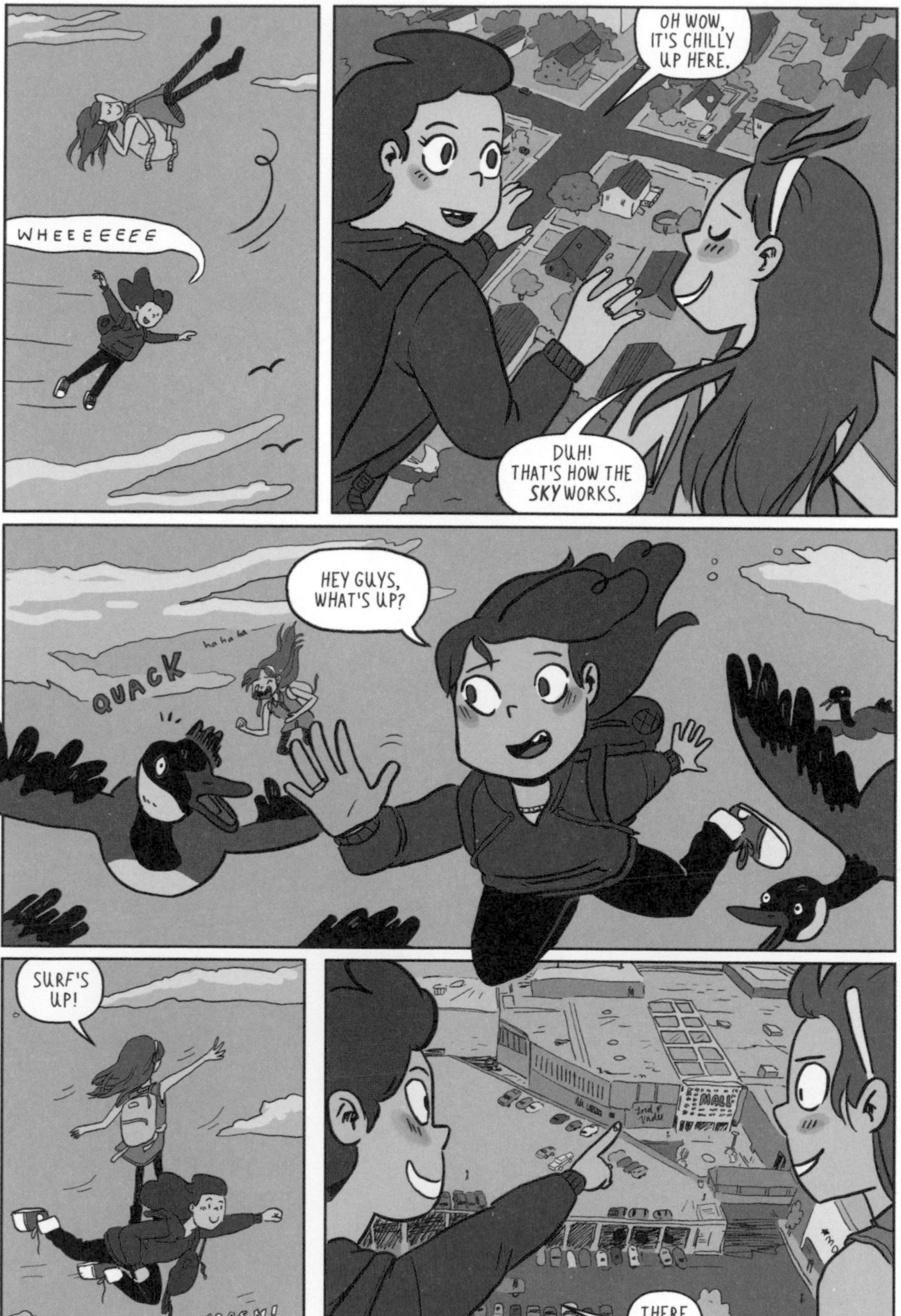
WHEEEEEEE
OH WOW, IT'S CHILLY UP HERE.
DUH! THAT'S HOW THE SKY WORKS.
HEY GUYS, WHAT'S UP?
ha ha ha
QUACK
SURF'S UP!
FWOOSH!
THERE IT IS!

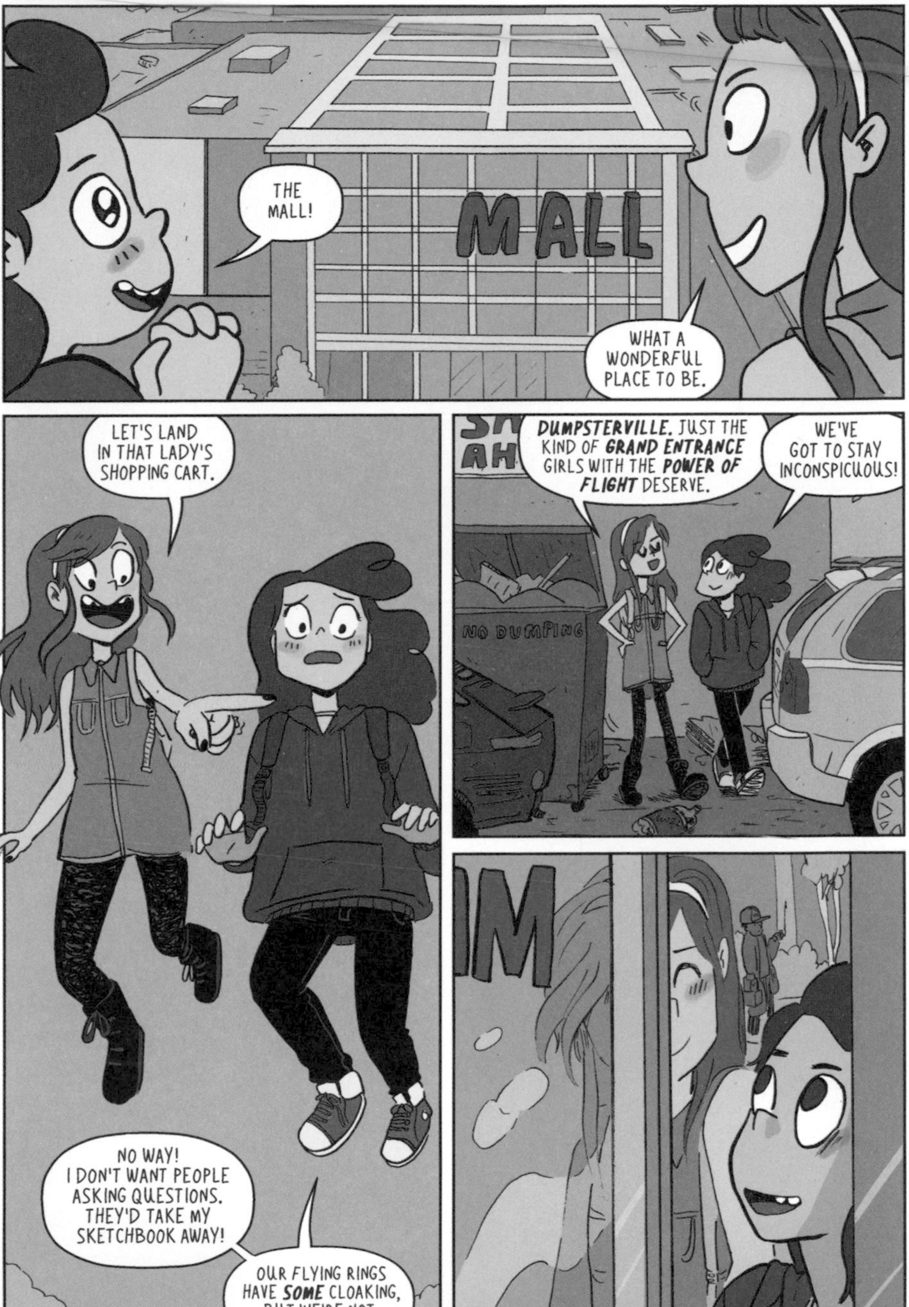
THE MALL!
WHAT A WONDERFUL PLACE TO BE.
MALL
LET'S LAND IN THAT LADY'S SHOPPING CART.
NO WAY! I DON'T WANT PEOPLE ASKING QUESTIONS. THEY'D TAKE MY SKETCHBOOK AWAY!
OUR FLYING RINGS HAVE **SOME** CLOAKING, BUT WE'RE NOT ***INVISIBLE...***
DUMPSTERVILLE. JUST THE KIND OF ***GRAND ENTRANCE*** GIRLS WITH THE ***POWER OF FLIGHT*** DESERVE.
WE'VE GOT TO STAY INCONSPICUOUS!
NO DUMPING

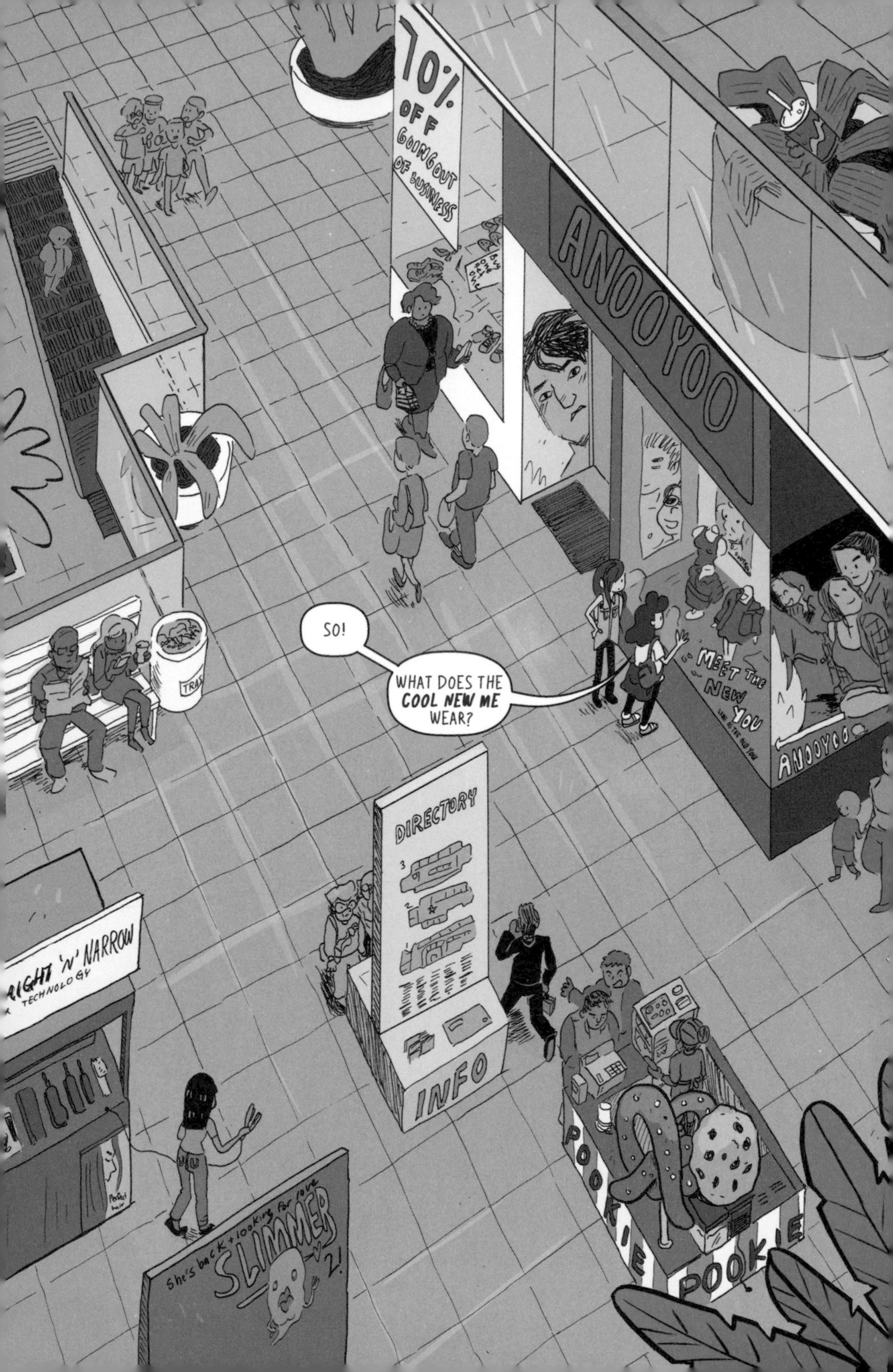

70% OFF GOING OUT OF BUSINESS
BUY ONE GET ONE
ANOOYOO
SO!
WHAT DOES THE **COOL NEW ME** WEAR?
MEET THE NEW YOU
SAME AS THE OLD YOU
ANOOYOO
DIRECTORY
INFO
AIGHT 'N' NARROW
TECHNOLOGY
She's back + looking for love
SLIMMER 2!
POOKIE POOKIE

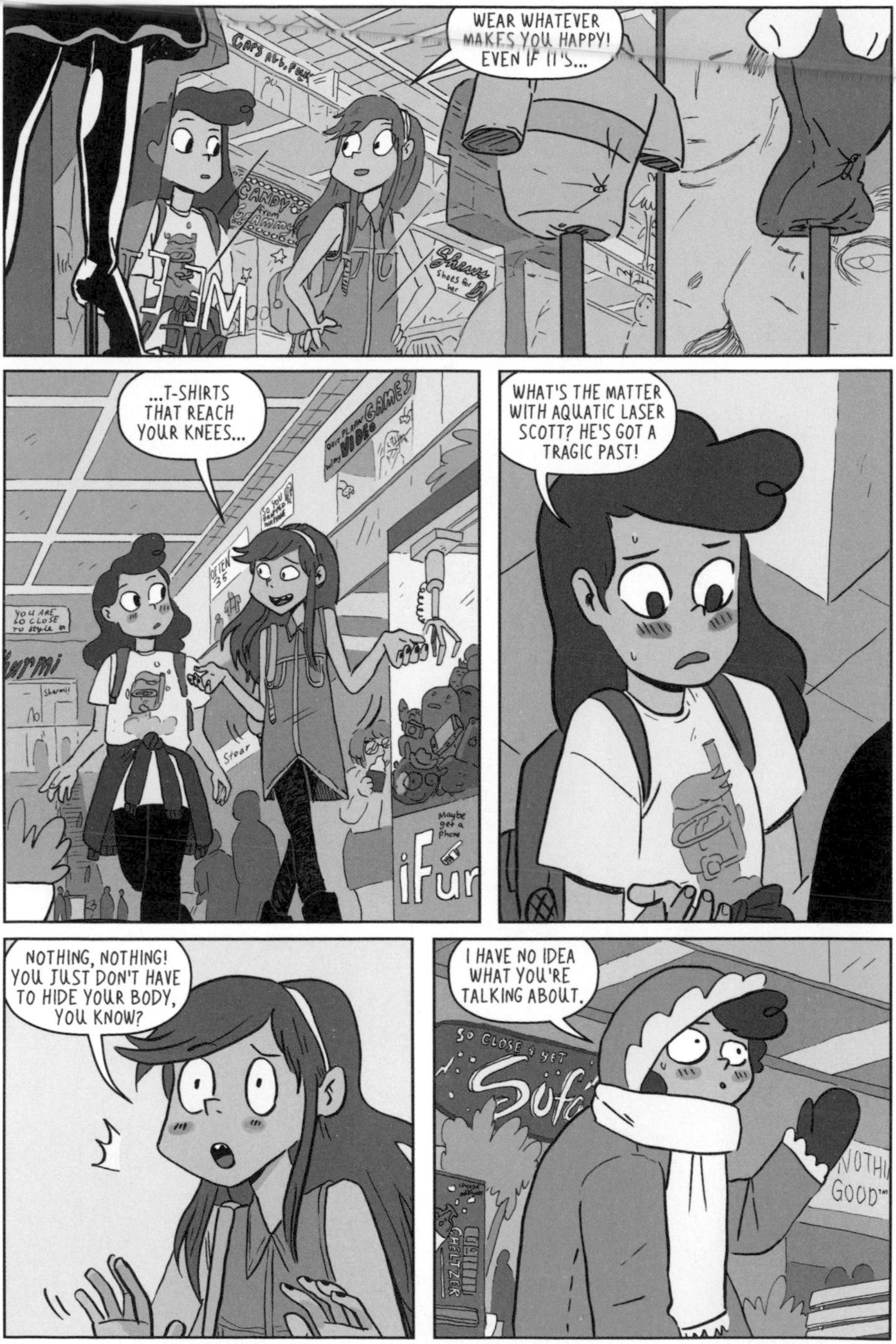
WEAR WHATEVER MAKES YOU HAPPY! EVEN IF IT'S...
...T-SHIRTS THAT REACH YOUR KNEES...
WHAT'S THE MATTER WITH AQUATIC LASER SCOTT? HE'S GOT A TRAGIC PAST!
NOTHING, NOTHING! YOU JUST DON'T HAVE TO HIDE YOUR BODY, YOU KNOW?
I HAVE NO IDEA WHAT YOU'RE TALKING ABOUT.

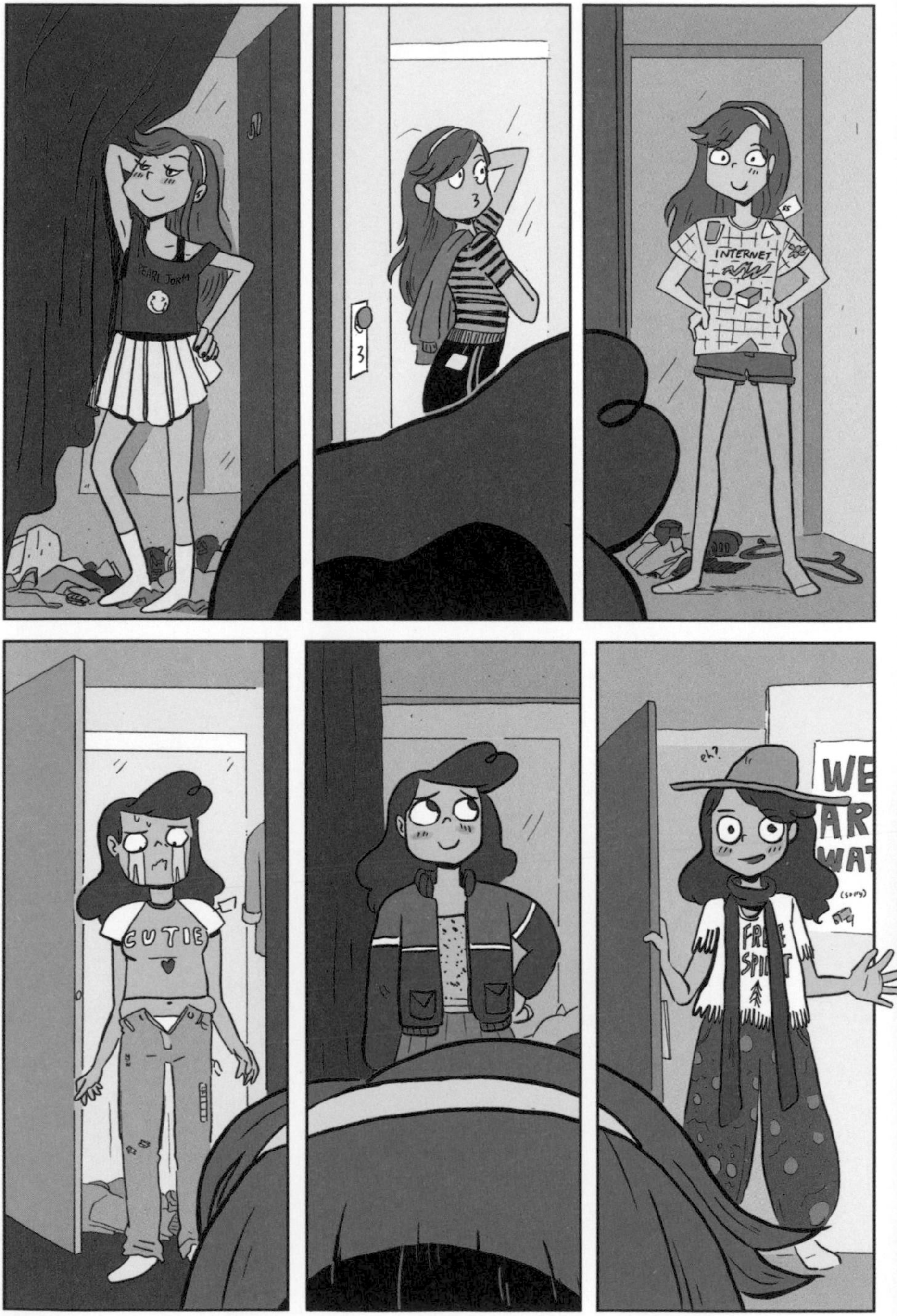
PEARL JORM
INTERNET
CUTIE
eh?

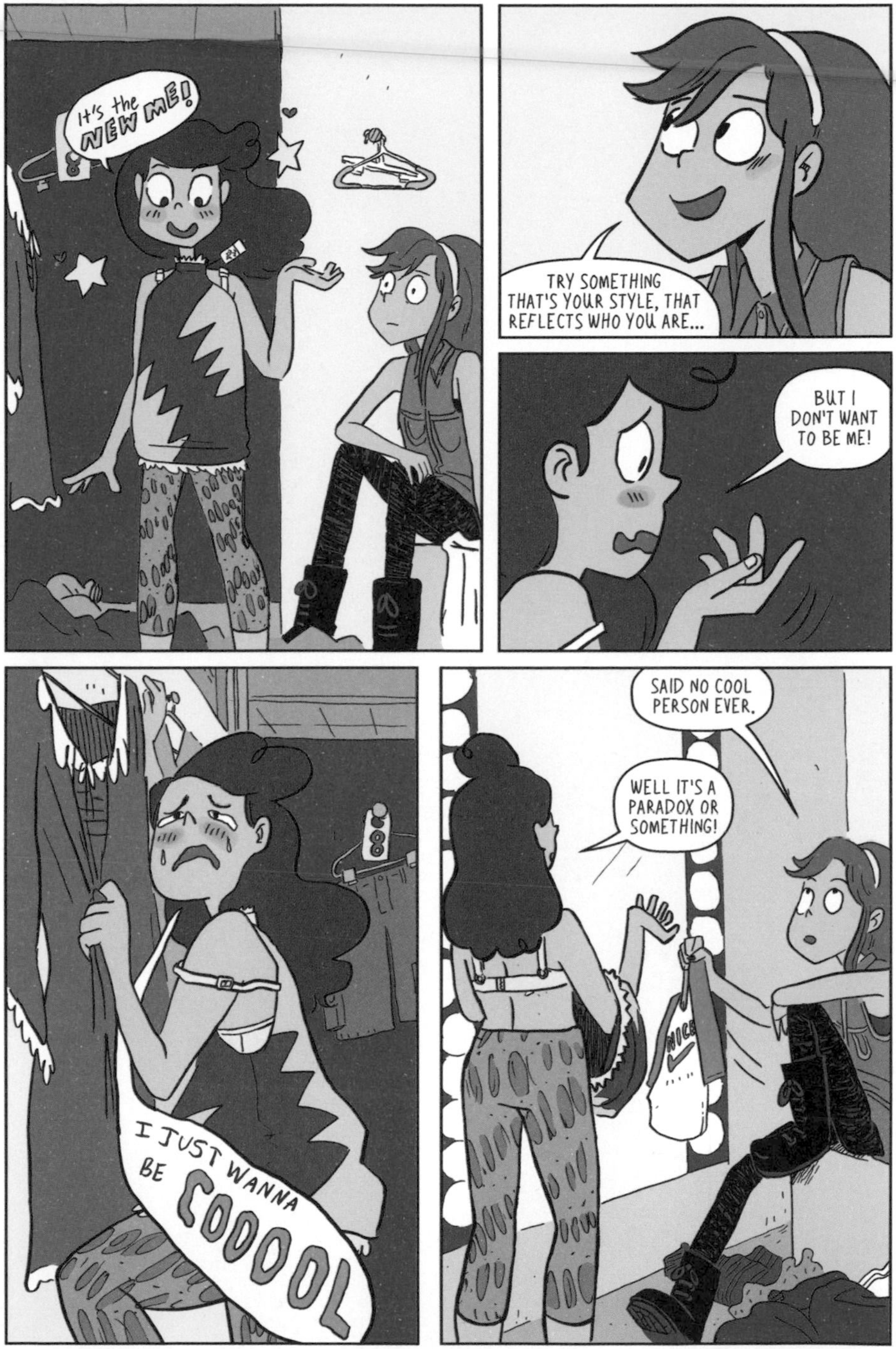
It's the NEW ME!
TRY SOMETHING THAT'S YOUR STYLE, THAT REFLECTS WHO YOU ARE...
BUT I DON'T WANT TO BE ME!
I JUST WANNA BE COOOOL
SAID NO COOL PERSON EVER.
WELL IT'S A PARADOX OR SOMETHING!

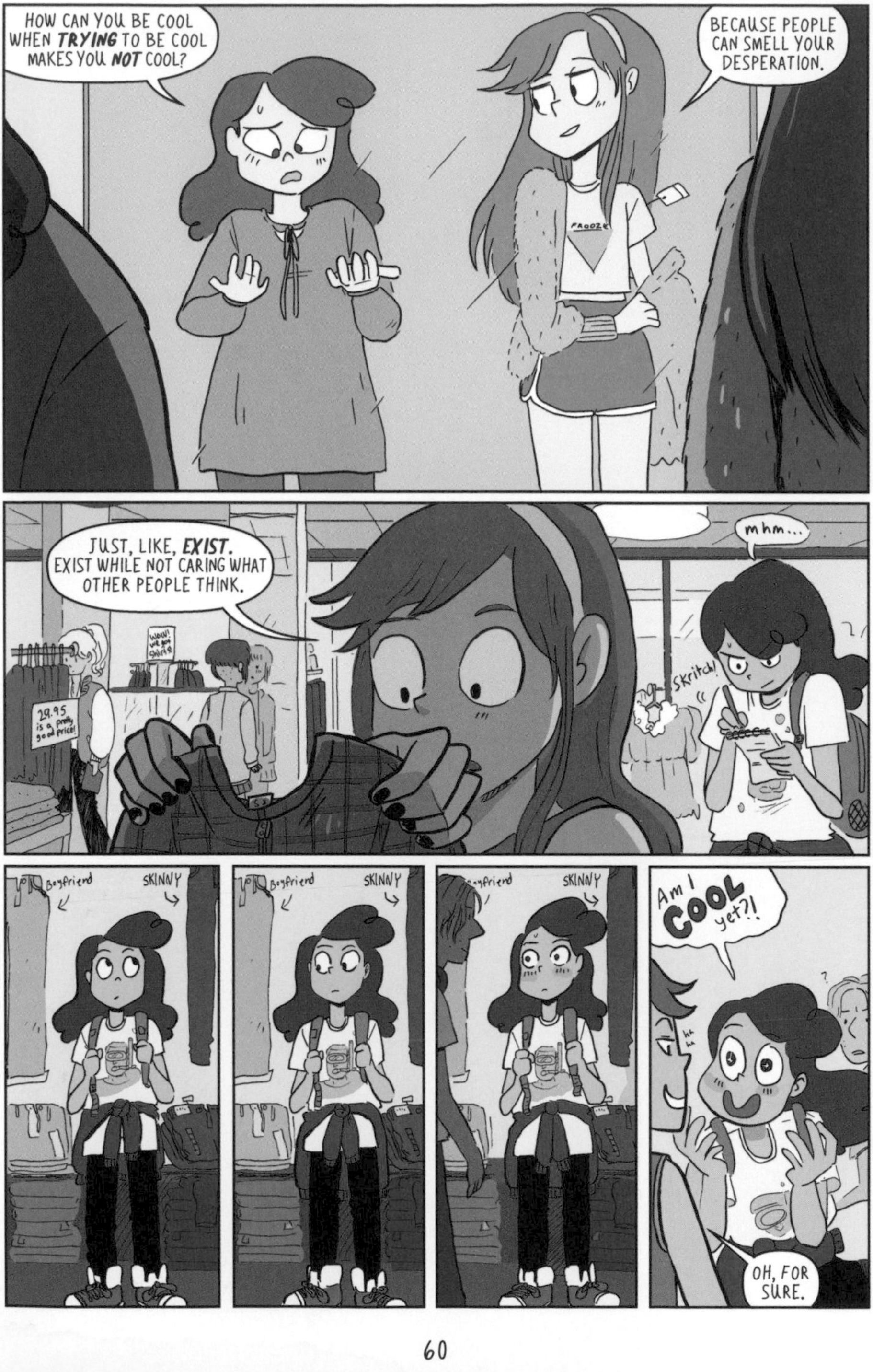
HOW CAN YOU BE COOL WHEN **TRYING** TO BE COOL MAKES YOU **NOT** COOL?
BECAUSE PEOPLE CAN SMELL YOUR DESPERATION.
FROOZE
JUST, LIKE, **EXIST.** EXIST WHILE NOT CARING WHAT OTHER PEOPLE THINK.
WOW! we got shirts
29.95 is a pretty good price!
mhm...
Skritch!
Boyfriend
SKINNY
Boyfriend
SKINNY
SKINNY
Am I COOL yet?!
OH, FOR SURE.

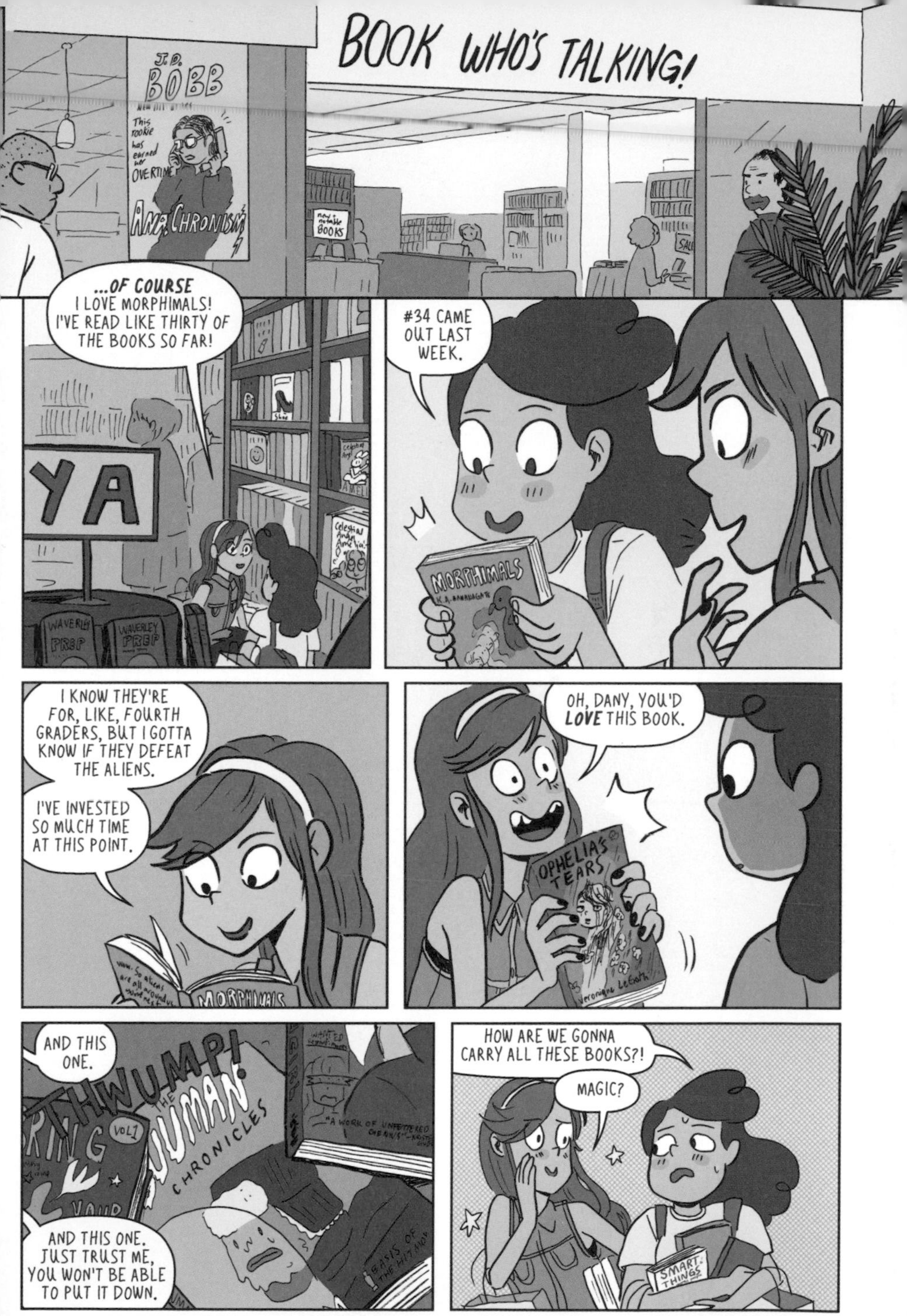
BOOK WHO'S TALKING!
J.D. BOBB
This rookie has earned her OVERTIME
ANA CHRONISM
new notable BOOKS
...OF COURSE I LOVE MORPHIMALS! I'VE READ LIKE THIRTY OF THE BOOKS SO FAR!
YA
WAVERLEY PREP
#34 CAME OUT LAST WEEK.
MORPHIMALS
I KNOW THEY'RE FOR, LIKE, FOURTH GRADERS, BUT I GOTTA KNOW IF THEY DEFEAT THE ALIENS.
I'VE INVESTED SO MUCH TIME AT THIS POINT.
OH, DANY, YOU'D **LOVE** THIS BOOK.
OPHELIA'S TEARS
AND THIS ONE.
THWUMP!
THE HUMAN CHRONICLES
AND THIS ONE. JUST TRUST ME, YOU WON'T BE ABLE TO PUT IT DOWN.
HOW ARE WE GONNA CARRY ALL THESE BOOKS?!
MAGIC?
SMART THINGS

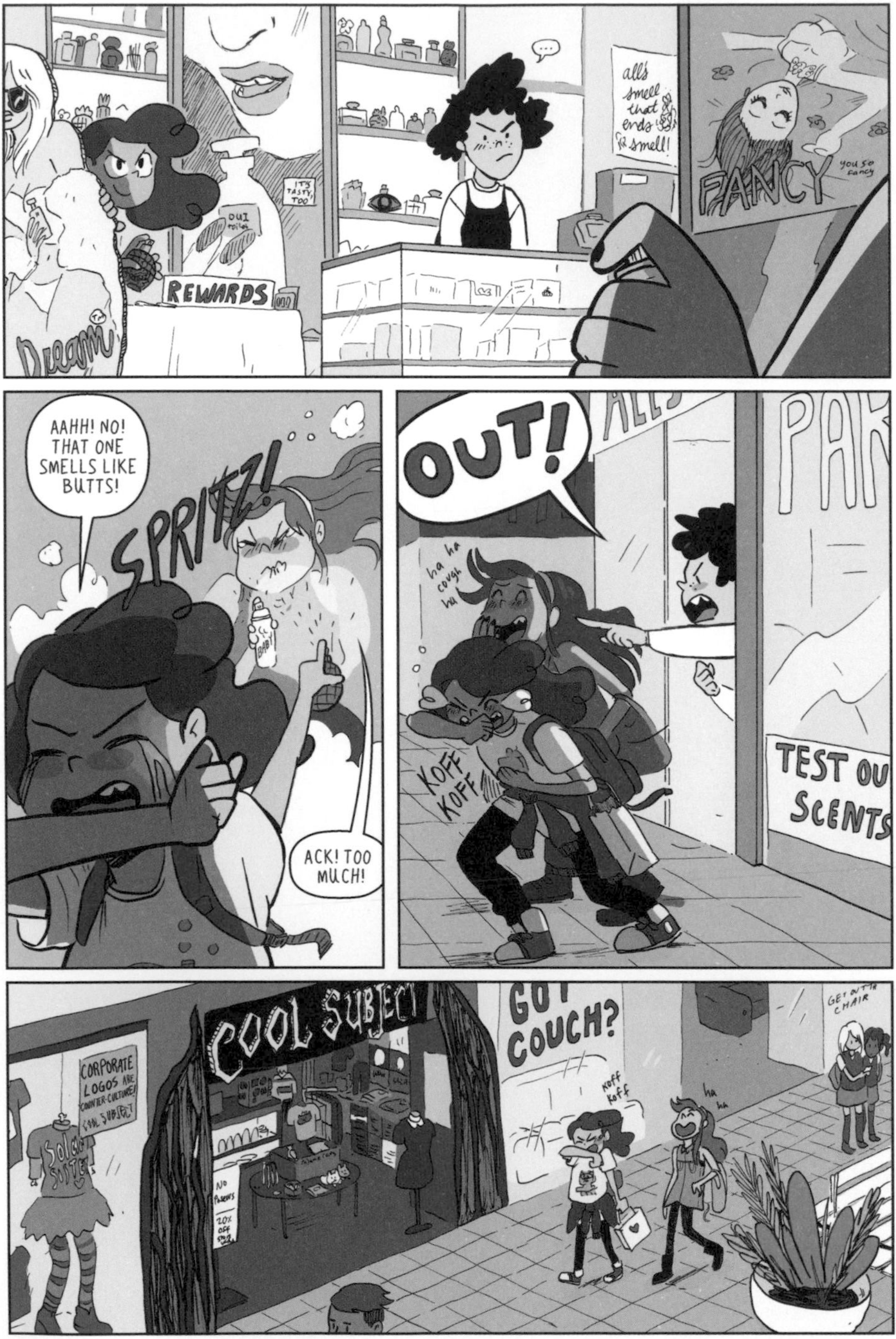
all's smell that ends smell!
IT'S TASTY, TOO
OUI
REWARDS
FANCY
you so fancy
AAHH! NO! THAT ONE SMELLS LIKE BUTTS!
SPRITZ!
BABY
ACK! TOO MUCH!
OUT!
ha ha cough ha
KOFF KOFF
TEST OU
SCENTS
COOL SUBJECT
CORPORATE LOGOS ARE COUNTER-CULTURE!
GOT COUCH?
GET OUTTA CHAIR
koff koff
ha ha

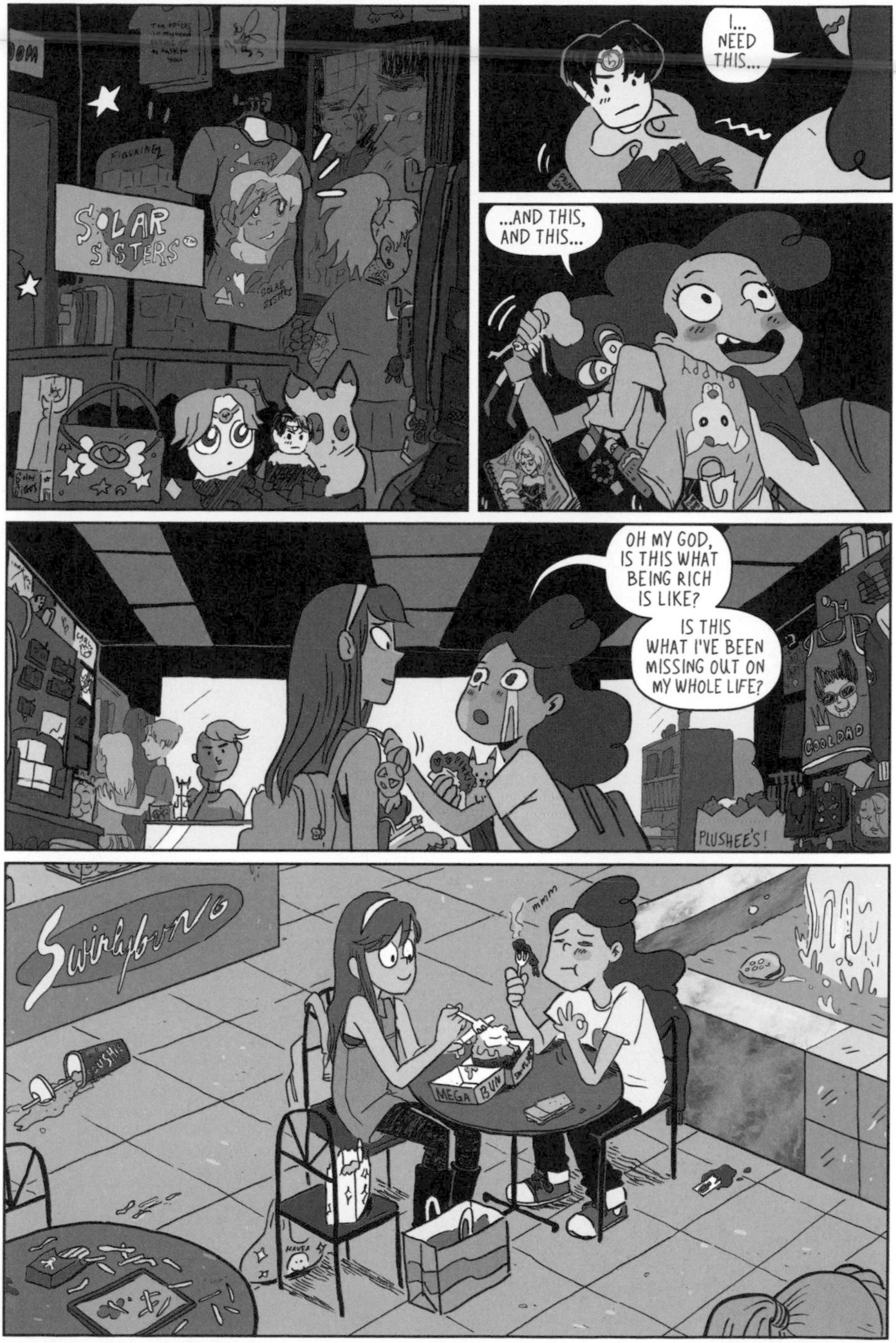
SOLAR SISTERS™
FIGURINES
I... NEED THIS...
...AND THIS, AND THIS...
OH MY GOD, IS THIS WHAT BEING RICH IS LIKE?
IS THIS WHAT I'VE BEEN MISSING OUT ON MY WHOLE LIFE?
COOLDAD
PLUSHEE'S!
Swirlybuns
mmm
MEGA BUN

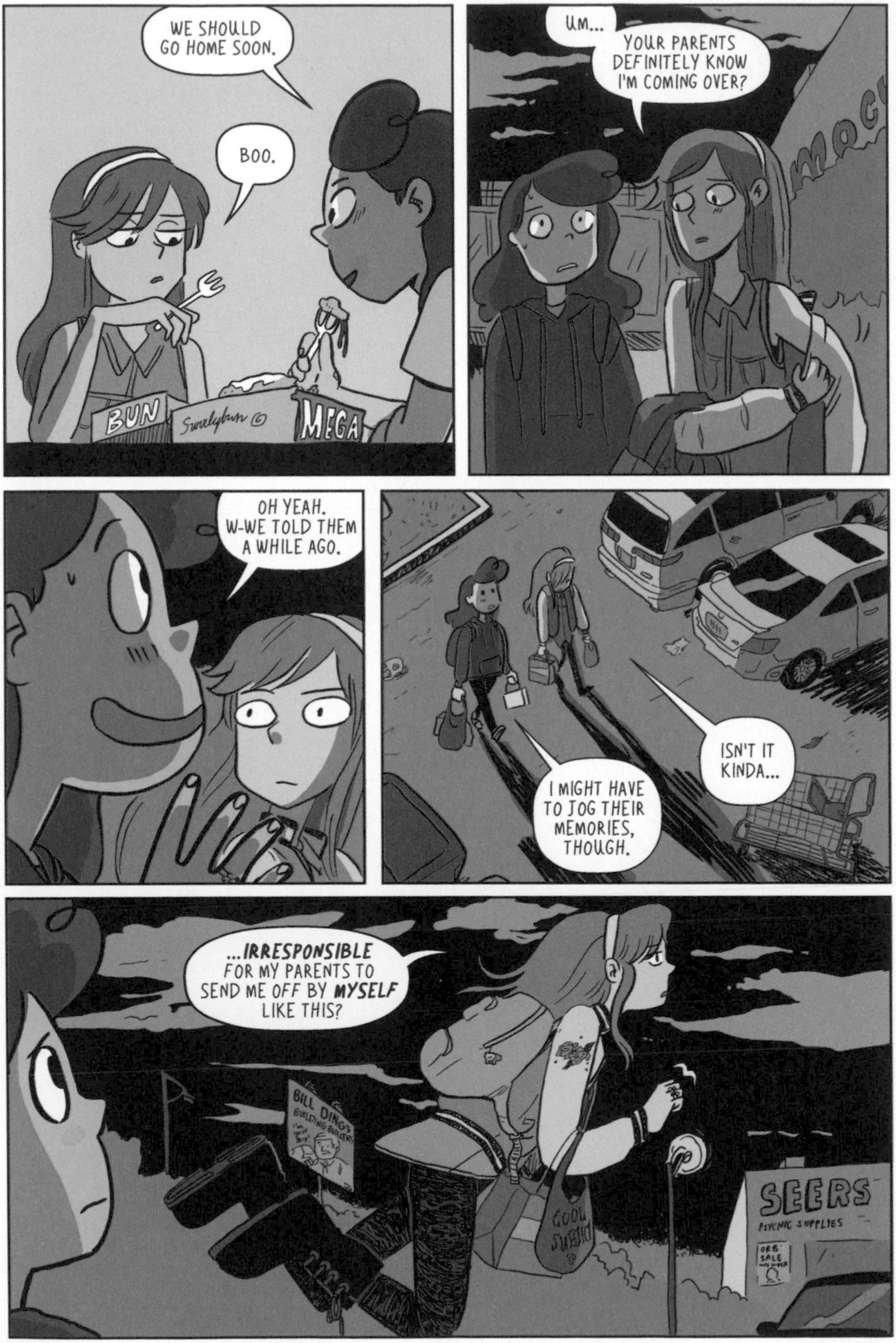
WE SHOULD GO HOME SOON.
BOO.
BUN
MEGA
UM...
YOUR PARENTS DEFINITELY KNOW I'M COMING OVER?
OH YEAH. W-WE TOLD THEM A WHILE AGO.
I MIGHT HAVE TO JOG THEIR MEMORIES, THOUGH.
ISN'T IT KINDA...
...IRRESPONSIBLE FOR MY PARENTS TO SEND ME OFF BY MYSELF LIKE THIS?
BILL DINGS BUILDING BUILDERS
SEERS
PSYCHIC SUPPLIES
ORB SALE

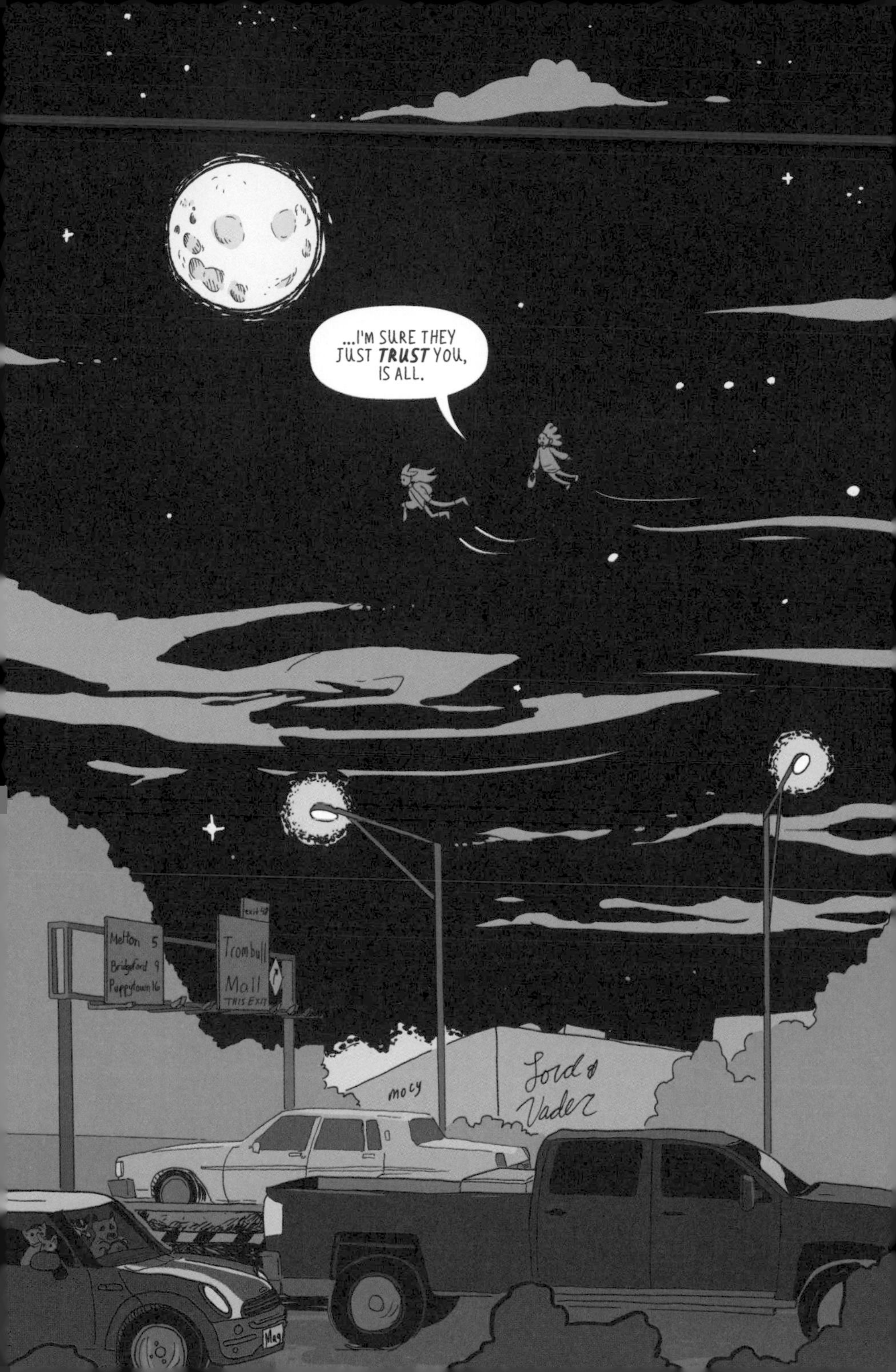
...I'M SURE THEY JUST **TRUST** YOU, IS ALL.
Melton 5
Bridgeford 9
Puppytown 16
Trombull Mall
THIS EXIT
mocy
Lord & Vader

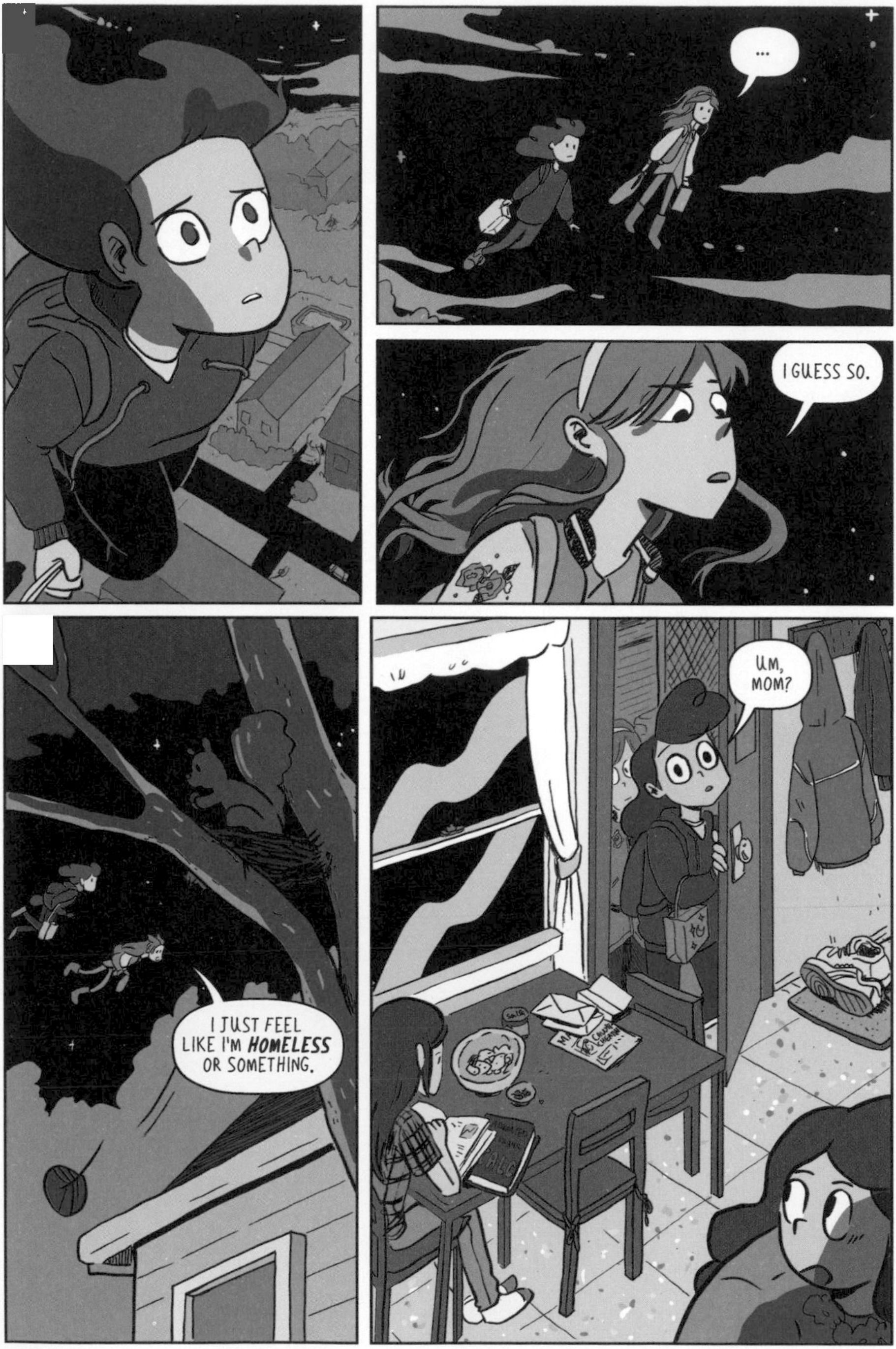
...
I GUESS SO.
I JUST FEEL LIKE I'M HOMELESS OR SOMETHING.
UM, MOM?

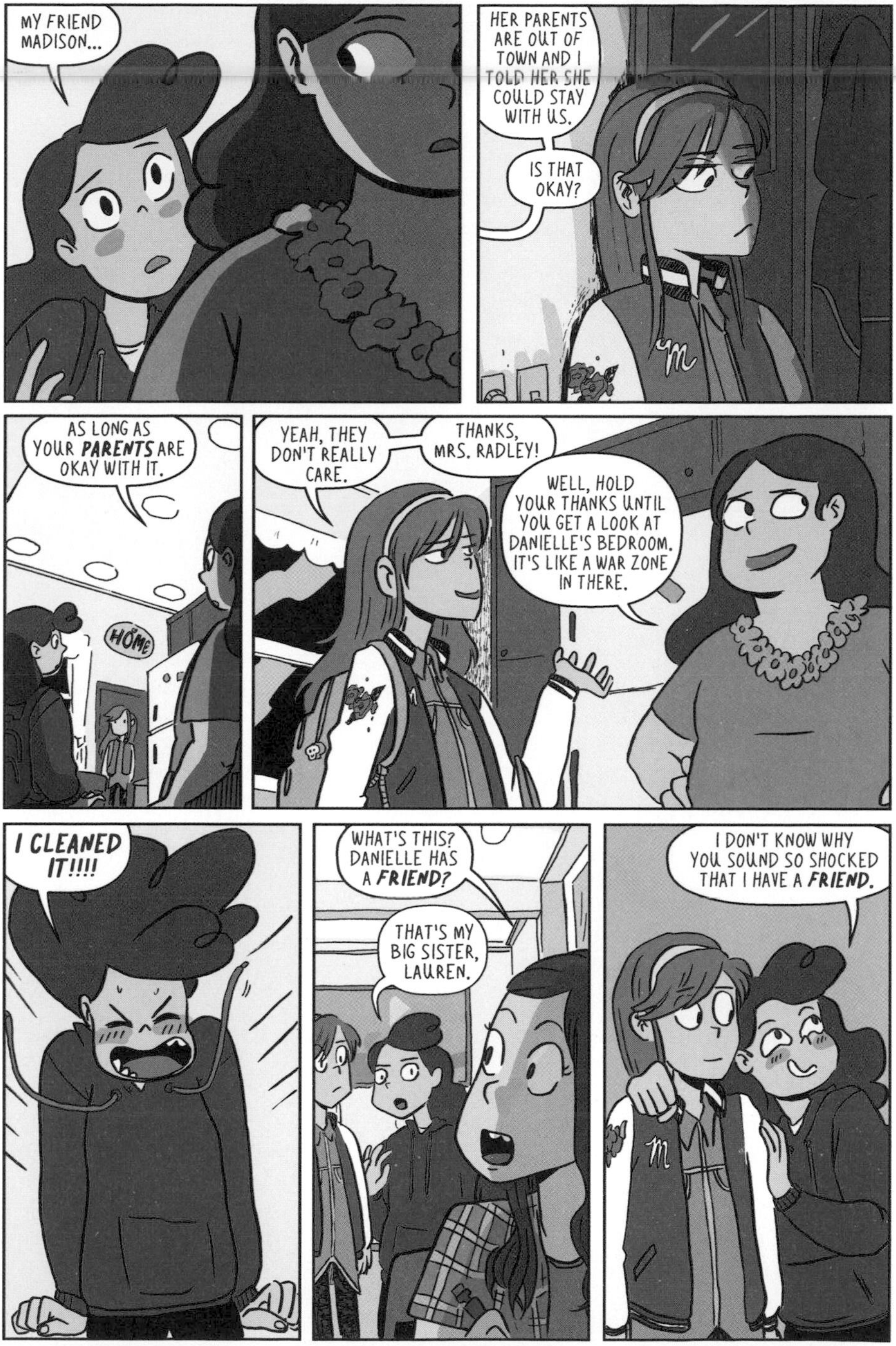
MY FRIEND MADISON...
HER PARENTS ARE OUT OF TOWN AND I TOLD HER SHE COULD STAY WITH US.
IS THAT OKAY?
AS LONG AS YOUR PARENTS ARE OKAY WITH IT.
HOME
YEAH, THEY DON'T REALLY CARE.
THANKS, MRS. RADLEY!
WELL, HOLD YOUR THANKS UNTIL YOU GET A LOOK AT DANIELLE'S BEDROOM. IT'S LIKE A WAR ZONE IN THERE.
I CLEANED IT!!!!
WHAT'S THIS? DANIELLE HAS A FRIEND?
THAT'S MY BIG SISTER, LAUREN.
I DON'T KNOW WHY YOU SOUND SO SHOCKED THAT I HAVE A FRIEND.

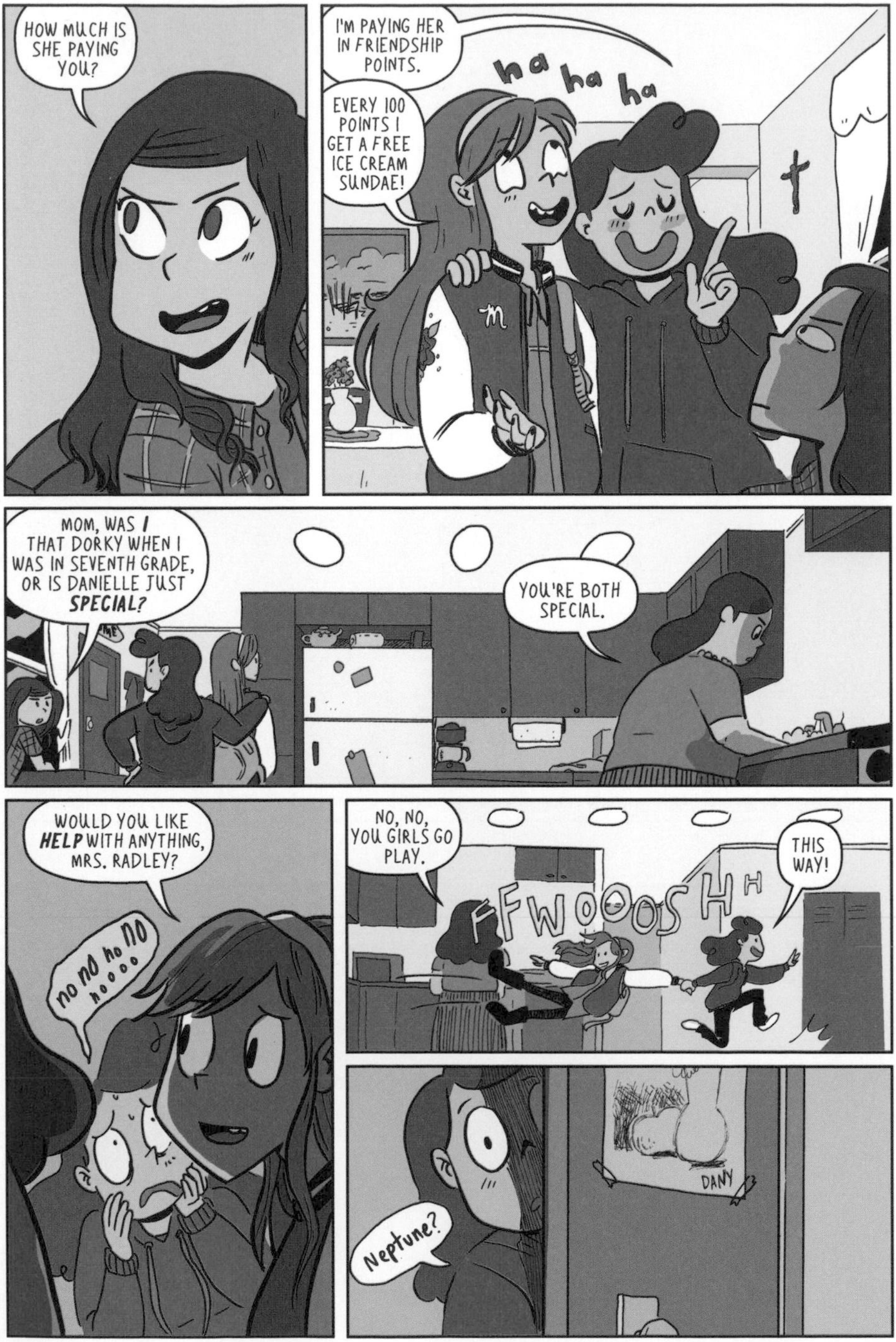
HOW MUCH IS SHE PAYING YOU?
I'M PAYING HER IN FRIENDSHIP POINTS.
ha ha ha
EVERY 100 POINTS I GET A FREE ICE CREAM SUNDAE!
MOM, WAS I THAT DORKY WHEN I WAS IN SEVENTH GRADE, OR IS DANIELLE JUST SPECIAL?
YOU'RE BOTH SPECIAL.
WOULD YOU LIKE HELP WITH ANYTHING, MRS. RADLEY?
no no no no nooooo
NO, NO, YOU GIRLS GO PLAY.
FFWOOOOSHHH
THIS WAY!
DANY
Neptune?

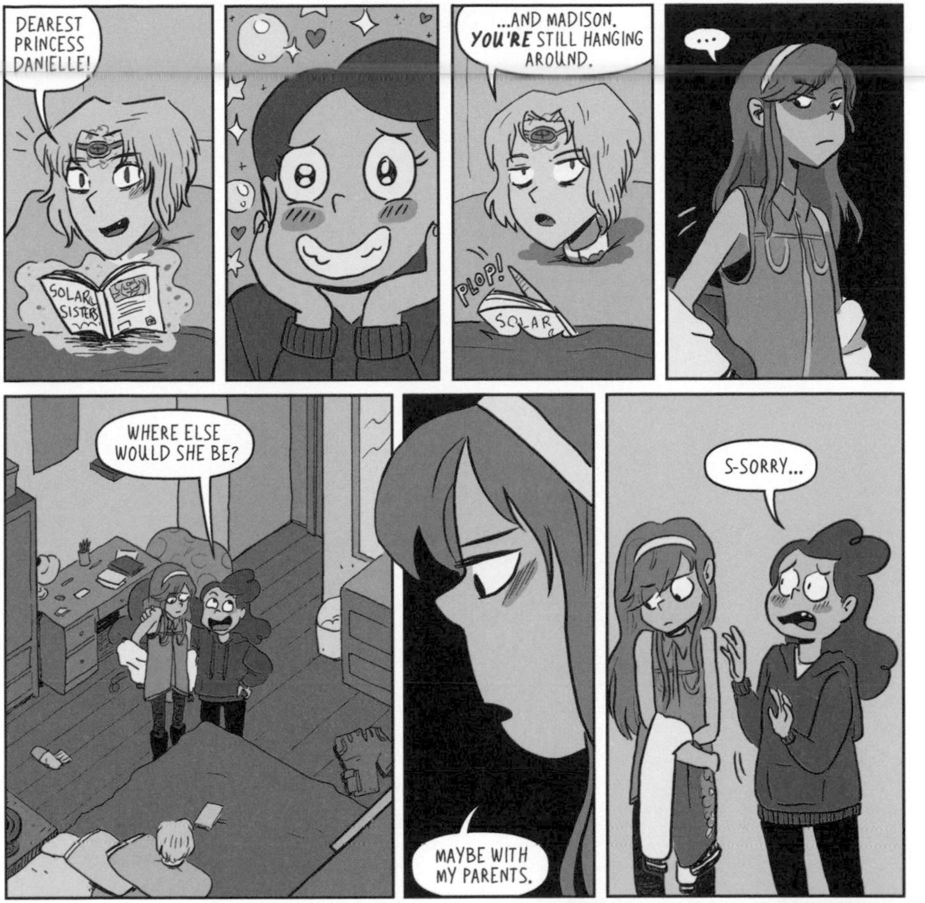
DEAREST PRINCESS DANIELLE!
SOLAR SISTERS
...AND MADISON. YOU'RE STILL HANGING AROUND.
PLOP!
SOLAR
...
WHERE ELSE WOULD SHE BE?
MAYBE WITH MY PARENTS.
S-SORRY...
I'VE BEEN THINKING ABOUT THAT MARVELOUS SKETCHBOOK OF YOURS, DANIELLE.
NOT THAT I MIND MY CURRENT STATE, BUT PERHAPS I COULD ACCOMPANY YOU TO SCHOOL IN A LESS...
...UNCOUTH... MANNER IF I WERE TO POSSESS A BODY OF MY OWN.

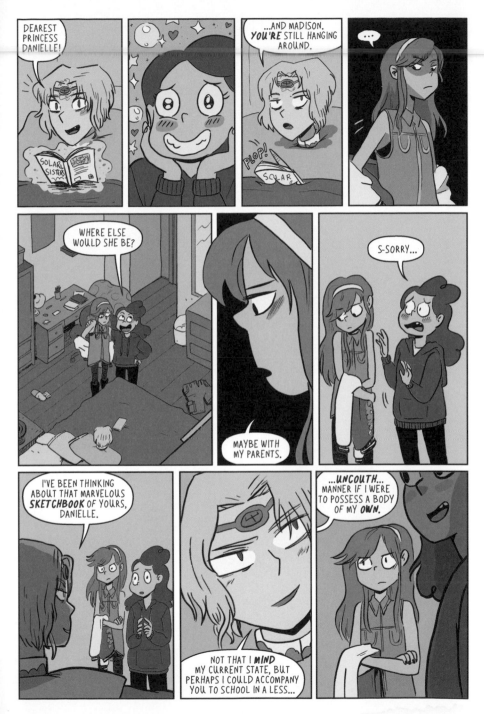

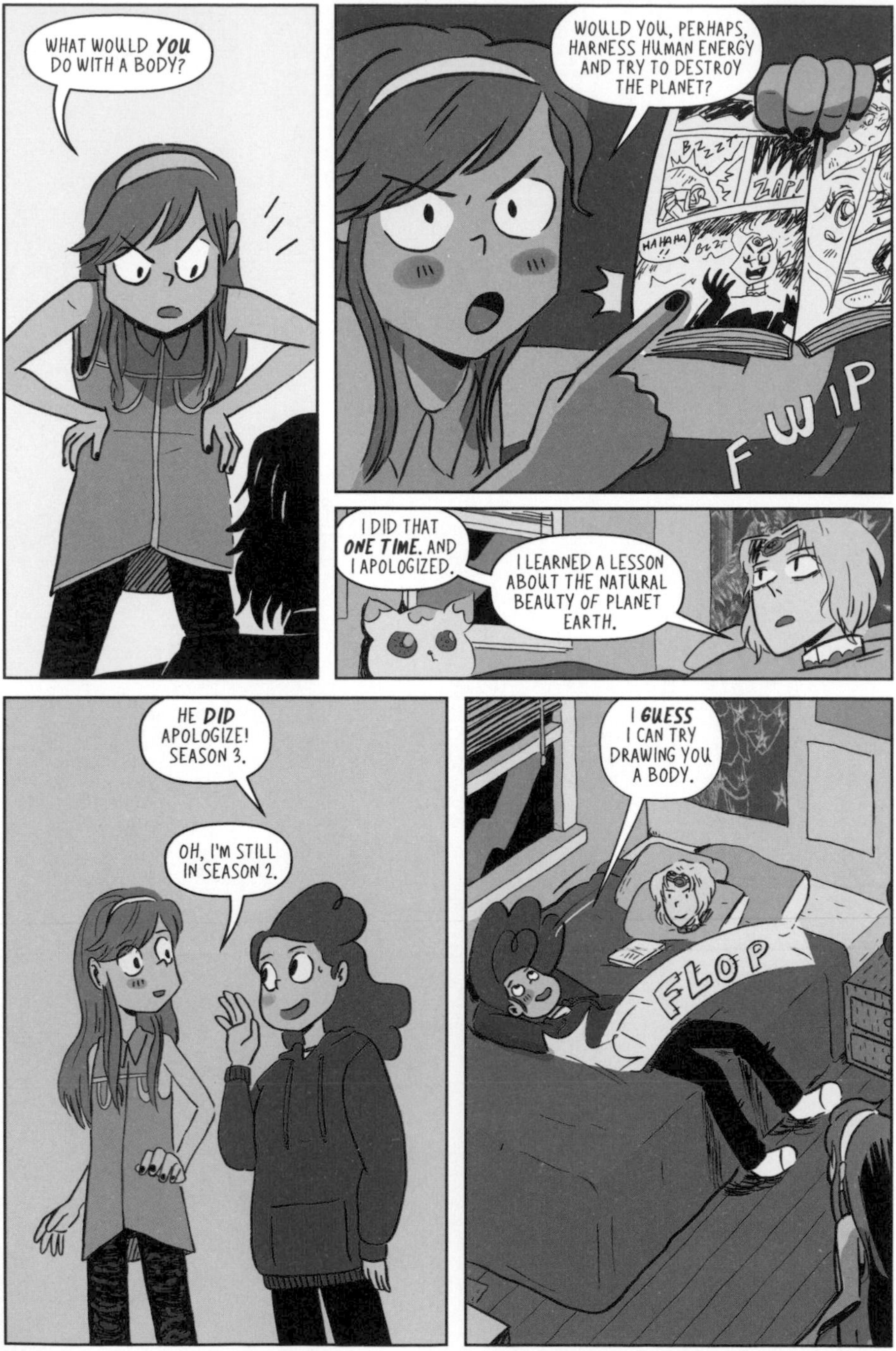
WHAT WOULD **YOU** DO WITH A BODY?
WOULD YOU, PERHAPS, HARNESS HUMAN ENERGY AND TRY TO DESTROY THE PLANET?
BZZZT
ZAP!
HAHAHA !!
BZZT
FWIP
I DID THAT **ONE TIME.** AND I APOLOGIZED.
I LEARNED A LESSON ABOUT THE NATURAL BEAUTY OF PLANET EARTH.
HE **DID** APOLOGIZE! SEASON 3.
OH, I'M STILL IN SEASON 2.
I **GUESS** I CAN TRY DRAWING YOU A BODY.
FLOP

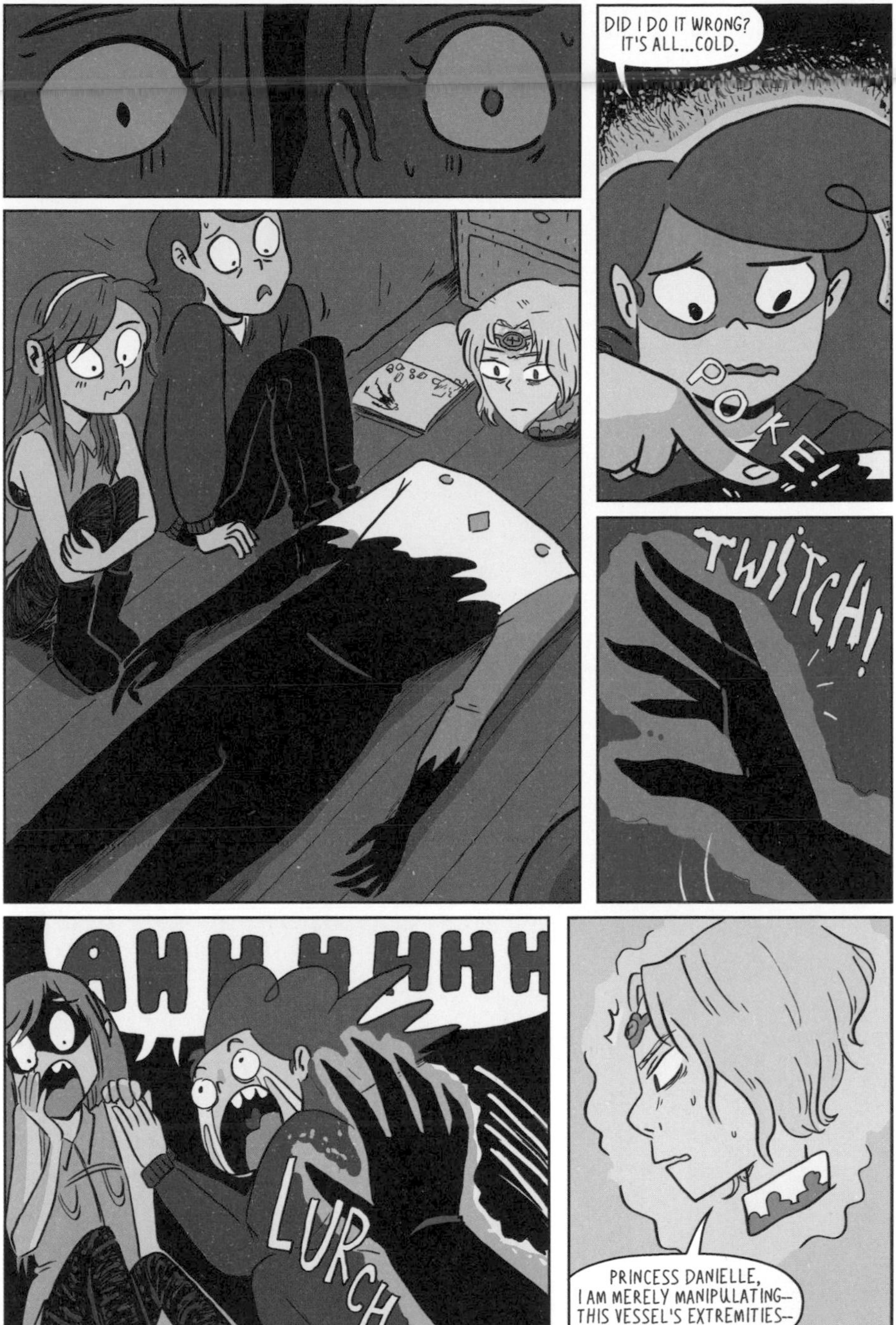
DID I DO IT WRONG? IT'S ALL...COLD.
POKE!
TWITCH!
AHHHHHHH
LURCH
PRINCESS DANIELLE, I AM MERELY MANIPULATING-- THIS VESSEL'S EXTREMITIES--

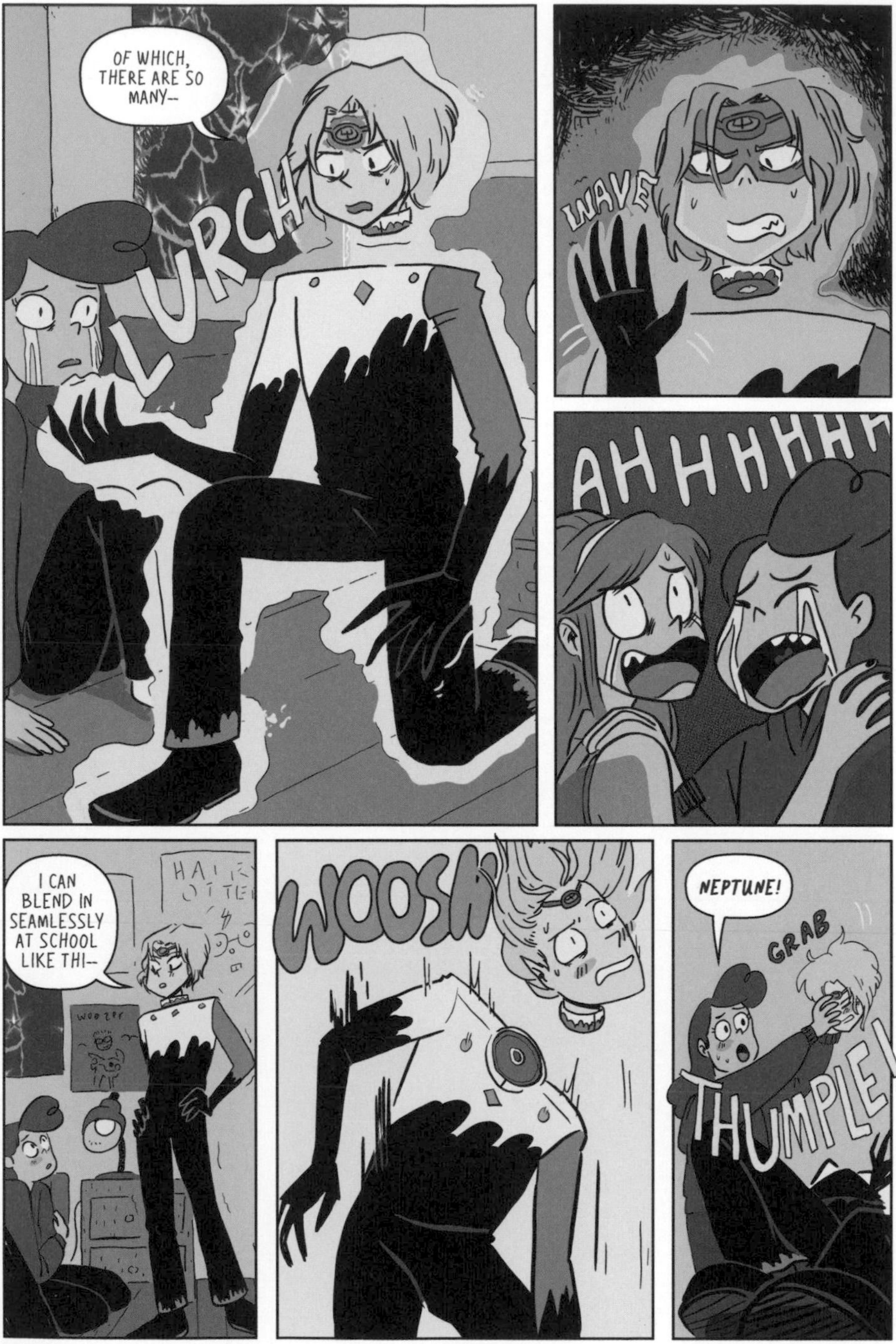
OF WHICH, THERE ARE SO MANY--
LURCH
WAVE
AHHHHHH
I CAN BLEND IN SEAMLESSLY AT SCHOOL LIKE THI--
WOOSH
NEPTUNE!
GRAB
THUMPLE!

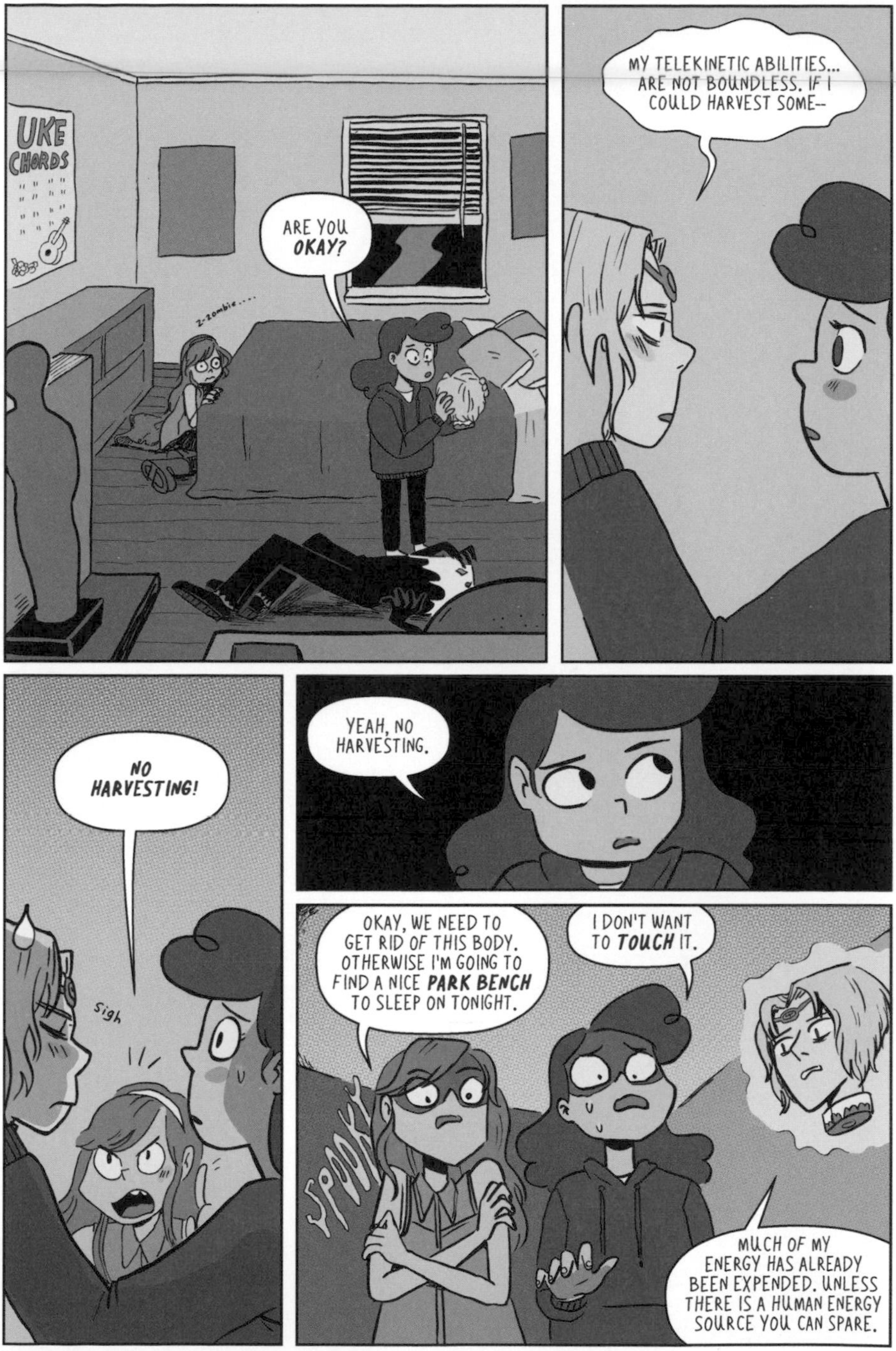
UKE CHORDS
z-zombie....
ARE YOU **OKAY?**
MY TELEKINETIC ABILITIES... ARE NOT BOUNDLESS. IF I COULD HARVEST SOME--
NO HARVESTING!
sigh
YEAH, NO HARVESTING.
OKAY, WE NEED TO GET RID OF THIS BODY. OTHERWISE I'M GOING TO FIND A NICE **PARK BENCH** TO SLEEP ON TONIGHT.
I DON'T WANT TO **TOUCH** IT.
SPOOKY
MUCH OF MY ENERGY HAS ALREADY BEEN EXPENDED. UNLESS THERE IS A HUMAN ENERGY SOURCE YOU CAN SPARE.

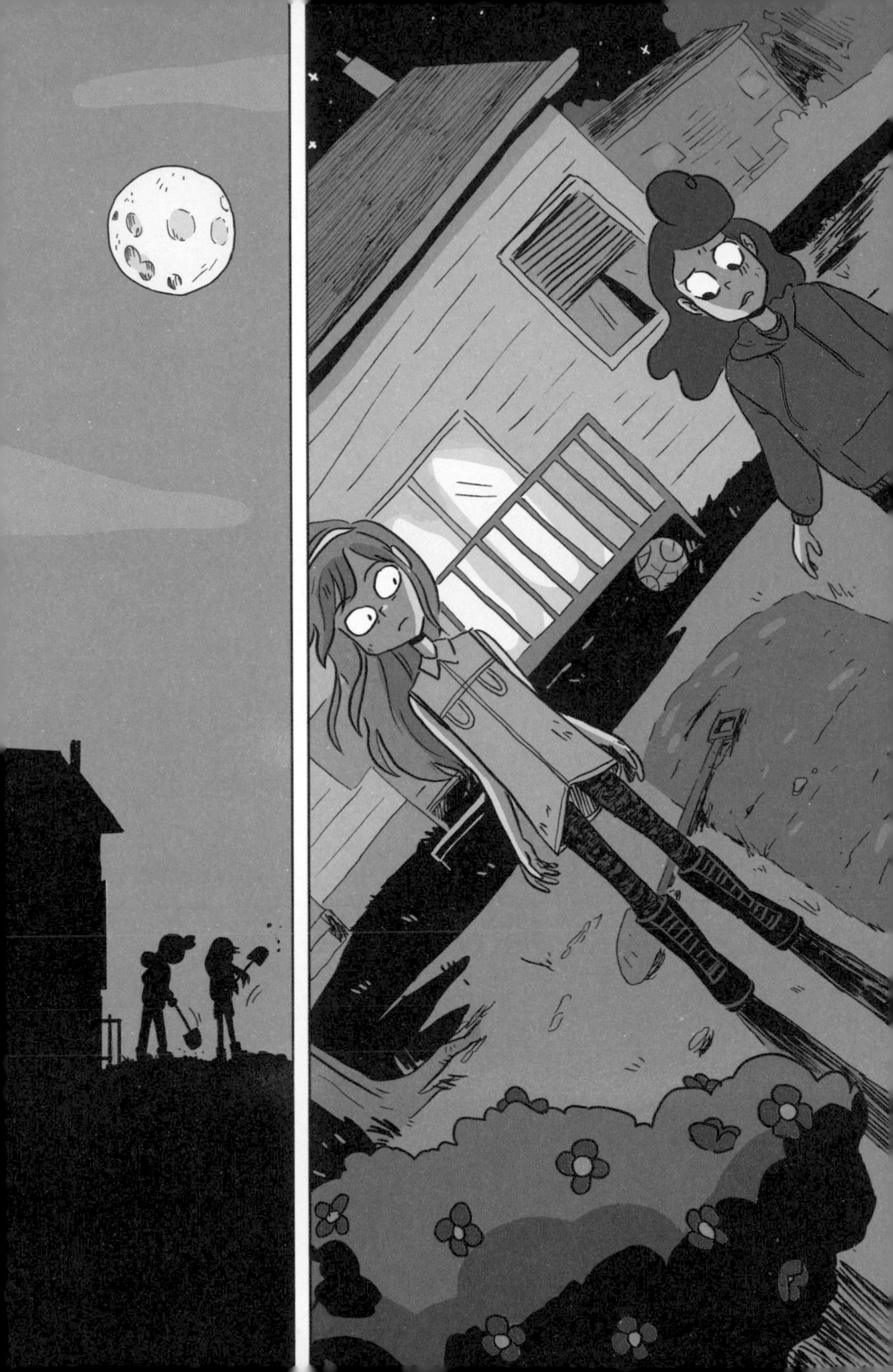

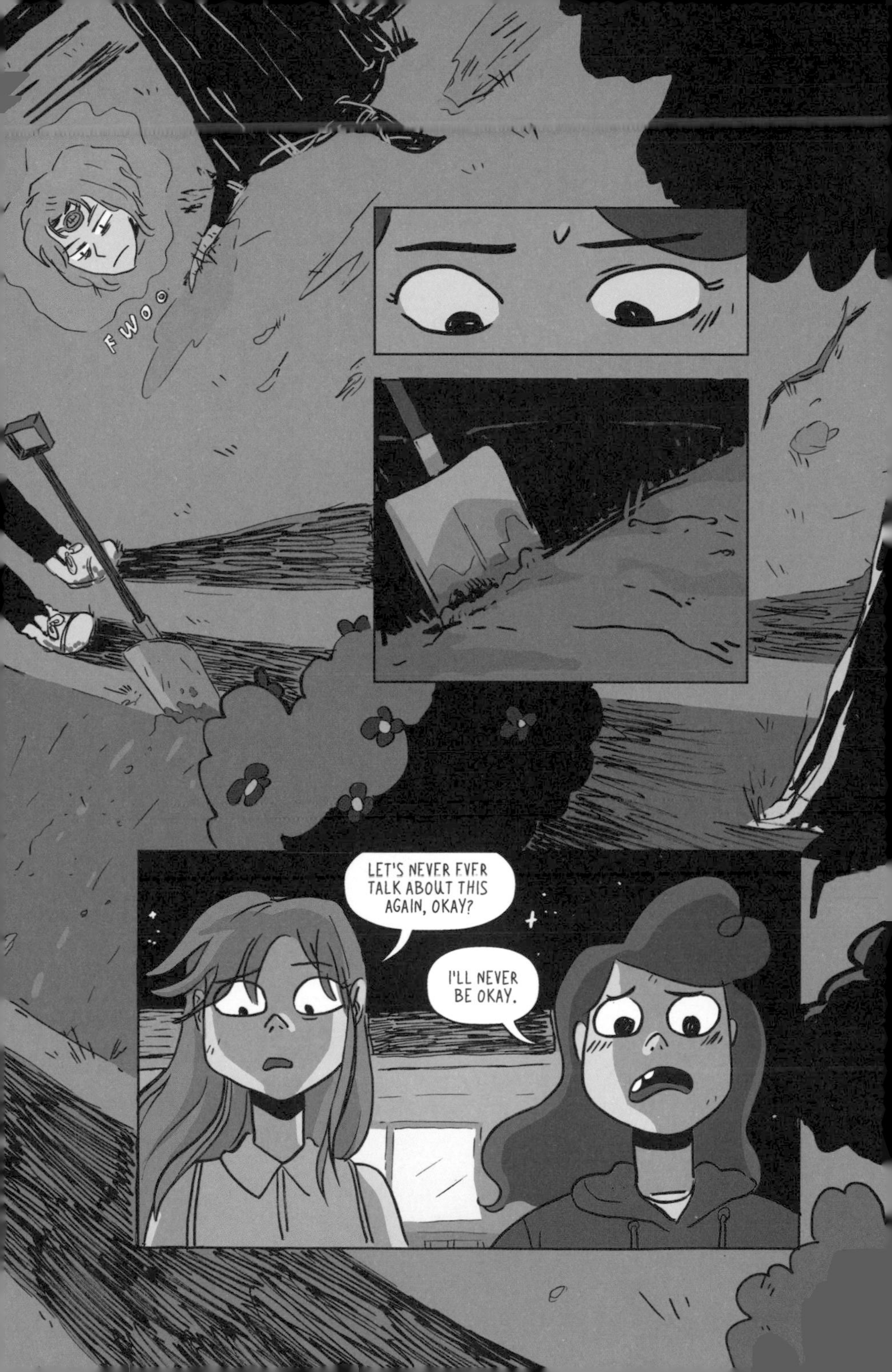
FWOO
LET'S NEVER EVER TALK ABOUT THIS AGAIN, OKAY?
I'LL NEVER BE OKAY.

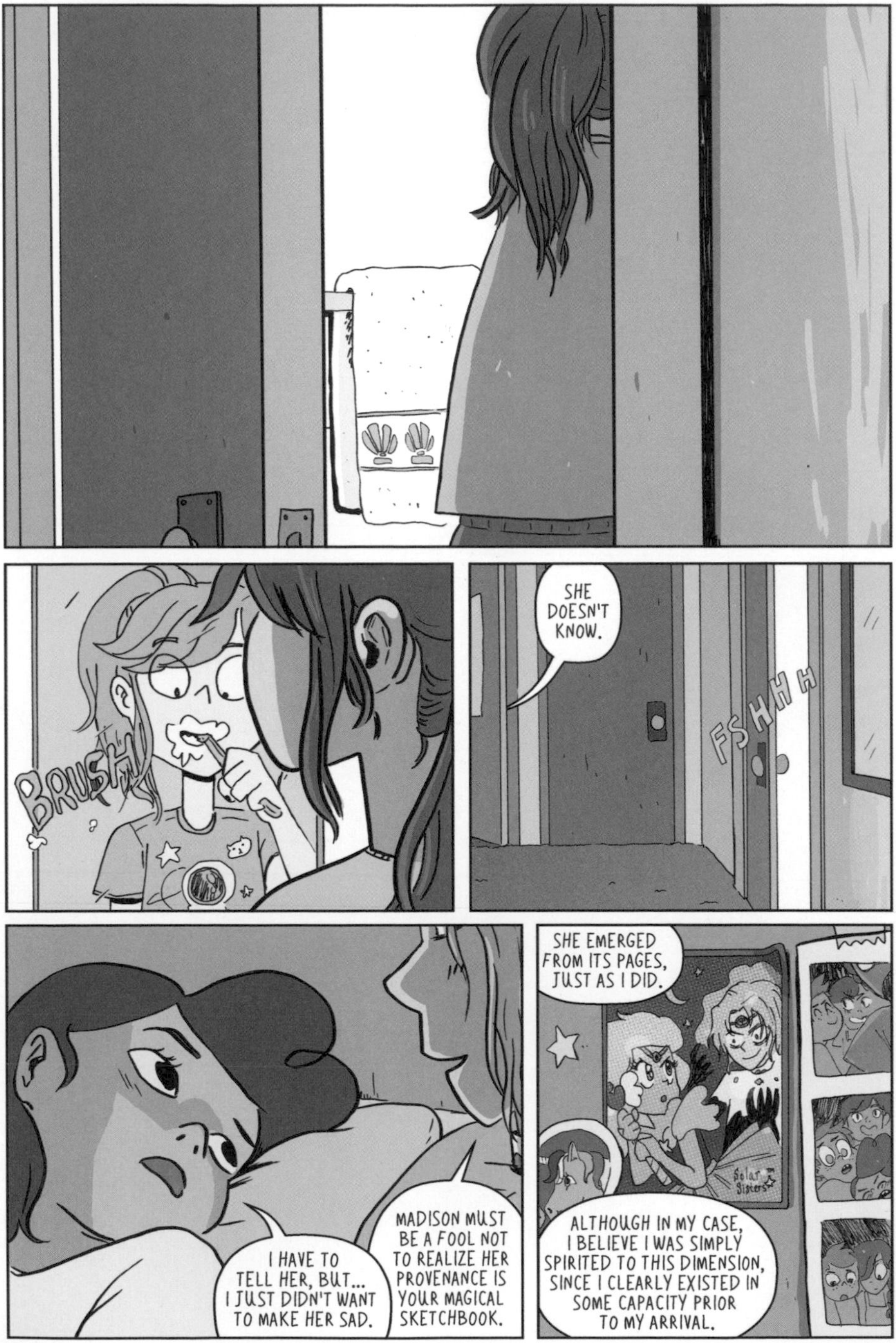
BRUSH
SHE DOESN'T KNOW.
FSHHHH
I HAVE TO TELL HER, BUT... I JUST DIDN'T WANT TO MAKE HER SAD.
MADISON MUST BE A FOOL NOT TO REALIZE HER PROVENANCE IS YOUR MAGICAL SKETCHBOOK.
SHE EMERGED FROM ITS PAGES, JUST AS I DID.
Solar Sisters
ALTHOUGH IN MY CASE, I BELIEVE I WAS SIMPLY SPIRITED TO THIS DIMENSION, SINCE I CLEARLY EXISTED IN SOME CAPACITY PRIOR TO MY ARRIVAL.

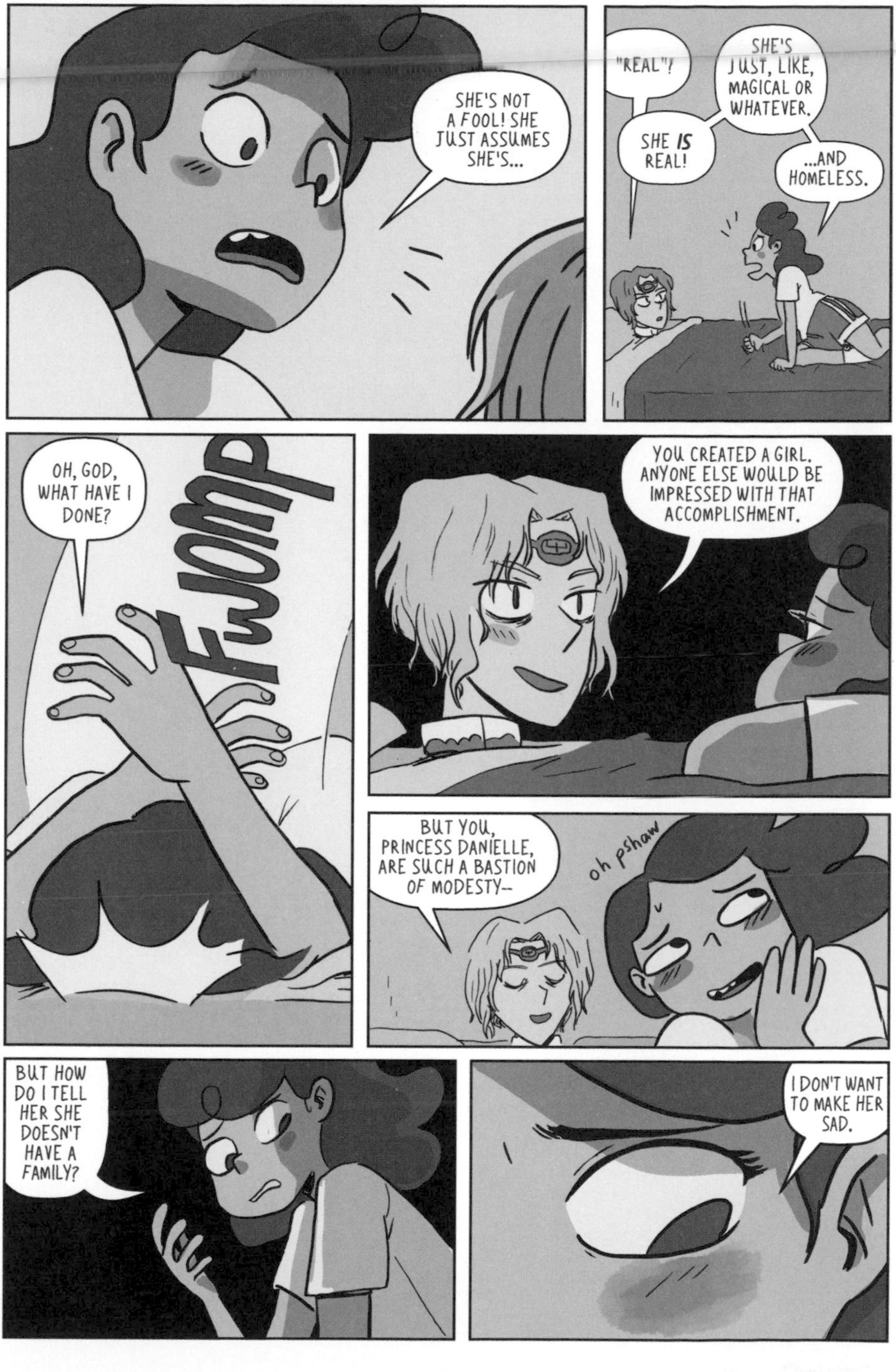
SHE'S NOT A FOOL! SHE JUST ASSUMES SHE'S...
"REAL"?
SHE IS REAL!
SHE'S JUST, LIKE, MAGICAL OR WHATEVER.
...AND HOMELESS.
OH, GOD, WHAT HAVE I DONE?
FWOMP
YOU CREATED A GIRL. ANYONE ELSE WOULD BE IMPRESSED WITH THAT ACCOMPLISHMENT.
BUT YOU, PRINCESS DANIELLE, ARE SUCH A BASTION OF MODESTY--
oh pshaw
BUT HOW DO I TELL HER SHE DOESN'T HAVE A FAMILY?
I DON'T WANT TO MAKE HER SAD.

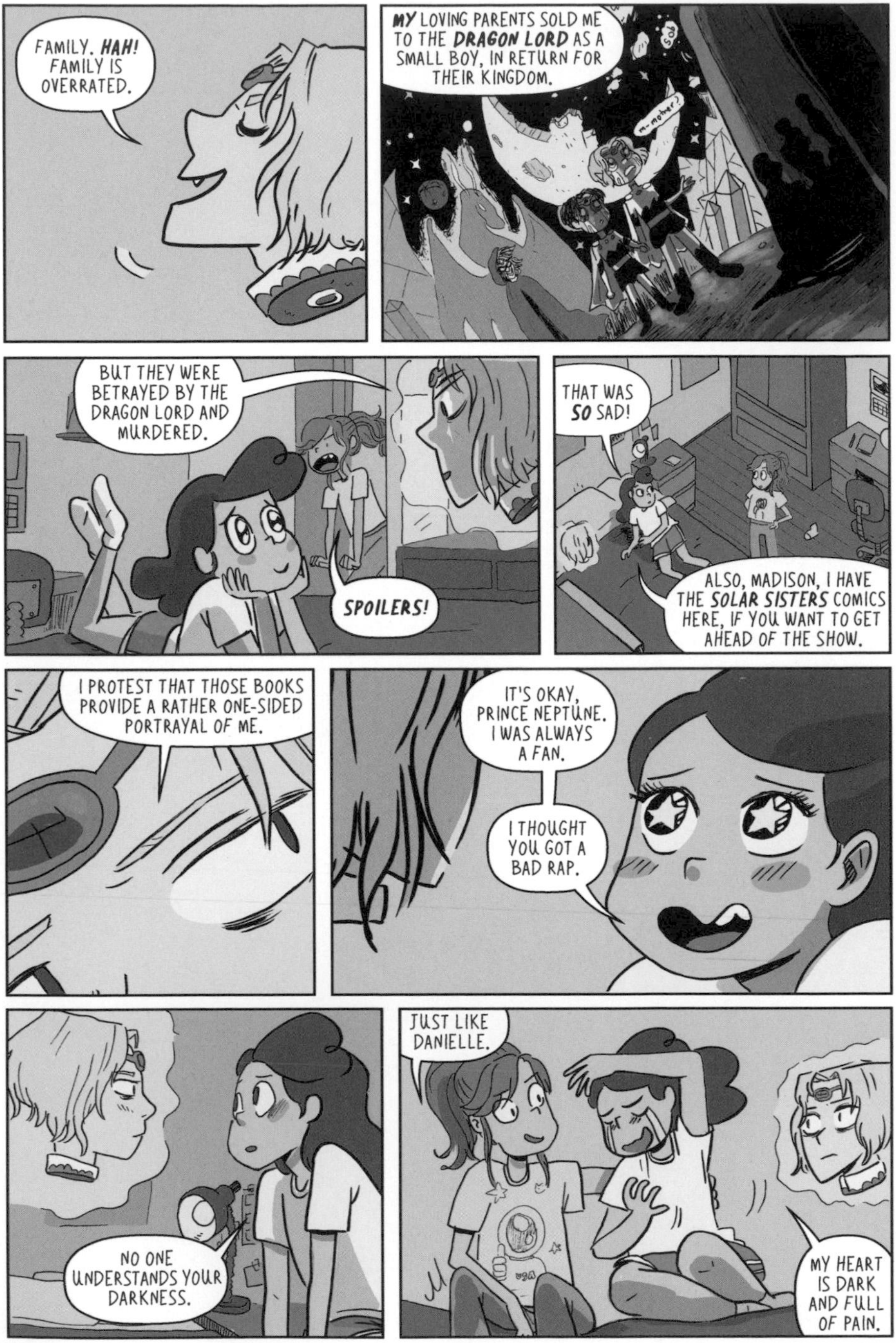

FAMILY. **HAH!** FAMILY IS OVERRATED.
MY LOVING PARENTS SOLD ME TO THE **DRAGON LORD** AS A SMALL BOY, IN RETURN FOR THEIR KINGDOM.
sob
m-mother?
BUT THEY WERE BETRAYED BY THE DRAGON LORD AND MURDERED.
SPOILERS!
THAT WAS **SO** SAD!
ALSO, MADISON, I HAVE THE **SOLAR SISTERS** COMICS HERE, IF YOU WANT TO GET AHEAD OF THE SHOW.
I PROTEST THAT THOSE BOOKS PROVIDE A RATHER ONE-SIDED PORTRAYAL OF ME.
IT'S OKAY, PRINCE NEPTUNE. I WAS ALWAYS A FAN.
I THOUGHT YOU GOT A BAD RAP.
NO ONE UNDERSTANDS YOUR DARKNESS.
JUST LIKE DANIELLE.
MY HEART IS DARK AND FULL OF PAIN.

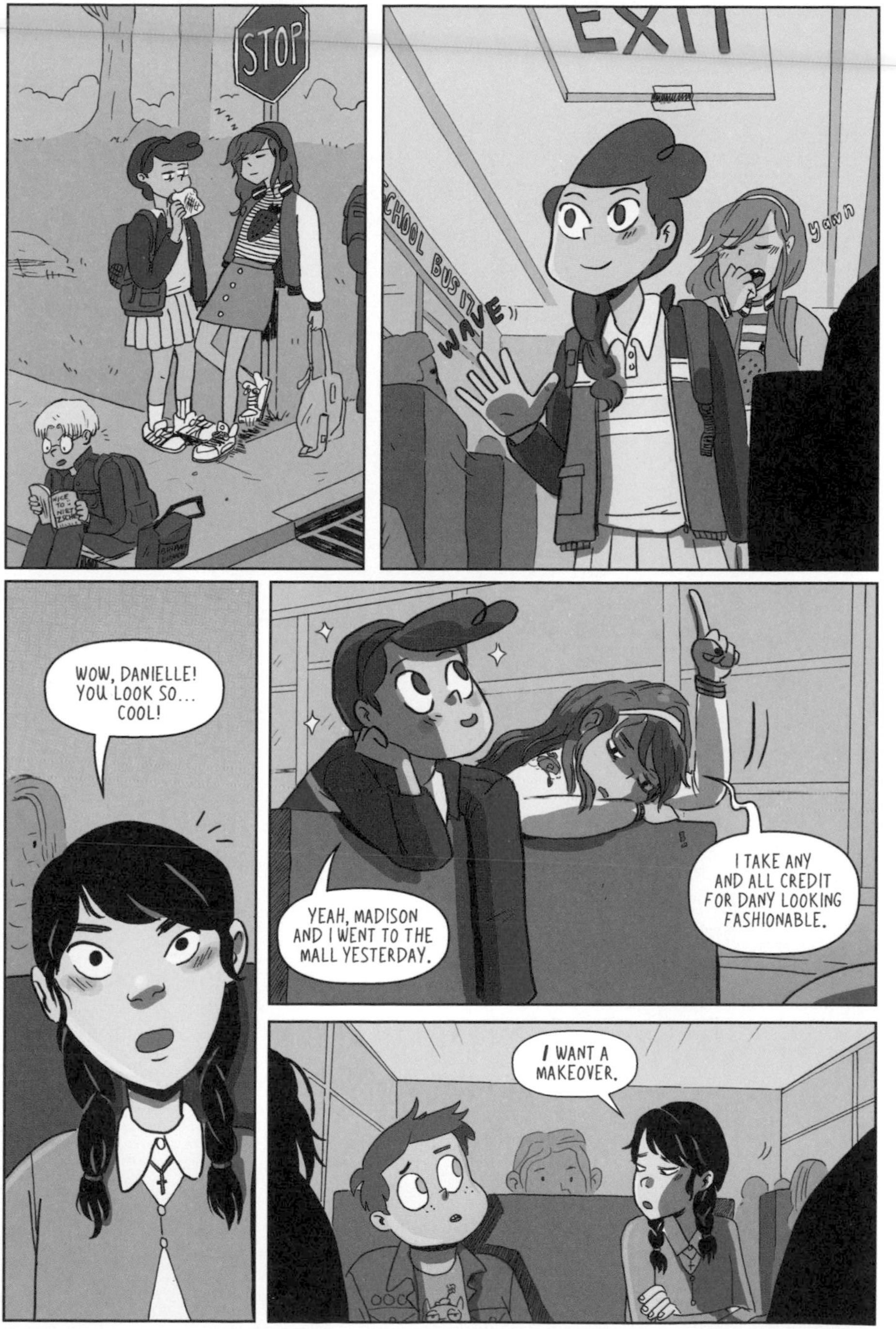
STOP
EXIT
SCHOOL BUS
WAVE
yawn
WOW, DANIELLE! YOU LOOK SO... COOL!
YEAH, MADISON AND I WENT TO THE MALL YESTERDAY.
I TAKE ANY AND ALL CREDIT FOR DANY LOOKING FASHIONABLE.
I WANT A MAKEOVER.

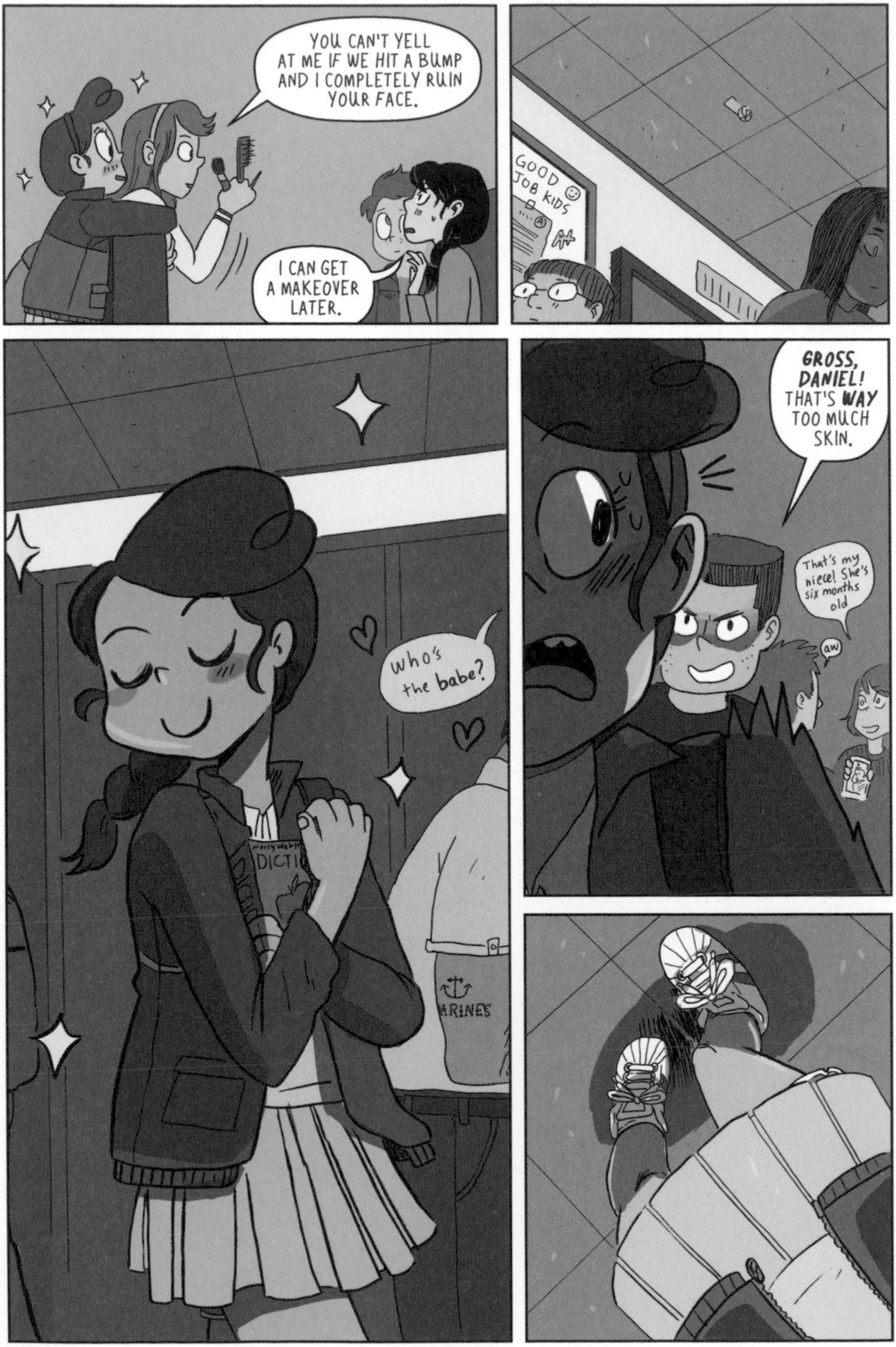

YOU CAN'T YELL AT ME IF WE HIT A BUMP AND I COMPLETELY RUIN YOUR FACE.
I CAN GET A MAKEOVER LATER.
GOOD JOB KIDS
who's the babe?
MARINES
DICTI
GROSS, DANIEL! THAT'S WAY TOO MUCH SKIN.
That's my niece! She's six months old
aw

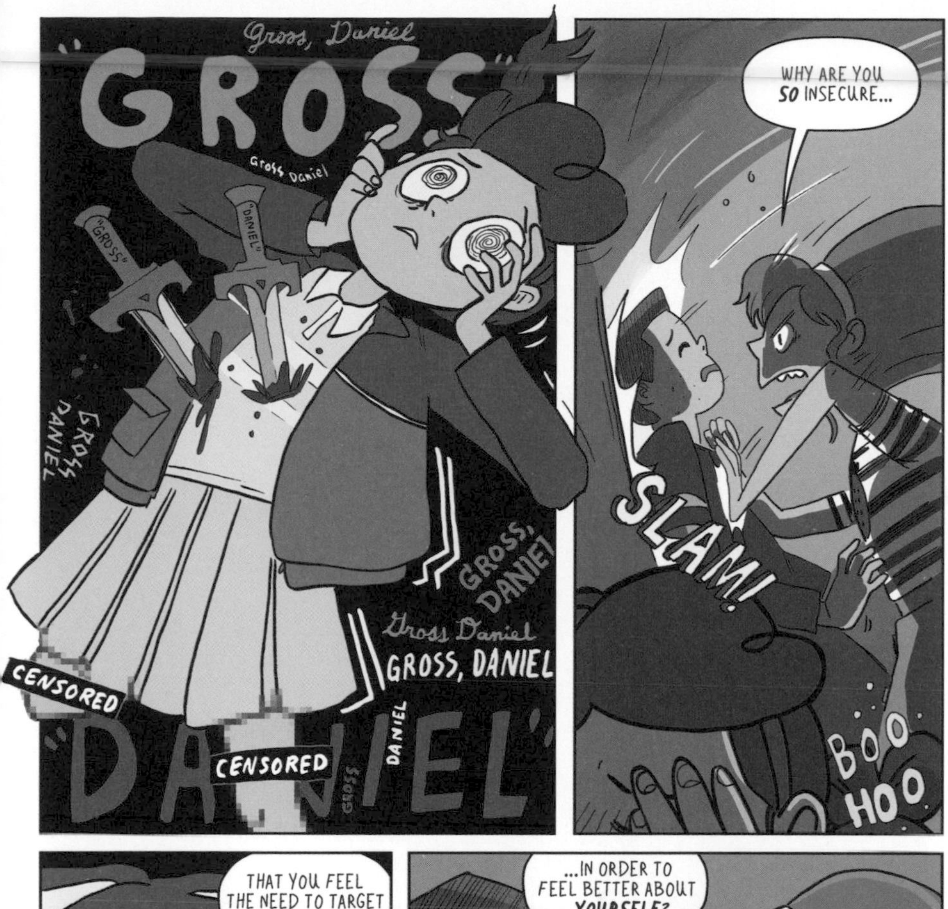
"GROSS"
Gross, Daniel
Gross Daniel
"GROSS"
"DANIEL"
GROSS DANIEL
GROSS, DANIEL
Gross Daniel
GROSS, DANIEL
CENSORED
"DA
CENSORED
IEL"
GROSS
DANIEL
WHY ARE YOU SO INSECURE...
SLAM!
BOO HOO
THAT YOU FEEL THE NEED TO TARGET MY FRIEND...
MY HERO
...IN ORDER TO FEEL BETTER ABOUT YOURSELF?

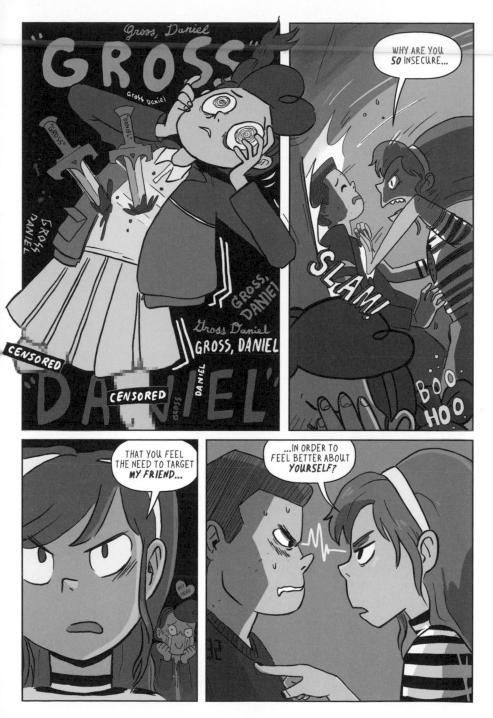

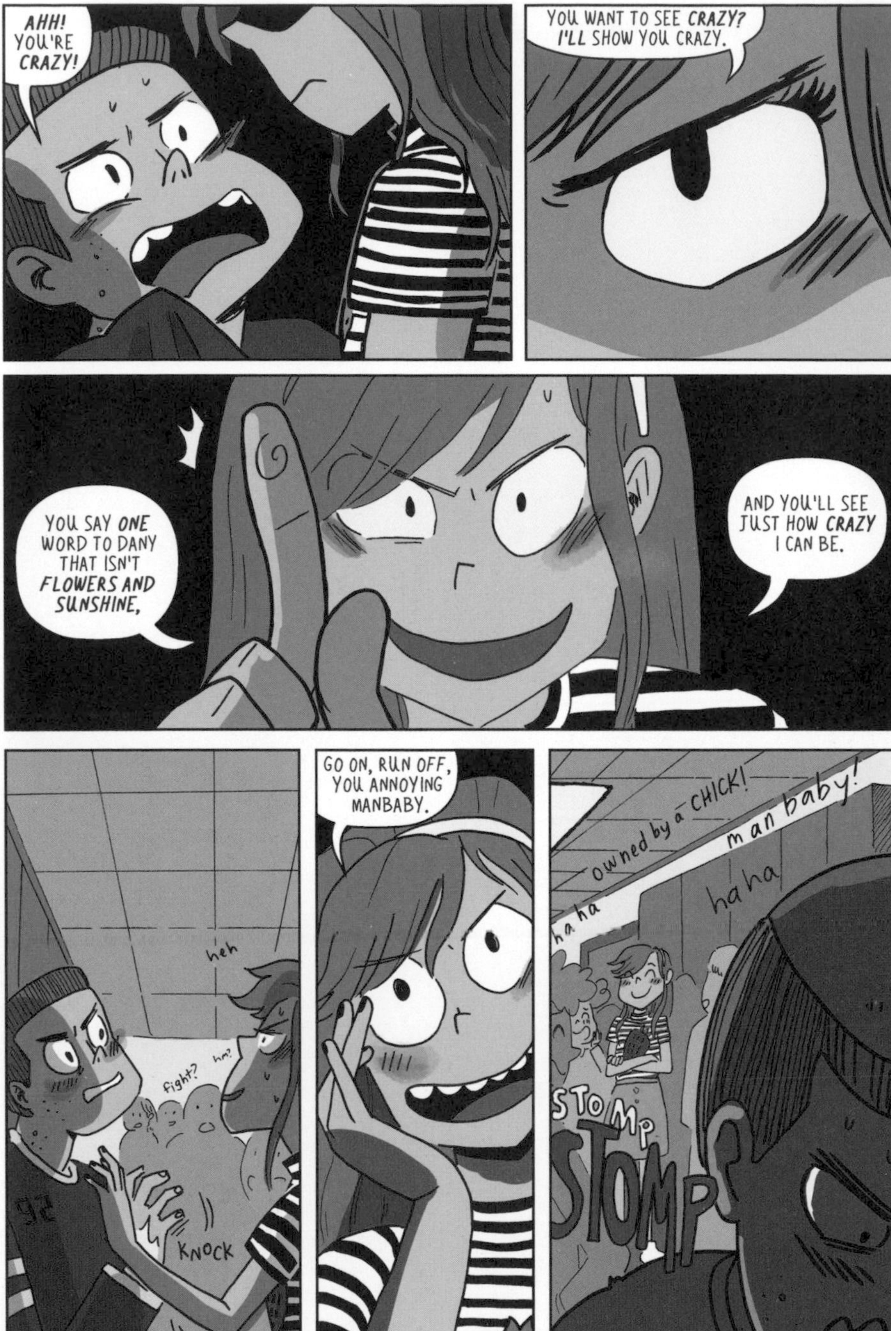

AHH! YOU'RE CRAZY!
YOU WANT TO SEE CRAZY? I'LL SHOW YOU CRAZY.
YOU SAY ONE WORD TO DANY THAT ISN'T FLOWERS AND SUNSHINE,
AND YOU'LL SEE JUST HOW CRAZY I CAN BE.
heh
fight?
hm?
KNOCK
GO ON, RUN OFF, YOU ANNOYING MANBABY.
owned by a CHICK!
man baby!
haha
ha ha
STOMP
STOMP

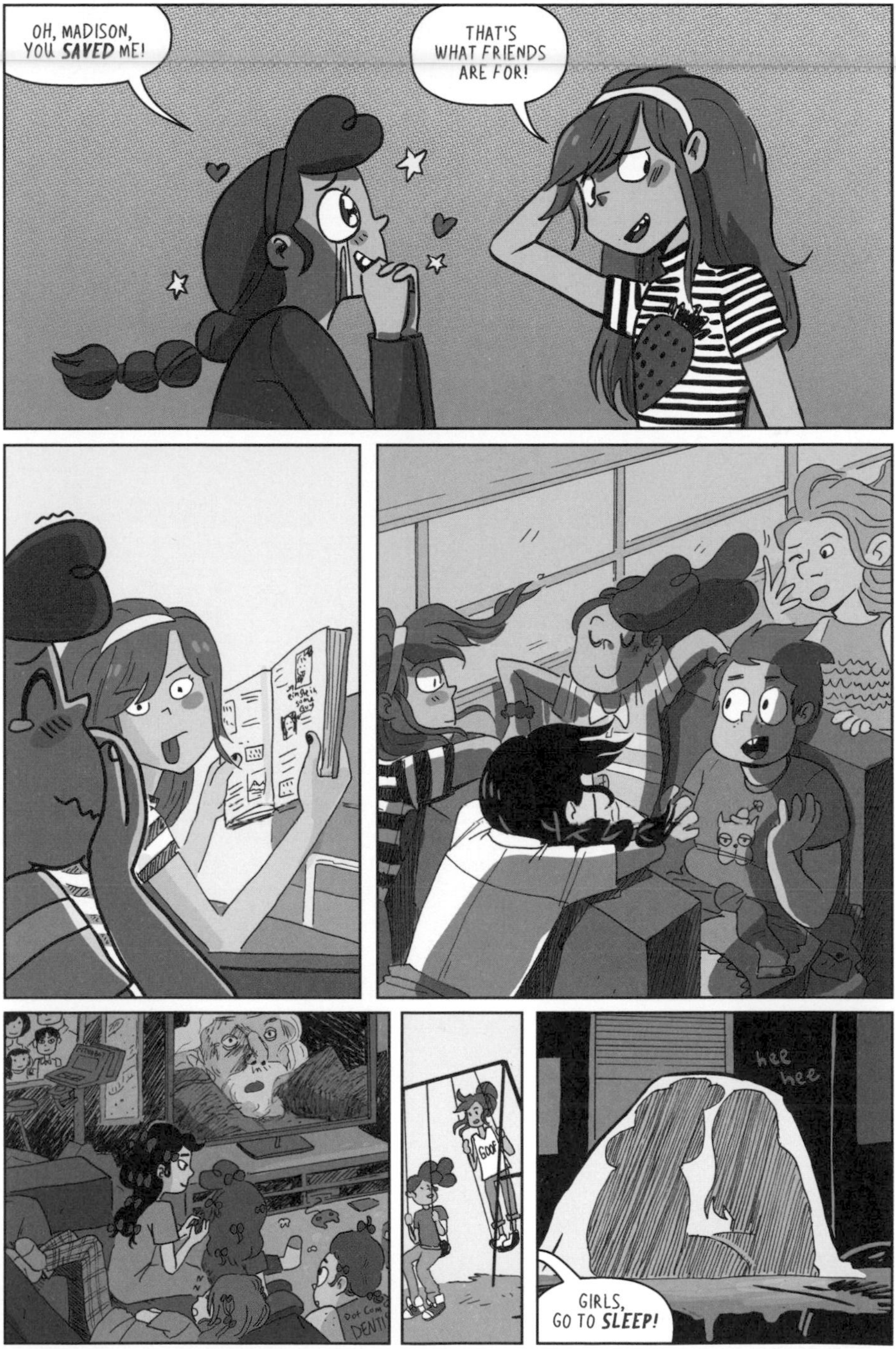
OH, MADISON, YOU **SAVED** ME!
THAT'S WHAT FRIENDS ARE FOR!
GOOF
hee hee
GIRLS, GO TO **SLEEP!**

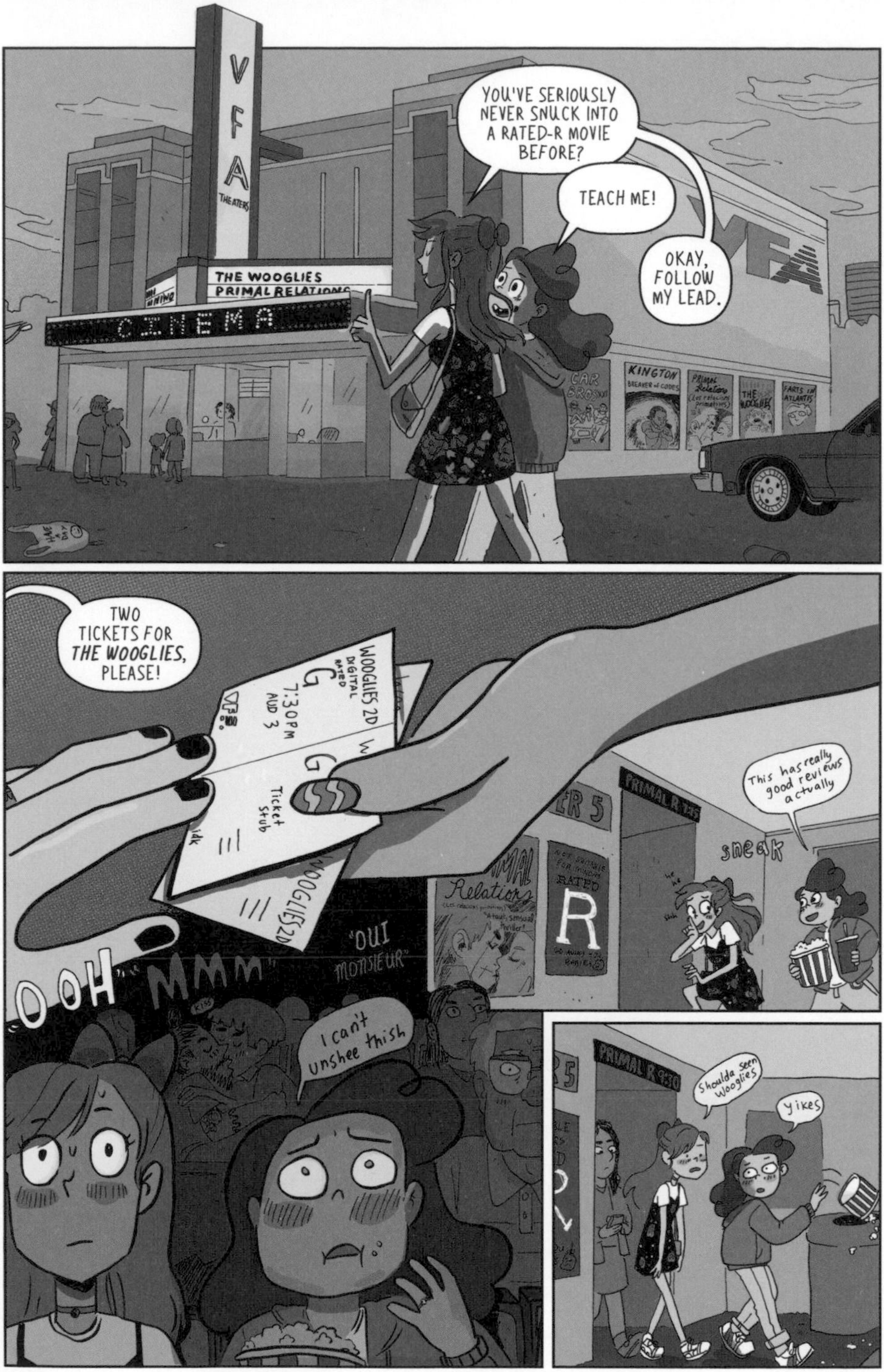
VFA
THEATERS
THE WOOGLIES
CINEMA
YOU'VE SERIOUSLY NEVER SNUCK INTO A RATED-R MOVIE BEFORE?
TEACH ME!
OKAY, FOLLOW MY LEAD.
KINGTON
BREAKER of CODES
FARTS IN ATLANTIS
TWO TICKETS FOR *THE WOOGLIES,* PLEASE!
WOOGLIES 2D
DIGITAL
RATED
G
7:30PM
AUG 3
Ticket stub
This has really good reviews actually
sneak
RATED
R
"OOH" "MMM"
"OUI MONSIEUR"
I can't unshee thish
PRIMAL R 9:30
Shoulda seen Wooglies
Yikes

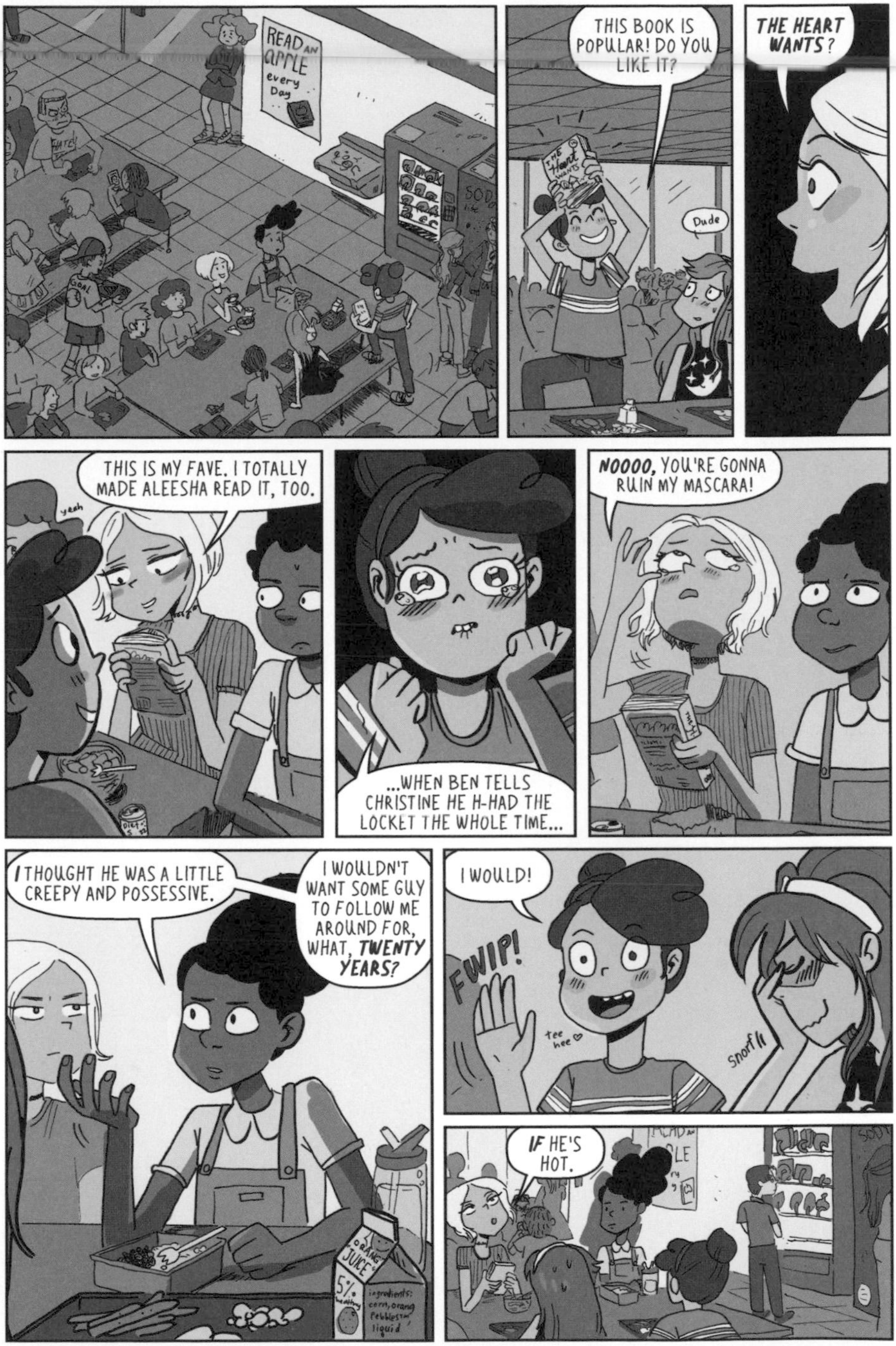
READ AN APPLE every Day
THIS BOOK IS POPULAR! DO YOU LIKE IT?
Dude
THE HEART WANTS?
THIS IS MY FAVE. I TOTALLY MADE ALEESHA READ IT, TOO.
yeah
...WHEN BEN TELLS CHRISTINE HE H-HAD THE LOCKET THE WHOLE TIME...
NOOOO, YOU'RE GONNA RUIN MY MASCARA!
I THOUGHT HE WAS A LITTLE CREEPY AND POSSESSIVE.
I WOULDN'T WANT SOME GUY TO FOLLOW ME AROUND FOR, WHAT, TWENTY YEARS?
ORANG JUICE
5% healthy
ingredients: corn, orang pebbles'n' liquid
I WOULD!
FWIP!
tee hee ♡
snorf
IF HE'S HOT.

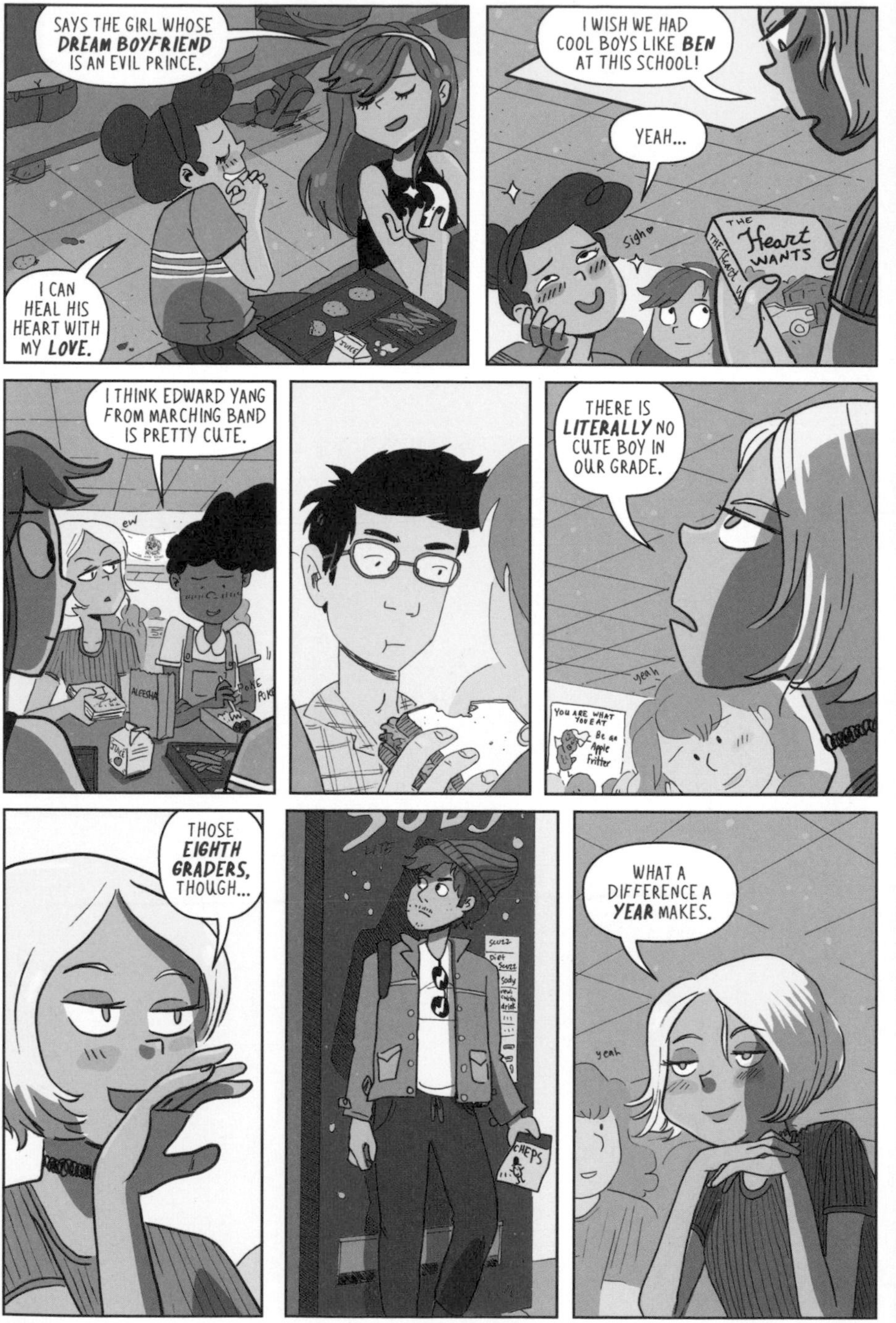
SAYS THE GIRL WHOSE DREAM BOYFRIEND IS AN EVIL PRINCE.
I CAN HEAL HIS HEART WITH MY LOVE.
JUICE
I WISH WE HAD COOL BOYS LIKE BEN AT THIS SCHOOL!
YEAH...
Sigh
THE Heart WANTS
I THINK EDWARD YANG FROM MARCHING BAND IS PRETTY CUTE.
ew
ALEESHA
POKE
POKE
JUICE
THERE IS LITERALLY NO CUTE BOY IN OUR GRADE.
yeah
YOU ARE WHAT YOU EAT
Be an Apple Fritter
THOSE EIGHTH GRADERS, THOUGH...
CHEPS
WHAT A DIFFERENCE A YEAR MAKES.
yeah

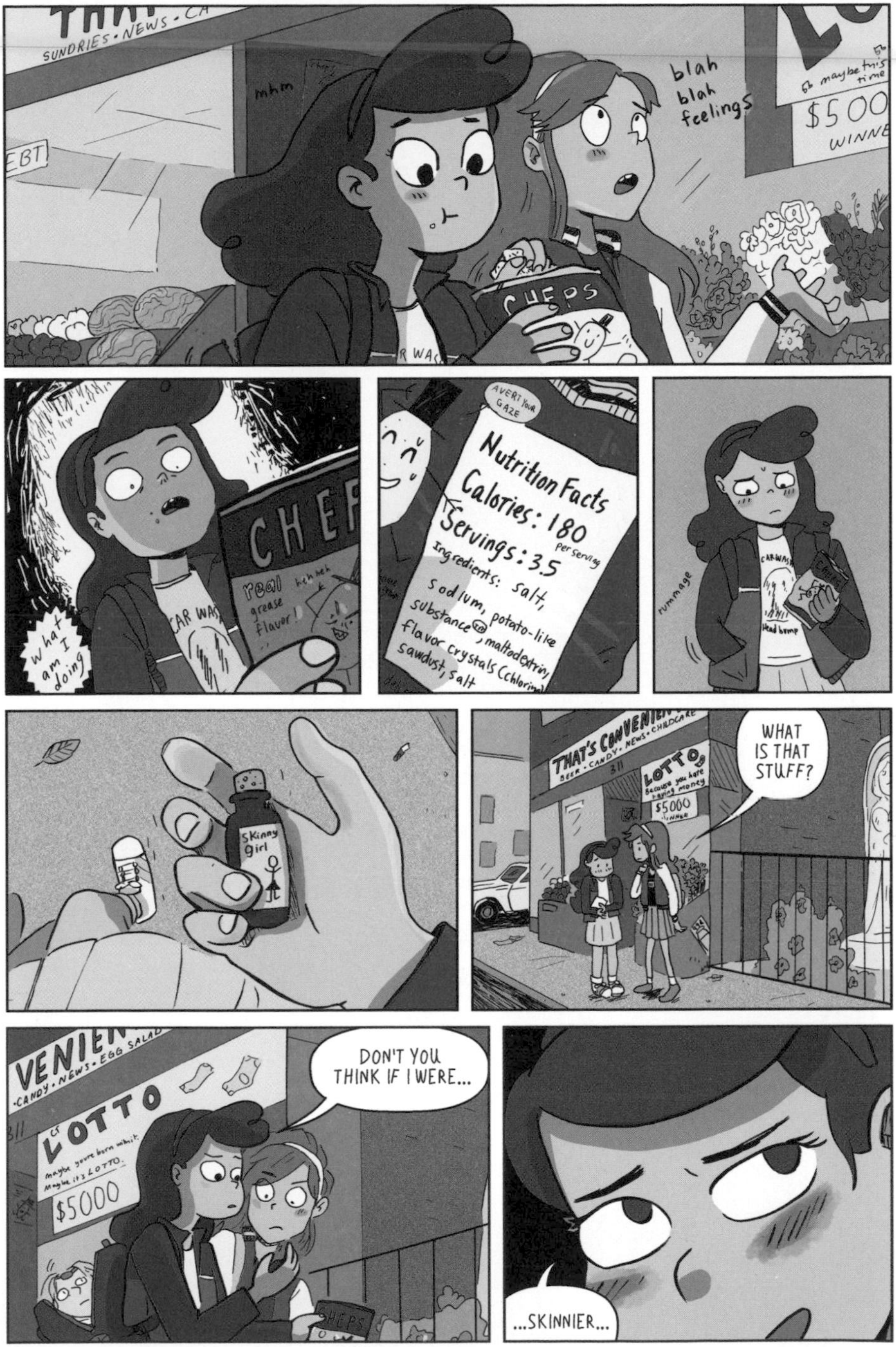

SUNDRIES • NEWS • CA
mhm
blah
blah
feelings
maybe this time
$5000
WINNE
EBT
CHEPS
CHEP
real grease flavor!
heh heh
what am I doing
AVERT YOUR GAZE
Nutrition Facts
Calories: 180 per serving
Servings: 3.5
Ingredients: salt, sodium, potato-like substance, maltodextrin, flavor crystals (Chlorine), sawdust, salt
rummage
CARWASH
dead bump
SKinny Girl
THAT'S CONVENIENT
BEER • CANDY • NEWS • CHILDCARE
311
LOTTO
Because you hate having money
$5000
WHAT IS THAT STUFF?
VENIEN
• CANDY • NEWS • EGG SALAD
LOTTO
maybe you're born with it. Maybe it's LOTTO.
$5000
DON'T YOU THINK IF I WERE...
...SKINNIER...

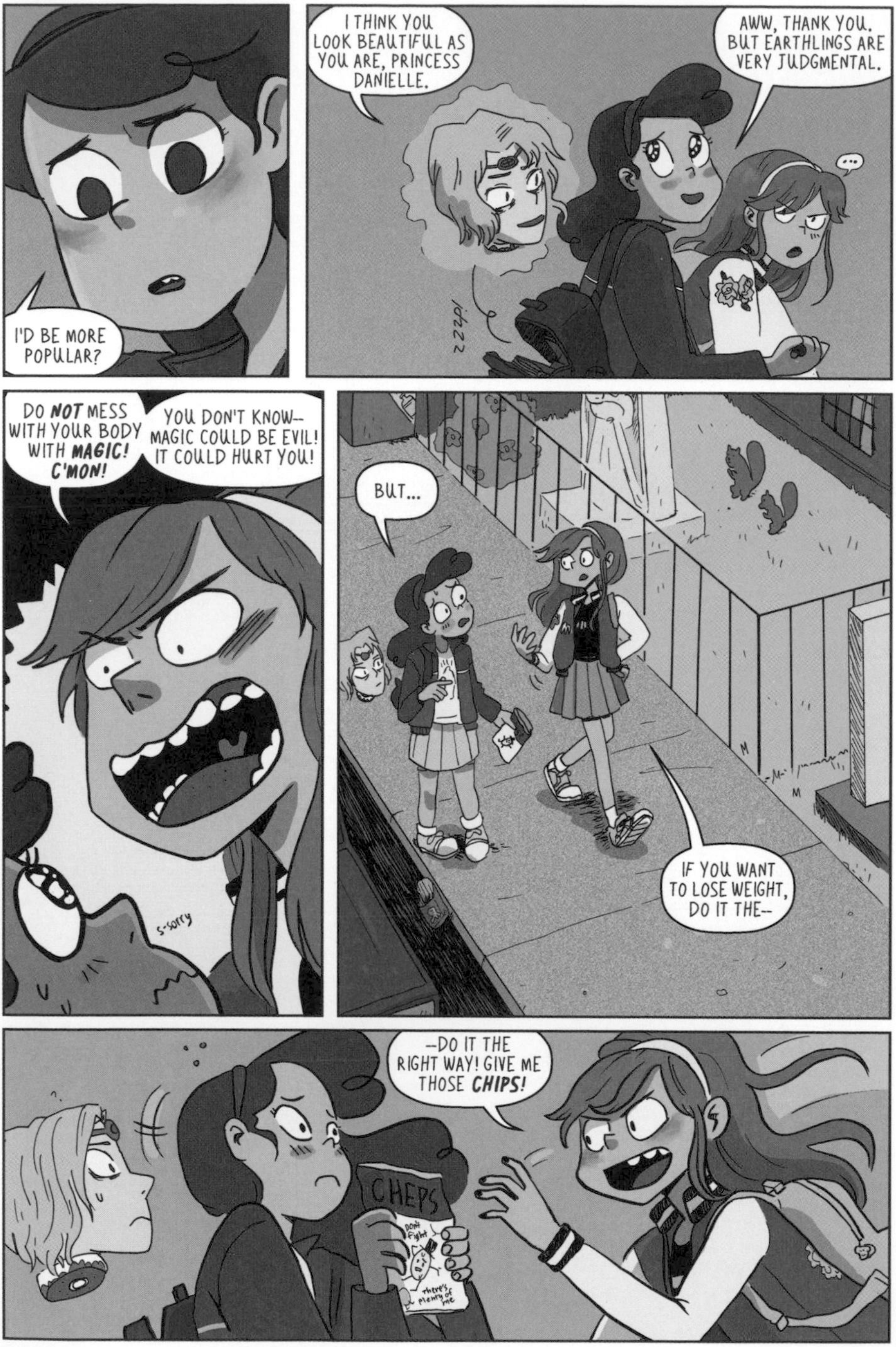
I'D BE MORE POPULAR?
I THINK YOU LOOK BEAUTIFUL AS YOU ARE, PRINCESS DANIELLE.
AWW, THANK YOU. BUT EARTHLINGS ARE VERY JUDGMENTAL.
DO NOT MESS WITH YOUR BODY WITH MAGIC! C'MON!
YOU DON'T KNOW-- MAGIC COULD BE EVIL! IT COULD HURT YOU!
s-sorry
BUT...
IF YOU WANT TO LOSE WEIGHT, DO IT THE--
--DO IT THE RIGHT WAY! GIVE ME THOSE CHIPS!
CHEPS
Don't Fight
there's plenty of me

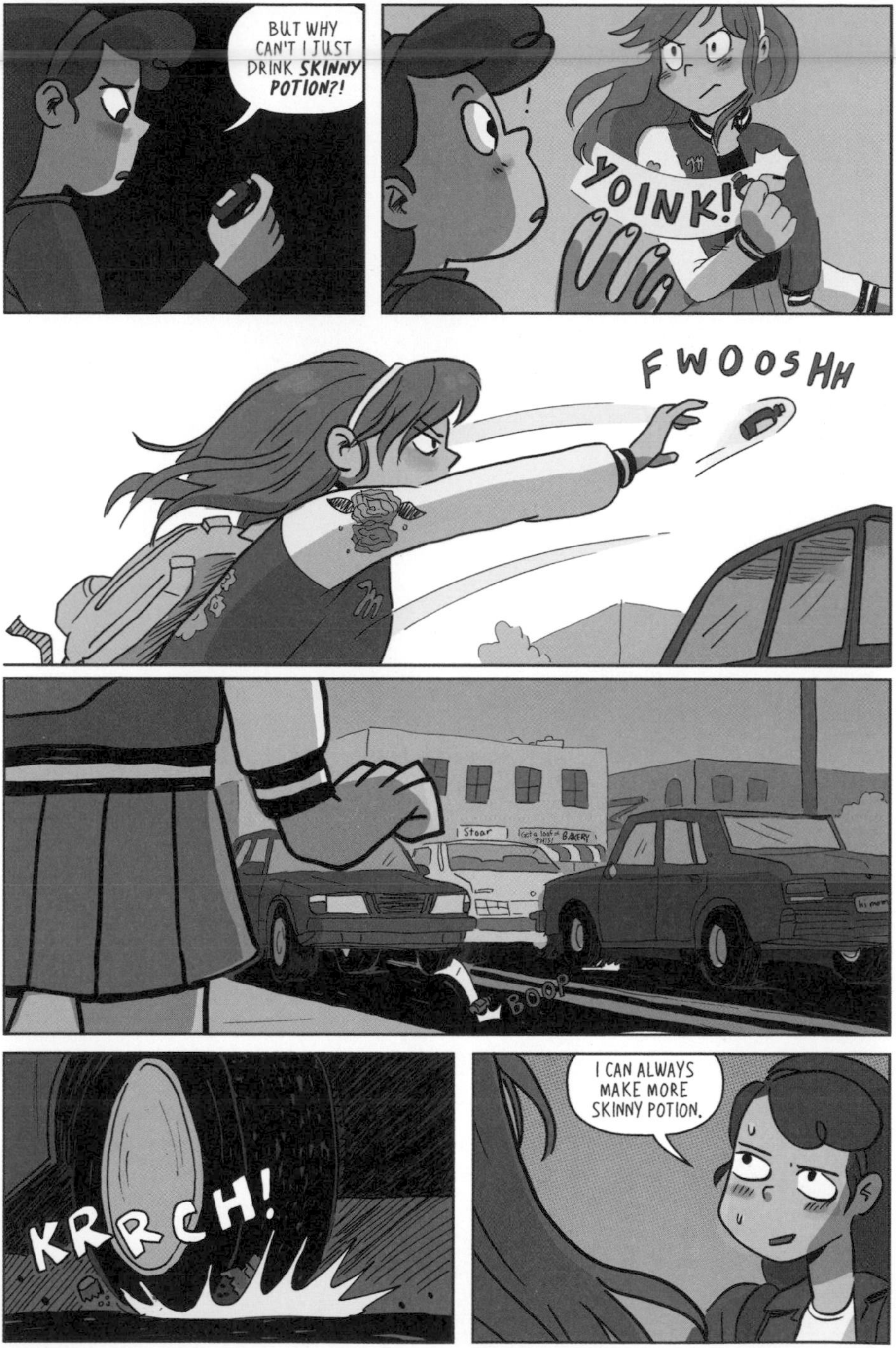
BUT WHY CAN'T I JUST DRINK **SKINNY POTION?!**
!
YOINK!
FWOOSHH
Stoar
Get a loaf of THIS!
BAKERY
BOOP
KRRCH!
I CAN ALWAYS MAKE MORE SKINNY POTION.

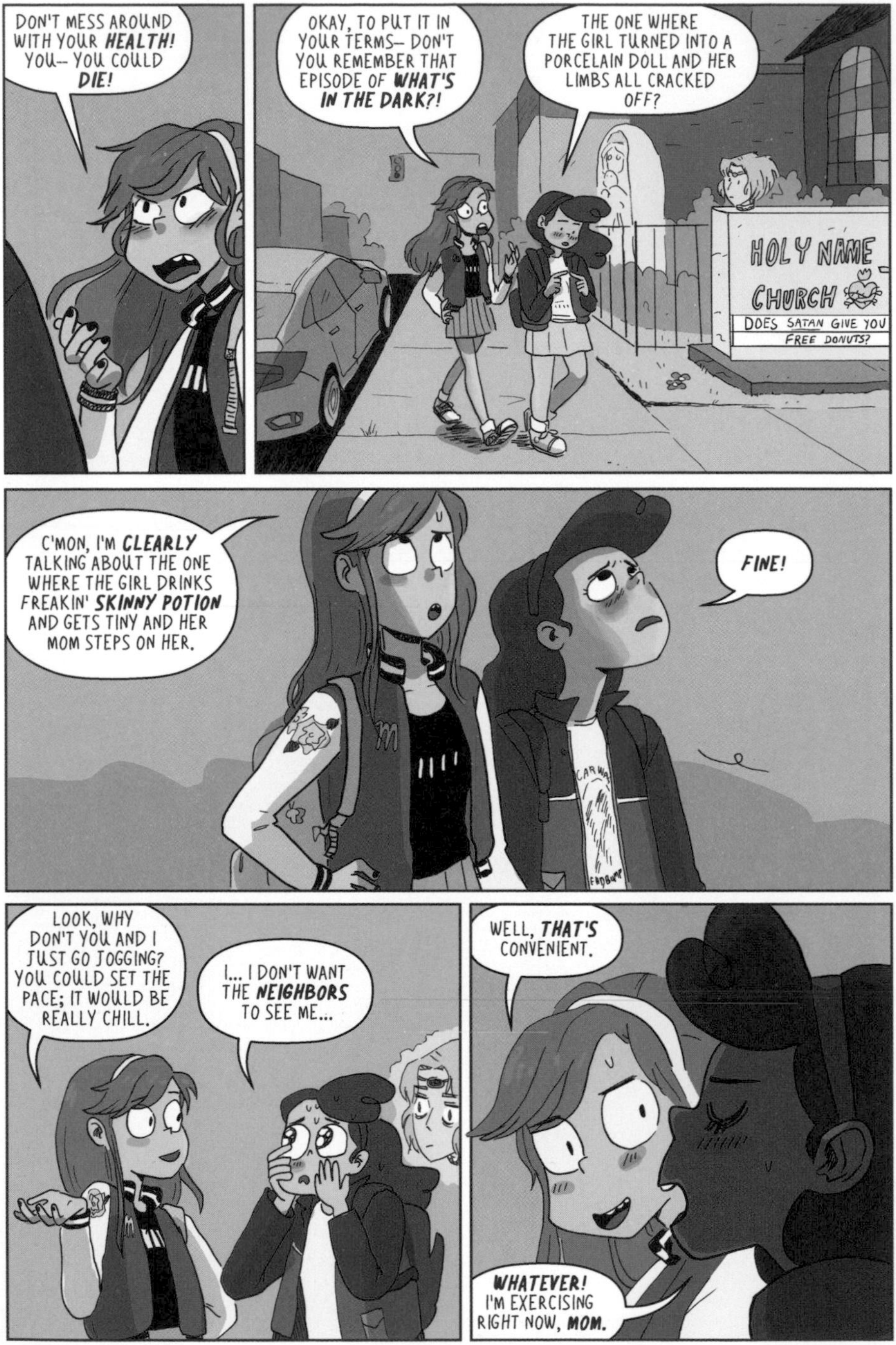
DON'T MESS AROUND WITH YOUR HEALTH! YOU-- YOU COULD DIE!
OKAY, TO PUT IT IN YOUR TERMS-- DON'T YOU REMEMBER THAT EPISODE OF WHAT'S IN THE DARK?!
THE ONE WHERE THE GIRL TURNED INTO A PORCELAIN DOLL AND HER LIMBS ALL CRACKED OFF?
HOLY NAME CHURCH
DOES SATAN GIVE YOU FREE DONUTS?
C'MON, I'M CLEARLY TALKING ABOUT THE ONE WHERE THE GIRL DRINKS FREAKIN' SKINNY POTION AND GETS TINY AND HER MOM STEPS ON HER.
FINE!
LOOK, WHY DON'T YOU AND I JUST GO JOGGING? YOU COULD SET THE PACE; IT WOULD BE REALLY CHILL.
I... I DON'T WANT THE NEIGHBORS TO SEE ME...
WELL, THAT'S CONVENIENT.
WHATEVER! I'M EXERCISING RIGHT NOW, MOM.

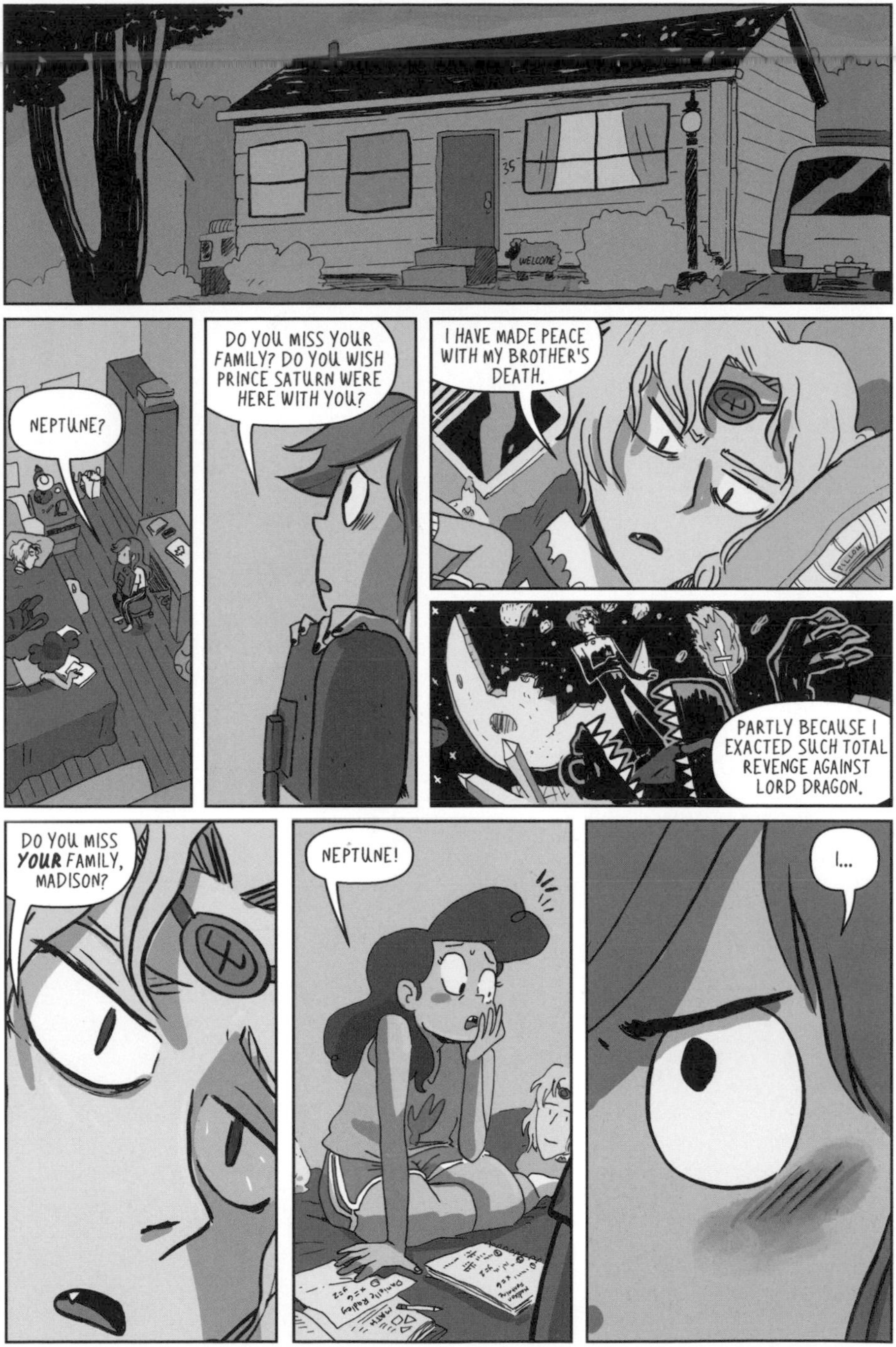
35
WELCOME
NEPTUNE?
DO YOU MISS YOUR FAMILY? DO YOU WISH PRINCE SATURN WERE HERE WITH YOU?
I HAVE MADE PEACE WITH MY BROTHER'S DEATH.
PILLOW
PARTLY BECAUSE I EXACTED SUCH TOTAL REVENGE AGAINST LORD DRAGON.
DO YOU MISS **YOUR** FAMILY, MADISON?
NEPTUNE!
I...

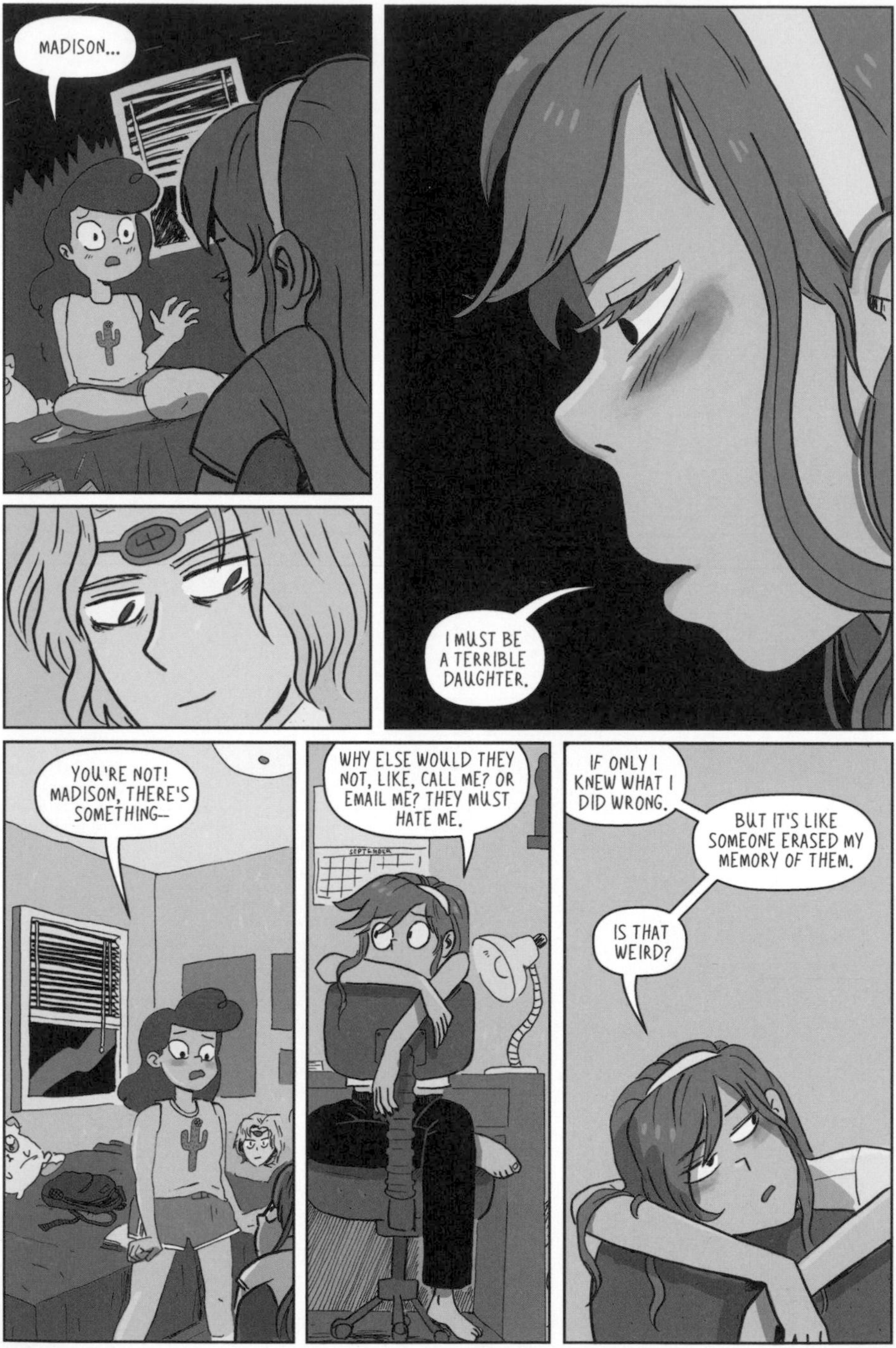
MADISON...
I MUST BE A TERRIBLE DAUGHTER.
YOU'RE NOT! MADISON, THERE'S SOMETHING--
WHY ELSE WOULD THEY NOT, LIKE, CALL ME? OR EMAIL ME? THEY MUST HATE ME.
IF ONLY I KNEW WHAT I DID WRONG.
BUT IT'S LIKE SOMEONE ERASED MY MEMORY OF THEM.
IS THAT WEIRD?

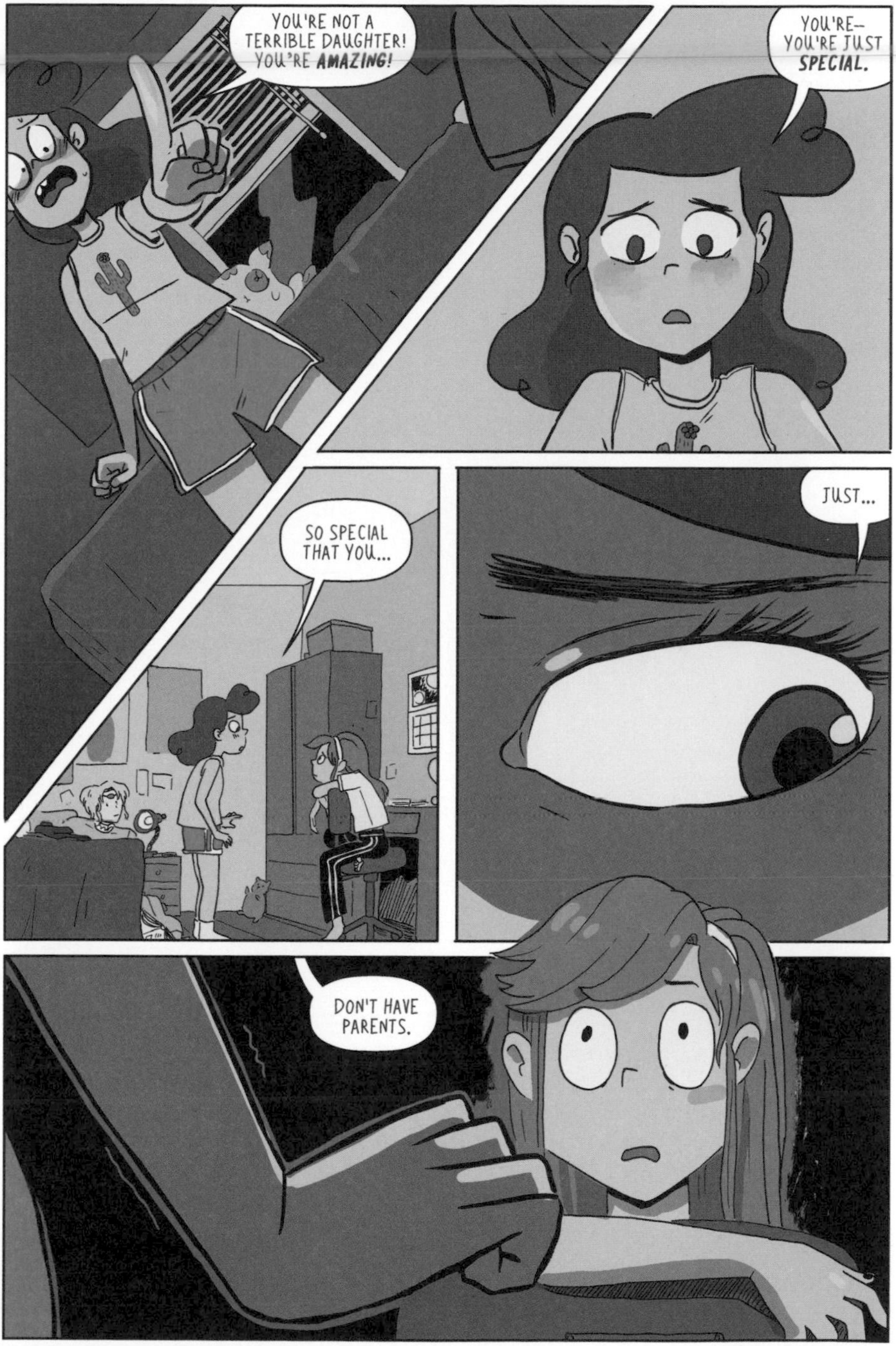
YOU'RE NOT A
TERRIBLE DAUGHTER!
YOU'RE **AMAZING!**
YOU'RE—
YOU'RE JUST
SPECIAL.
SO SPECIAL
THAT YOU...
JUST...
DON'T HAVE
PARENTS.

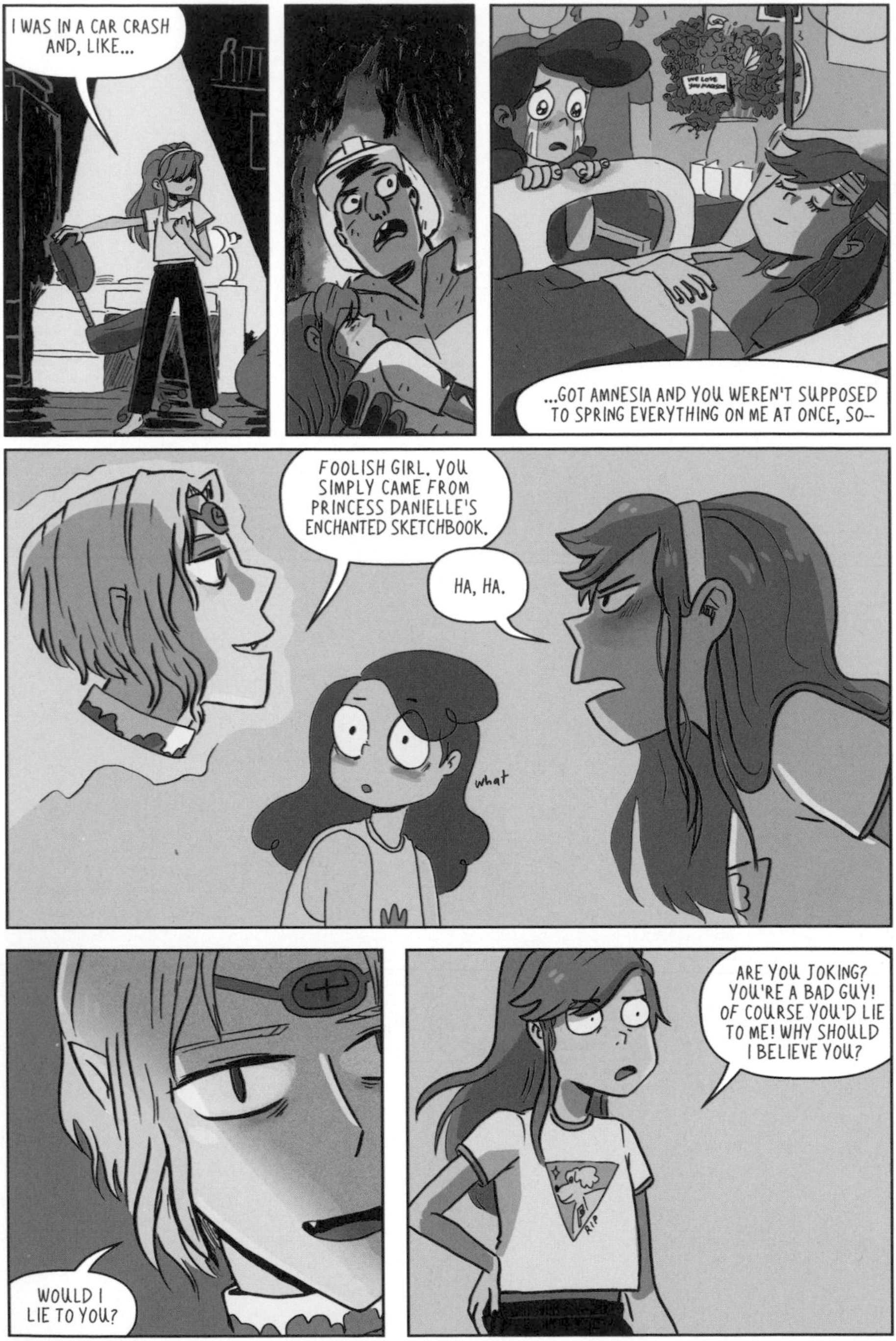
I WAS IN A CAR CRASH AND, LIKE...
...GOT AMNESIA AND YOU WEREN'T SUPPOSED TO SPRING EVERYTHING ON ME AT ONCE, SO--
FOOLISH GIRL. YOU SIMPLY CAME FROM PRINCESS DANIELLE'S ENCHANTED SKETCHBOOK.
HA, HA.
what
WOULD I LIE TO YOU?
ARE YOU JOKING? YOU'RE A BAD GUY! OF COURSE YOU'D LIE TO ME! WHY SHOULD I BELIEVE YOU?
RIP

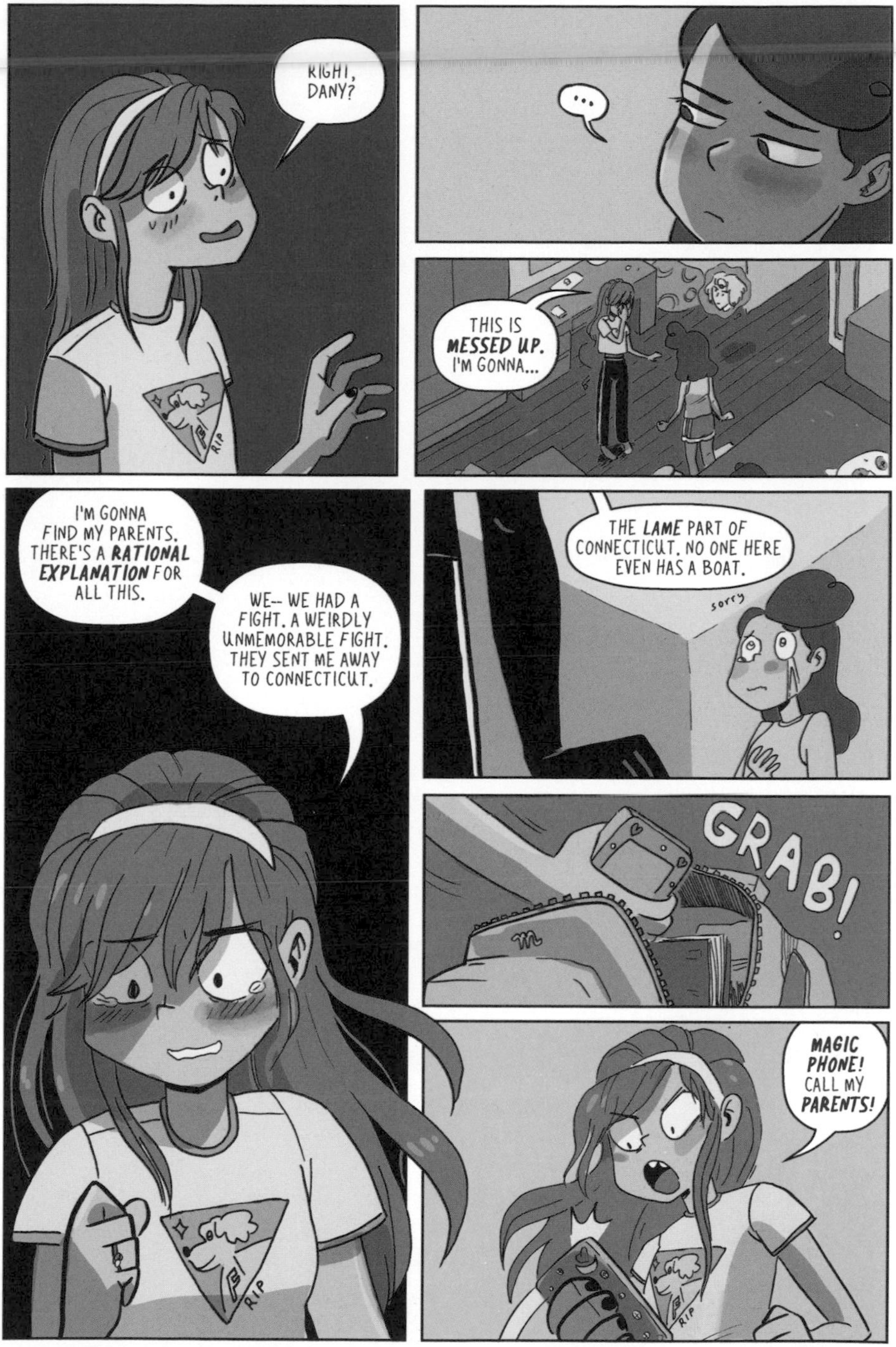

RIGHT, DANY?
...
THIS IS MESSED UP. I'M GONNA...
I'M GONNA FIND MY PARENTS. THERE'S A RATIONAL EXPLANATION FOR ALL THIS.
WE-- WE HAD A FIGHT. A WEIRDLY UNMEMORABLE FIGHT. THEY SENT ME AWAY TO CONNECTICUT.
THE LAME PART OF CONNECTICUT. NO ONE HERE EVEN HAS A BOAT.
sorry
GRAB!
MAGIC PHONE! CALL MY PARENTS!

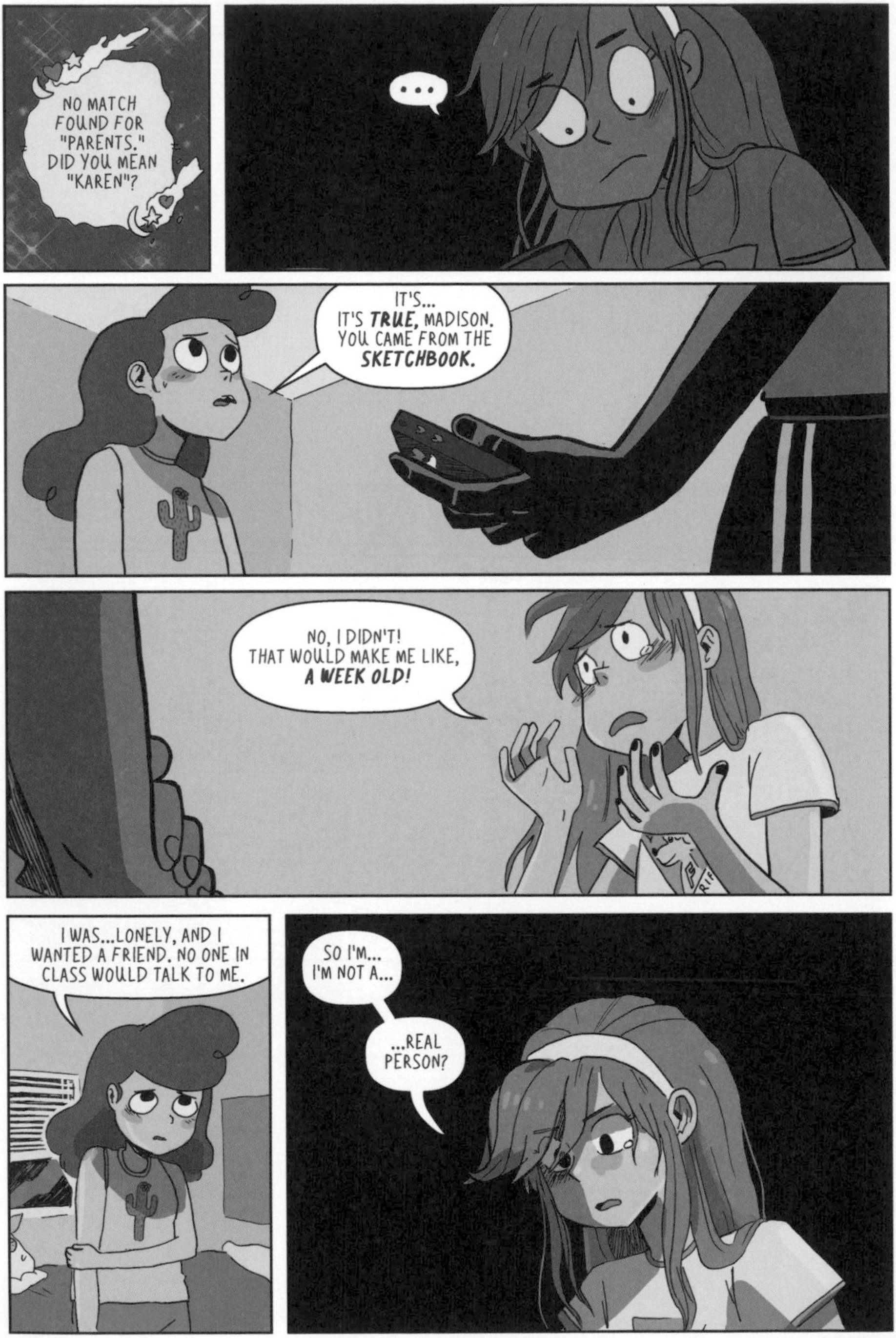
NO MATCH FOUND FOR "PARENTS." DID YOU MEAN "KAREN"?
...
IT'S... IT'S **TRUE,** MADISON. YOU CAME FROM THE **SKETCHBOOK.**
NO, I DIDN'T! THAT WOULD MAKE ME LIKE, **A WEEK OLD!**
I WAS...LONELY, AND I WANTED A FRIEND. NO ONE IN CLASS WOULD TALK TO ME.
SO I'M... I'M NOT A...
...REAL PERSON?

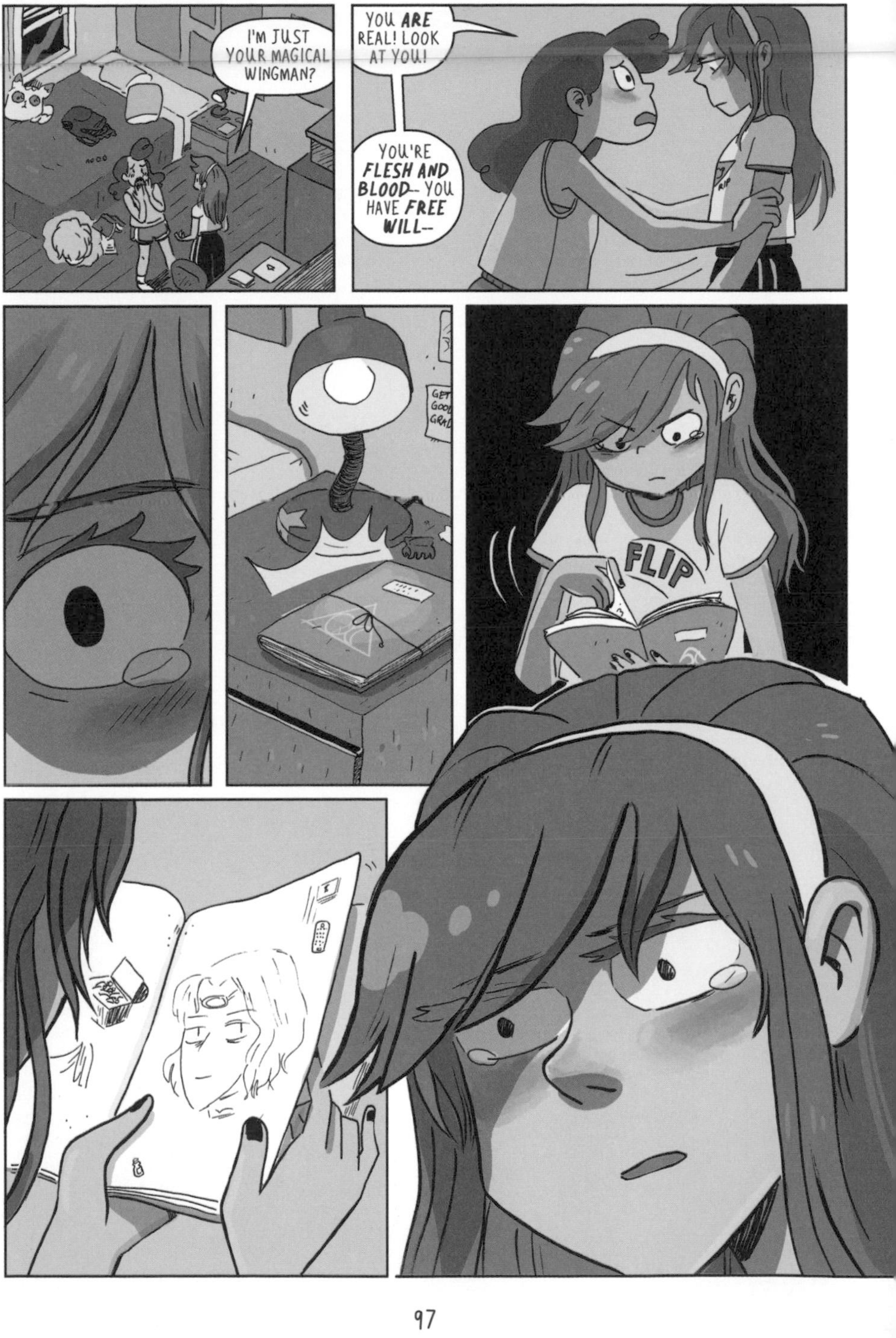
I'M JUST YOUR MAGICAL WINGMAN?
YOU **ARE** REAL! LOOK AT YOU!
YOU'RE **FLESH AND BLOOD**-- YOU HAVE **FREE WILL**--
FLIP

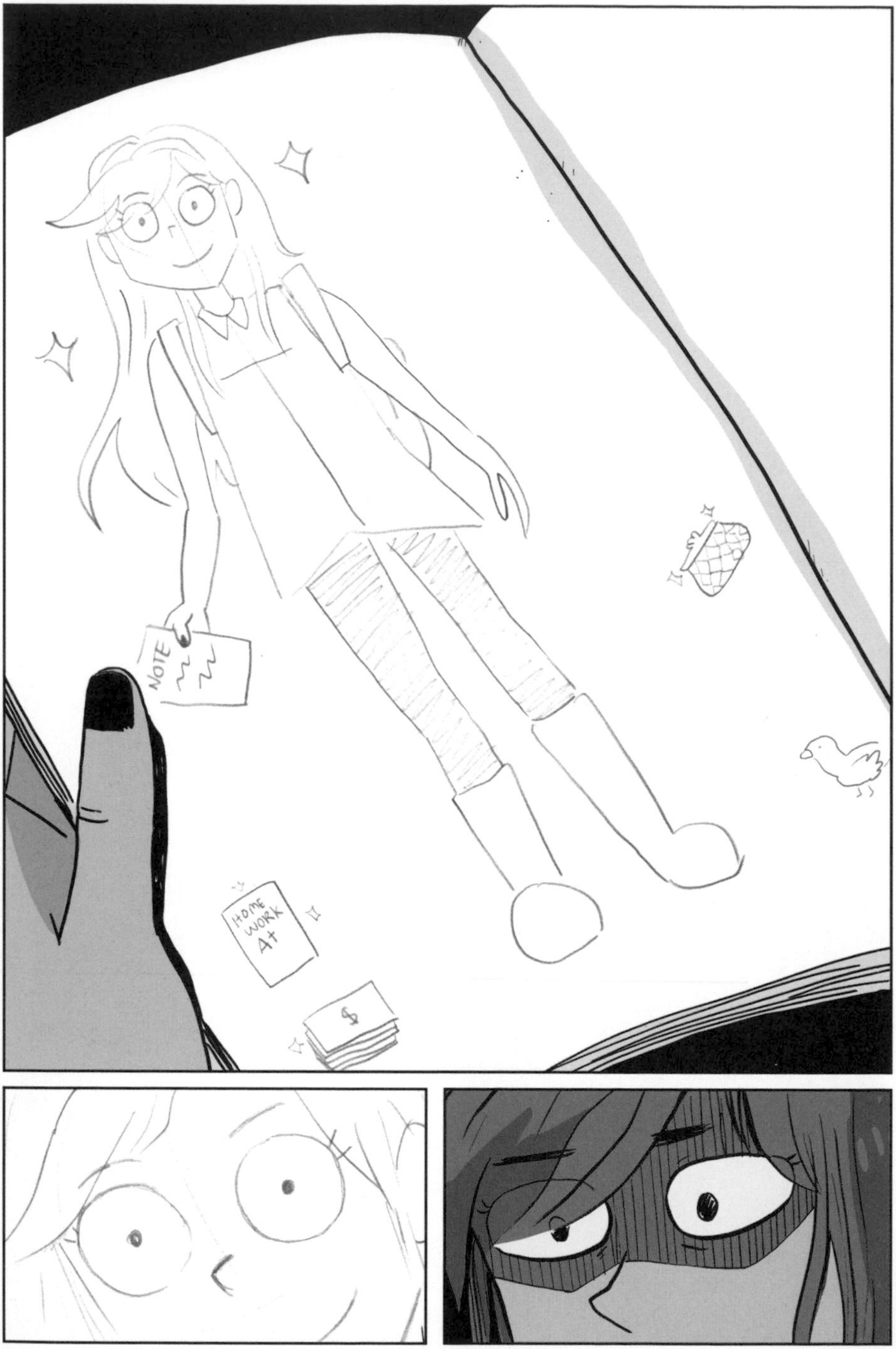
NOTE
HOME WORK A+
$

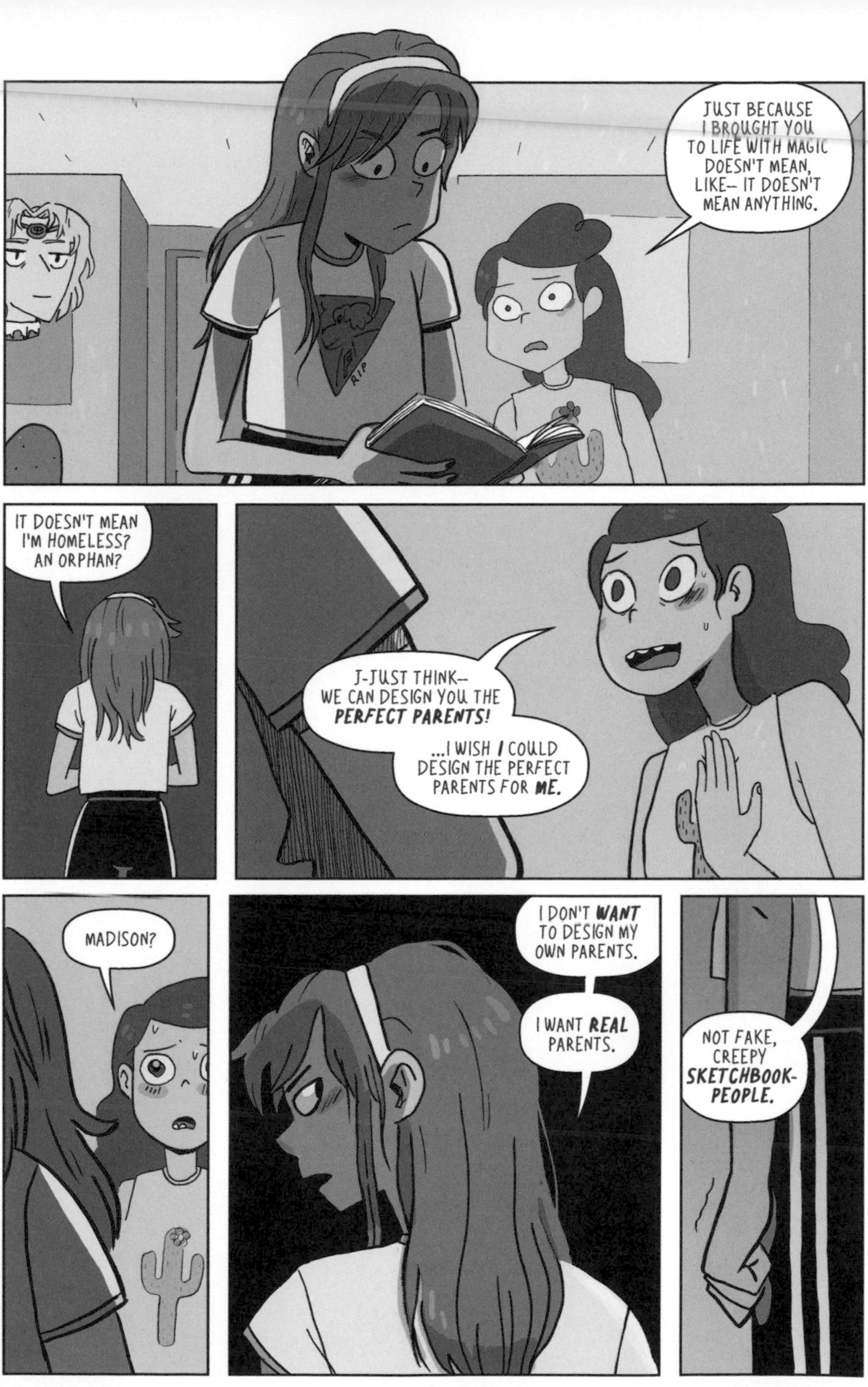
JUST BECAUSE I BROUGHT YOU TO LIFE WITH MAGIC DOESN'T MEAN, LIKE-- IT DOESN'T MEAN ANYTHING.
RIP
IT DOESN'T MEAN I'M HOMELESS? AN ORPHAN?
J-JUST THINK-- WE CAN DESIGN YOU THE **PERFECT PARENTS!**
...I WISH **I** COULD DESIGN THE PERFECT PARENTS FOR **ME.**
MADISON?
I DON'T **WANT** TO DESIGN MY OWN PARENTS.
I WANT **REAL** PARENTS.
NOT FAKE, CREEPY **SKETCHBOOK-PEOPLE.**

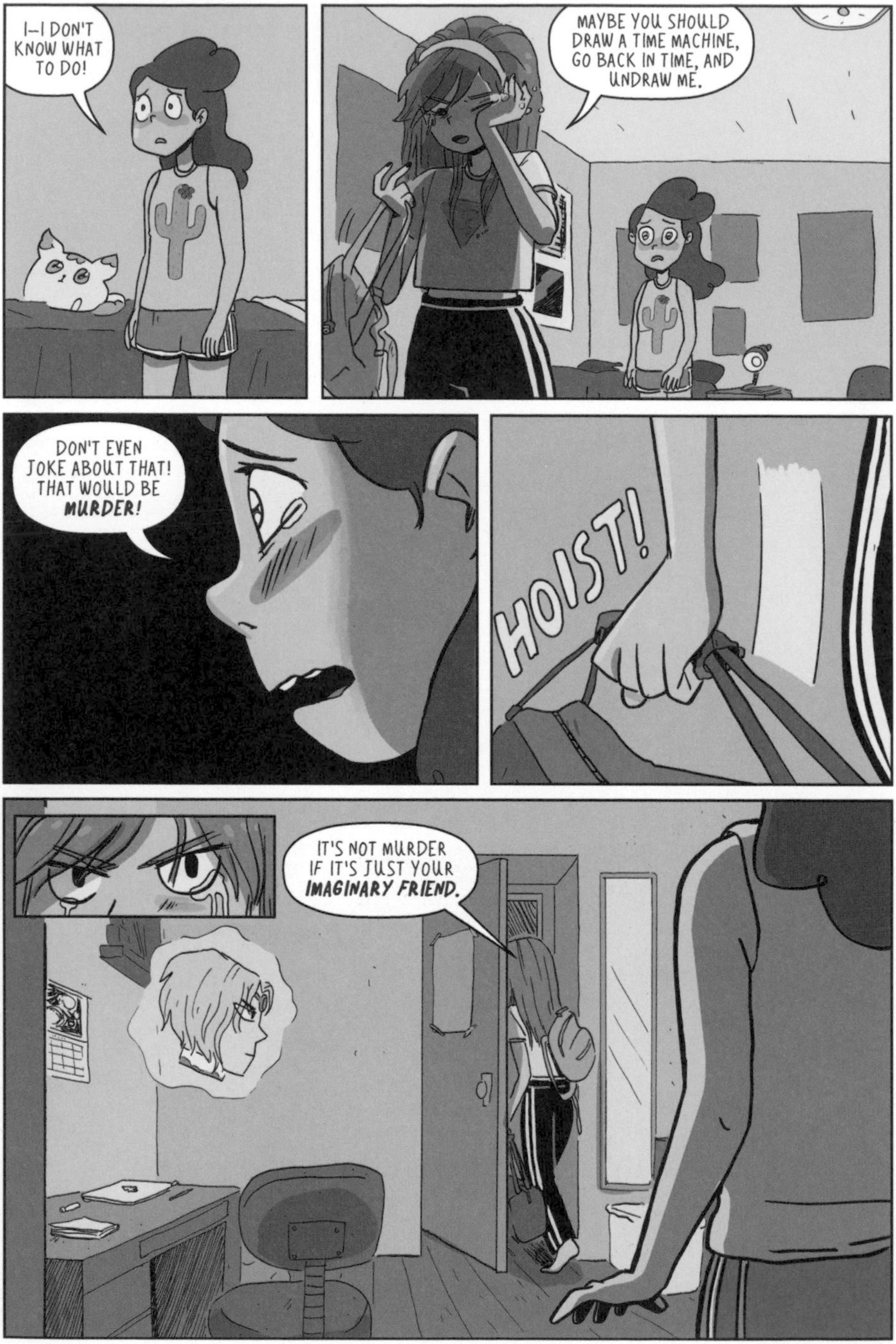
I—I DON'T KNOW WHAT TO DO!
MAYBE YOU SHOULD DRAW A TIME MACHINE, GO BACK IN TIME, AND UNDRAW ME.
DON'T EVEN JOKE ABOUT THAT! THAT WOULD BE MURDER!
HOIST!
IT'S NOT MURDER IF IT'S JUST YOUR IMAGINARY FRIEND.

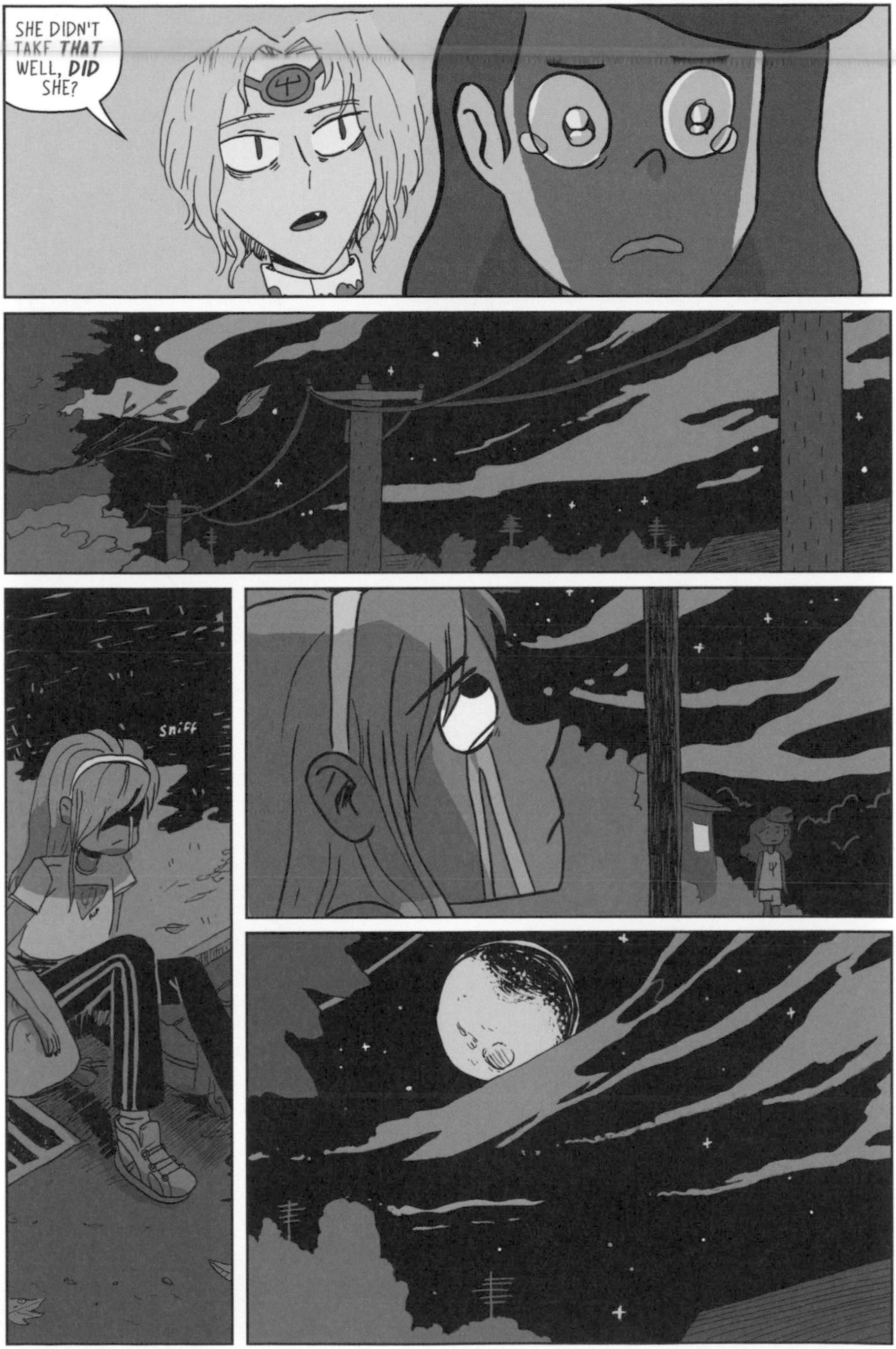
SHE DIDN'T TAKE **THAT** WELL, **DID** SHE?
sniff

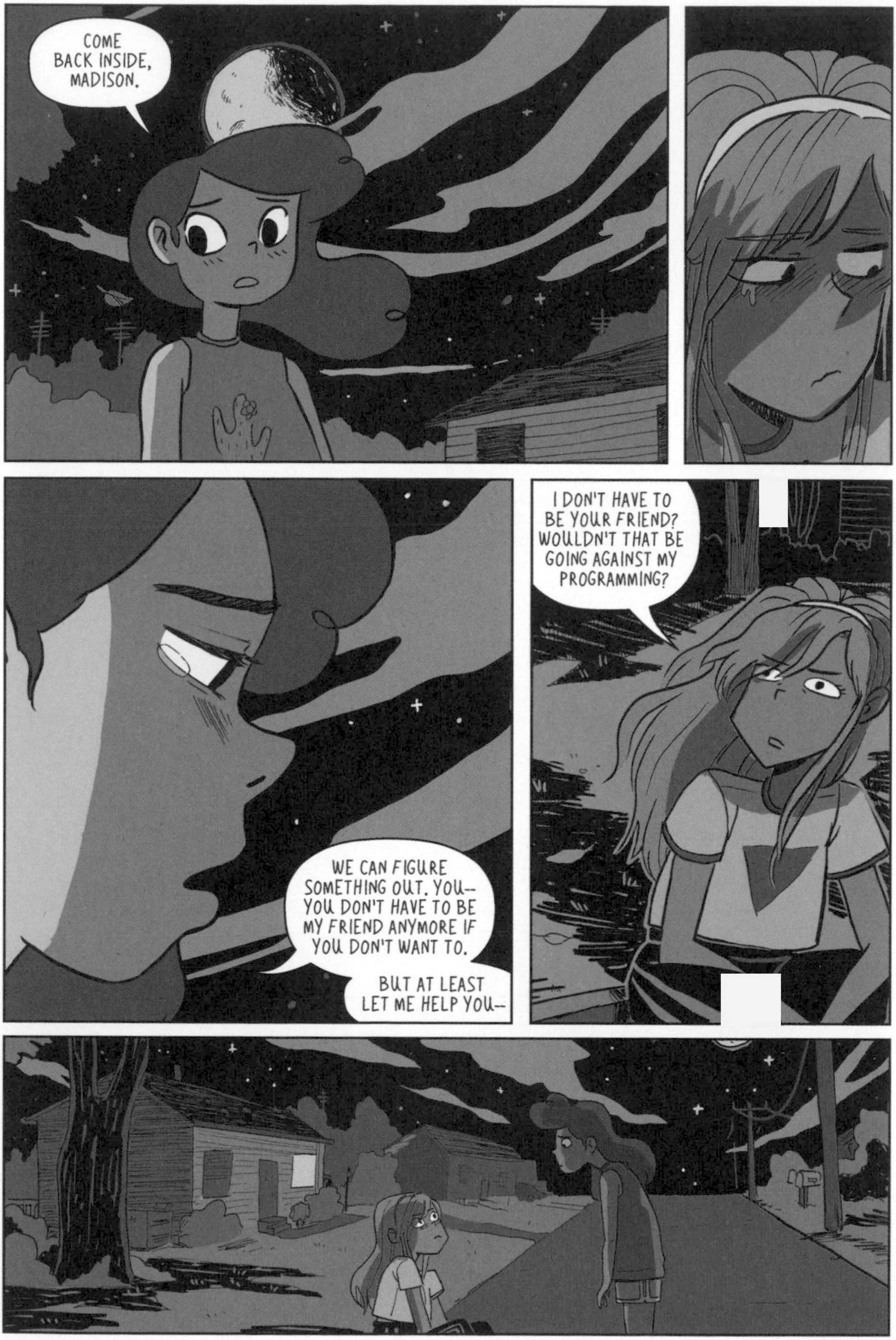
COME BACK INSIDE, MADISON.
WE CAN FIGURE SOMETHING OUT. YOU-- YOU DON'T HAVE TO BE MY FRIEND ANYMORE IF YOU DON'T WANT TO.
BUT AT LEAST LET ME HELP YOU--
I DON'T HAVE TO BE YOUR FRIEND? WOULDN'T THAT BE GOING AGAINST MY PROGRAMMING?

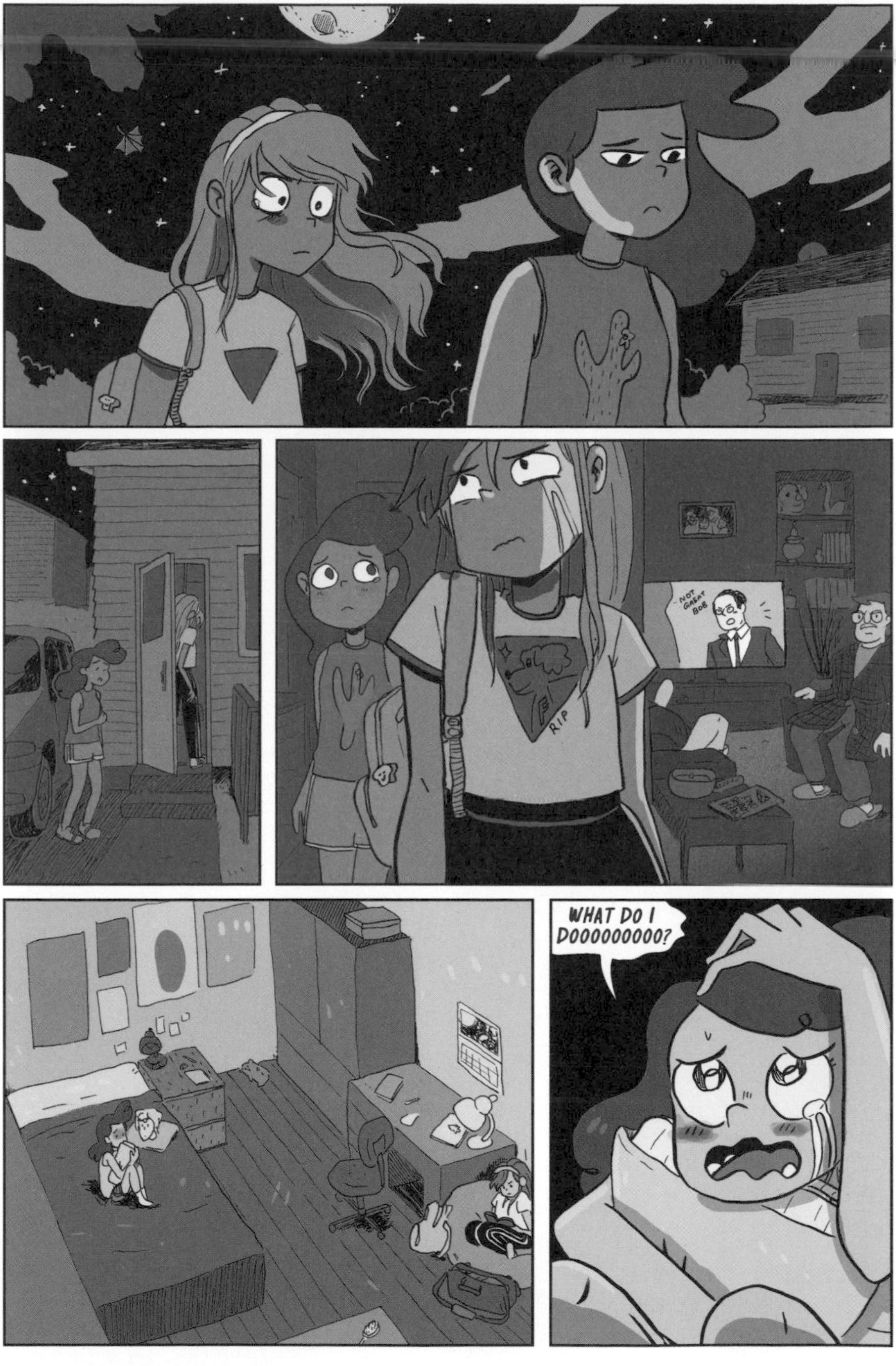
- NOT GREAT BOB
RIP
WHAT DO I DOOOOOOOOO?

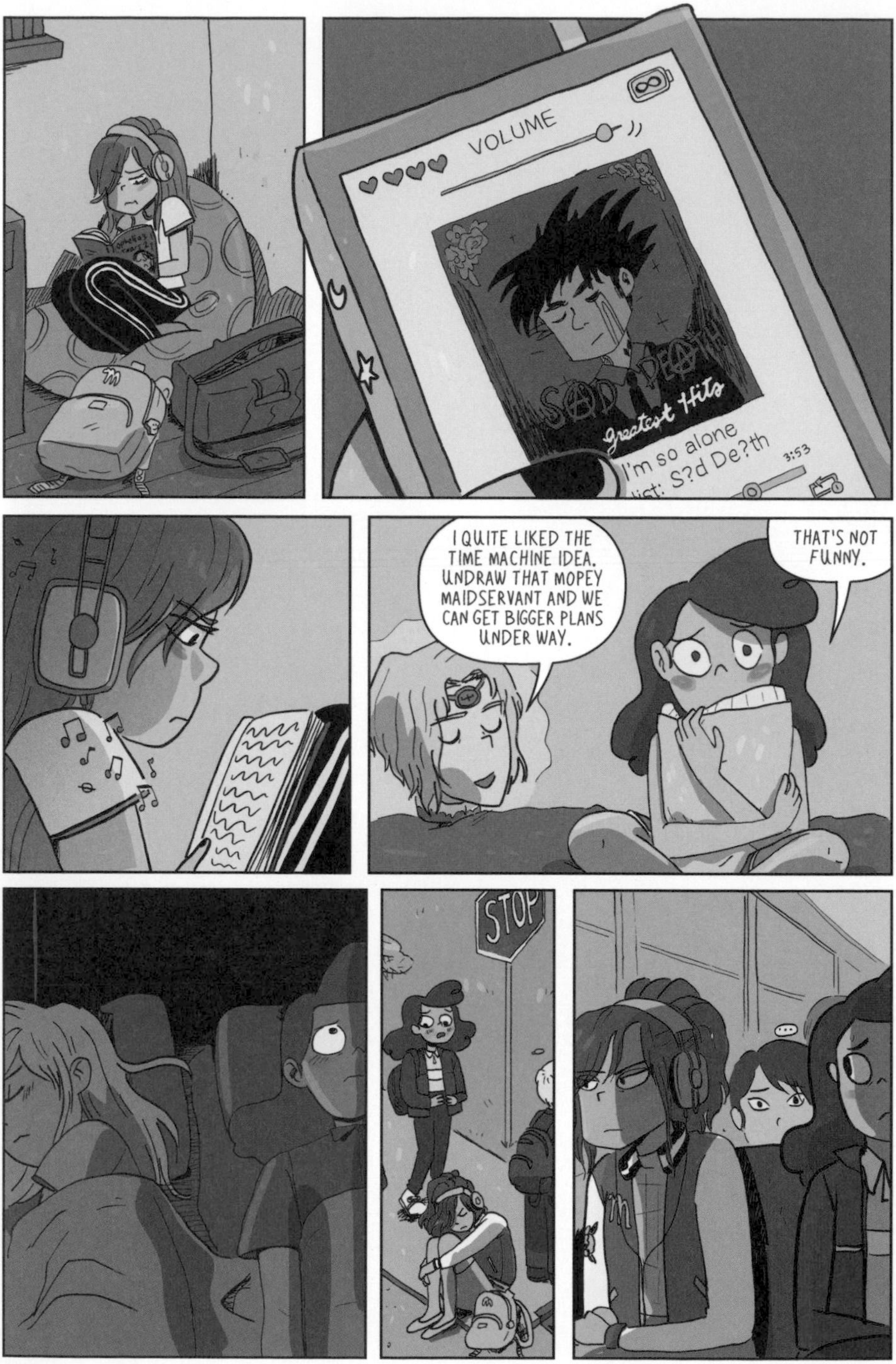
VOLUME
Greatest Hits
I'm so alone
3:53
I QUITE LIKED THE TIME MACHINE IDEA. UNDRAW THAT MOPEY MAIDSERVANT AND WE CAN GET BIGGER PLANS UNDER WAY.
THAT'S NOT FUNNY.
STOP

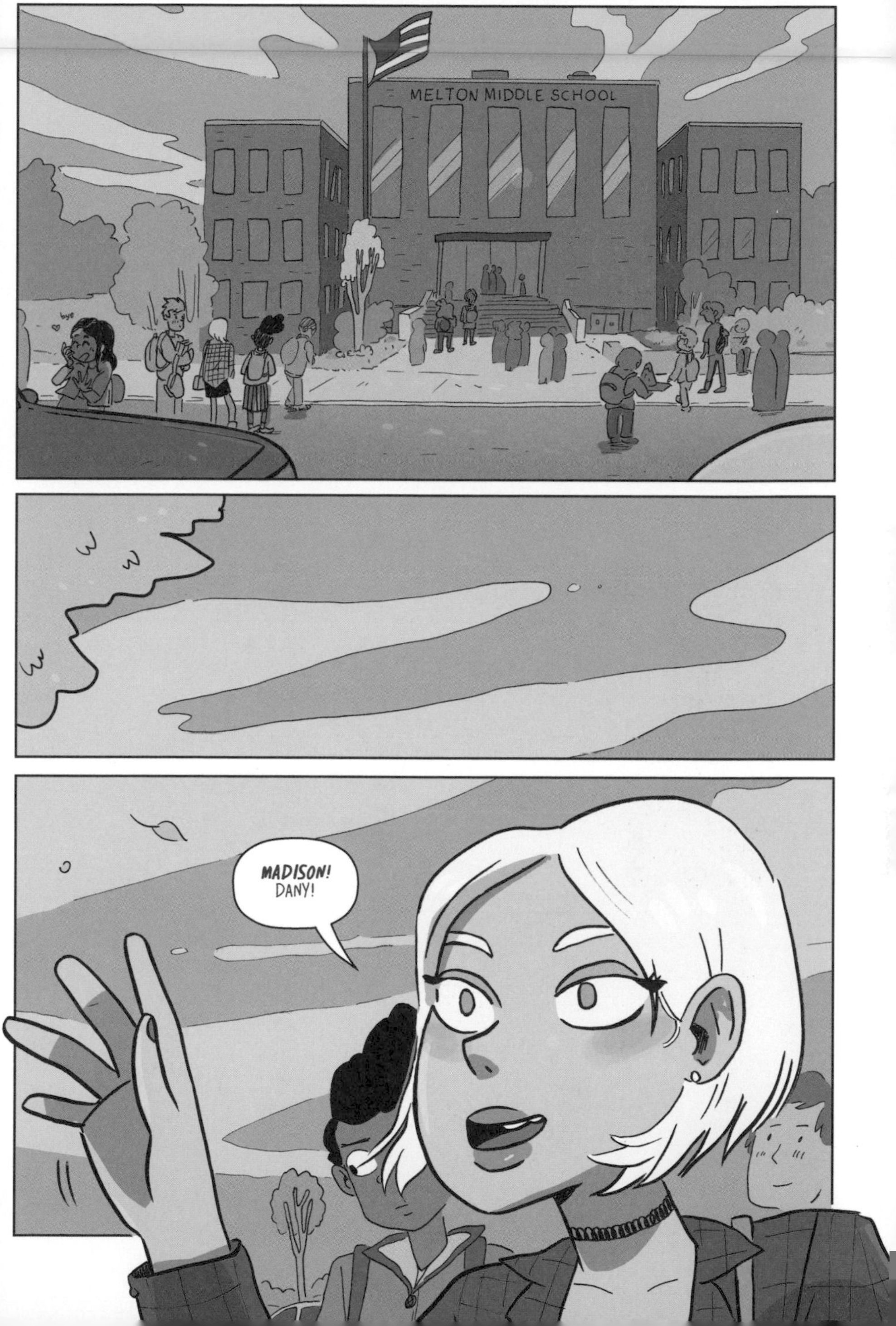
MELTON MIDDLE SCHOOL
bye
MADISON!
DANY!

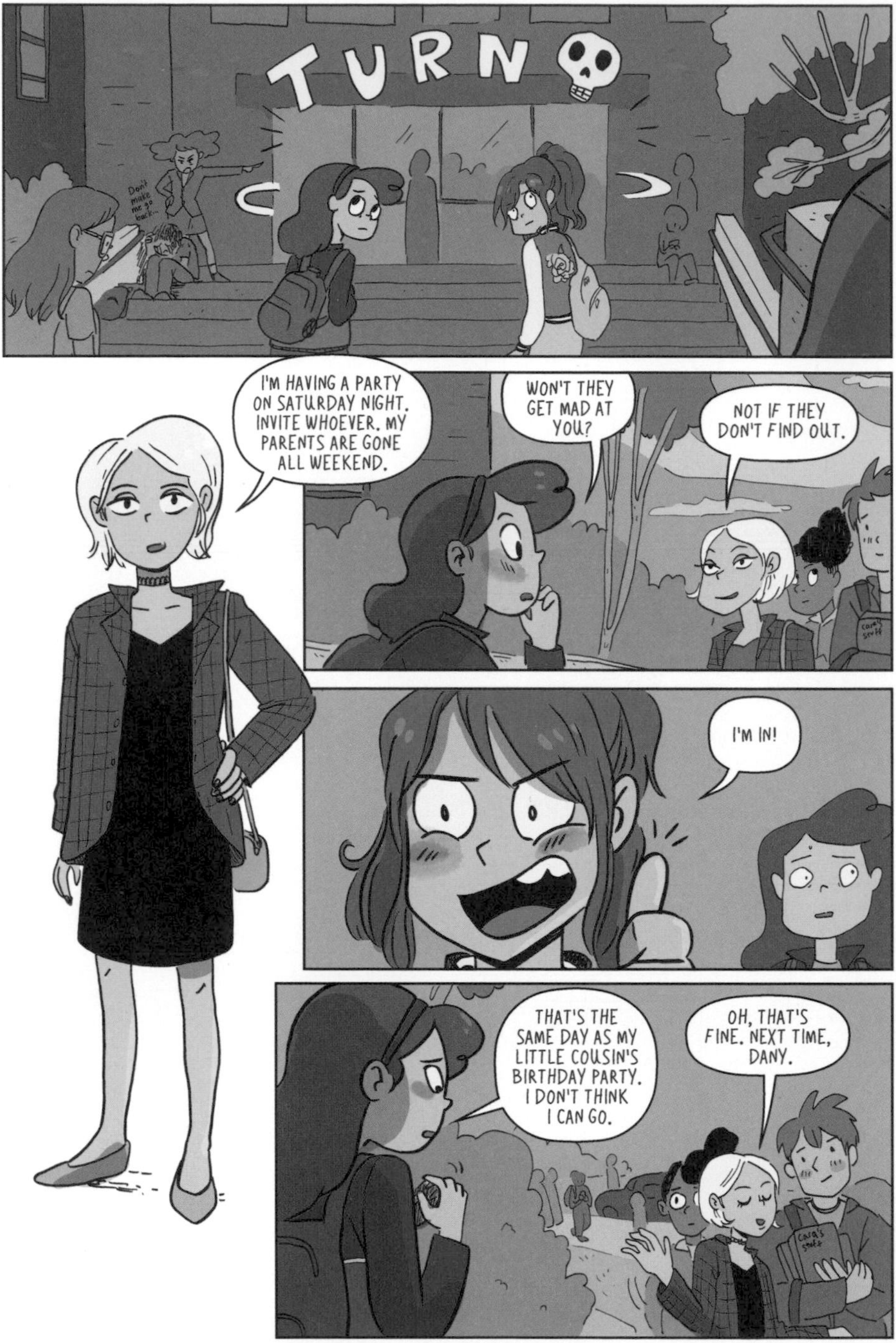
TURN
Don't make me go back...
I'M HAVING A PARTY ON SATURDAY NIGHT. INVITE WHOEVER. MY PARENTS ARE GONE ALL WEEKEND.
WON'T THEY GET MAD AT YOU?
NOT IF THEY DON'T FIND OUT.
I'M IN!
THAT'S THE SAME DAY AS MY LITTLE COUSIN'S BIRTHDAY PARTY. I DON'T THINK I CAN GO.
OH, THAT'S FINE. NEXT TIME, DANY.
Cara's stuff

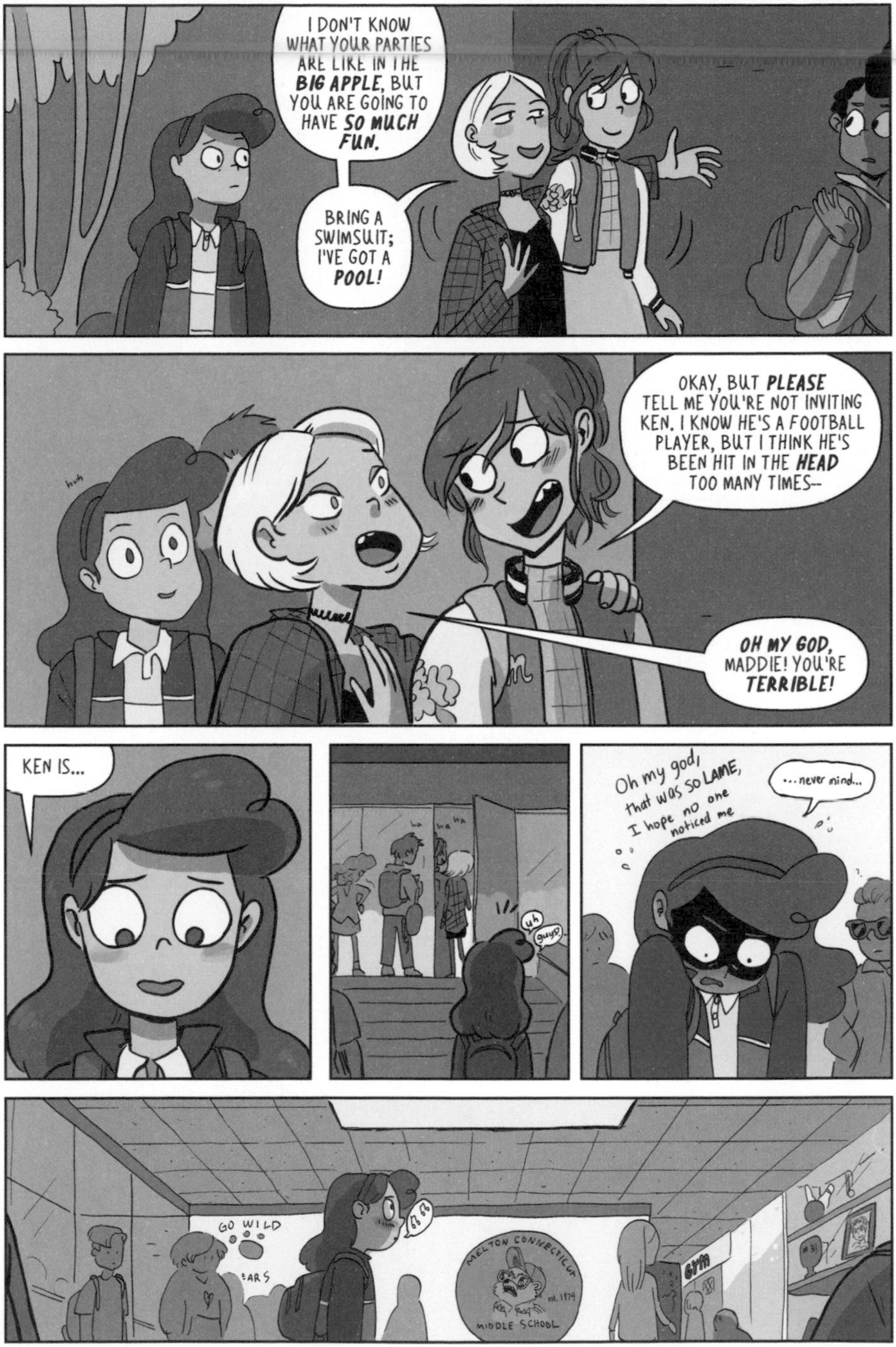
I DON'T KNOW WHAT YOUR PARTIES ARE LIKE IN THE **BIG APPLE**, BUT YOU ARE GOING TO HAVE **SO MUCH FUN.**
BRING A SWIMSUIT; I'VE GOT A **POOL!**
OKAY, BUT **PLEASE** TELL ME YOU'RE NOT INVITING KEN. I KNOW HE'S A FOOTBALL PLAYER, BUT I THINK HE'S BEEN HIT IN THE **HEAD** TOO MANY TIMES--
huh
OH MY GOD, MADDIE! YOU'RE **TERRIBLE!**
KEN IS...
ha ha ha
uh guys?
Oh my god, that was so LAME, I hope no one noticed me
...never mind...
GO WILD
MELTON CONNECTICUT
est. 1974
MIDDLE SCHOOL
GYM
#31

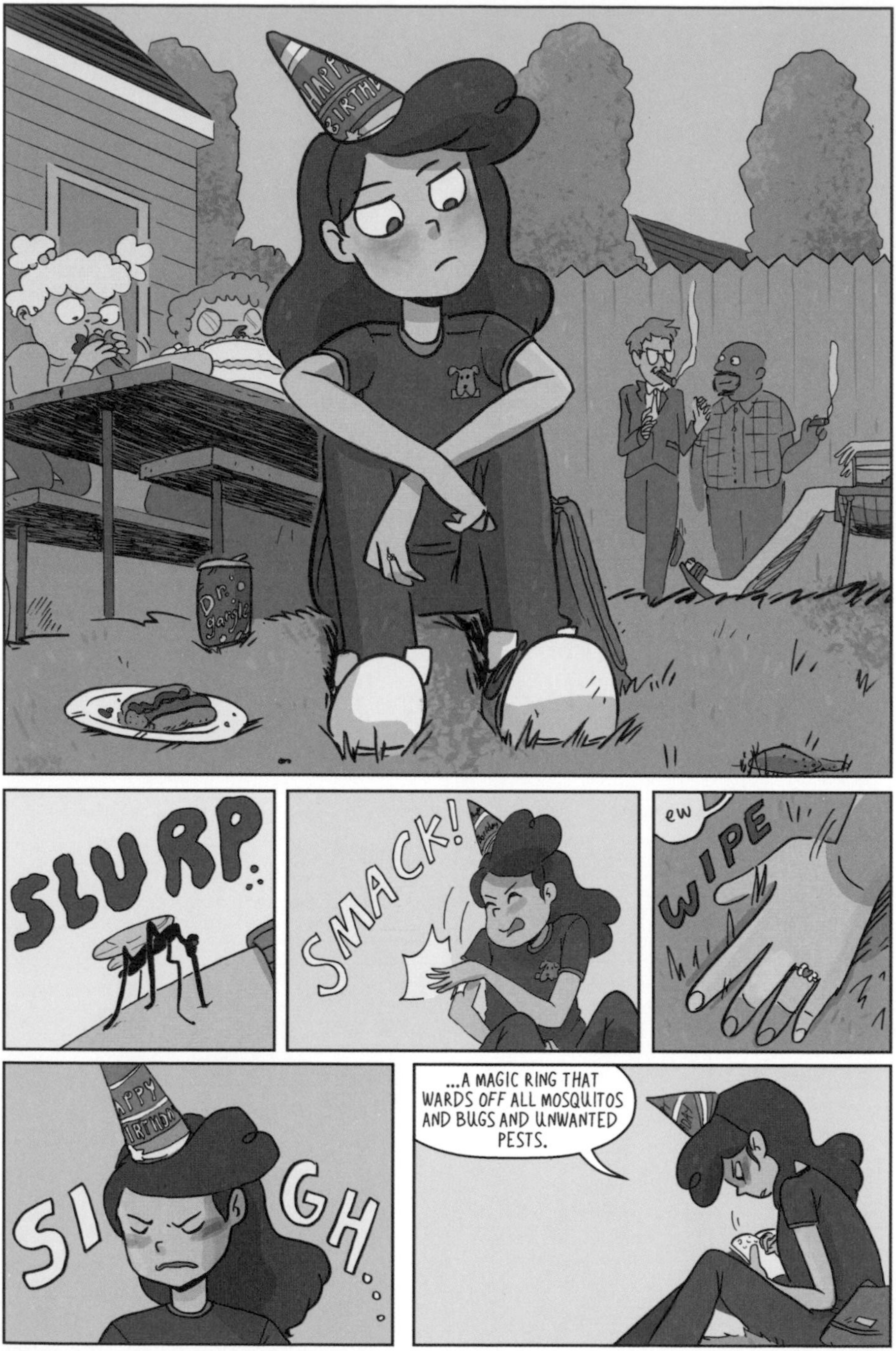
HAPPY BIRTHDAY
Dr. gargle
SLURP
SMACK!
ew
WIPE
HAPPY BIRTHDAY
SIGH
...A MAGIC RING THAT WARDS OFF ALL MOSQUITOS AND BUGS AND UNWANTED PESTS.

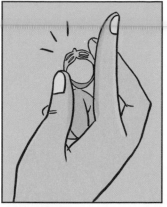

A TONKO TRUCK! WHAT DO YOU SAY TO AUNT TRACY?

I DON'T LIKE IT!

THAT'S *IT*, CHARLIE.

YOU KNOW WHAT?

YOU'RE NOT GETTING ANY BIRTHDAY CAKE.

NOOOOO!!!!

HRGH

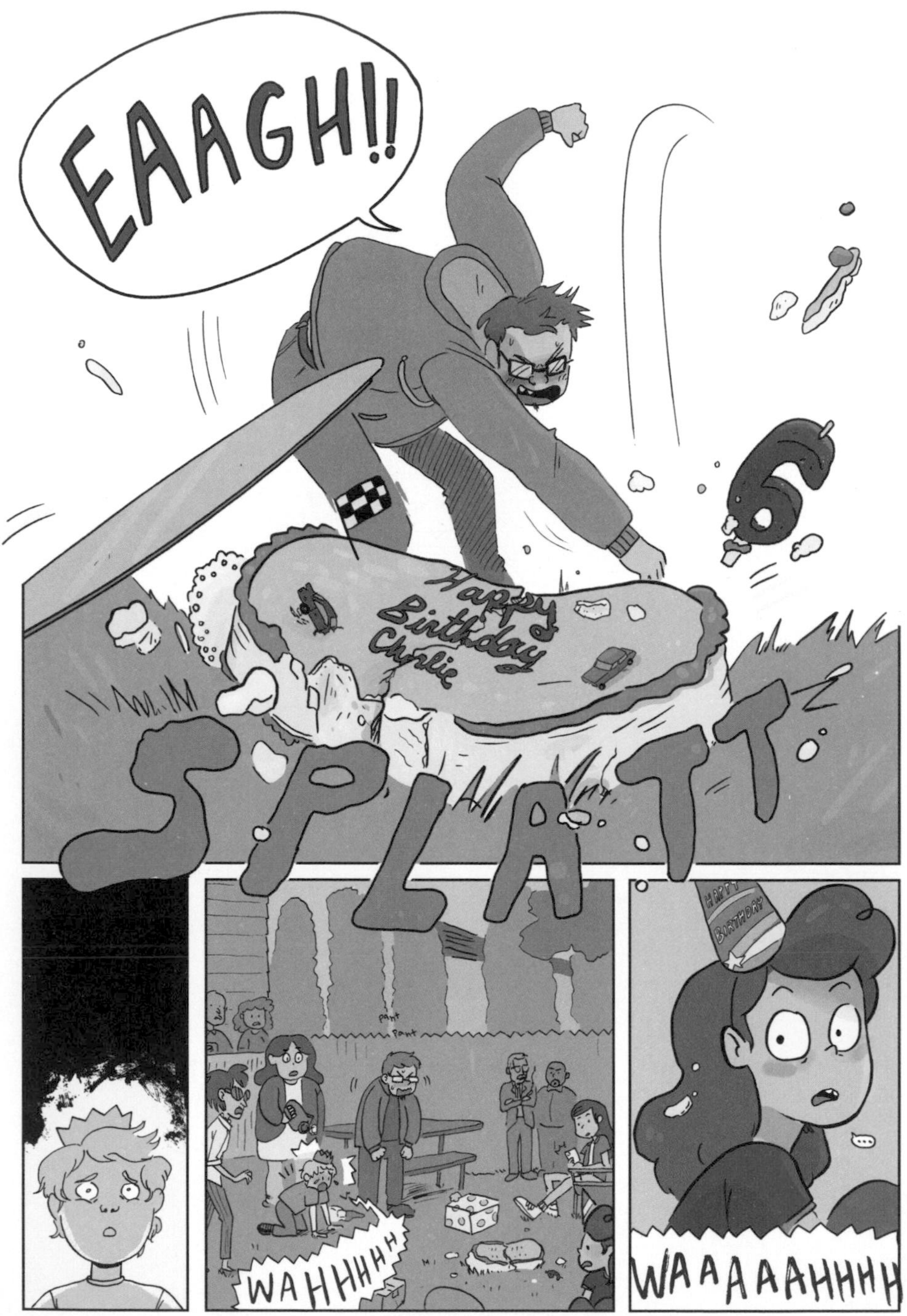
EAAGH!!
Happy Birthday Charlie
SPLATT
pant
pant
WAHHHHH
HAPPY BIRTHDAY
WAAAAAHHHH

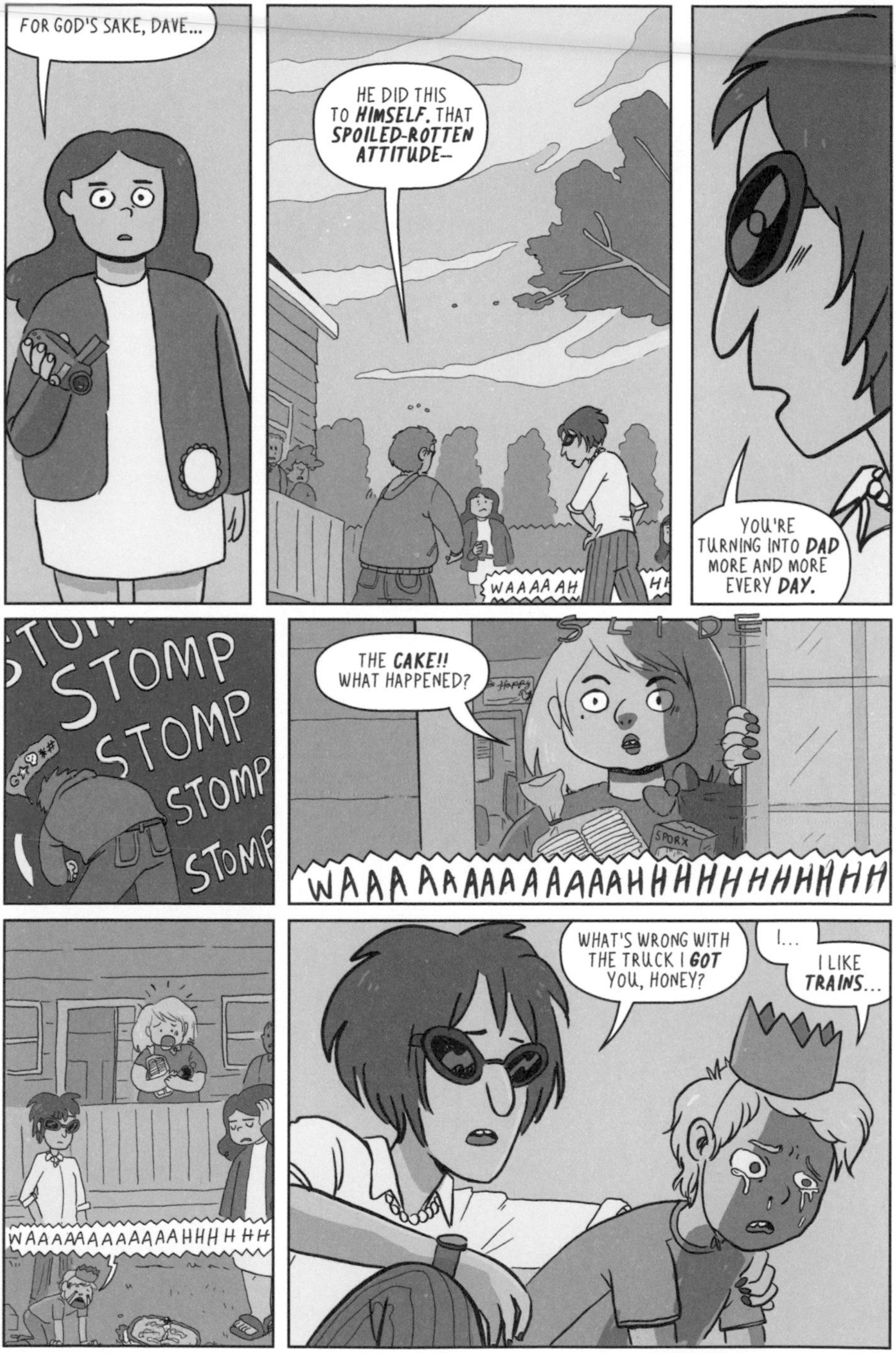
FOR GOD'S SAKE, DAVE...
HE DID THIS TO **HIMSELF.** THAT **SPOILED-ROTTEN ATTITUDE**--
WAAAAAH
YOU'RE TURNING INTO **DAD** MORE AND MORE EVERY **DAY.**
STOMP
STOMP
STOMP
STOMP
STOMP
SLIDE
THE **CAKE!!** WHAT HAPPENED?
SPORX
WAAAAAAAAAAAAHHHHHHHHHHH
WAAAAAAAAAAAAHHHHHH
WHAT'S WRONG WITH THE TRUCK I **GOT** YOU, HONEY?
I...
I LIKE **TRAINS**...

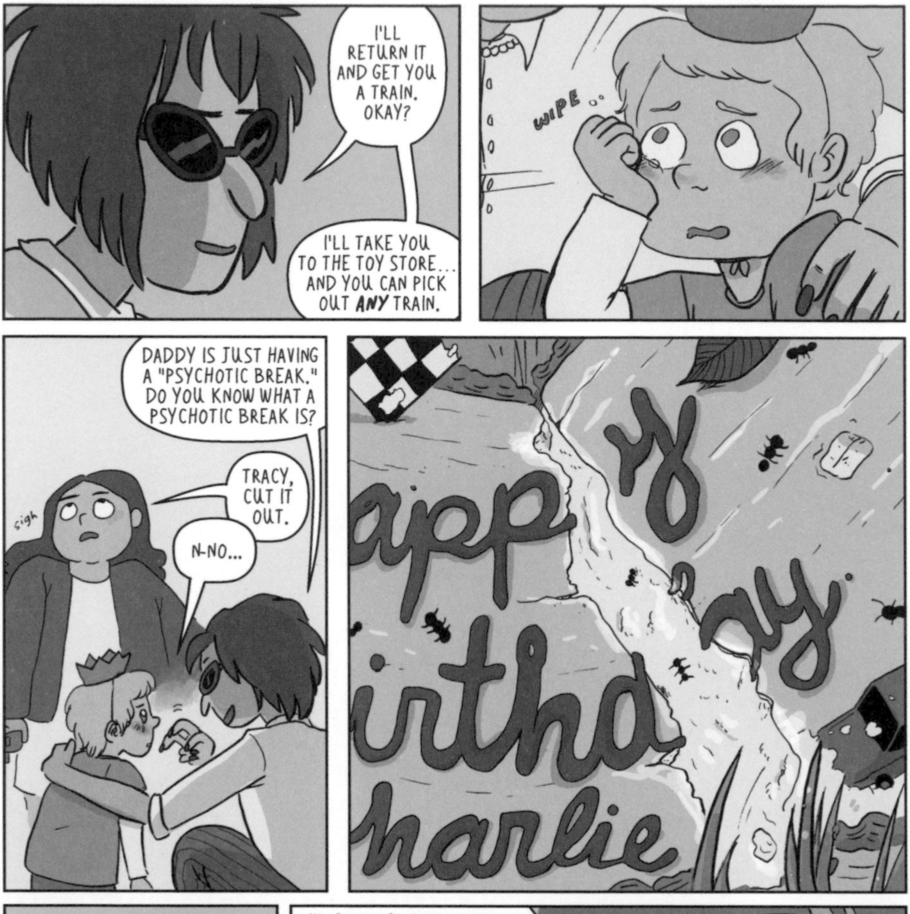
I'LL RETURN IT AND GET YOU A TRAIN. OKAY?
I'LL TAKE YOU TO THE TOY STORE... AND YOU CAN PICK OUT **ANY** TRAIN.
WIPE
DADDY IS JUST HAVING A "PSYCHOTIC BREAK." DO YOU KNOW WHAT A PSYCHOTIC BREAK IS?
sigh
TRACY, CUT IT OUT.
N-NO...
blah blah sick of thi
SIGH
I'M GONNA GO FOR A WALK. TELL MOM IT'S GETTING TOO CRAZY FOR ME IF SHE ASKS.
Promise me you'll euthanize me if I ever get like that, Linda.
FINE.
UGH, I CAN'T BELIEVE HE RUINED THE **CAKE.**
I **ONLY** CAME HERE FOR THE CAKE.

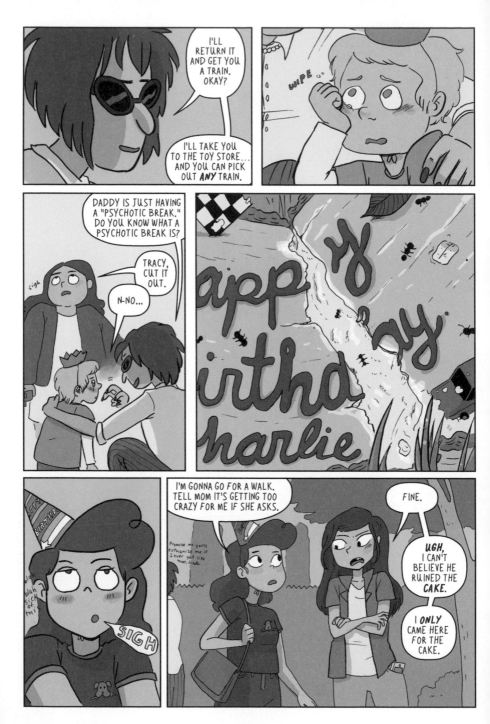

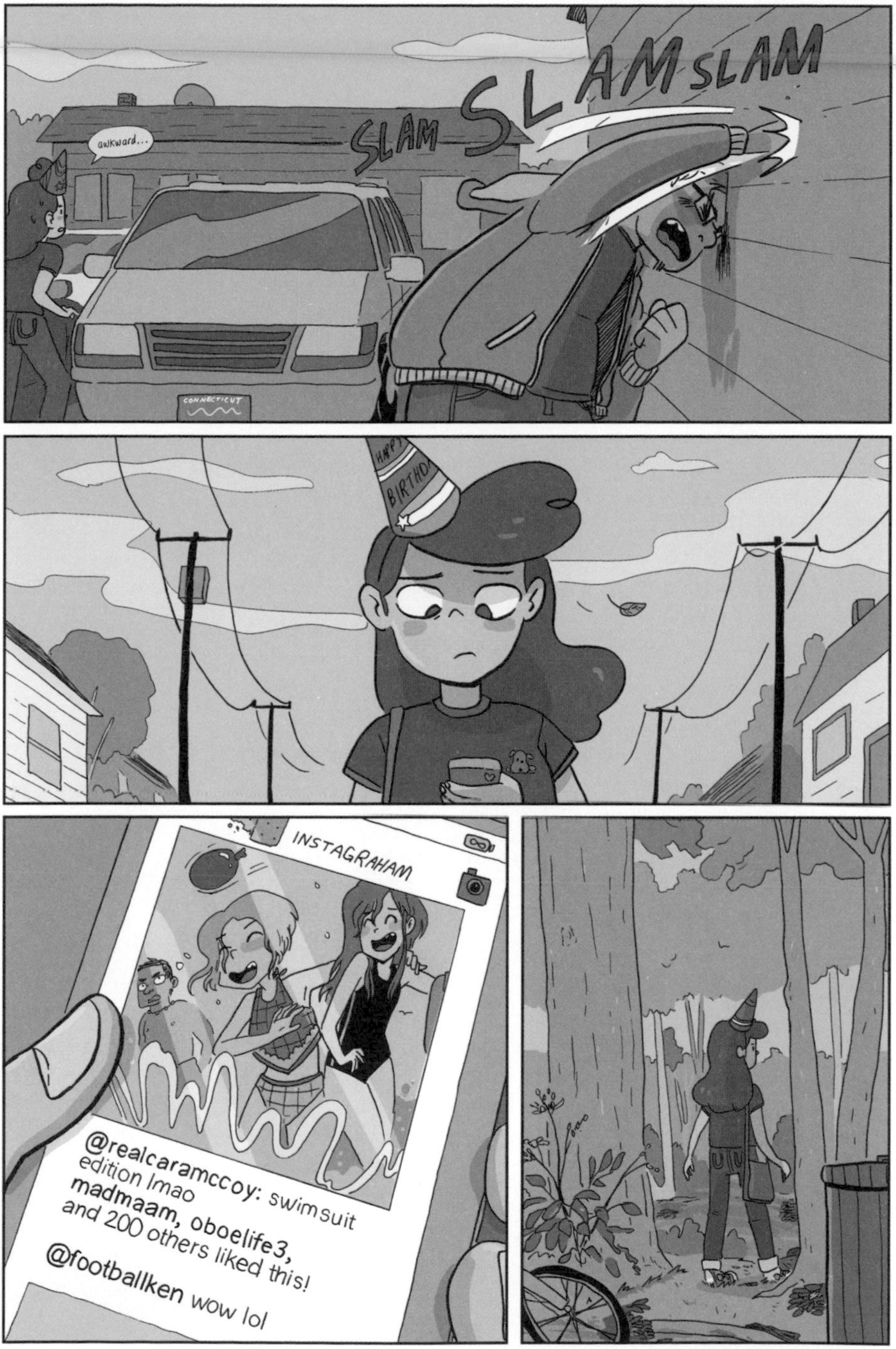
awkward...
SLAM SLAM SLAM SLAM
CONNECTICUT
HAPPY BIRTHDAY
INSTAGRAHAM
@realcaramccoy: swimsuit edition lmao
madmaam, oboelife3, and 200 others liked this!
@footballken wow lol

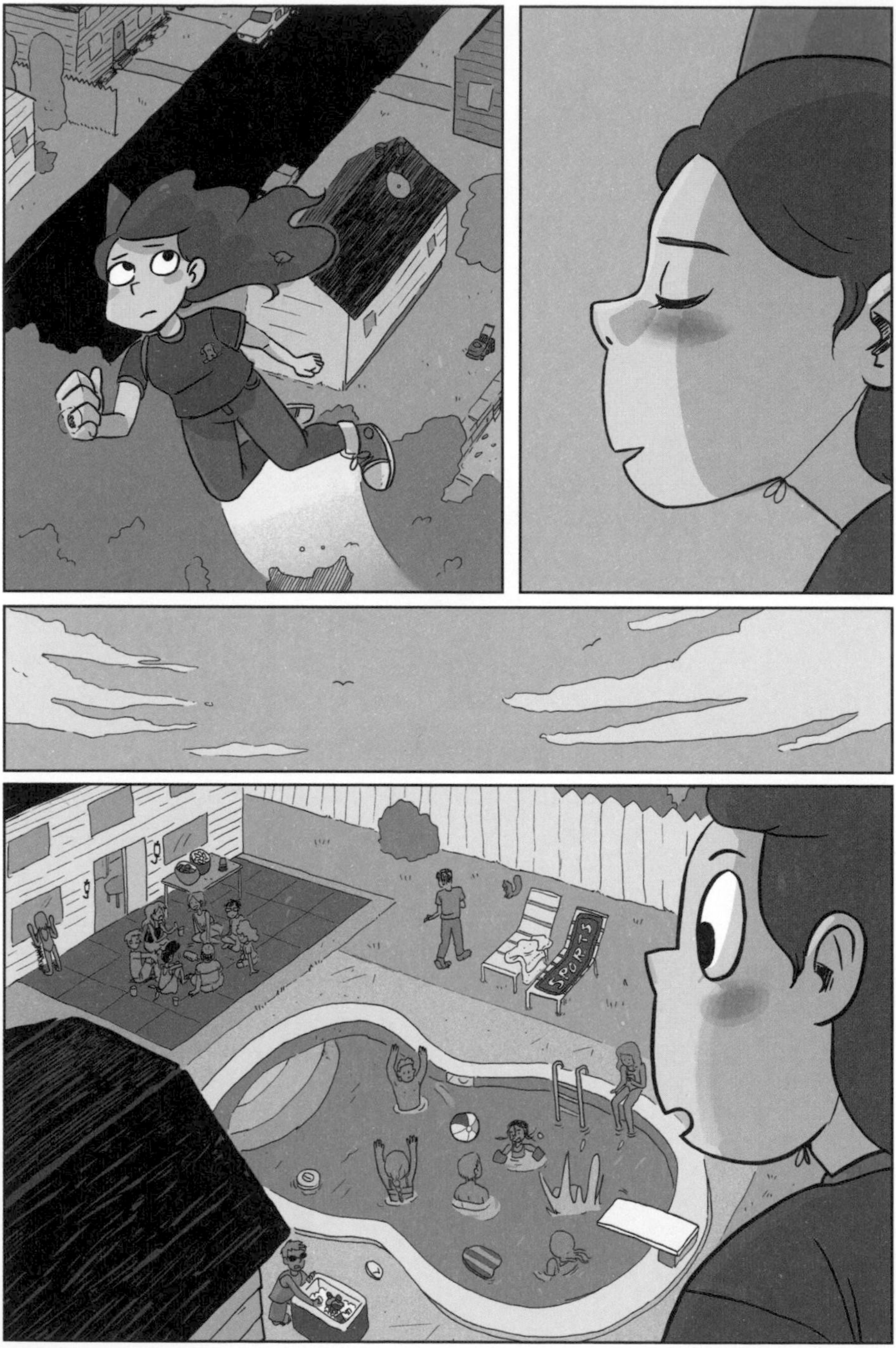
SPORTS

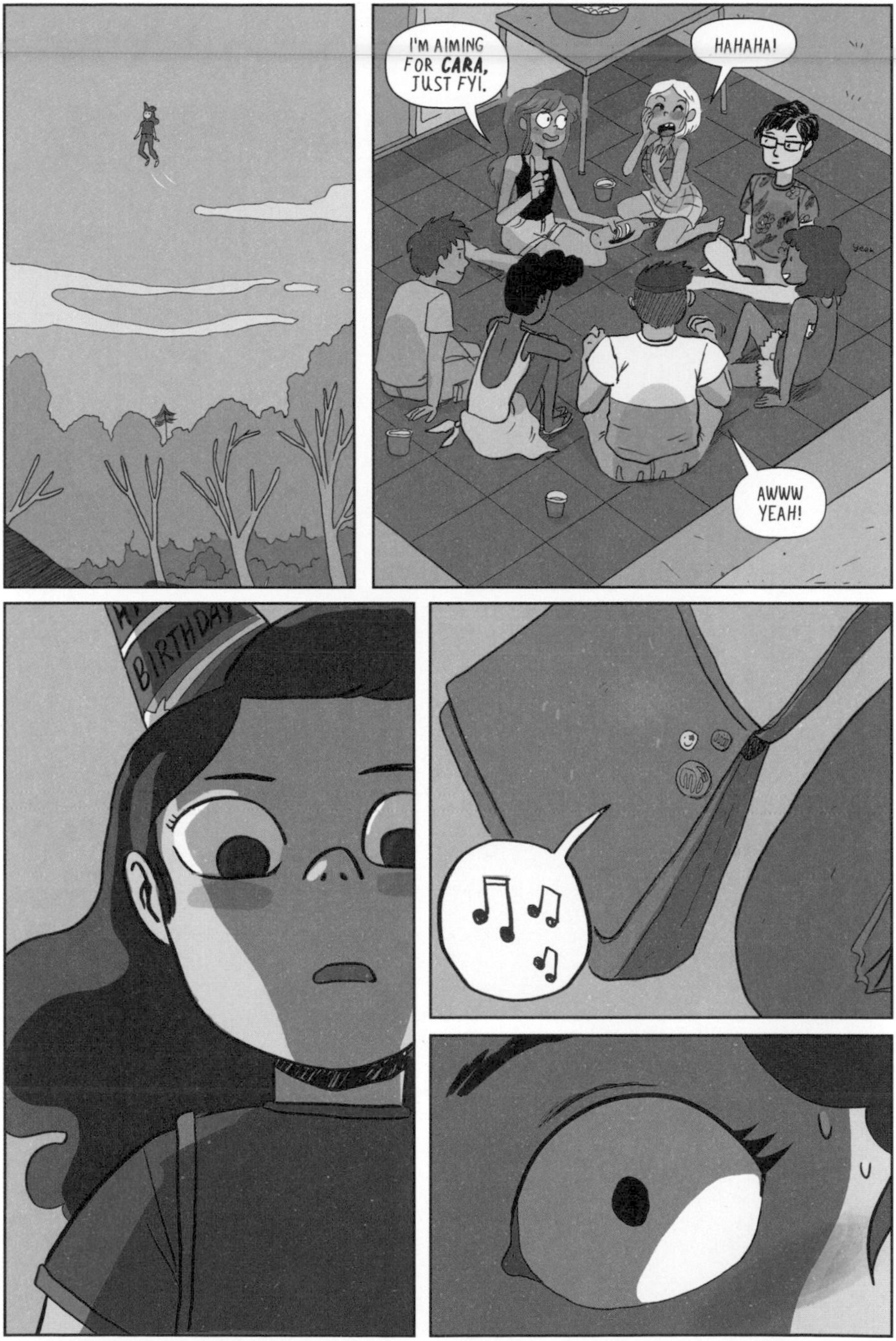
I'M AIMING FOR **CARA**, JUST FYI.
HAHAHA!
AWWW YEAH!
BIRTHDAY

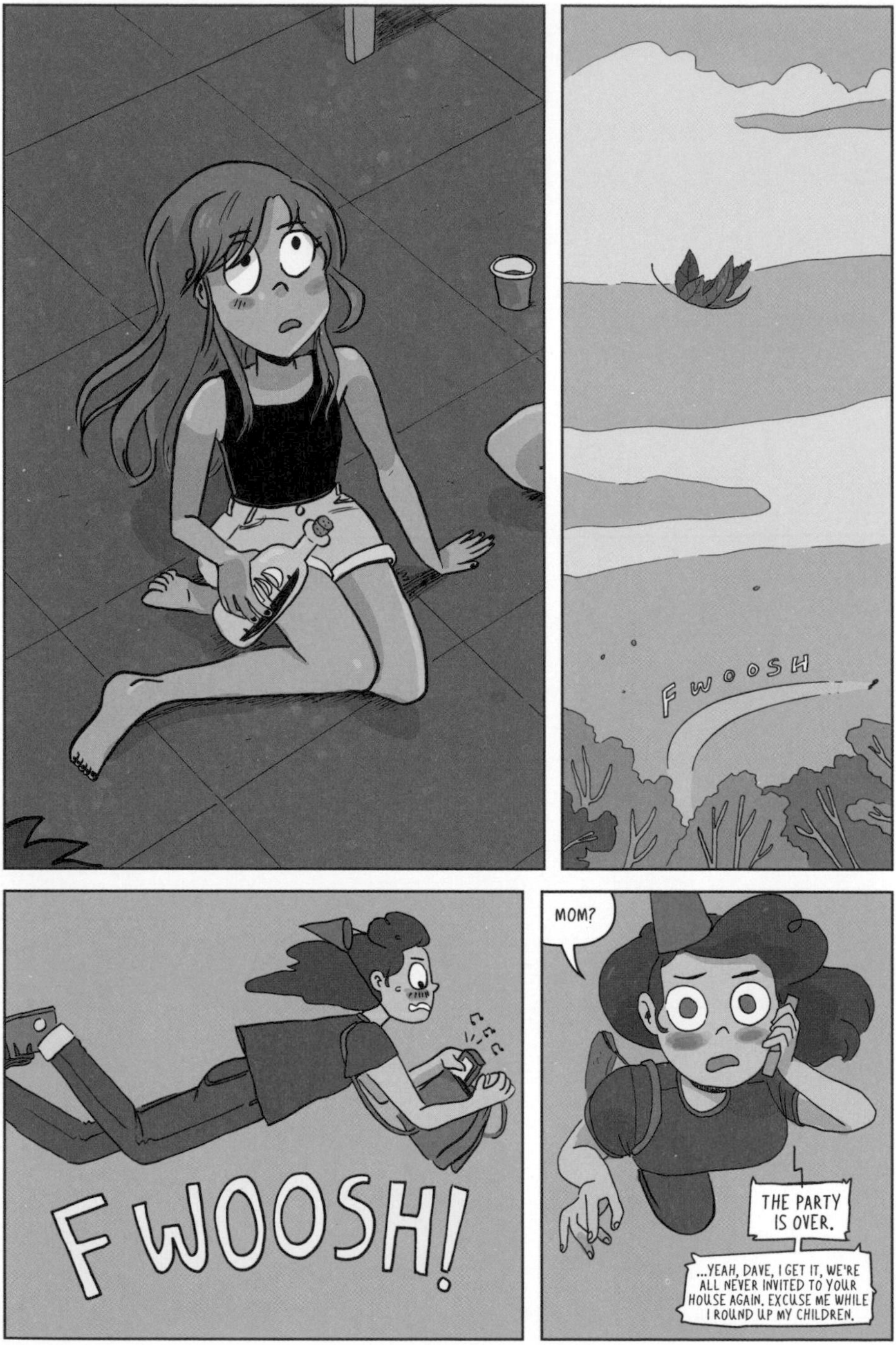
FWOOSH
FWOOSH!
MOM?
THE PARTY IS OVER.
...YEAH, DAVE, I GET IT, WE'RE ALL NEVER INVITED TO YOUR HOUSE AGAIN. EXCUSE ME WHILE I ROUND UP MY CHILDREN.

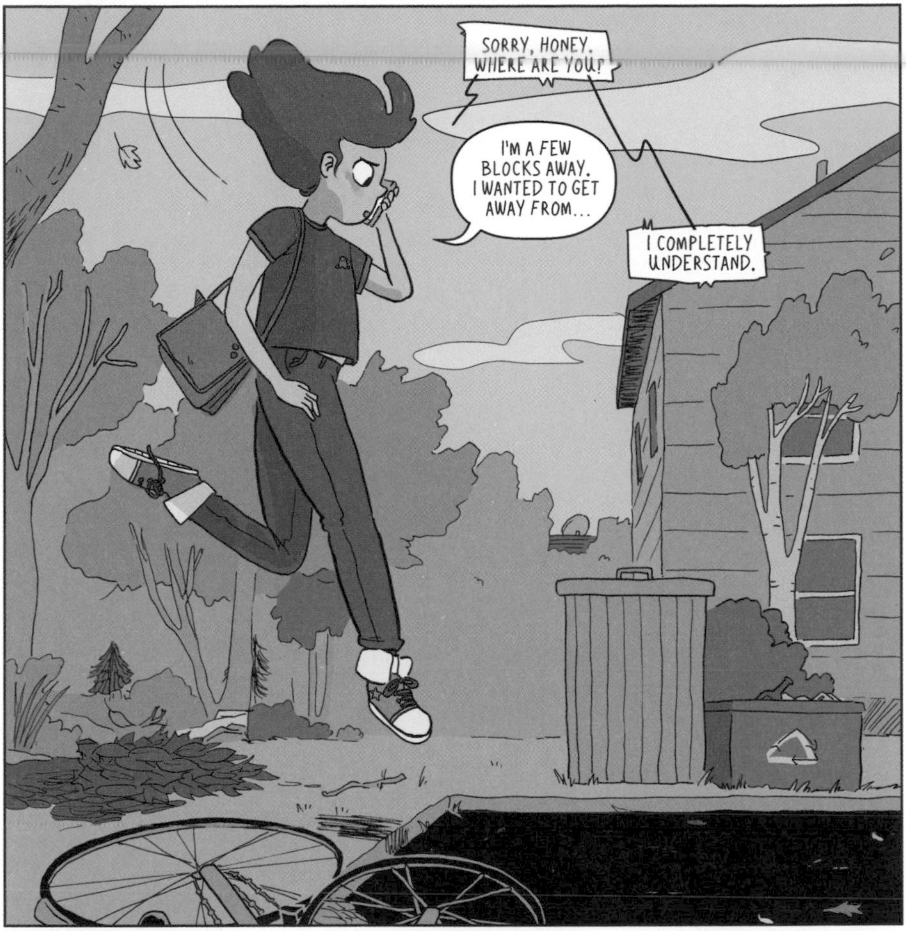
SORRY, HONEY. WHERE ARE YOU?
I'M A FEW BLOCKS AWAY. I WANTED TO GET AWAY FROM...
I COMPLETELY UNDERSTAND.

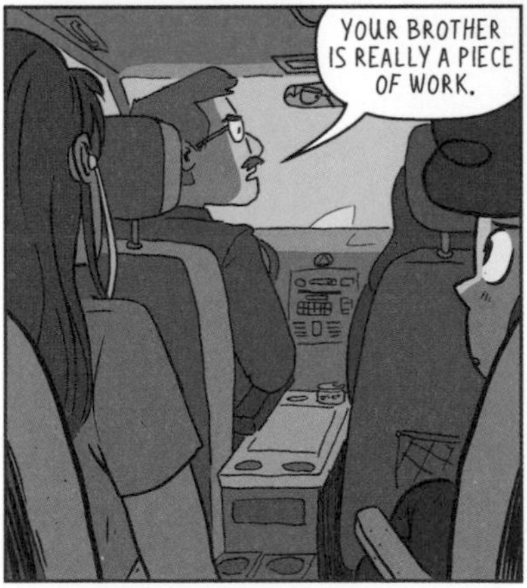
YOUR BROTHER IS REALLY A PIECE OF WORK.

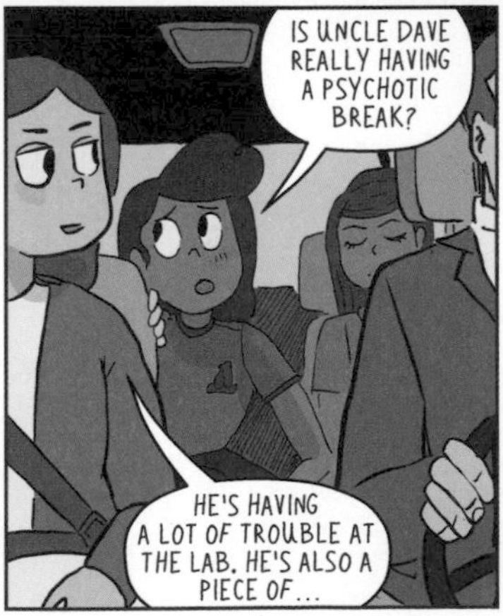
IS UNCLE DAVE REALLY HAVING A PSYCHOTIC BREAK?
HE'S HAVING A LOT OF TROUBLE AT THE LAB. HE'S ALSO A PIECE OF...

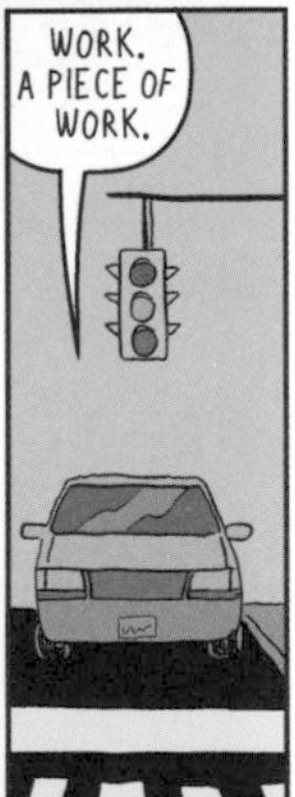
WORK. A PIECE OF WORK.

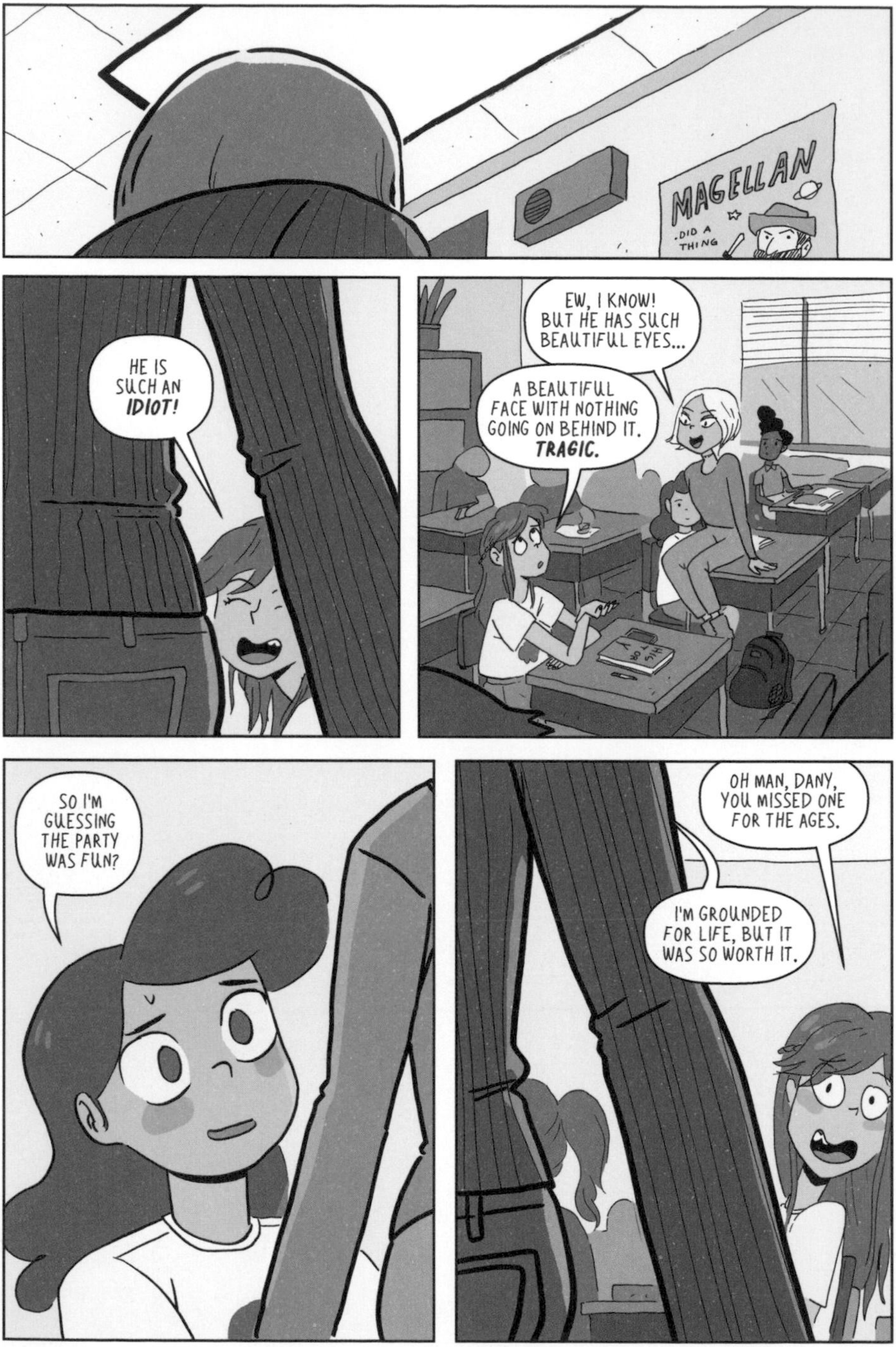
MAGELLAN
DID A THING
HE IS SUCH AN ***IDIOT!***
EW, I KNOW! BUT HE HAS SUCH BEAUTIFUL EYES...
A BEAUTIFUL FACE WITH NOTHING GOING ON BEHIND IT. **TRAGIC.**
HISTORY
SO I'M GUESSING THE PARTY WAS FUN?
OH MAN, DANY, YOU MISSED ONE FOR THE AGES.
I'M GROUNDED FOR LIFE, BUT IT WAS SO WORTH IT.

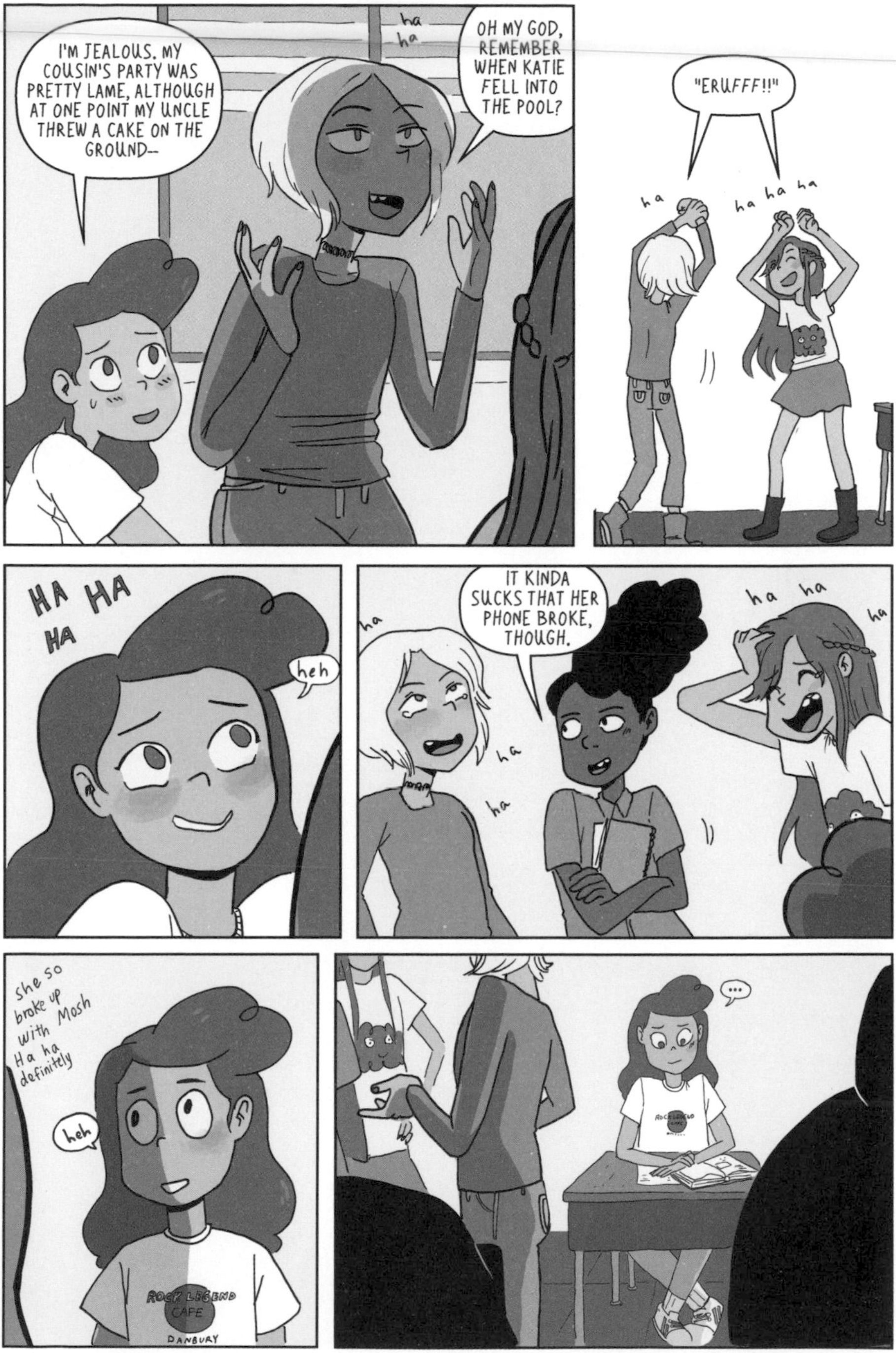
I'M JEALOUS. MY COUSIN'S PARTY WAS PRETTY LAME, ALTHOUGH AT ONE POINT MY UNCLE THREW A CAKE ON THE GROUND--
ha ha
OH MY GOD, REMEMBER WHEN KATIE FELL INTO THE POOL?
"ERUFFF!!"
ha
ha ha ha
HA HA HA
heh
IT KINDA SUCKS THAT HER PHONE BROKE, THOUGH.
ha
ha ha
ha
ha
ha
she so broke up with Mosh Ha ha definitely
heh
ROCK LEGEND CAFE DANBURY
...

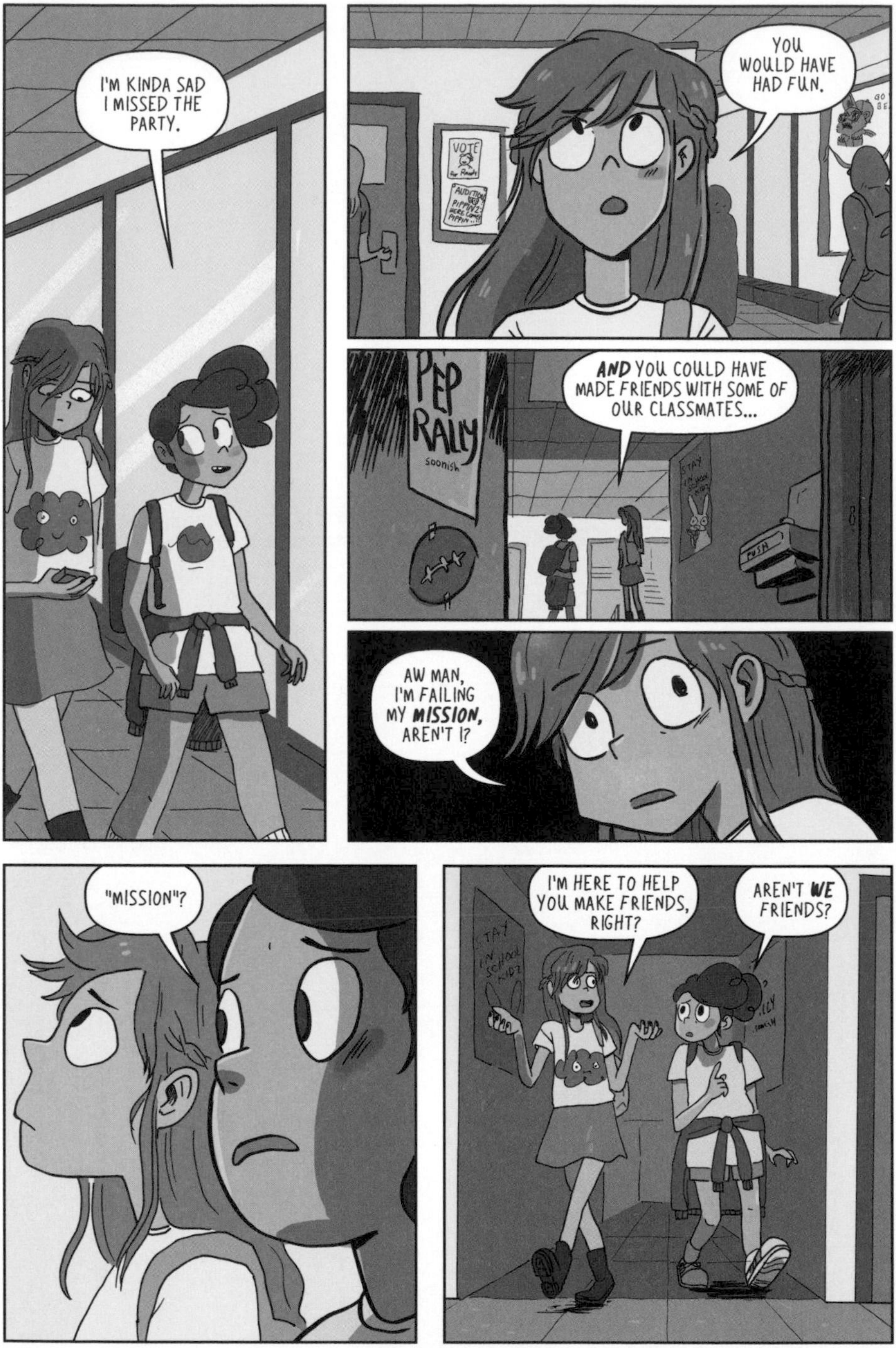
I'M KINDA SAD I MISSED THE PARTY.
YOU WOULD HAVE HAD FUN.
VOTE
PEP RALLY
soonish
AND YOU COULD HAVE MADE FRIENDS WITH SOME OF OUR CLASSMATES...
STAY IN SCHOOL KIDZ
AW MAN, I'M FAILING MY **MISSION,** AREN'T I?
"MISSION"?
I'M HERE TO HELP YOU MAKE FRIENDS, RIGHT?
AREN'T **WE** FRIENDS?

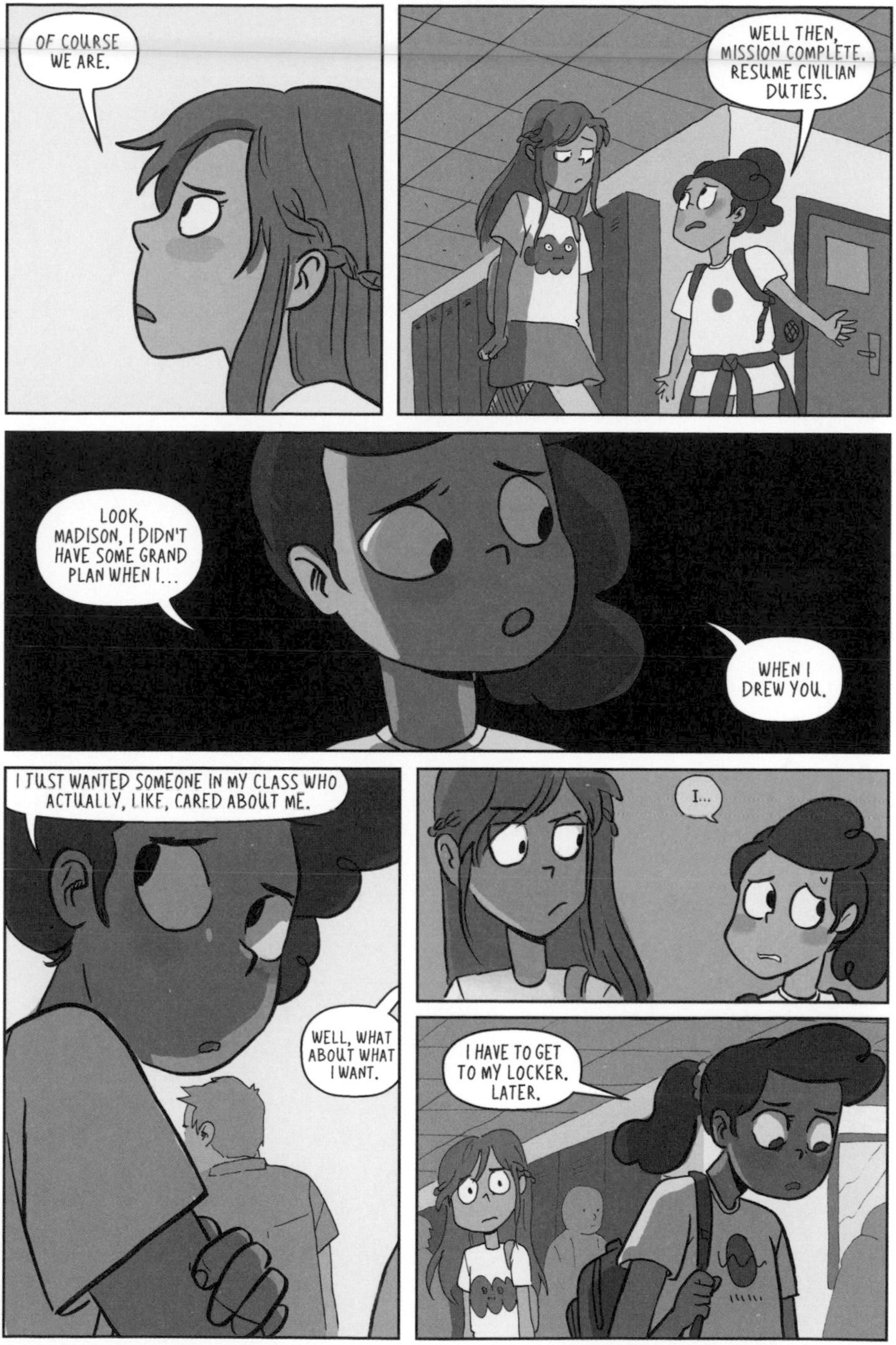
OF COURSE WE ARE.
WELL THEN, MISSION COMPLETE. RESUME CIVILIAN DUTIES.
LOOK, MADISON, I DIDN'T HAVE SOME GRAND PLAN WHEN I...
WHEN I DREW YOU.
I JUST WANTED SOMEONE IN MY CLASS WHO ACTUALLY, LIKE, CARED ABOUT ME.
WELL, WHAT ABOUT WHAT I WANT.
I...
I HAVE TO GET TO MY LOCKER. LATER.

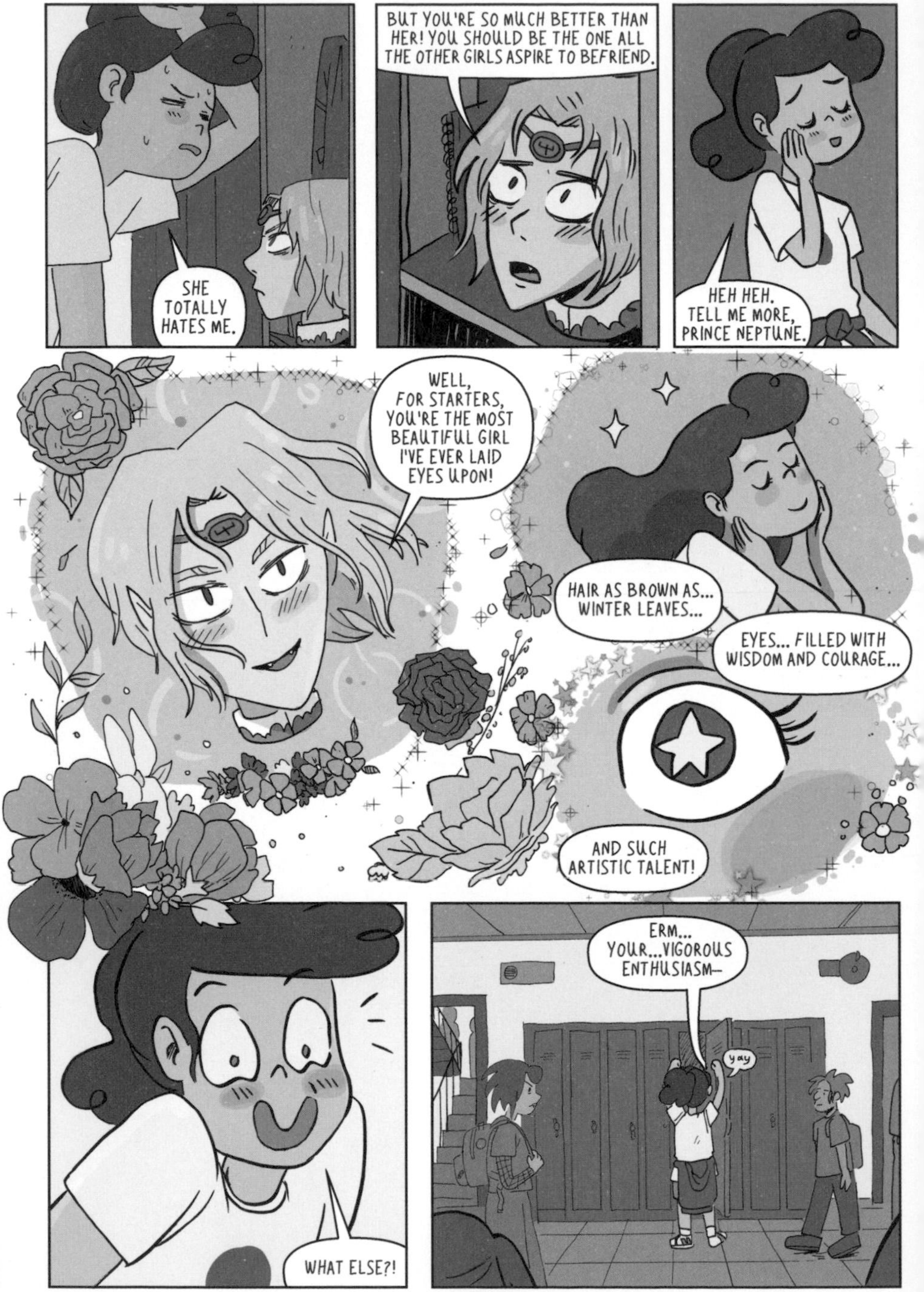
SHE TOTALLY HATES ME.
BUT YOU'RE SO MUCH BETTER THAN HER! YOU SHOULD BE THE ONE ALL THE OTHER GIRLS ASPIRE TO BEFRIEND.
HEH HEH. TELL ME MORE, PRINCE NEPTUNE.
WELL, FOR STARTERS, YOU'RE THE MOST BEAUTIFUL GIRL I'VE EVER LAID EYES UPON!
HAIR AS BROWN AS... WINTER LEAVES...
EYES... FILLED WITH WISDOM AND COURAGE...
AND SUCH ARTISTIC TALENT!
WHAT ELSE?!
ERM... YOUR...VIGOROUS ENTHUSIASM—
yay

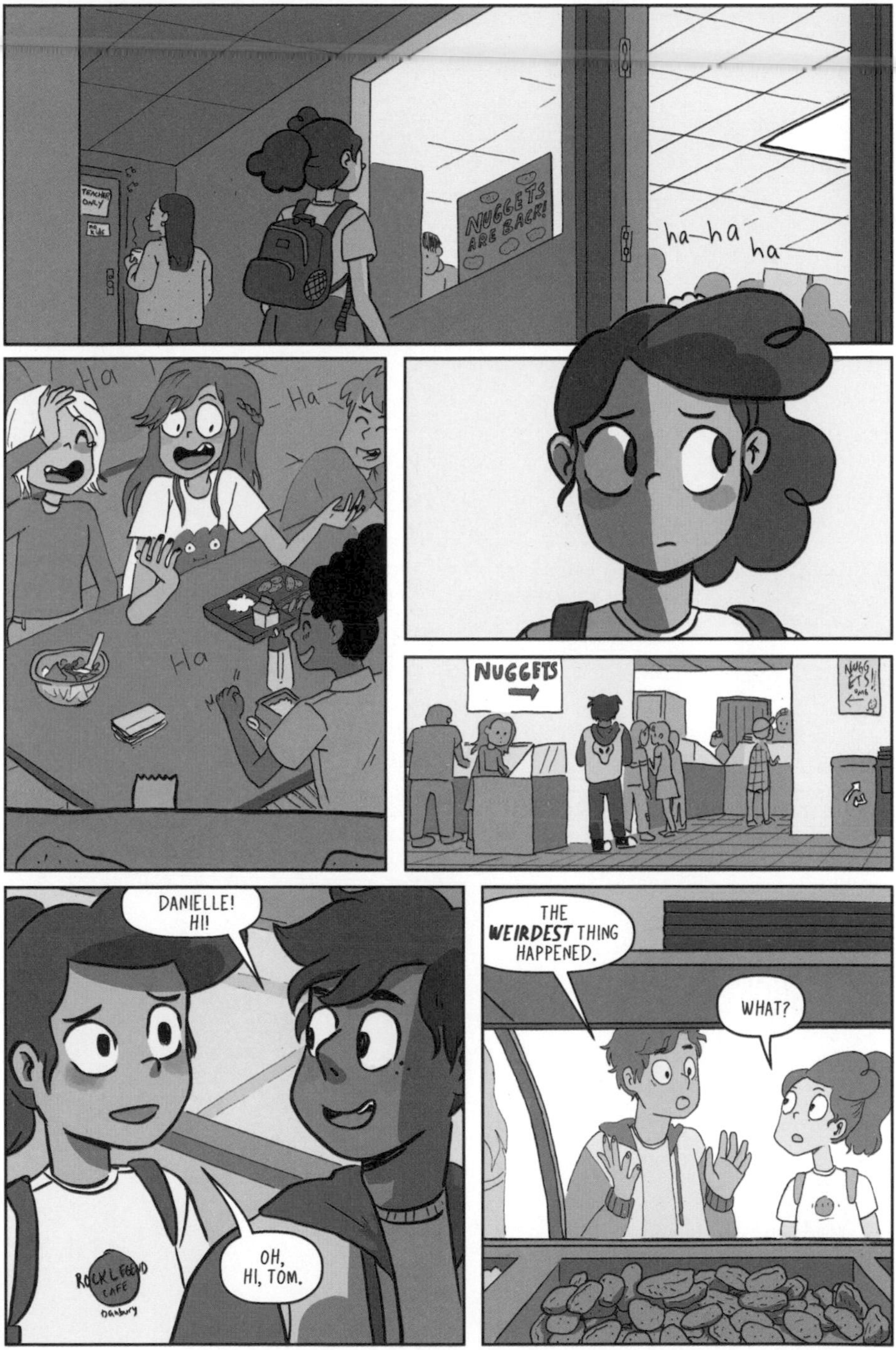
NUGGETS ARE BACK!
TEACHER ONLY
ha-ha ha
Ha
-Ha
Ha
NUGGETS
DANIELLE! HI!
OH, HI, TOM.
ROCK LEGEND CAFE
THE WEIRDEST THING HAPPENED.
WHAT?

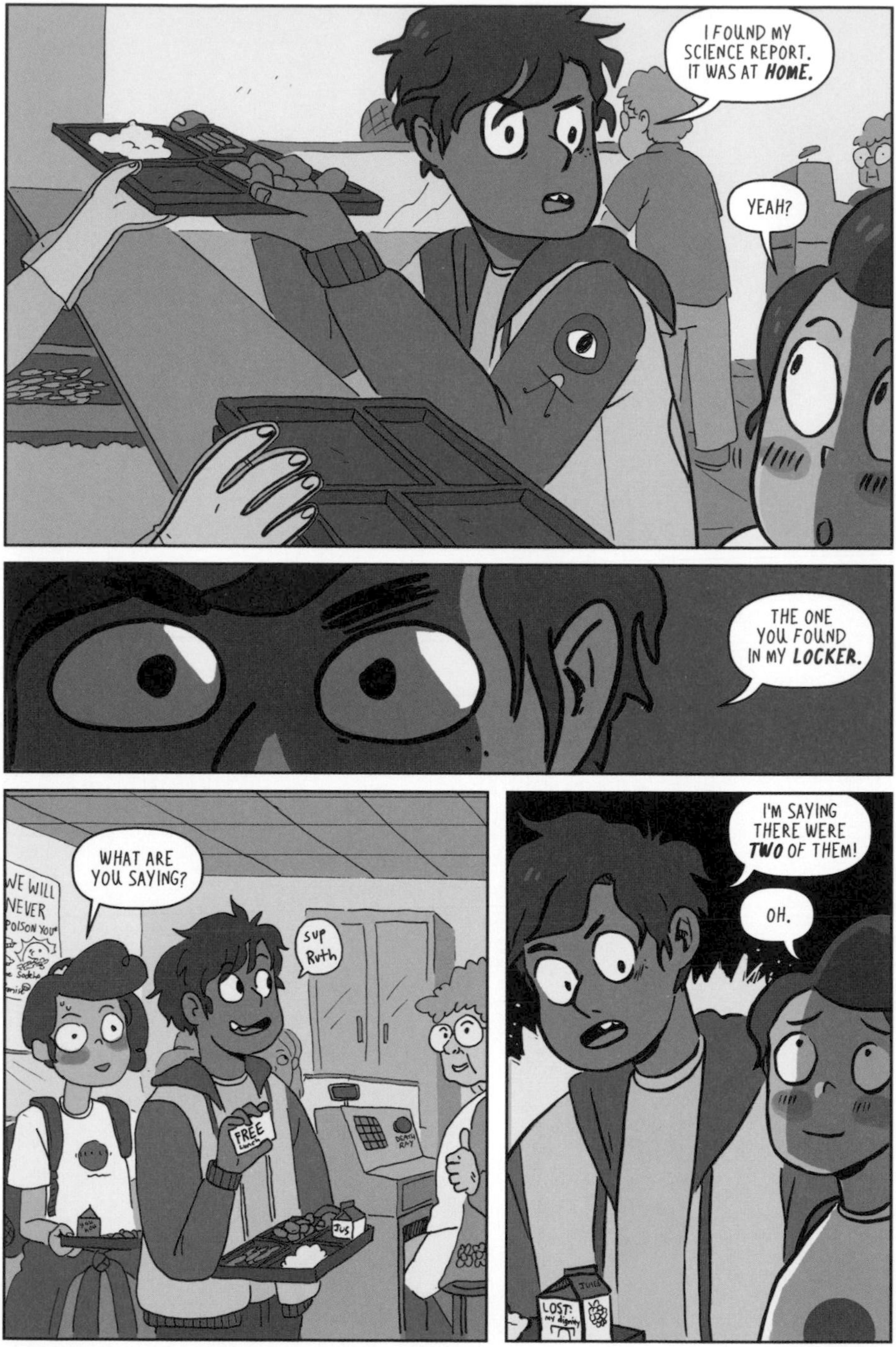
I FOUND MY SCIENCE REPORT. IT WAS AT **HOME.**
YEAH?
THE ONE YOU FOUND IN MY **LOCKER.**
WHAT ARE YOU SAYING?
sup Ruth
FREE
I'M SAYING THERE WERE **TWO** OF THEM!
OH.

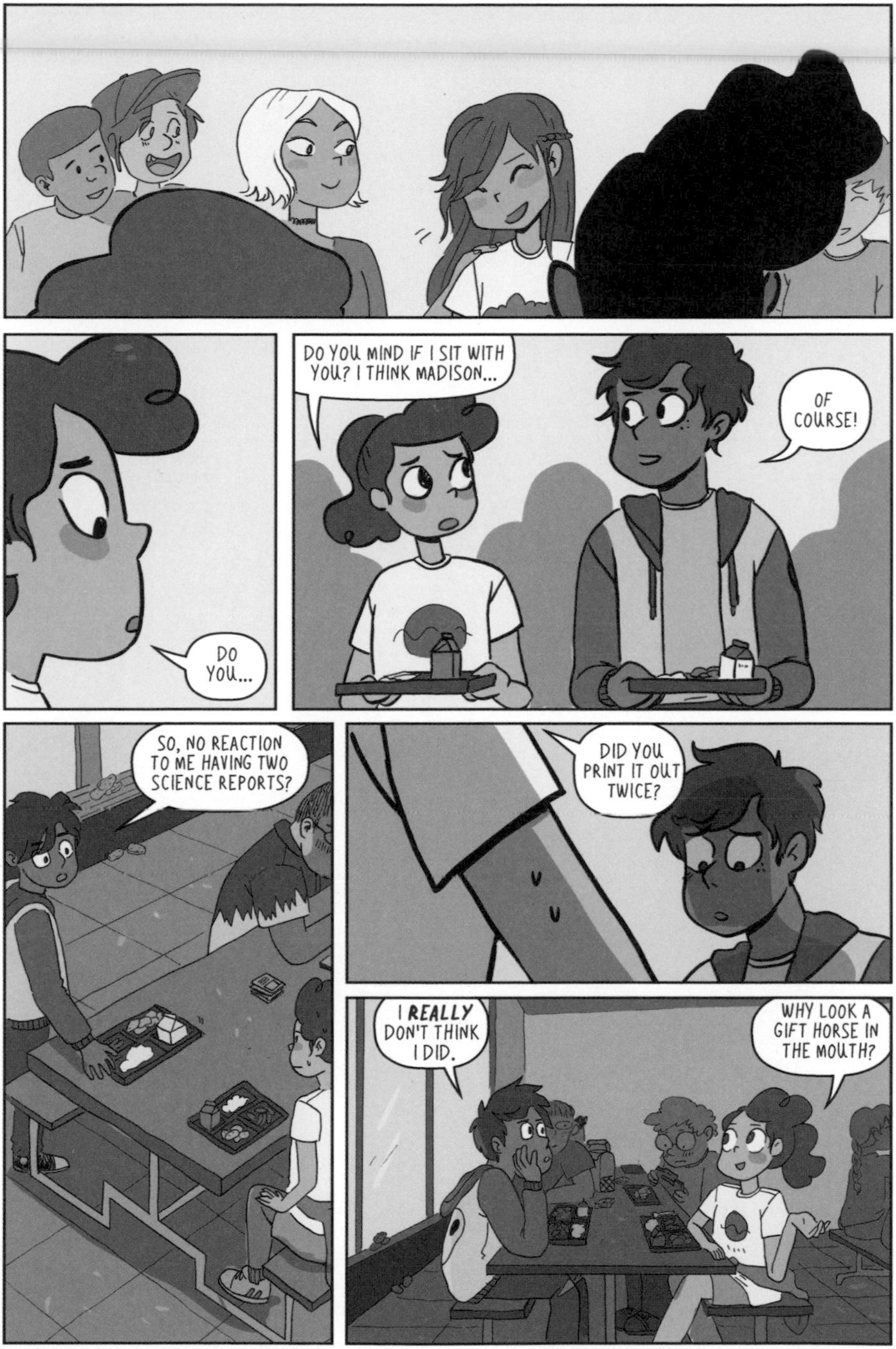
DO YOU...
DO YOU MIND IF I SIT WITH YOU? I THINK MADISON...
OF COURSE!
SO, NO REACTION TO ME HAVING TWO SCIENCE REPORTS?
DID YOU PRINT IT OUT TWICE?
I **REALLY** DON'T THINK I DID.
WHY LOOK A GIFT HORSE IN THE MOUTH?

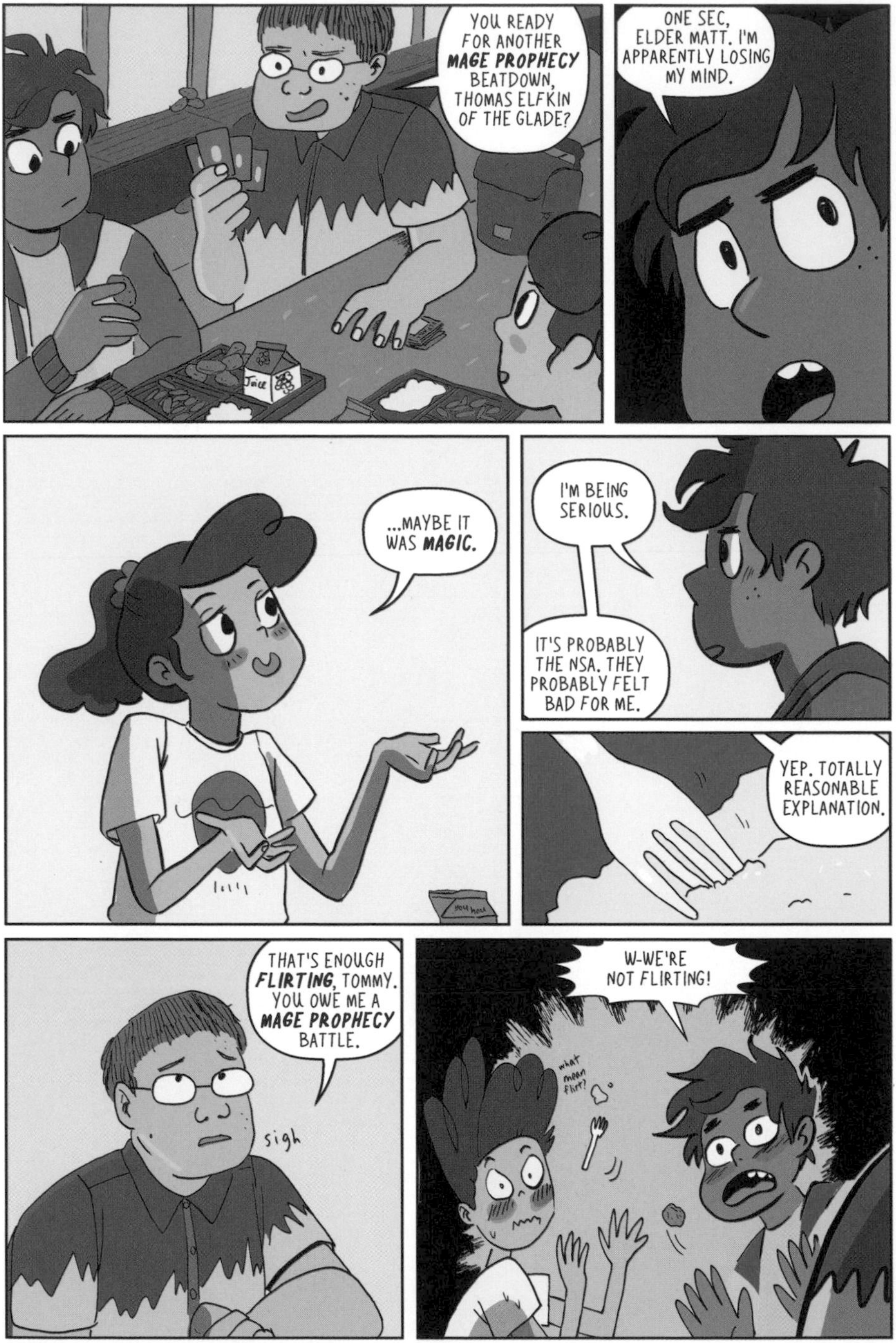
YOU READY FOR ANOTHER **MAGE PROPHECY** BEATDOWN, THOMAS ELFKIN OF THE GLADE?
ONE SEC, ELDER MATT. I'M APPARENTLY LOSING MY MIND.
...MAYBE IT WAS **MAGIC.**
I'M BEING SERIOUS.
IT'S PROBABLY THE NSA. THEY PROBABLY FELT BAD FOR ME.
YEP. TOTALLY REASONABLE EXPLANATION.
THAT'S ENOUGH **FLIRTING**, TOMMY. YOU OWE ME A **MAGE PROPHECY** BATTLE.
sigh
W-WE'RE NOT FLIRTING!
what mean flirt?

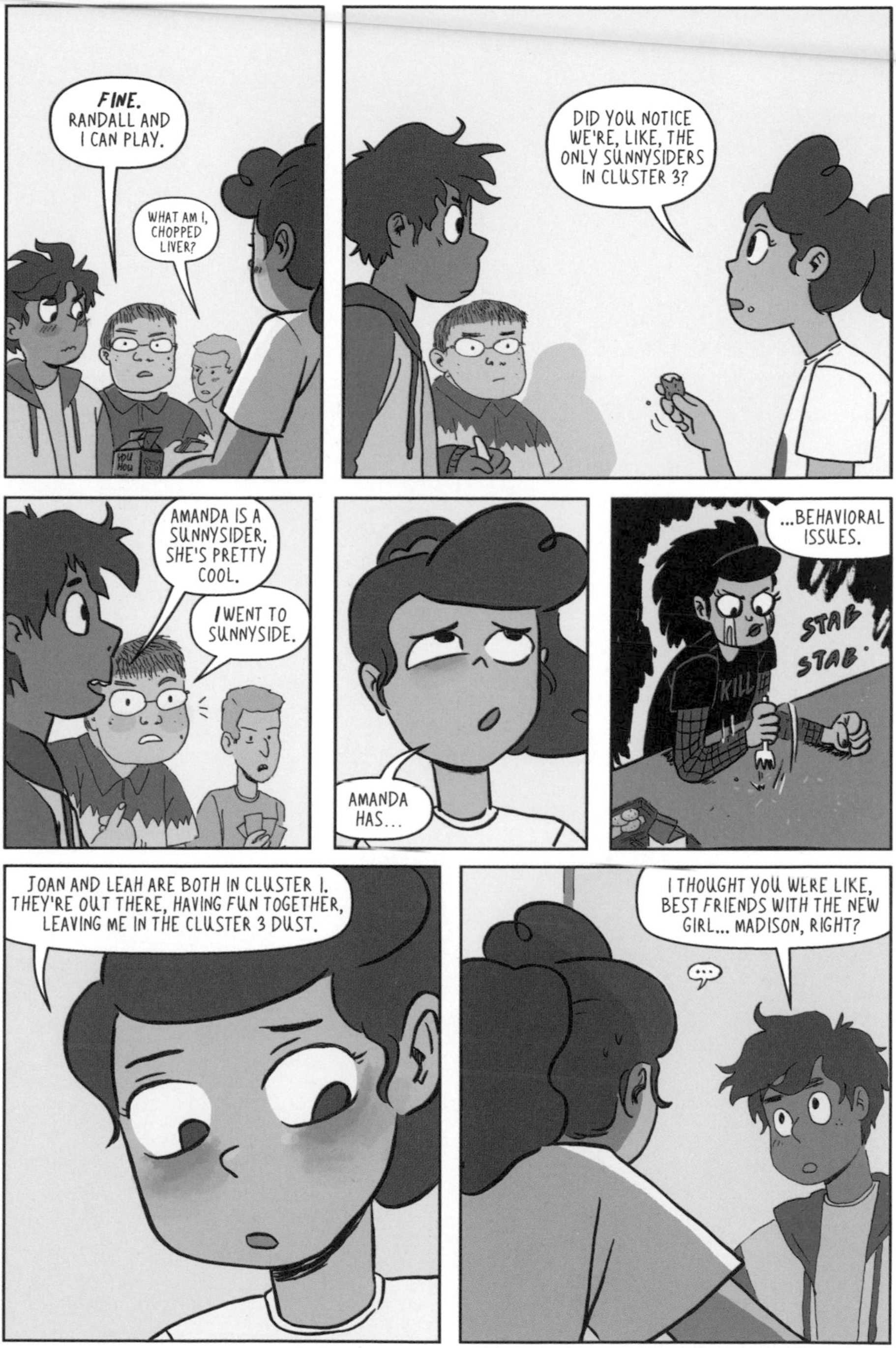
FINE. RANDALL AND I CAN PLAY.
WHAT AM I, CHOPPED LIVER?
DID YOU NOTICE WE'RE, LIKE, THE ONLY SUNNYSIDERS IN CLUSTER 3?
AMANDA IS A SUNNYSIDER. SHE'S PRETTY COOL.
I WENT TO SUNNYSIDE.
AMANDA HAS...
...BEHAVIORAL ISSUES.
KILL
STAB
STAB
JOAN AND LEAH ARE BOTH IN CLUSTER 1. THEY'RE OUT THERE, HAVING FUN TOGETHER, LEAVING ME IN THE CLUSTER 3 DUST.
I THOUGHT YOU WERE LIKE, BEST FRIENDS WITH THE NEW GIRL... MADISON, RIGHT?
...

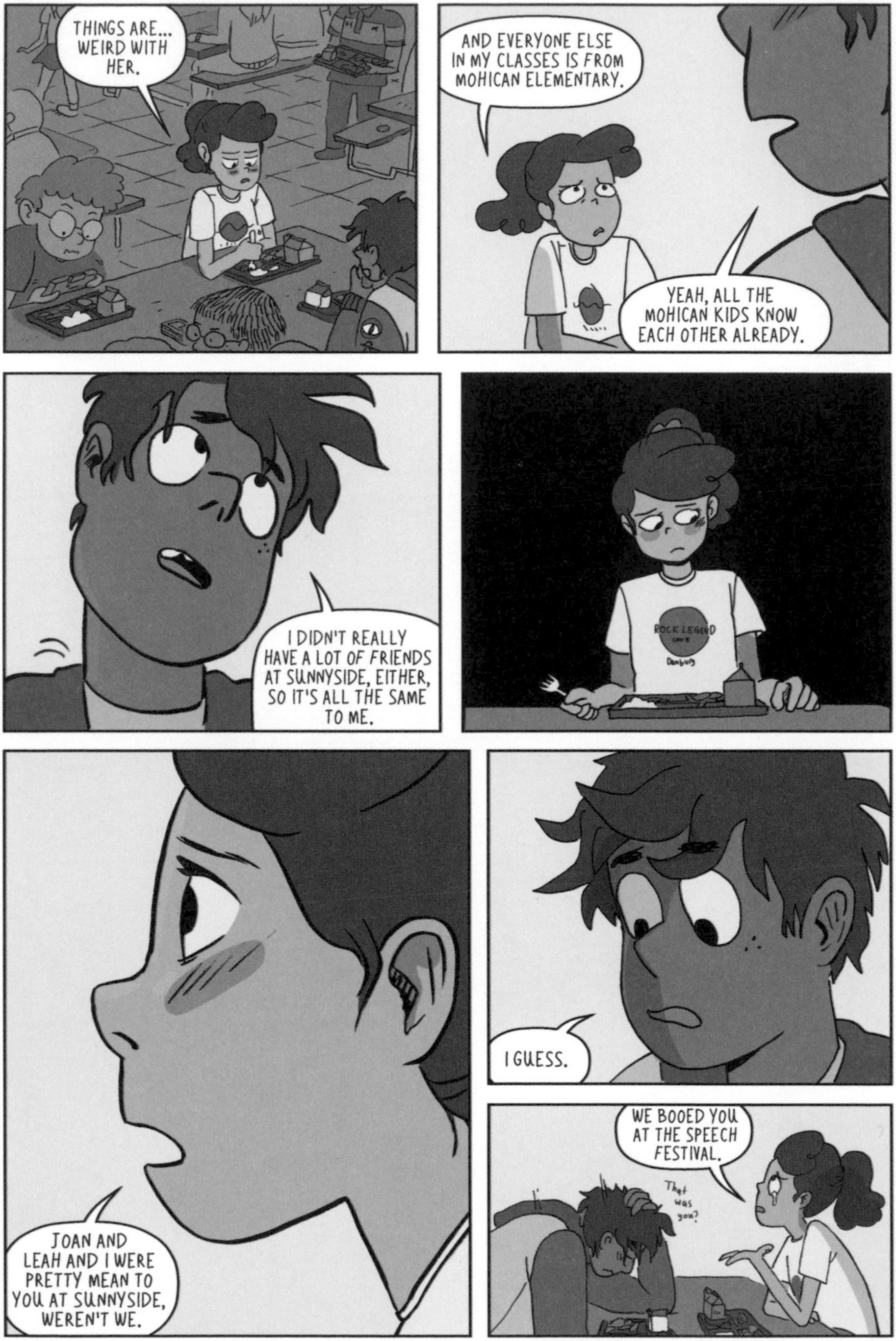
THINGS ARE... WEIRD WITH HER.
AND EVERYONE ELSE IN MY CLASSES IS FROM MOHICAN ELEMENTARY.
YEAH, ALL THE MOHICAN KIDS KNOW EACH OTHER ALREADY.
I DIDN'T REALLY HAVE A LOT OF FRIENDS AT SUNNYSIDE, EITHER, SO IT'S ALL THE SAME TO ME.
JOAN AND LEAH AND I WERE PRETTY MEAN TO YOU AT SUNNYSIDE, WEREN'T WE.
I GUESS.
WE BOOED YOU AT THE SPEECH FESTIVAL.
That was you?

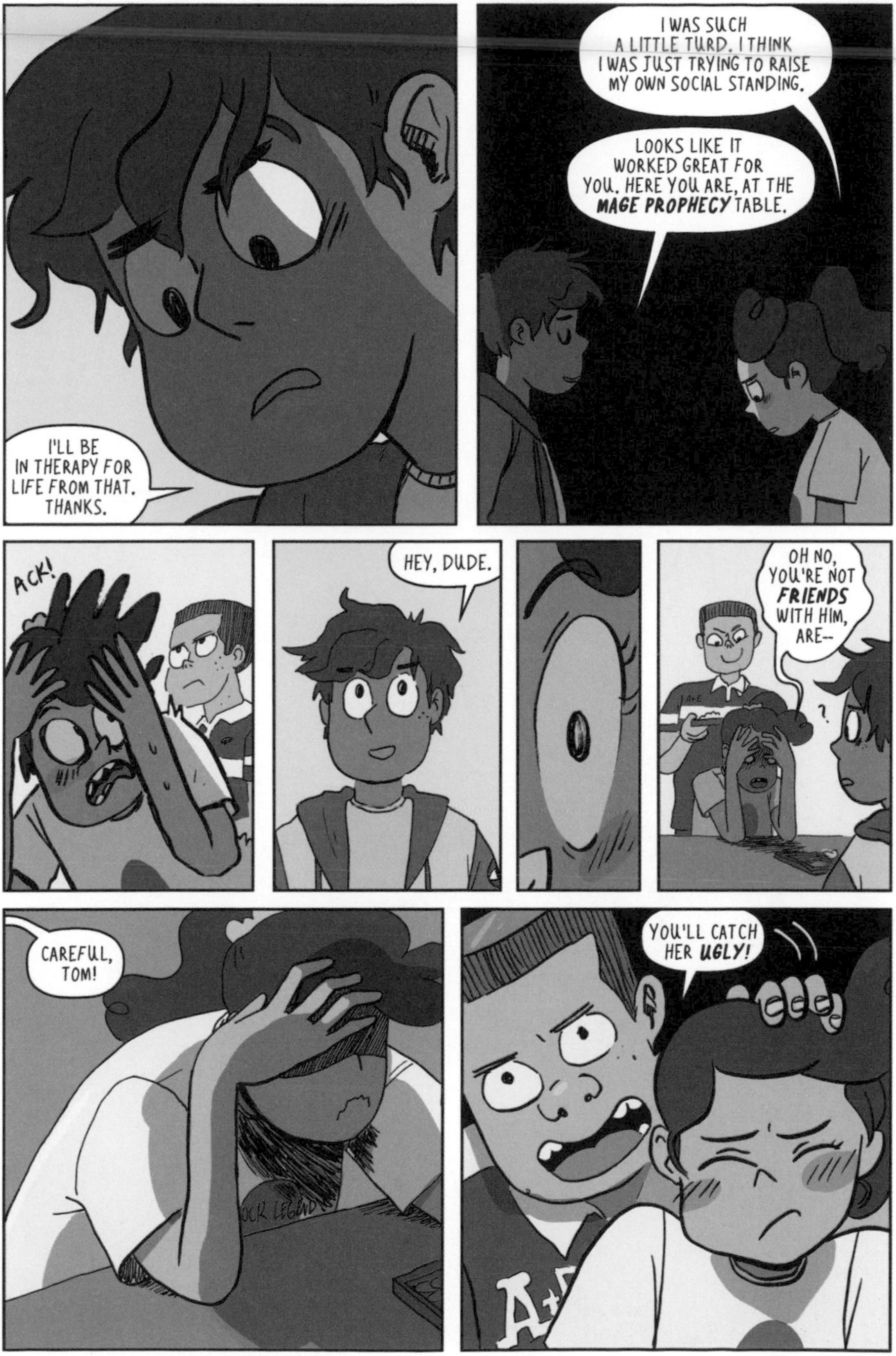
I'LL BE IN THERAPY FOR LIFE FROM THAT. THANKS.
I WAS SUCH A LITTLE TURD. I THINK I WAS JUST TRYING TO RAISE MY OWN SOCIAL STANDING.
LOOKS LIKE IT WORKED GREAT FOR YOU. HERE YOU ARE, AT THE **MAGE PROPHECY** TABLE.
ACK!
HEY, DUDE.
OH NO, YOU'RE NOT **FRIENDS** WITH HIM, ARE--
?
CAREFUL, TOM!
YOU'LL CATCH HER **UGLY!**

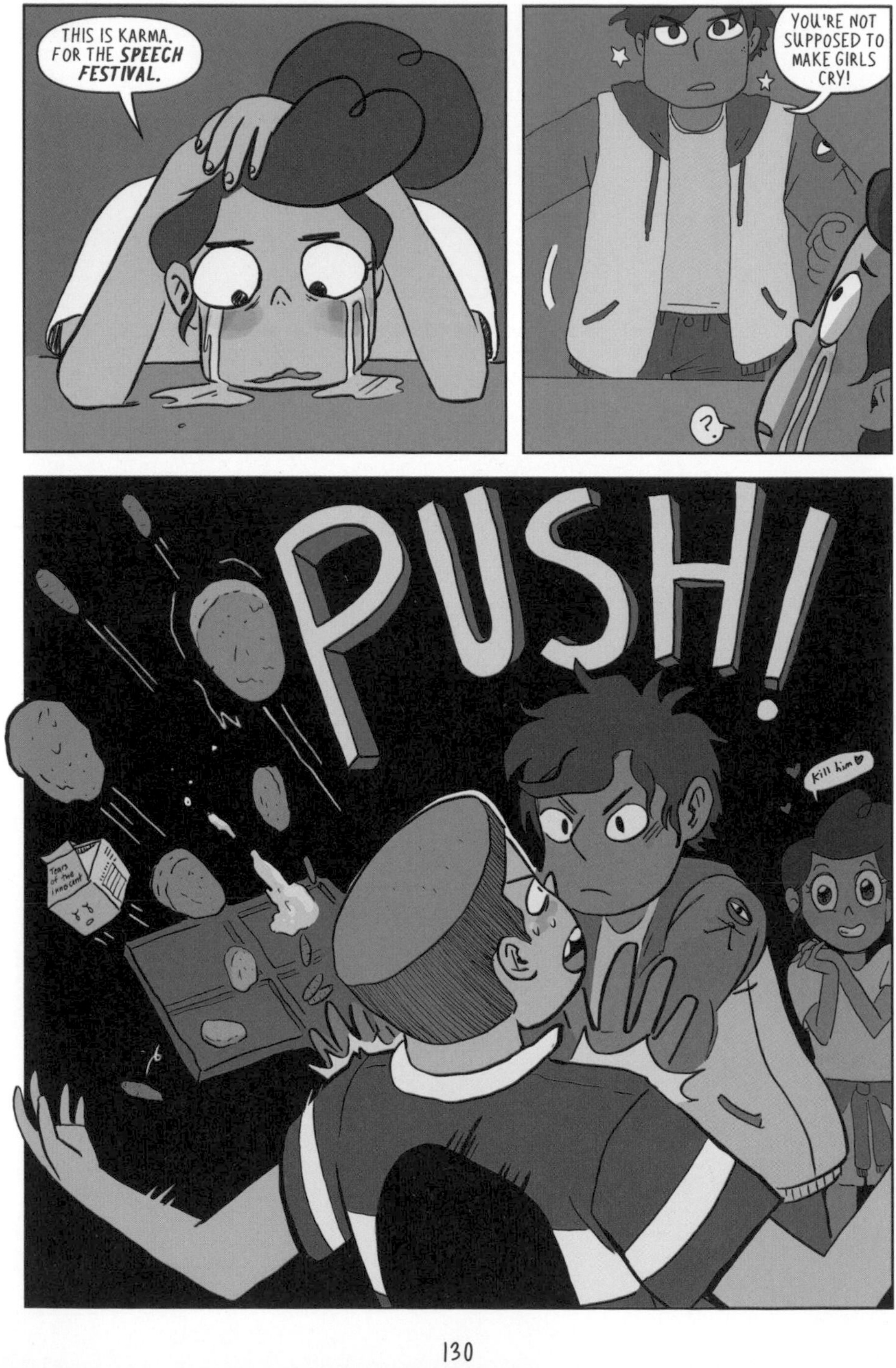
THIS IS KARMA. FOR THE **SPEECH FESTIVAL.**
YOU'RE NOT SUPPOSED TO MAKE GIRLS CRY!
?
PUSH!
Tears of the innocent
Kill him

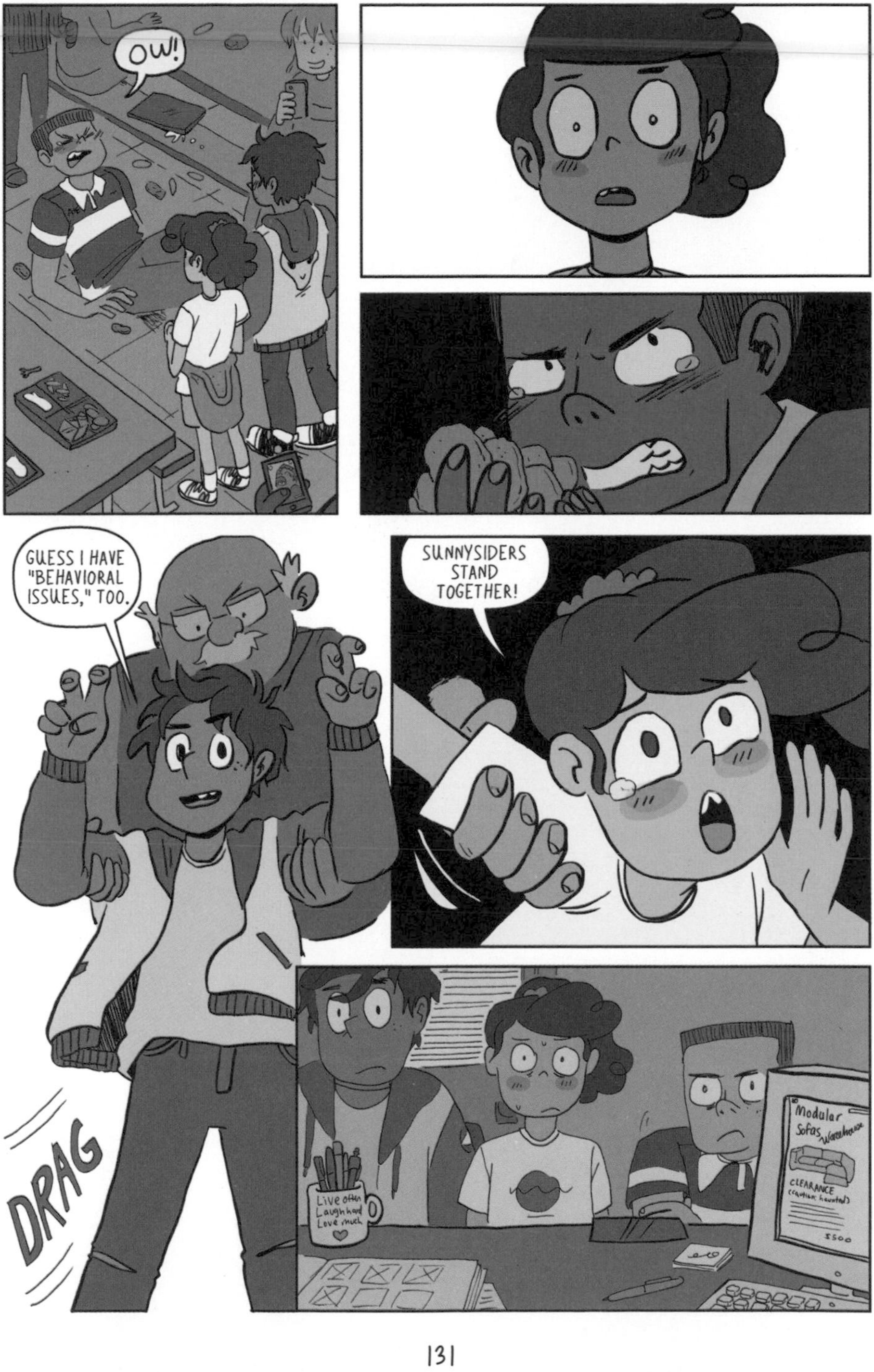
OW!
GUESS I HAVE "BEHAVIORAL ISSUES," TOO.
SUNNYSIDERS STAND TOGETHER!
DRAG
Live often Laugh hard Love much
Modular Sofas Warehouse
CLEARANCE
(caution: haunted)

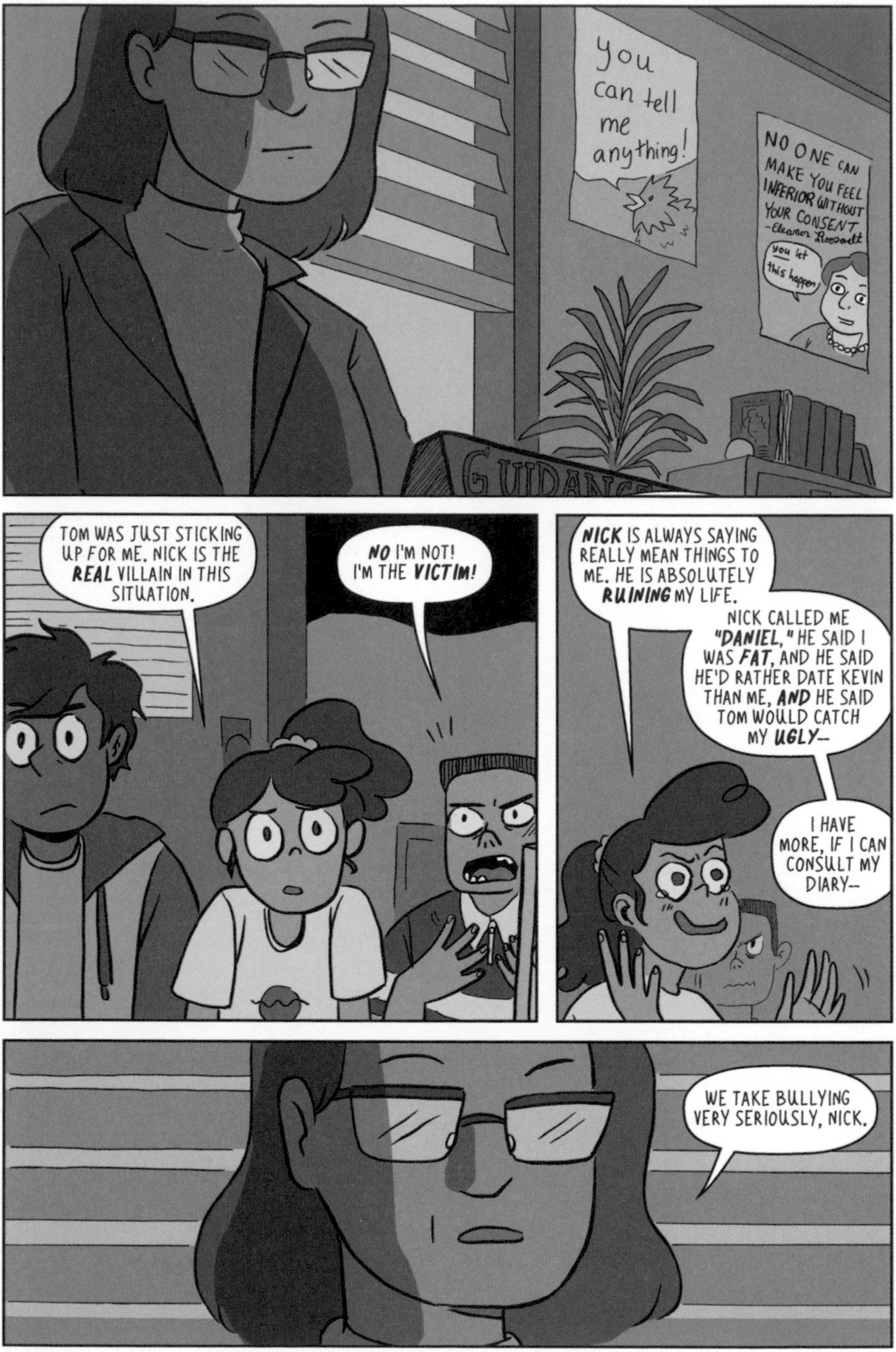
you can tell me anything!
NO ONE CAN MAKE YOU FEEL INFERIOR WITHOUT YOUR CONSENT
-Eleanor Roosevelt
you let this happen
GUIDANCE
TOM WAS JUST STICKING UP FOR ME. NICK IS THE REAL VILLAIN IN THIS SITUATION.
NO I'M NOT! I'M THE VICTIM!
NICK IS ALWAYS SAYING REALLY MEAN THINGS TO ME. HE IS ABSOLUTELY RUINING MY LIFE.
NICK CALLED ME "DANIEL," HE SAID I WAS FAT, AND HE SAID HE'D RATHER DATE KEVIN THAN ME, AND HE SAID TOM WOULD CATCH MY UGLY--
I HAVE MORE, IF I CAN CONSULT MY DIARY--
WE TAKE BULLYING VERY SERIOUSLY, NICK.

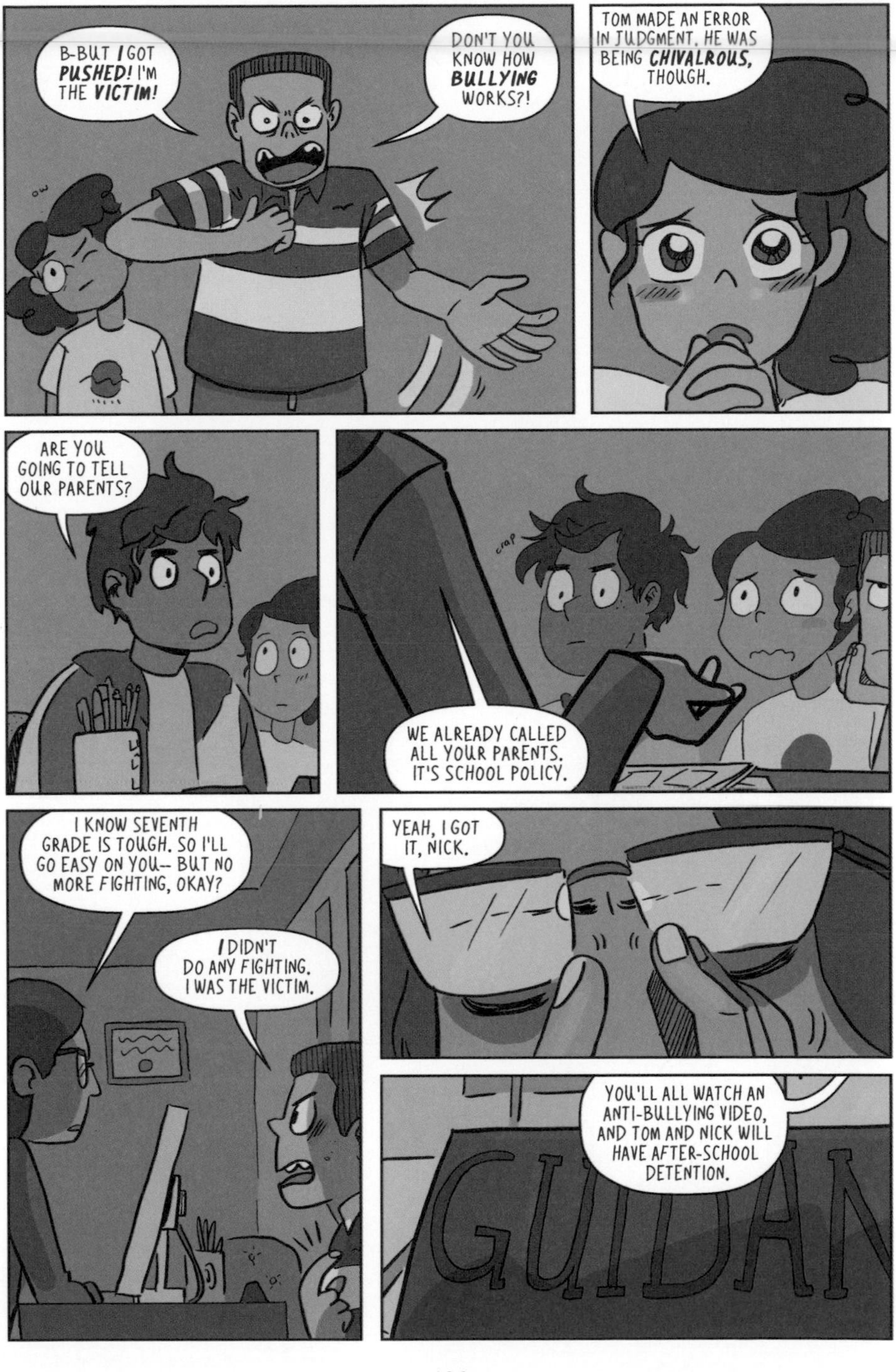
B-BUT I GOT PUSHED! I'M THE VICTIM!
ow
DON'T YOU KNOW HOW BULLYING WORKS?!
TOM MADE AN ERROR IN JUDGMENT. HE WAS BEING CHIVALROUS, THOUGH.
ARE YOU GOING TO TELL OUR PARENTS?
crap
WE ALREADY CALLED ALL YOUR PARENTS. IT'S SCHOOL POLICY.
I KNOW SEVENTH GRADE IS TOUGH. SO I'LL GO EASY ON YOU-- BUT NO MORE FIGHTING, OKAY?
I DIDN'T DO ANY FIGHTING. I WAS THE VICTIM.
YEAH, I GOT IT, NICK.
YOU'LL ALL WATCH AN ANTI-BULLYING VIDEO, AND TOM AND NICK WILL HAVE AFTER-SCHOOL DETENTION.
GUIDAN

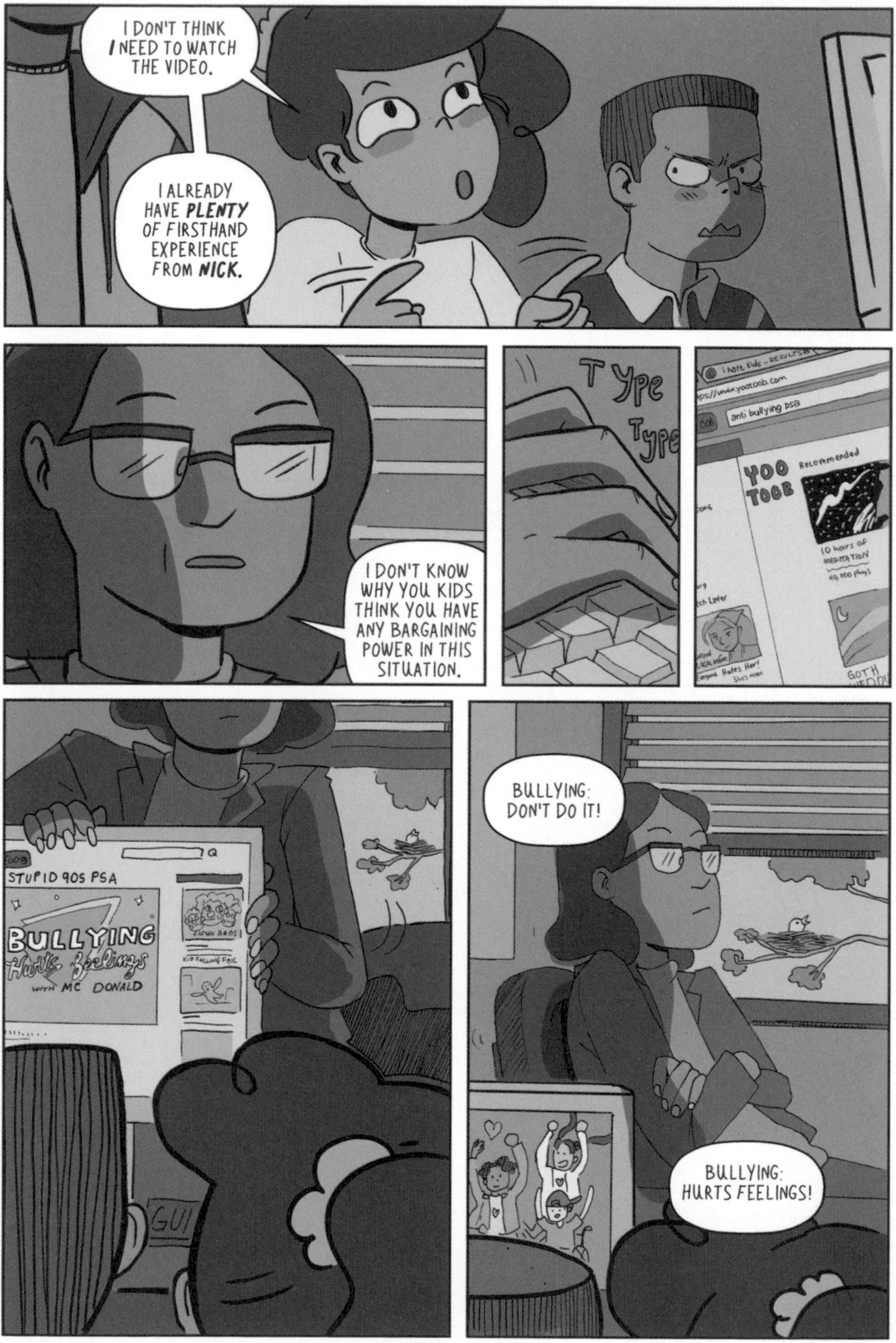
I DON'T THINK *I* NEED TO WATCH THE VIDEO.
I ALREADY HAVE **PLENTY** OF FIRSTHAND EXPERIENCE FROM **NICK.**
I DON'T KNOW WHY YOU KIDS THINK YOU HAVE ANY BARGAINING POWER IN THIS SITUATION.
TYPE
TYPE
anti bullying psa
YOO TOOB
Recommended
10 hours of MEDITATION
STUPID 90S PSA
BULLYING Hurts Feelings WITH MC DONALD
BULLYING: DON'T DO IT!
BULLYING: HURTS FEELINGS!

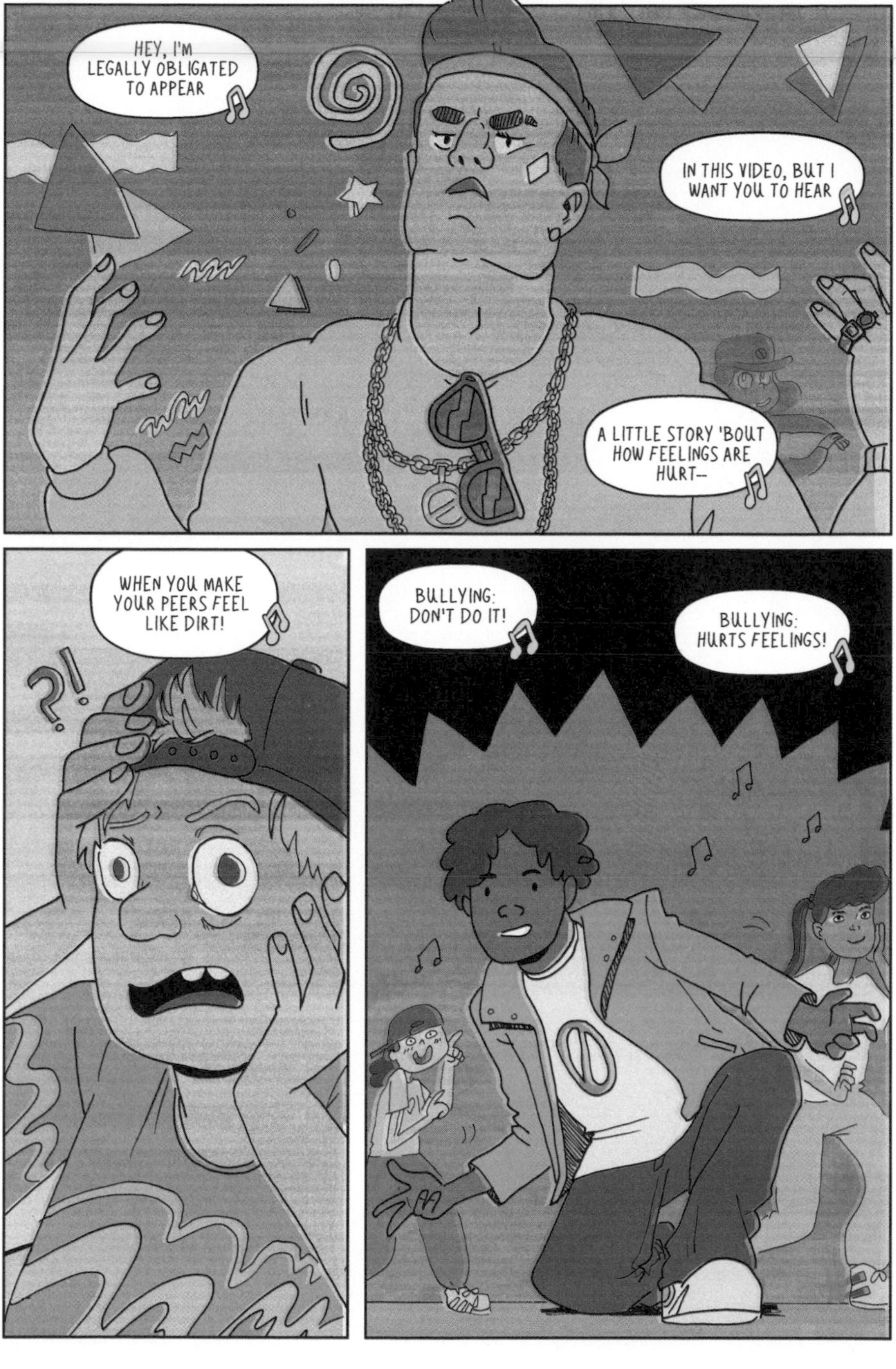
HEY, I'M LEGALLY OBLIGATED TO APPEAR
IN THIS VIDEO, BUT I WANT YOU TO HEAR
A LITTLE STORY 'BOUT HOW FEELINGS ARE HURT--
WHEN YOU MAKE YOUR PEERS FEEL LIKE DIRT!
?!
BULLYING: DON'T DO IT!
BULLYING: HURTS FEELINGS!

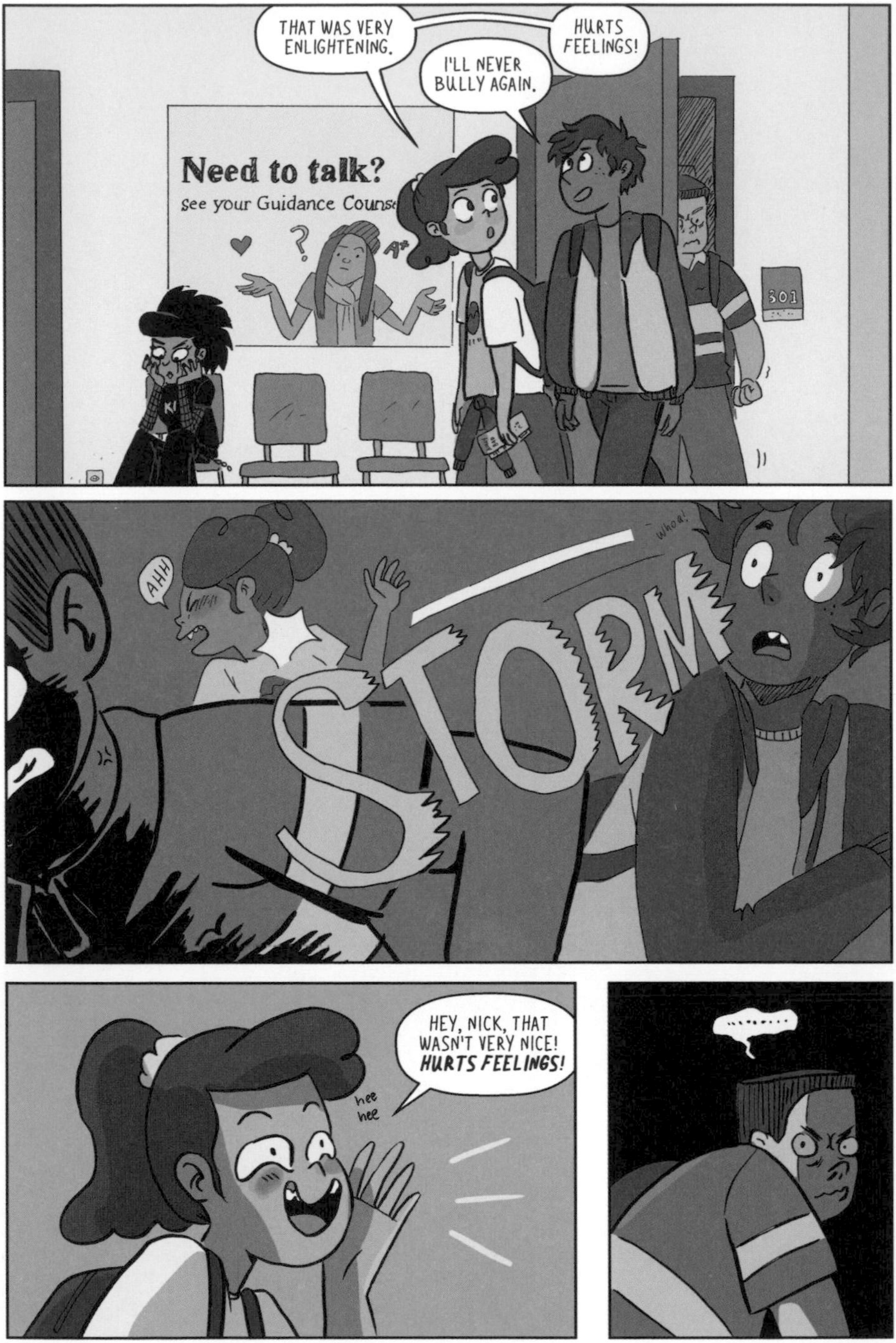
THAT WAS VERY ENLIGHTENING.
I'LL NEVER BULLY AGAIN.
HURTS FEELINGS!
Need to talk?
see your Guidance Couns
301
AHH!
Whoa!
STORM
HEY, NICK, THAT WASN'T VERY NICE! **HURTS FEELINGS!**
hee hee
....

140

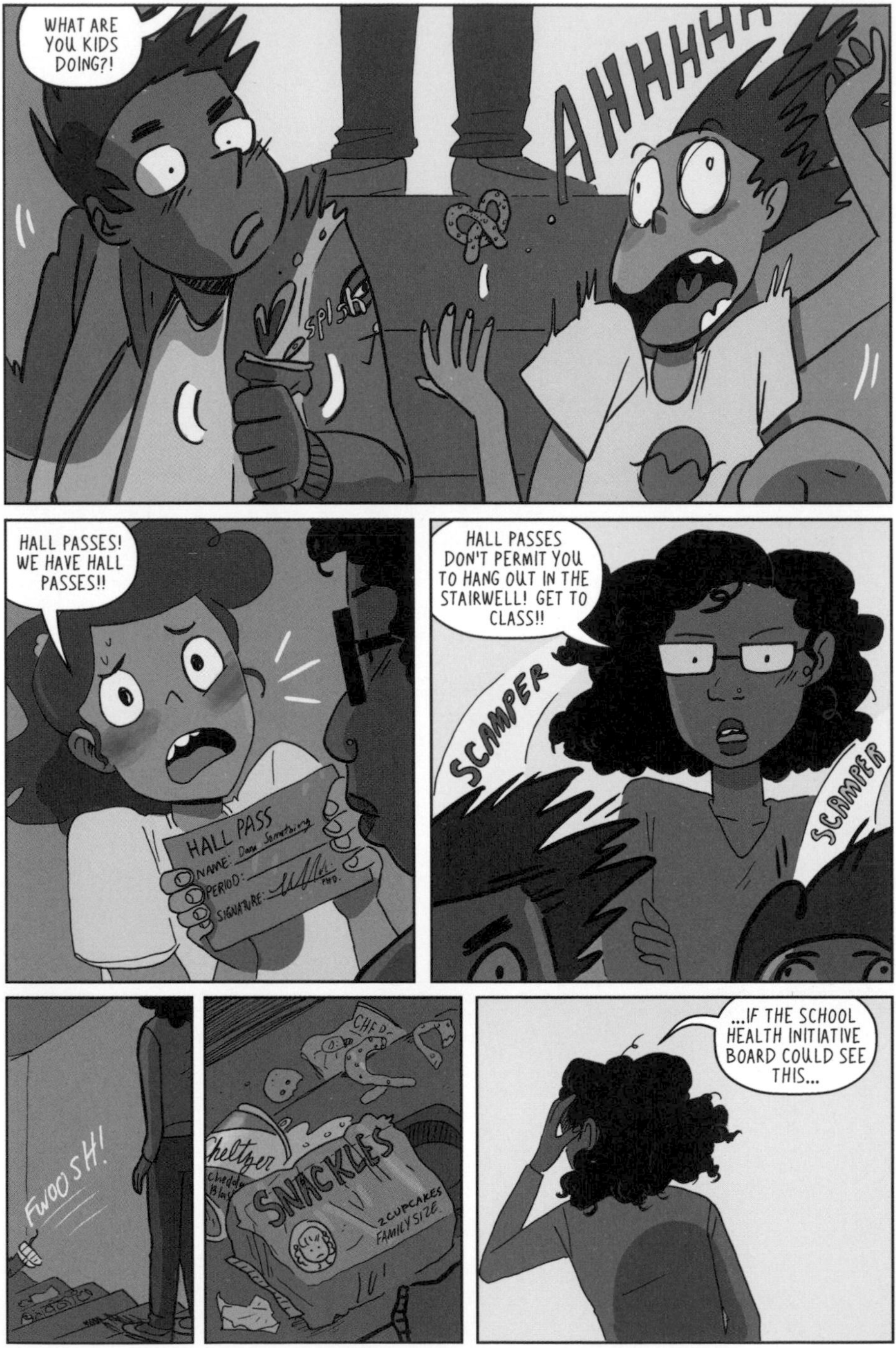
WHAT ARE YOU KIDS DOING?!
AHHHHH
splsh
HALL PASSES! WE HAVE HALL PASSES!!
HALL PASS
NAME:
PERIOD:
SIGNATURE:
HALL PASSES DON'T PERMIT YOU TO HANG OUT IN THE STAIRWELL! GET TO CLASS!!
SCAMPER
SCAMPER
FWOOSH!
SNACKLES
2CUPCAKES
FAMILY SIZE
...IF THE SCHOOL HEALTH INITIATIVE BOARD COULD SEE THIS...

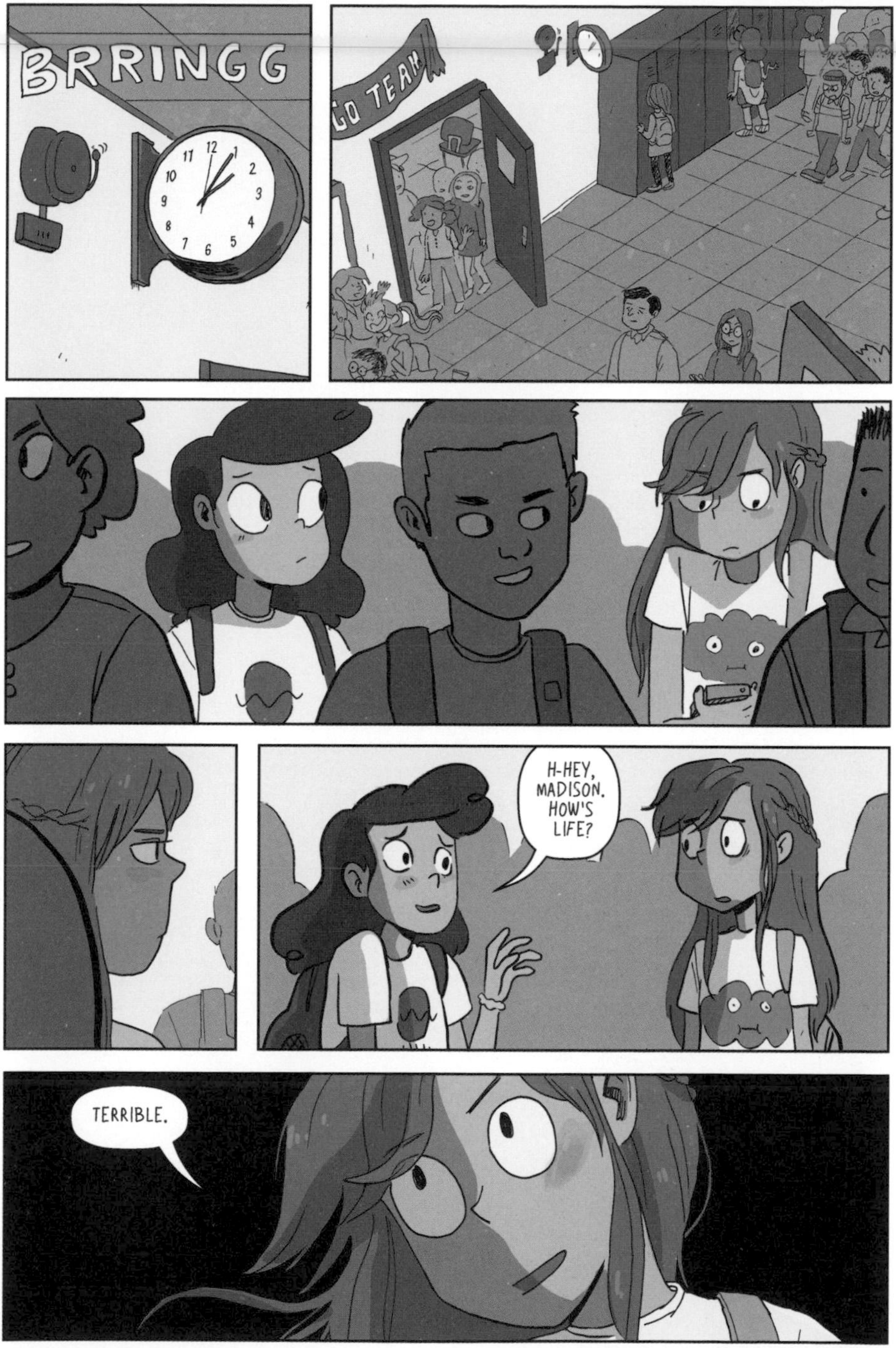
BRRINGG
GO TEAM
H-HEY, MADISON. HOW'S LIFE?
TERRIBLE.

144

146

147

148

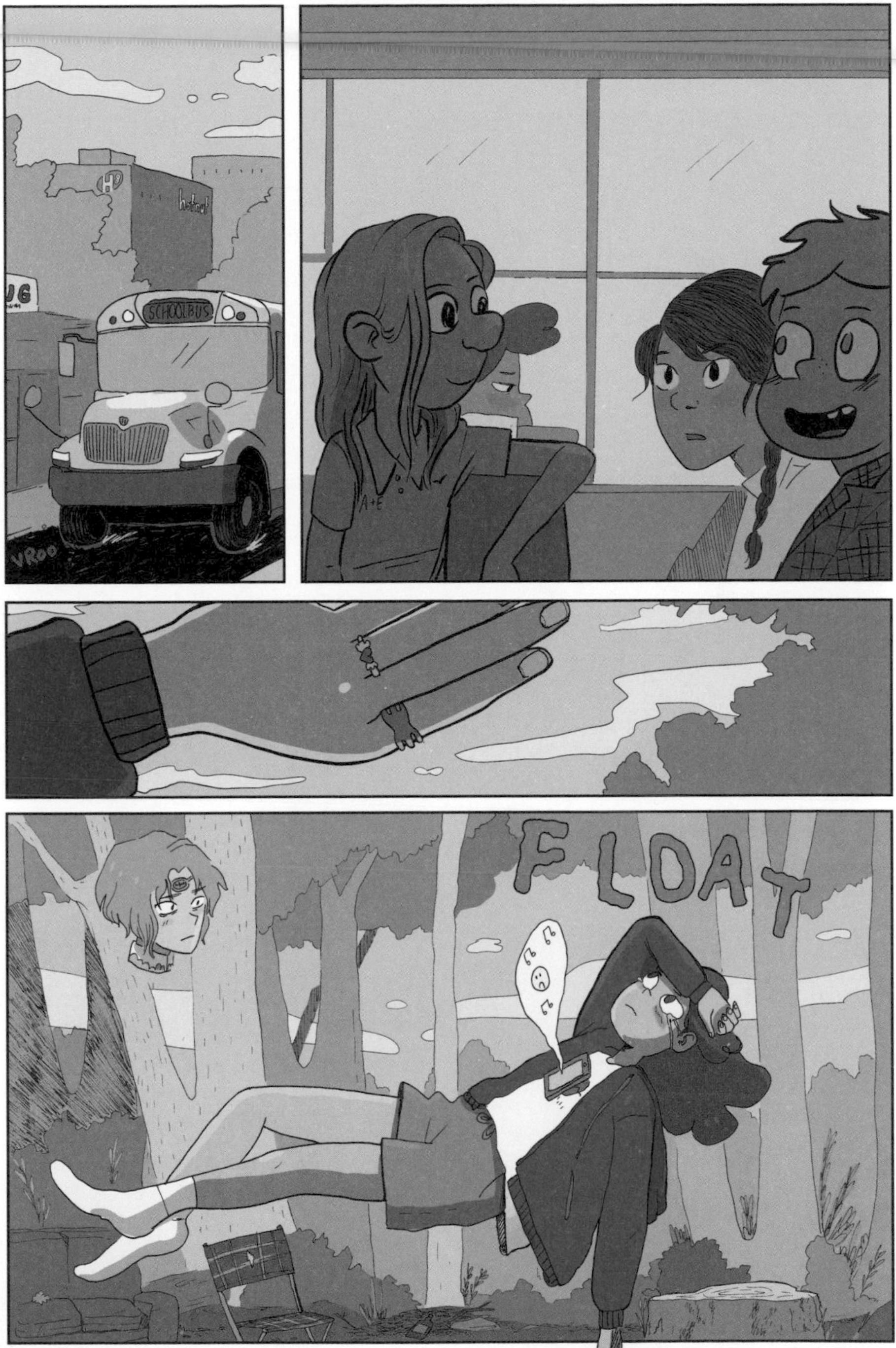
SCHOOLBUS
VROO
A+E
FLOAT

150

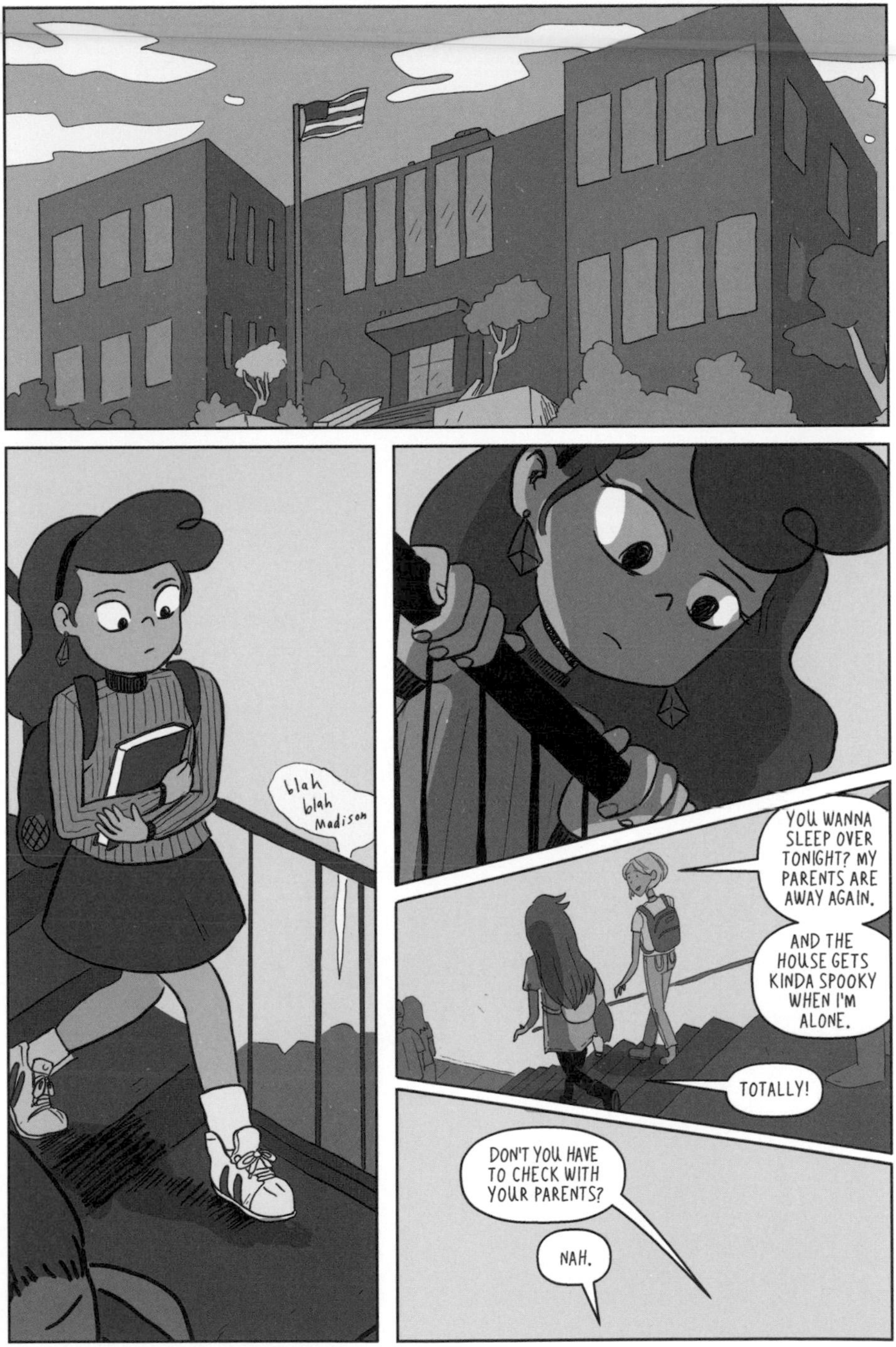

blah blah Madison
YOU WANNA SLEEP OVER TONIGHT? MY PARENTS ARE AWAY AGAIN.
AND THE HOUSE GETS KINDA SPOOKY WHEN I'M ALONE.
TOTALLY!
DON'T YOU HAVE TO CHECK WITH YOUR PARENTS?
NAH.

YEAH?

MAYBE WE CAN CHECK IT OUT SOMETIME.

THAT... COULD BE FUN? BYE?

bye

SCAMPER

THIS BOY DOES *NOT* IMPRESS ME.

TOM? TOM'S NOT SO BAD! YOU'VE JUST GOTTA GIVE HIM A CHANCE.

AND I CAN'T SAY *BATTLEMAN X* IS STUPID! IT'S MY THIRD FAVORITE SHOW *OF ALL TIME!*

I CRIED SO MUCH WHEN BOKU FELL INTO THE TIME-PIT TRYING TO SAVE HAMMY—

158

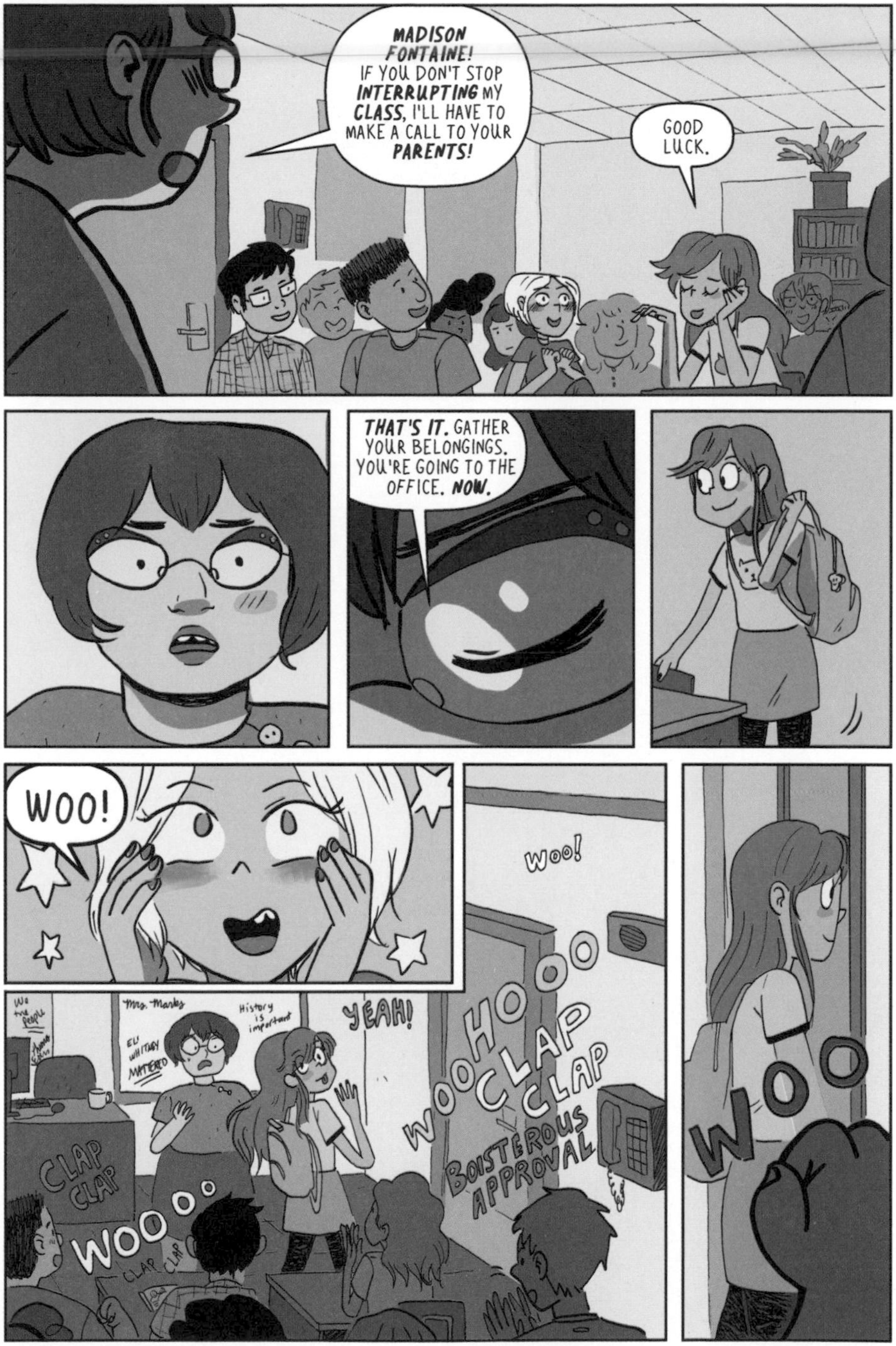
MADISON FONTAINE! IF YOU DON'T STOP INTERRUPTING MY CLASS, I'LL HAVE TO MAKE A CALL TO YOUR PARENTS!
GOOD LUCK.
THAT'S IT. GATHER YOUR BELONGINGS. YOU'RE GOING TO THE OFFICE. NOW.
WOO!
WOO!
HOOOO
WOO CLAP CLAP CLAP
BOISTEROUS APPROVAL
YEAH!
Mrs. Marks
History is important
ELI WHITNEY MATTERED
CLAP CLAP
WOO O O
CLAP CLAP
WOO

162

165

170

171

174

176

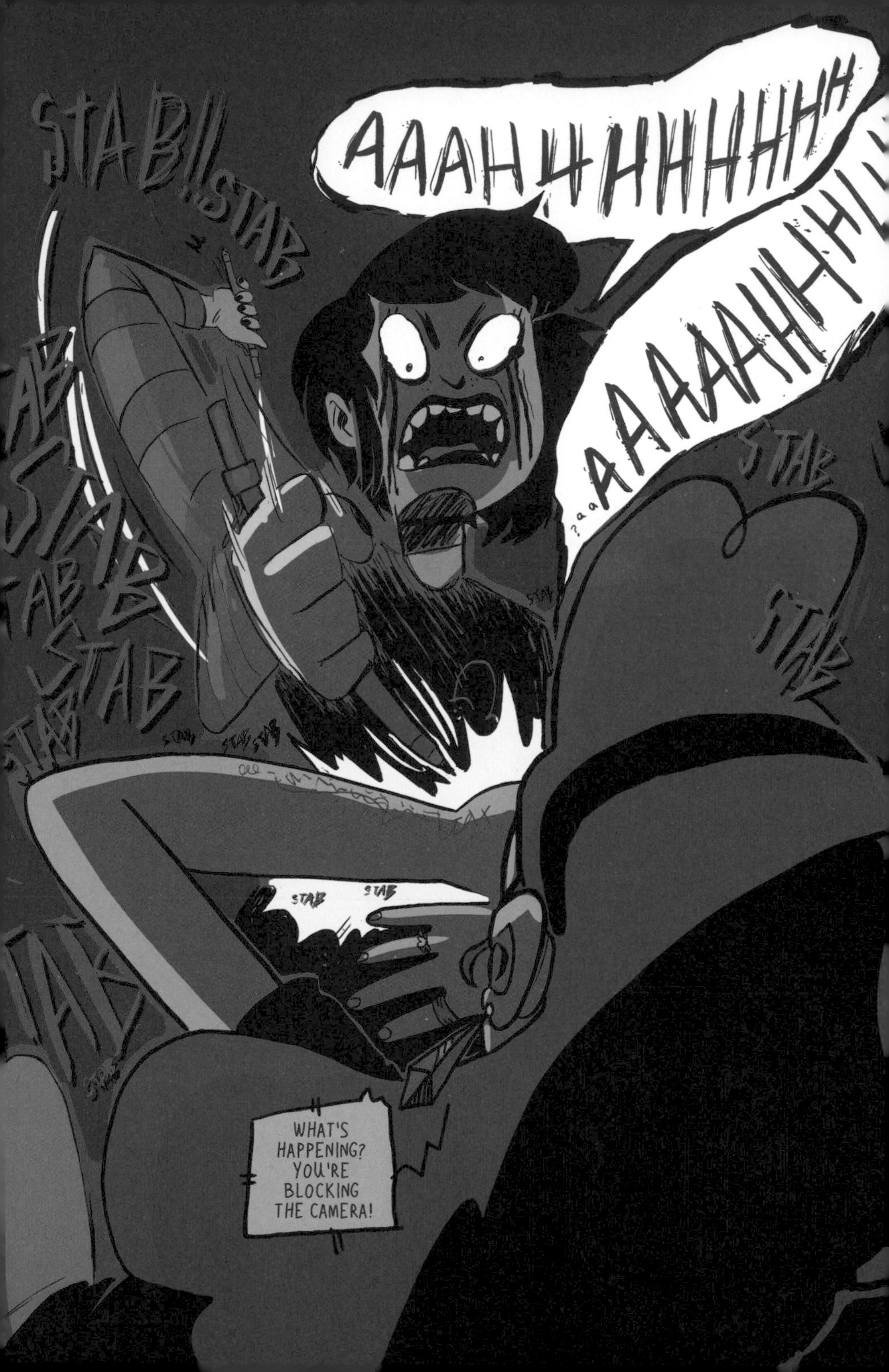
STAB!! STAB!! STAB
AAAHHHHHHH
AAAAAHHHH
STAB STAB STAB STAB STAB STAB
STAB STAB
WHAT'S HAPPENING? YOU'RE BLOCKING THE CAMERA!

179

180

182

184

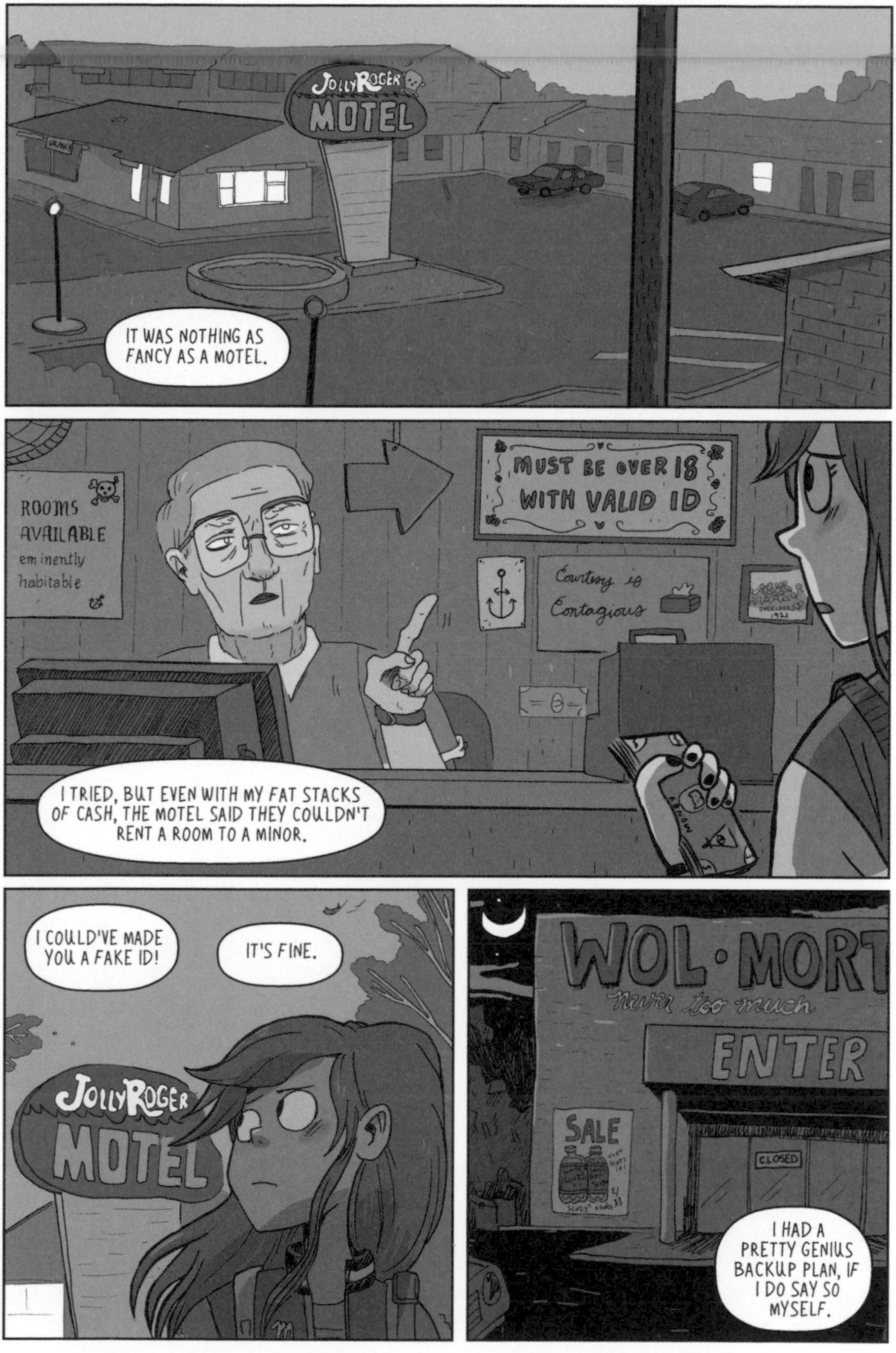

JOLLY ROGER
MOTEL
IT WAS NOTHING AS FANCY AS A MOTEL.
ROOMS AVAILABLE
eminently habitable
MUST BE OVER 18 WITH VALID ID
Courtesy is Contagious
I TRIED, BUT EVEN WITH MY FAT STACKS OF CASH, THE MOTEL SAID THEY COULDN'T RENT A ROOM TO A MINOR.
I COULD'VE MADE YOU A FAKE ID!
IT'S FINE.
JOLLY ROGER
MOTEL
WOL·MORT
never too much
ENTER
SALE
CLOSED
I HAD A PRETTY GENIUS BACKUP PLAN, IF I DO SAY SO MYSELF.

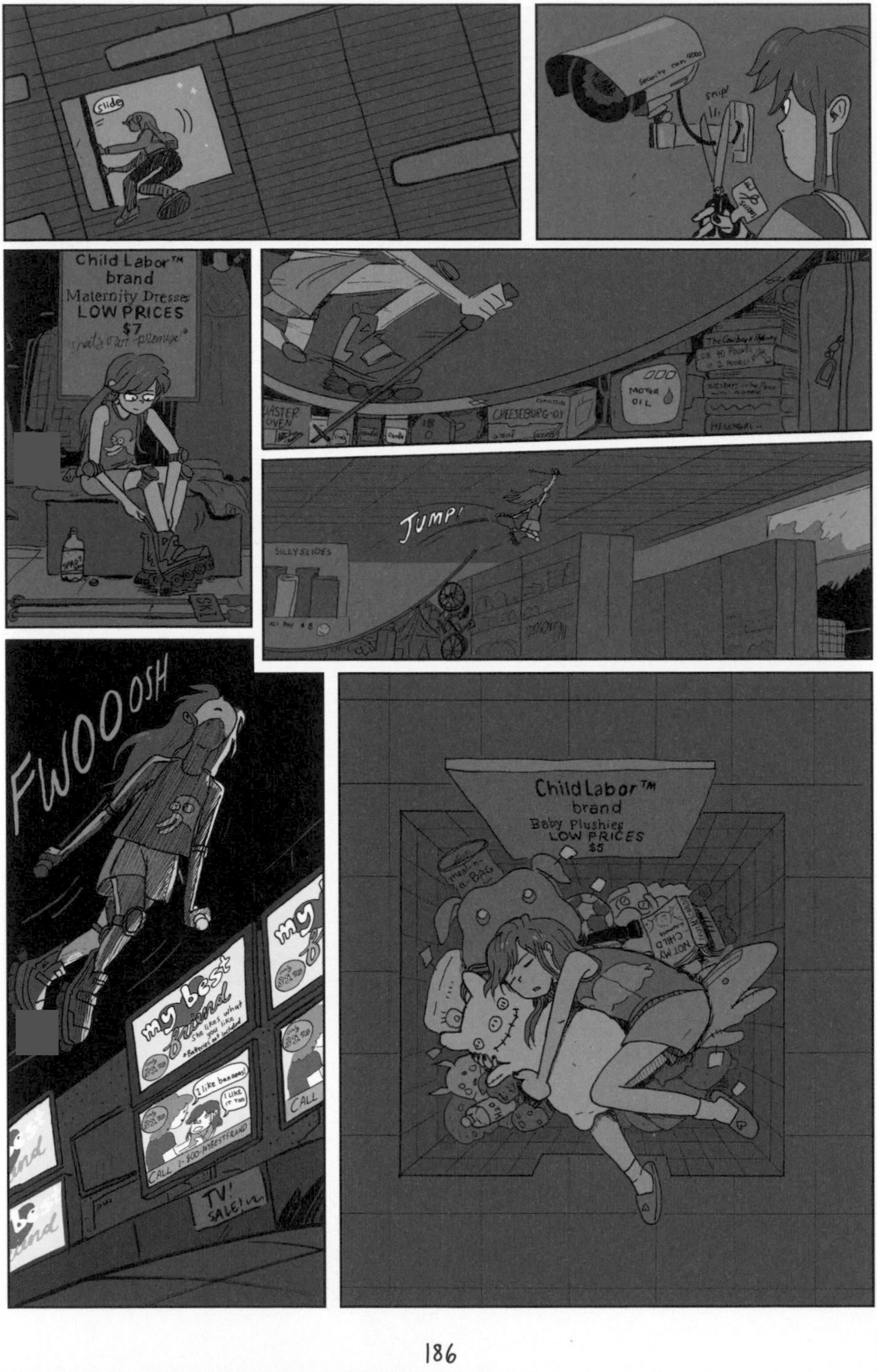

slide
snip!
Child Labor™
brand
Maternity Dresses
LOW PRICES
$7
The Cowboy's Highway
MOTOR OIL
CHEESEBURG-OS
JUMP!
SILLY SLIDES
FWOOOSH
my best friend
She likes what you like
*Batteries not included
I like bananas!
I LIKE IT TOO
TV! SALE!
Child Labor™
brand
Baby Plushies
LOW PRICES
$5
meal-in-a-BAG
NOT MY CHILD

THIS IS A **BOY-FREE** ZONE.

never mind...

TURN

NO, NO, HE'S COOL.

heh

it was no biggie

WHAT?

DRAMA

...WHO'S NICK MALONEY?

NO CLUE.

...YEAH, DURING LUNCH LAST WEEK. WE ALL GOT SENT TO THE OFFICE.

TOM BEAT UP **NICK MALONEY** FOR ME.

FIRST LUNCH WAVE IS **SO** MUCH COOLER THAN SECOND LUNCH WAVE.

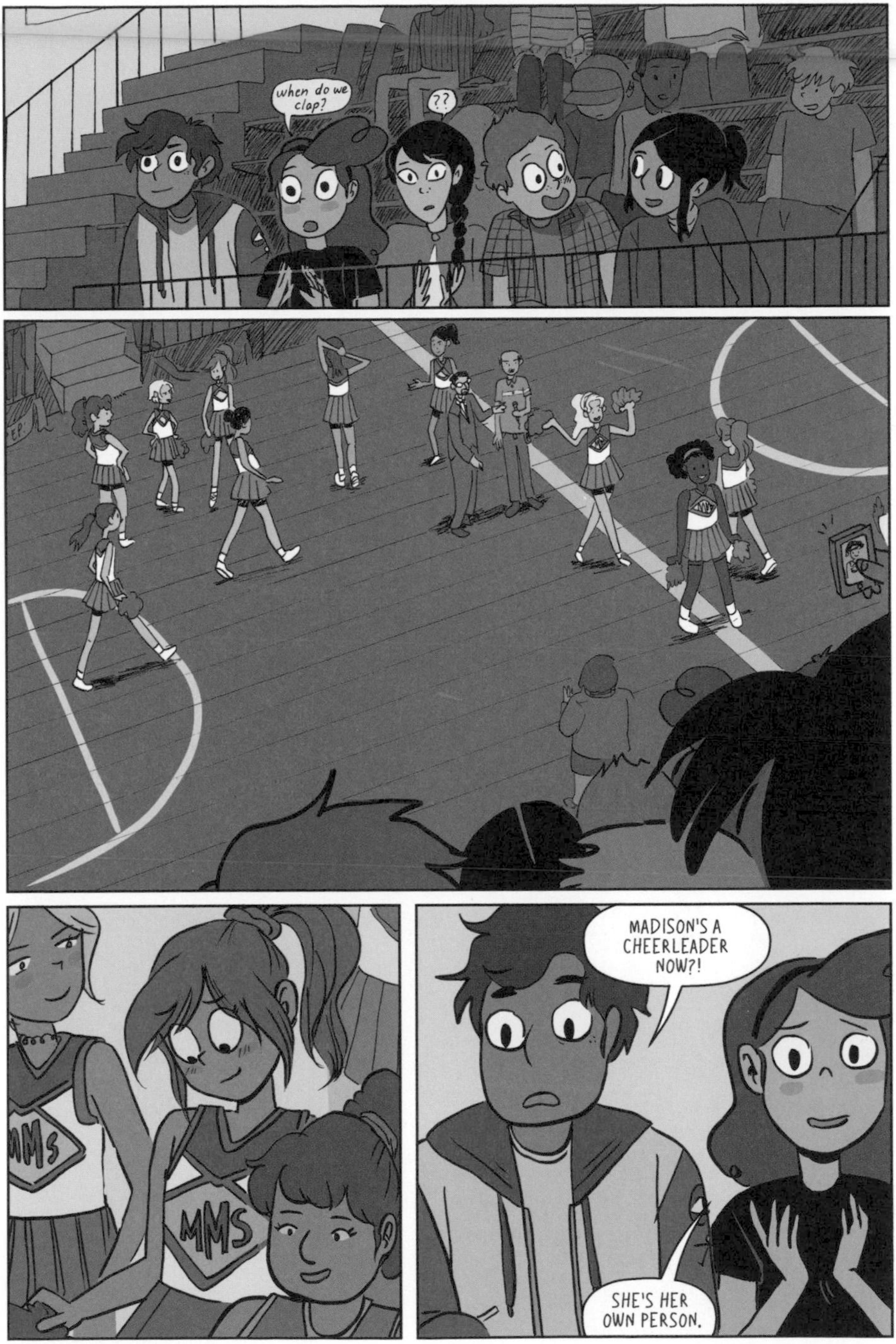
when do we clap?
??
MADISON'S A CHEERLEADER NOW?!
SHE'S HER OWN PERSON.

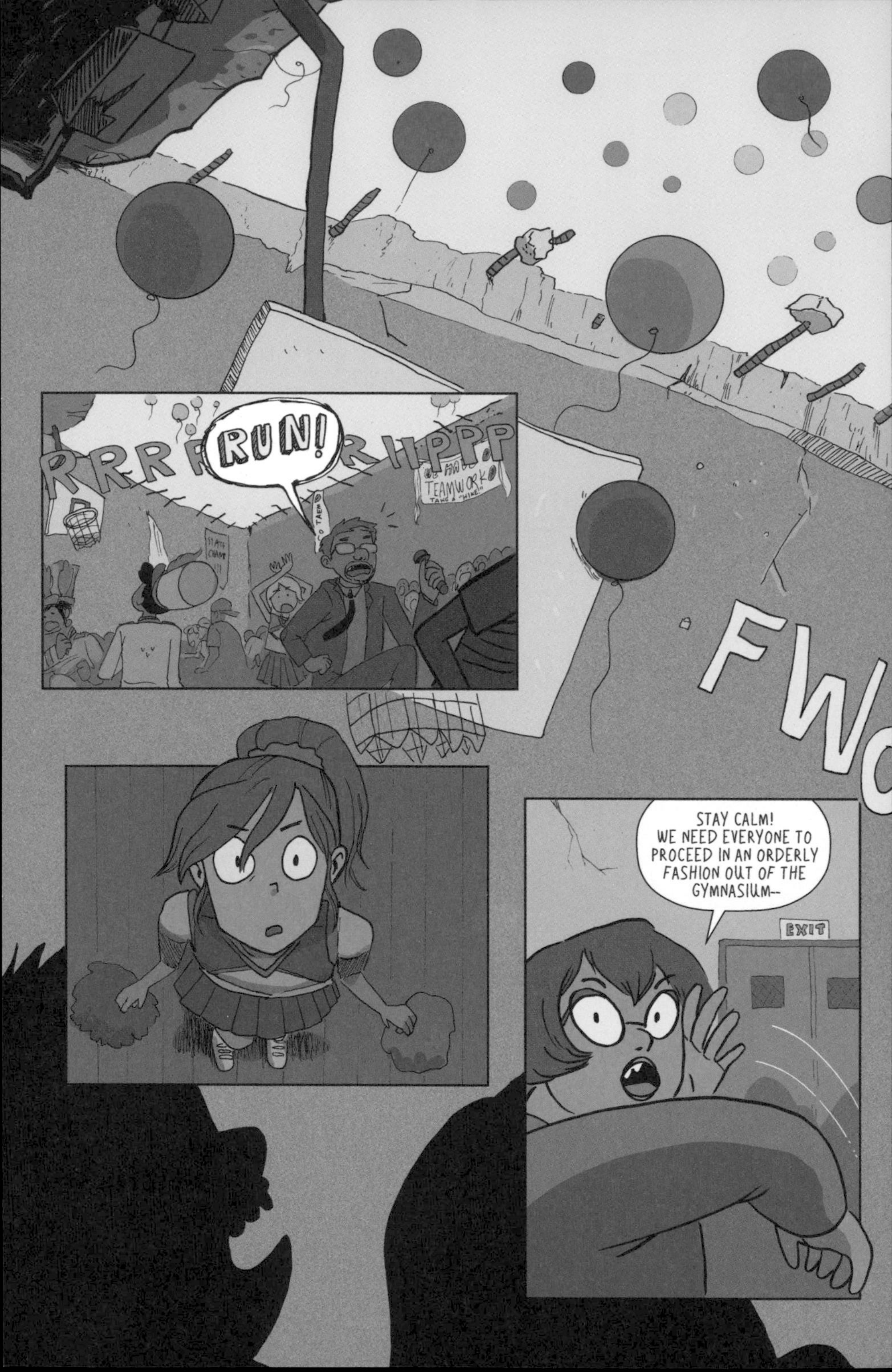
RRRR
RUN!
RIIPPPP
TEAMWORK
FWO
STAY CALM!
WE NEED EVERYONE TO PROCEED IN AN ORDERLY FASHION OUT OF THE GYMNASIUM--
EXIT

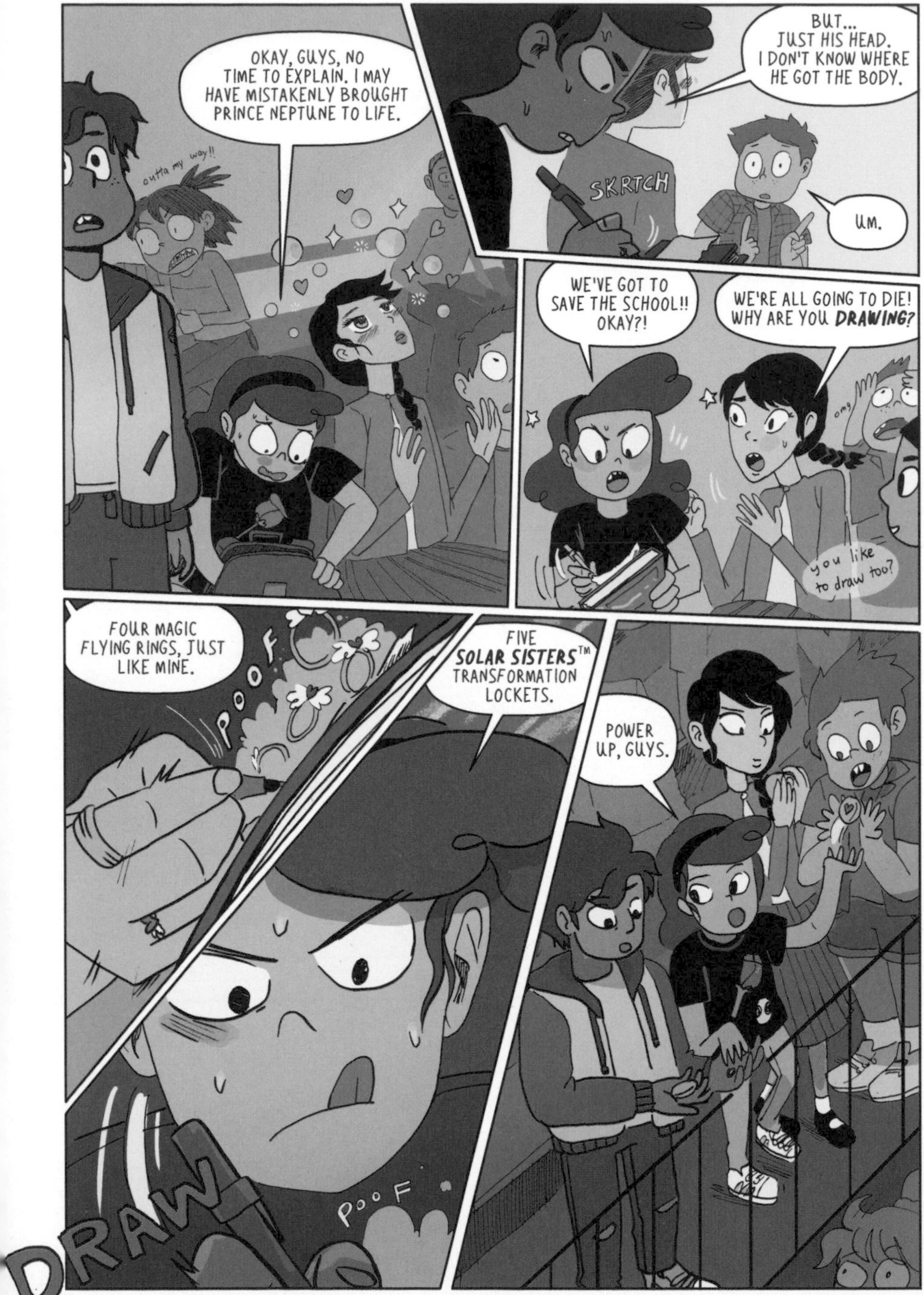
OKAY, GUYS, NO TIME TO EXPLAIN. I MAY HAVE MISTAKENLY BROUGHT PRINCE NEPTUNE TO LIFE.
outta my way!!
BUT... JUST HIS HEAD. I DON'T KNOW WHERE HE GOT THE BODY.
SKRTCH
UM.
WE'VE GOT TO SAVE THE SCHOOL!! OKAY?!
WE'RE ALL GOING TO DIE! WHY ARE YOU DRAWING?
omg
you like to draw too?
FOUR MAGIC FLYING RINGS, JUST LIKE MINE.
POOF
FIVE SOLAR SISTERS™ TRANSFORMATION LOCKETS.
DRAW
POOF
POWER UP, GUYS.

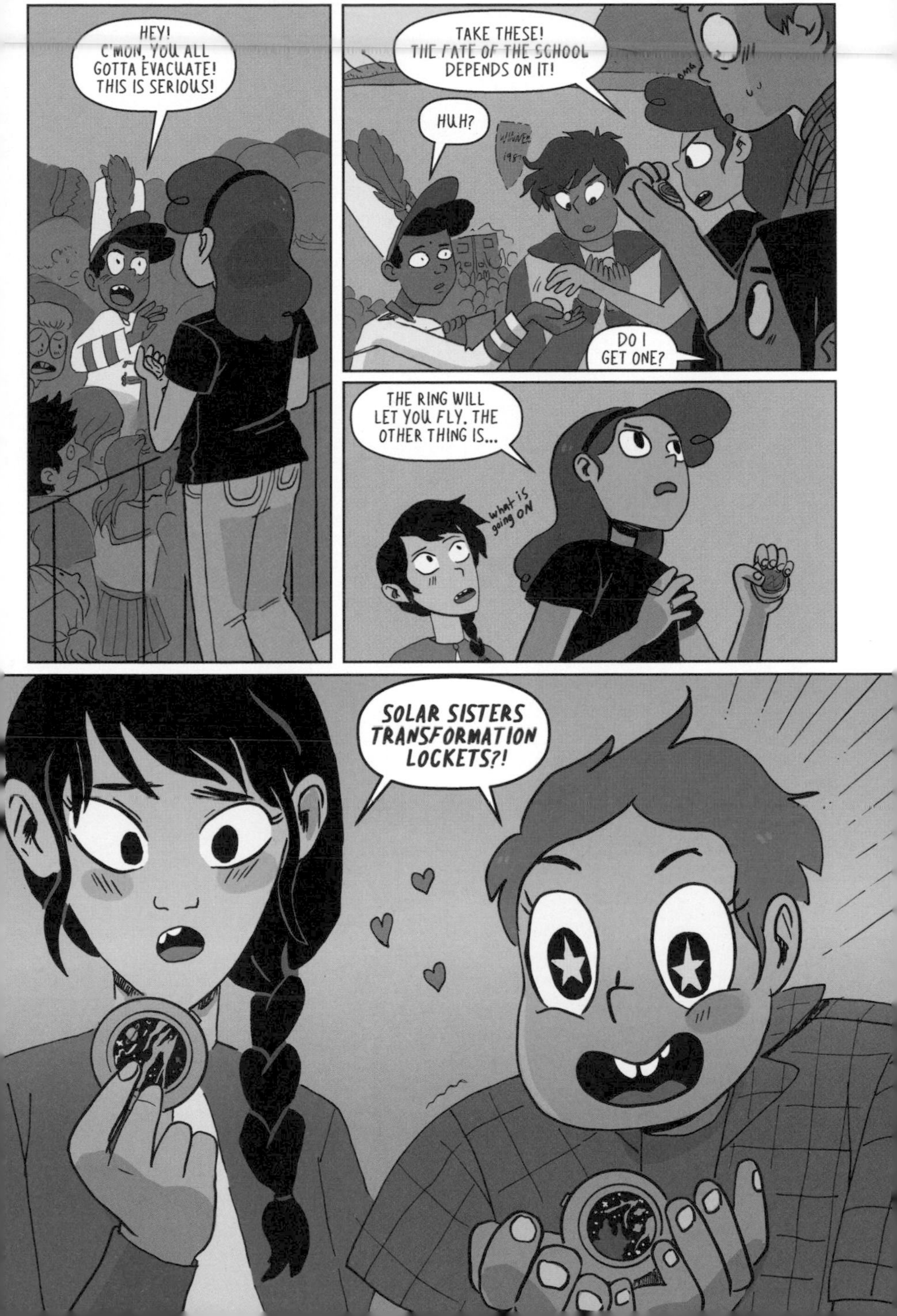
HEY!
C'MON, YOU ALL
GOTTA EVACUATE!
THIS IS SERIOUS!
TAKE THESE!
THE FATE OF THE SCHOOL
DEPENDS ON IT!
OMG
HUH?
DO I
GET ONE?
THE RING WILL
LET YOU *FLY*. THE
OTHER THING IS...
what is
going ON
SOLAR SISTERS
TRANSFORMATION
LOCKETS?!

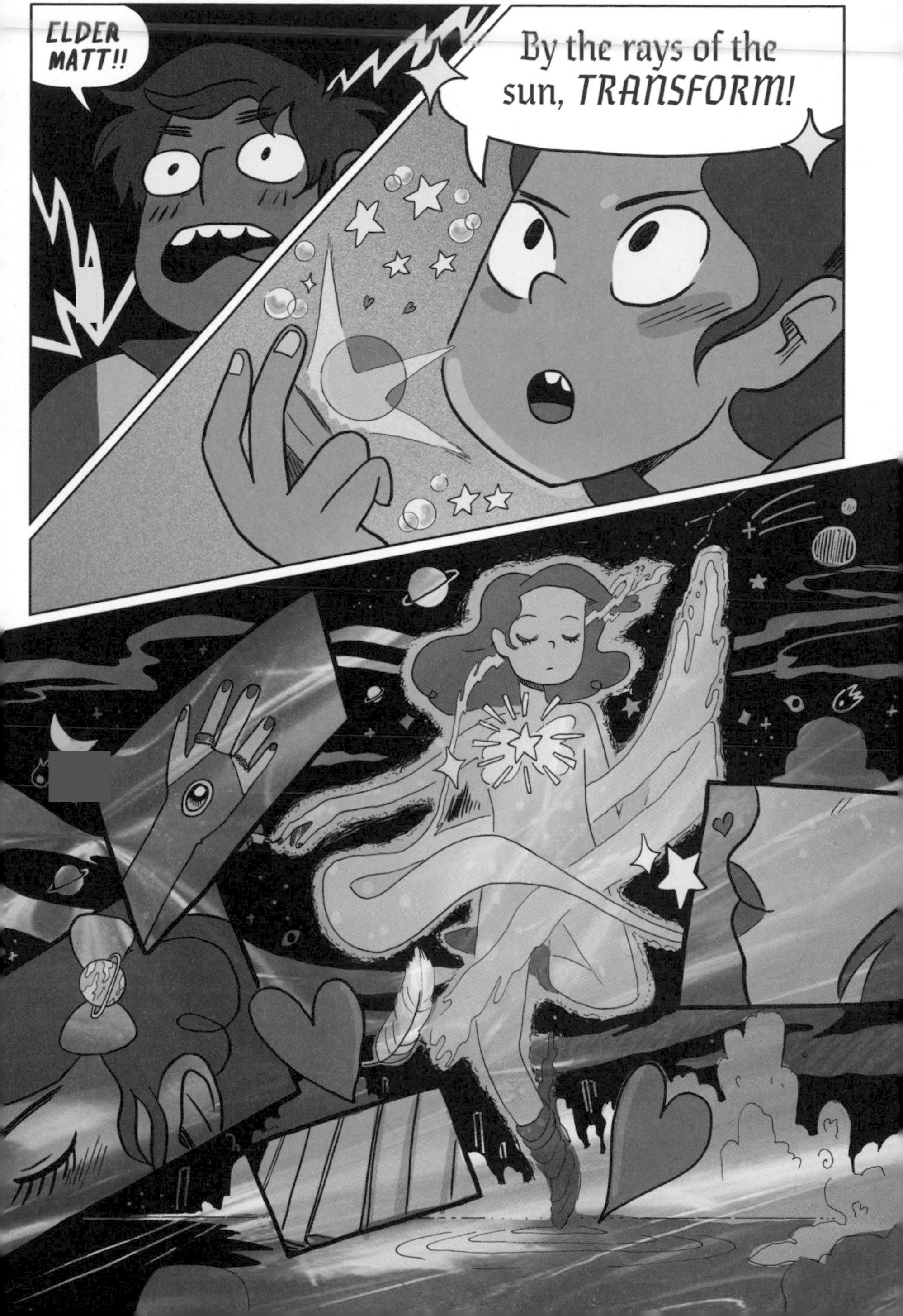
ELDER MATT!!
By the rays of the sun, TRANSFORM!

FWOOO

Lengthens

Princess Form

FWOO

HOW MANY MAKEOVERS DOES DANY NEED?!

Dany's evolving!!

THAT'S BETTER.

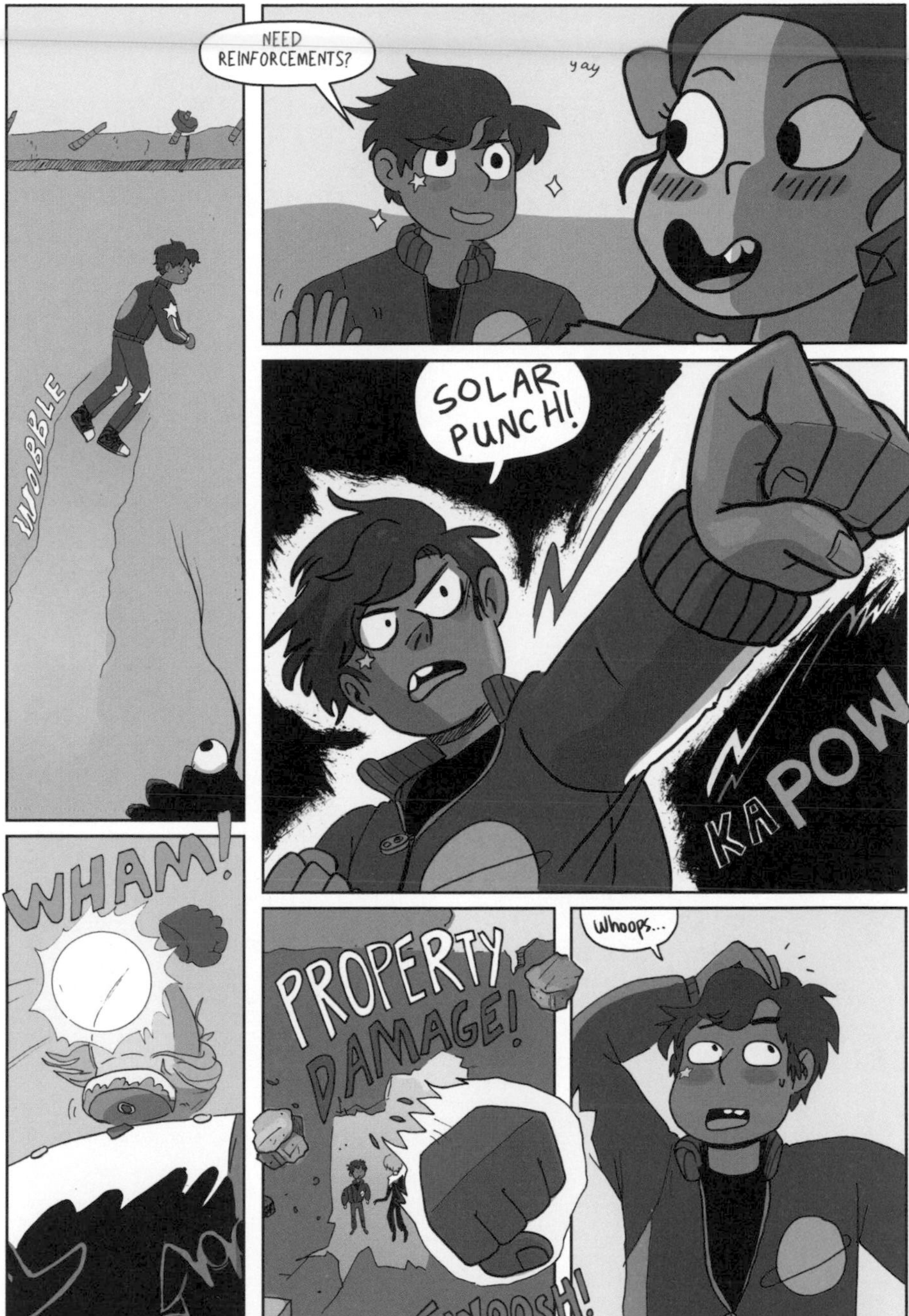
WOBBLE
NEED REINFORCEMENTS?
yay
SOLAR PUNCH!
KAPOW
WHAM!
PROPERTY DAMAGE!
FWOOSH!
Whoops...

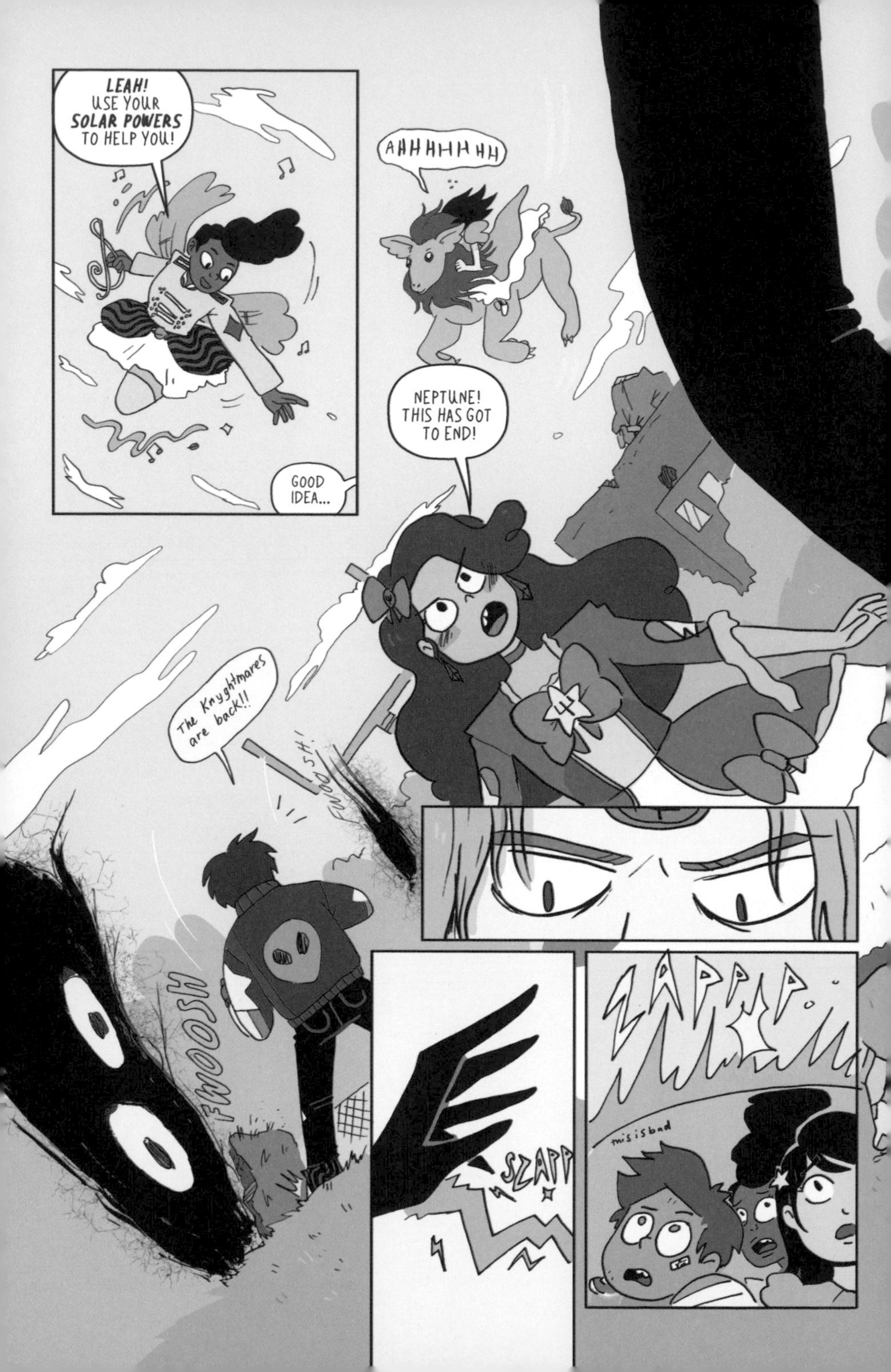
LEAH! USE YOUR SOLAR POWERS TO HELP YOU!
GOOD IDEA...
AHHHHHHH
NEPTUNE! THIS HAS GOT TO END!
The Knyghtmares are back!!
FWOOSH!
FWOOOSH
ZAPPP
SLAPP
this is bad

222

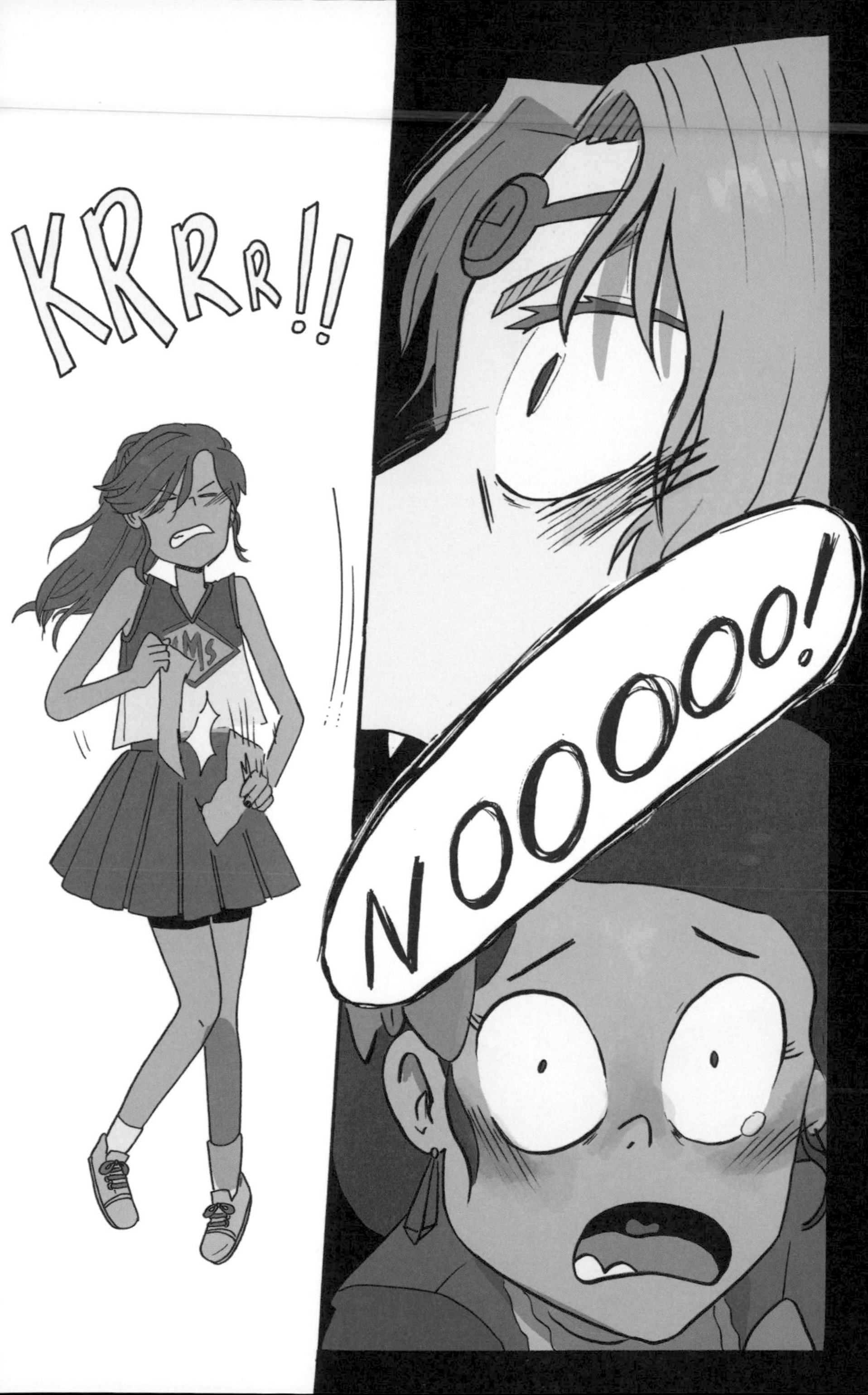
KRRR!!
NOOOOOOO!

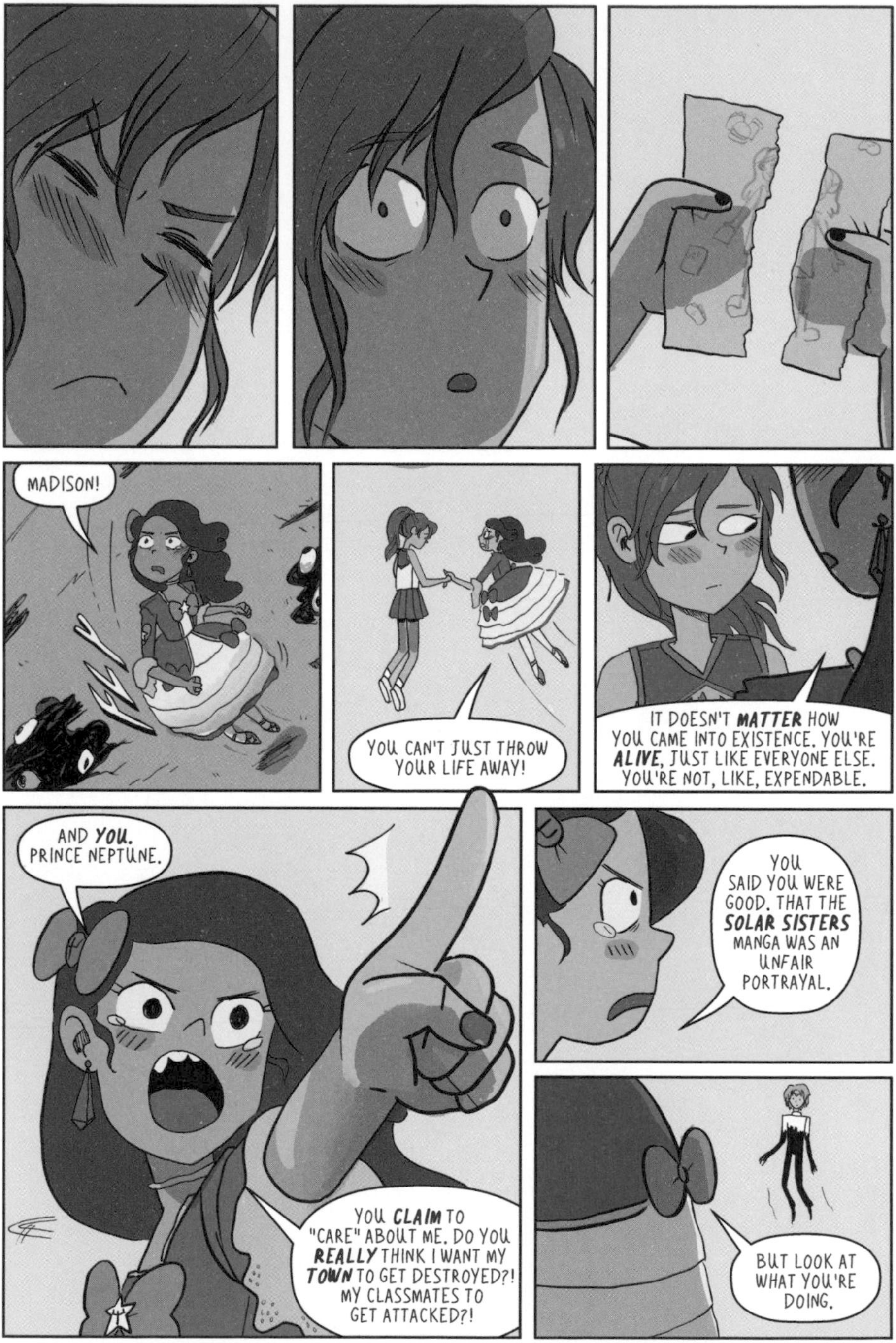
MADISON!
YOU CAN'T JUST THROW YOUR LIFE AWAY!
IT DOESN'T MATTER HOW YOU CAME INTO EXISTENCE. YOU'RE ALIVE, JUST LIKE EVERYONE ELSE. YOU'RE NOT, LIKE, EXPENDABLE.
AND YOU. PRINCE NEPTUNE.
YOU CLAIM TO "CARE" ABOUT ME. DO YOU REALLY THINK I WANT MY TOWN TO GET DESTROYED?! MY CLASSMATES TO GET ATTACKED?!
YOU SAID YOU WERE GOOD. THAT THE SOLAR SISTERS MANGA WAS AN UNFAIR PORTRAYAL.
BUT LOOK AT WHAT YOU'RE DOING.

YOU NEED A KINGDOM—

NO ONE *HAS* KINGDOMS HERE.

IT'S 'MURICA!

WE HAVE ELECTED OFFICIALS HERE. IT'S NOT PERFECT, BUT AT LEAST WE GET TO TRY AGAIN EVERY FEW YEARS.

I DON'T WANT TO BE A PRINCESS.

I'LL BE A PRINCESS!

hee hee

THEN WHY DID YOU EVEN BRING ME INTO EXISTENCE?

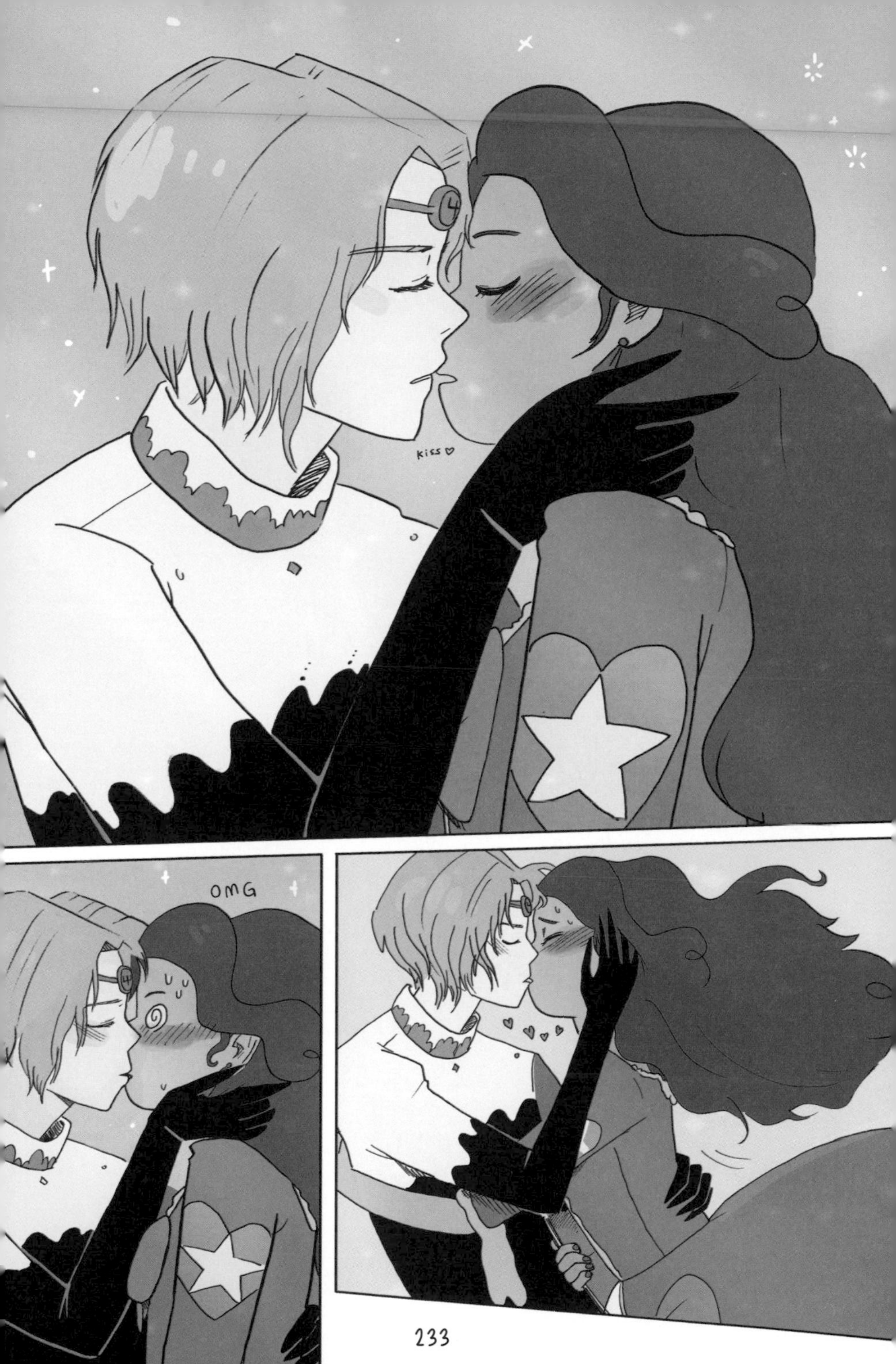
kiss ♡
OMG

234

239

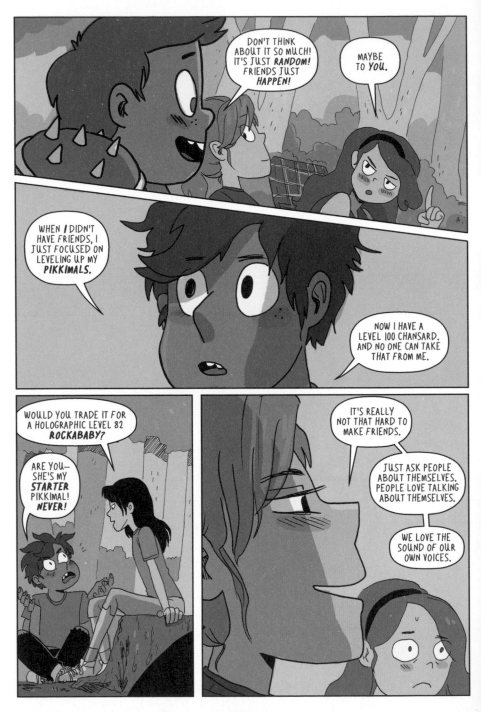

250

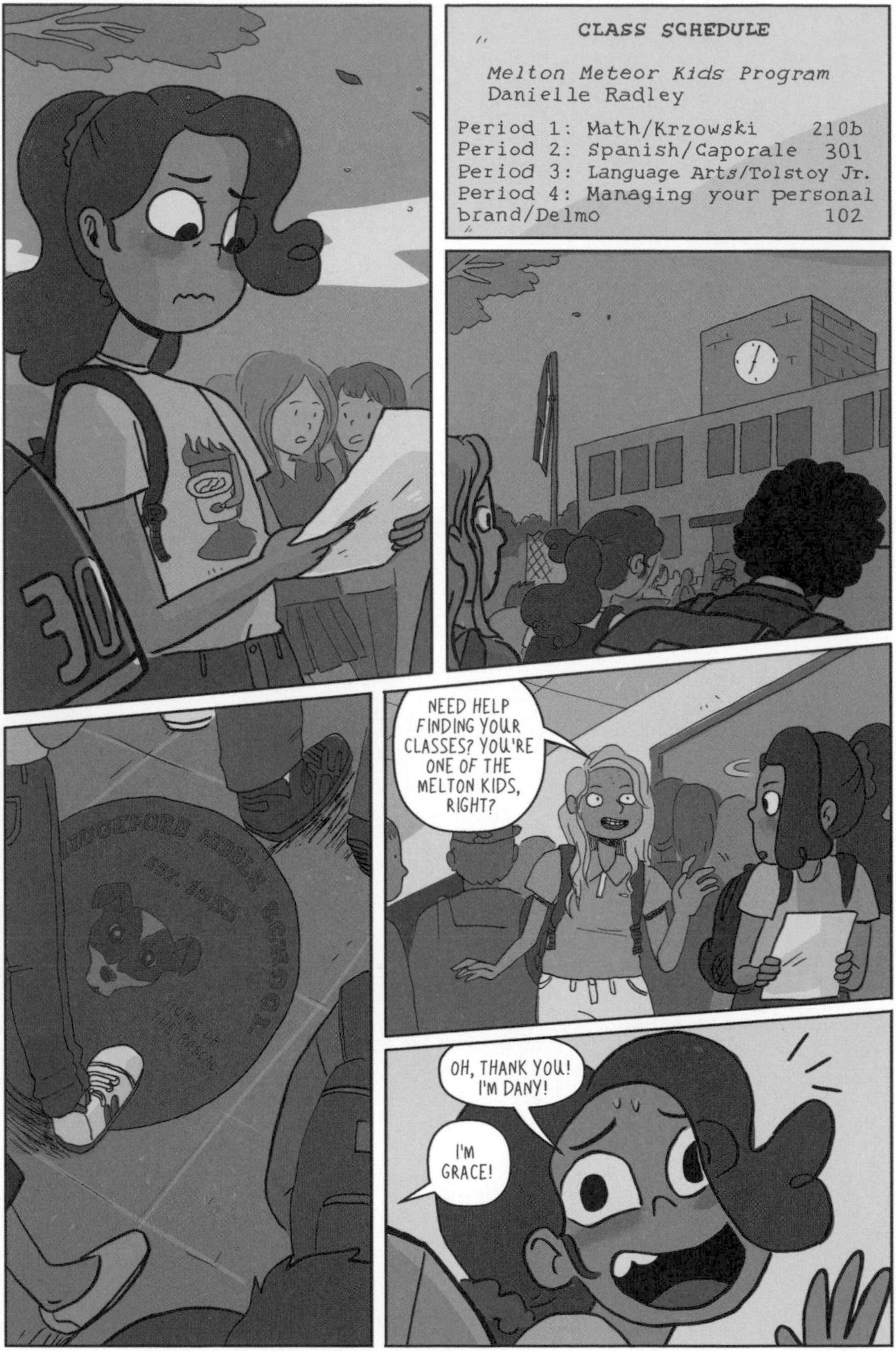
CLASS SCHEDULE
Melton Meteor Kids Program
Danielle Radley
Period 1: Math/Krzowski 210b
Period 2: Spanish/Caporale 301
Period 3: Language Arts/Tolstoy Jr.
Period 4: Managing your personal brand/Delmo 102
NEED HELP FINDING YOUR CLASSES? YOU'RE ONE OF THE MELTON KIDS, RIGHT?
OH, THANK YOU! I'M DANY!
I'M GRACE!

SQUEEE!

OiNK OiNK

NICK MALONEY? IS THAT YOU?!

255

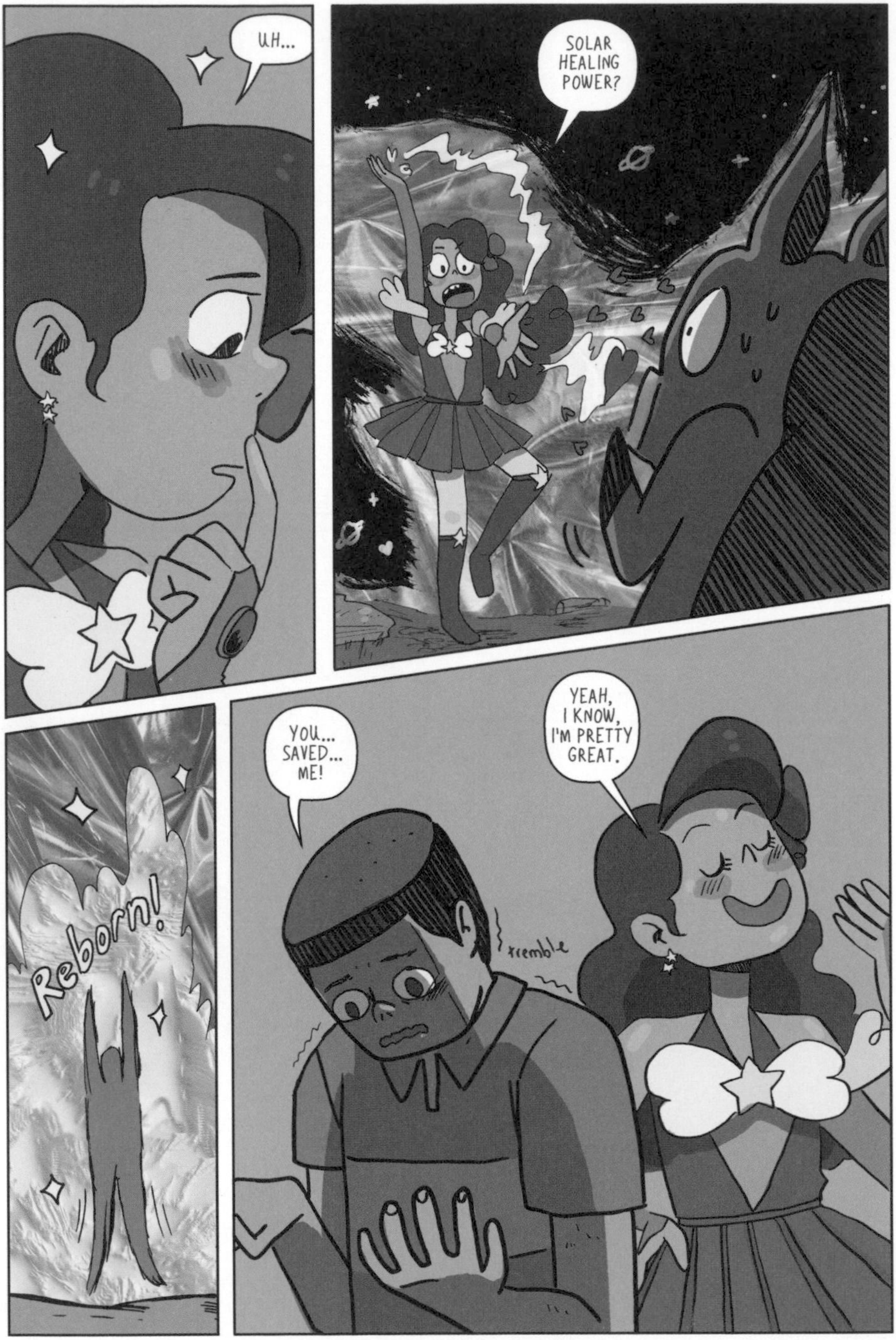
UH...
SOLAR HEALING POWER?
Reborn!
YOU... SAVED... ME!
YEAH, I KNOW, I'M PRETTY GREAT.
tremble

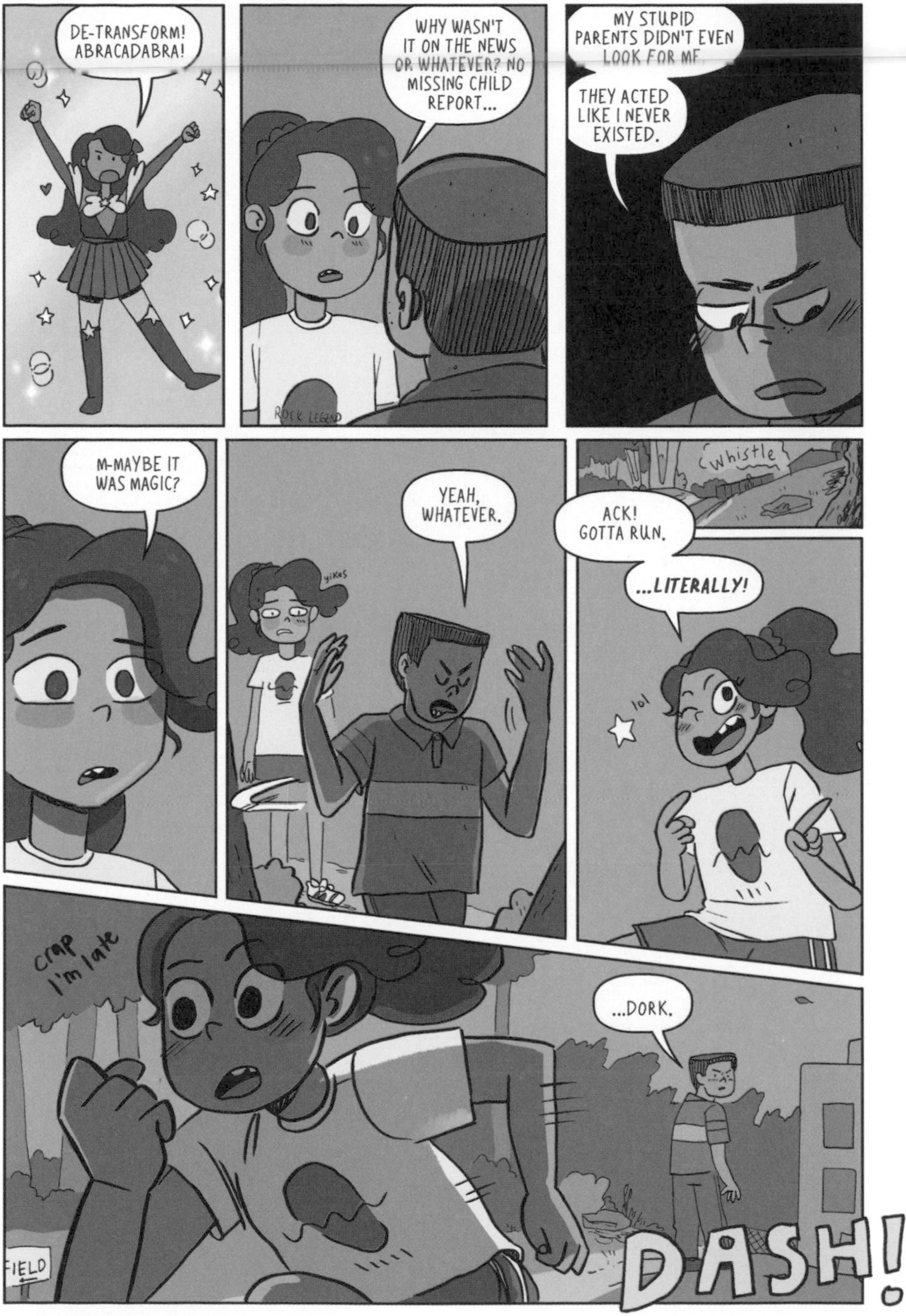
DE-TRANSFORM! ABRACADABRA!
WHY WASN'T IT ON THE NEWS OR WHATEVER? NO MISSING CHILD REPORT...
ROCK LEGEND
MY STUPID PARENTS DIDN'T EVEN LOOK FOR ME.
THEY ACTED LIKE I NEVER EXISTED.
M-MAYBE IT WAS MAGIC?
YEAH, WHATEVER.
yikes
whistle
ACK! GOTTA RUN.
...LITERALLY!
lol
crap I'm late
...DORK.
FIELD
DASH!

259

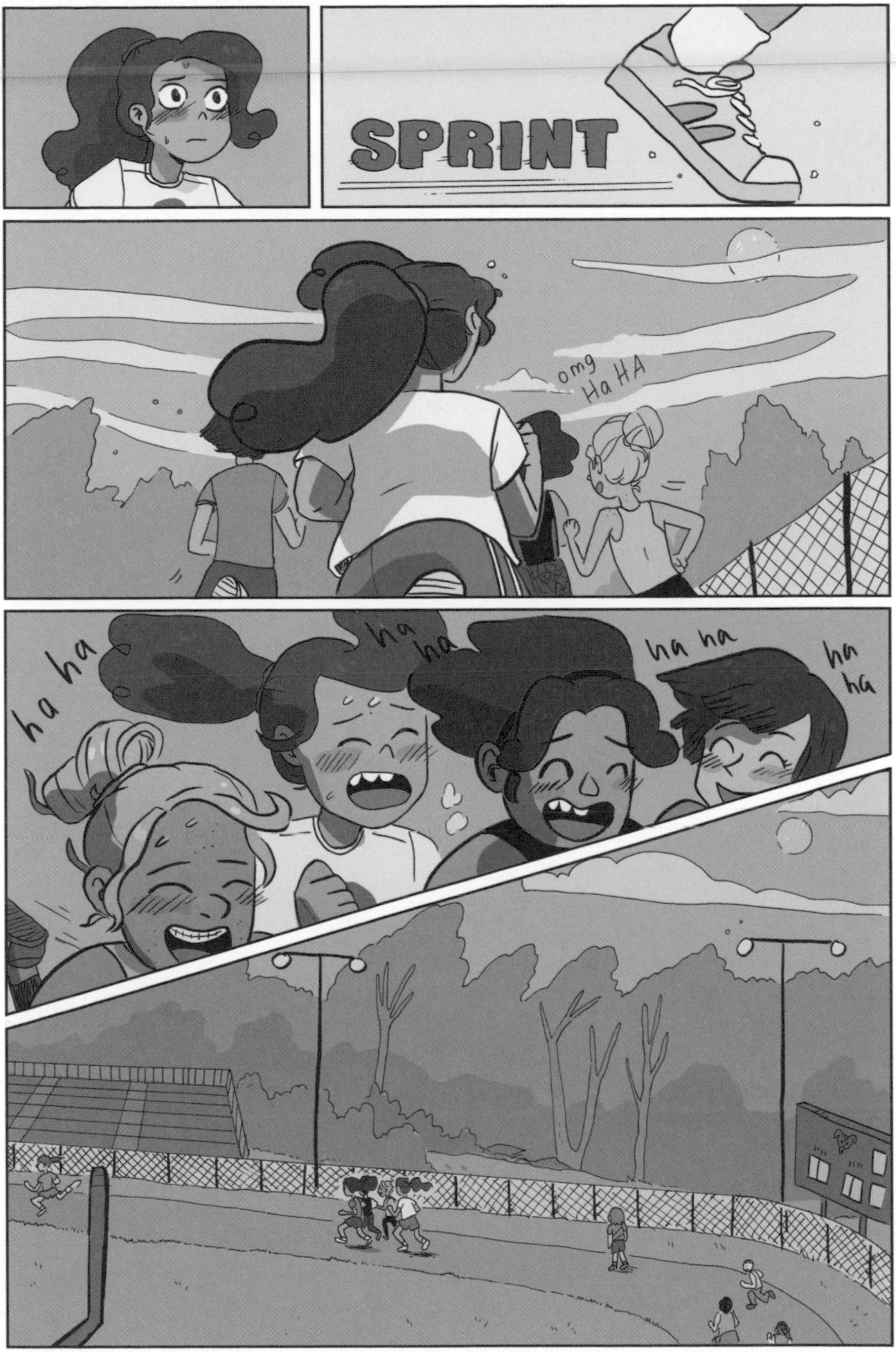
SPRINT
omg
Ha HA
ha ha
ha ha
ha ha
ha ha

Hi, everyone! Thanks for reading

MAKiNG FRiENDS

Here are some extra gags that didn't make it into the book.

Enjoy!

"...Well, it works on MY world..."

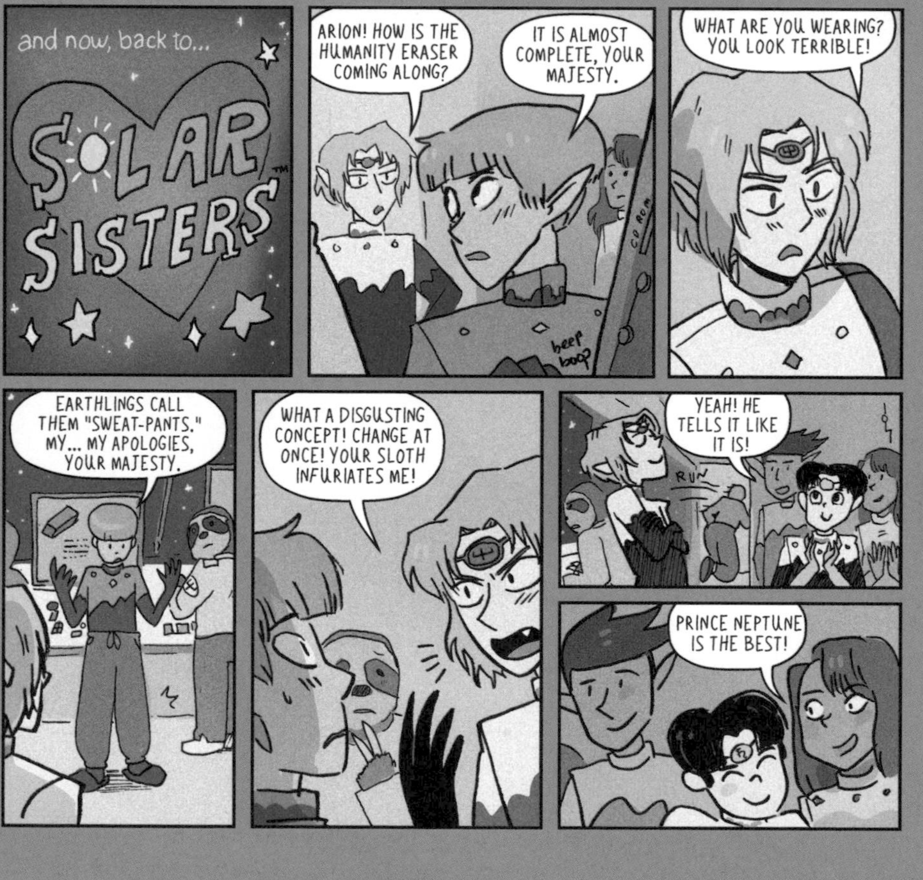
and now, back to...
SOLAR SISTERS™
ARION! HOW IS THE HUMANITY ERASER COMING ALONG?
IT IS ALMOST COMPLETE, YOUR MAJESTY.
beep boop
WHAT ARE YOU WEARING? YOU LOOK TERRIBLE!
EARTHLINGS CALL THEM "SWEAT-PANTS." MY... MY APOLOGIES, YOUR MAJESTY.
WHAT A DISGUSTING CONCEPT! CHANGE AT ONCE! YOUR SLOTH INFURIATES ME!
YEAH! HE TELLS IT LIKE IT IS!
PRINCE NEPTUNE IS THE BEST!

Locker Girl

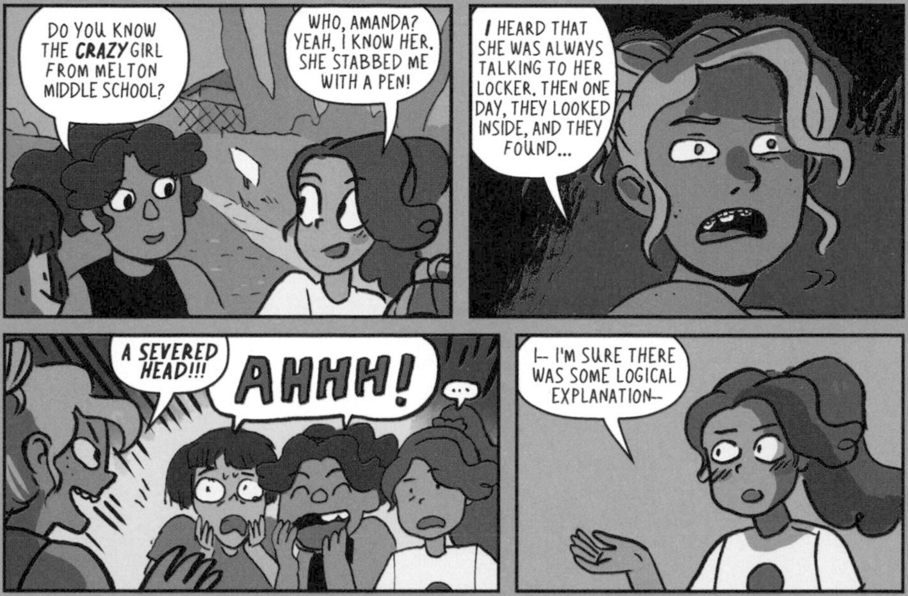
DO YOU KNOW THE CRAZY GIRL FROM MELTON MIDDLE SCHOOL?
WHO, AMANDA? YEAH, I KNOW HER. SHE STABBED ME WITH A PEN!
I HEARD THAT SHE WAS ALWAYS TALKING TO HER LOCKER. THEN ONE DAY, THEY LOOKED INSIDE, AND THEY FOUND...
A SEVERED HEAD!!!
AHHH!
...
I– I'M SURE THERE WAS SOME LOGICAL EXPLANATION–

Sorry, Rhonda

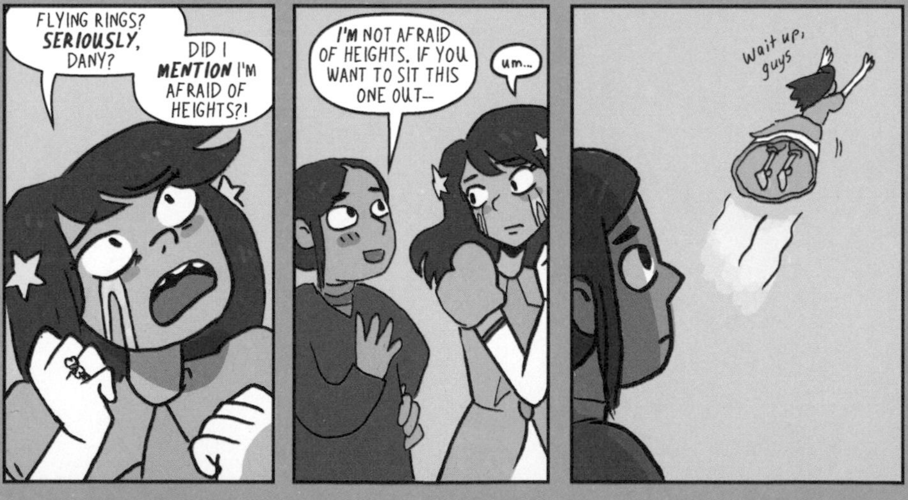
FLYING RINGS? SERIOUSLY, DANY?
DID I MENTION I'M AFRAID OF HEIGHTS?!
I'M NOT AFRAID OF HEIGHTS. IF YOU WANT TO SIT THIS ONE OUT–
um...
wait up, guys

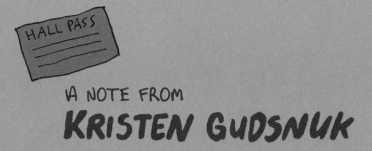

A NOTE FROM
KRISTEN GUDSNUK

The germ of MAKING FRIENDS was planted when I was in elementary school. My class read a Chinese folktale, THE MAGIC PAINTBRUSH, about an artist who gets a paintbrush that makes anything she draws come to life. She uses it to help people, but child-me was a lot more captivated by the concept of having anything I could draw—anything I could imagine!—materialize before my eyes. I would doodle stacks of money and fantastical inventions in the margins of my notebooks, preparing for the off chance I might get a magic paintbrush of my own. I guess in a way, comics ended up being my magic paintbrush, which is why I'm so glad to have shared this little world with you.

KRISTEN GUDSNUK

was born in suburbia, didn't go to art school, and now lives in Queens, New York, with her boyfriend and her dog. She is the creator of the comic series Henchgirl as well as the illustrator of the VIP series by Jen Calonita.

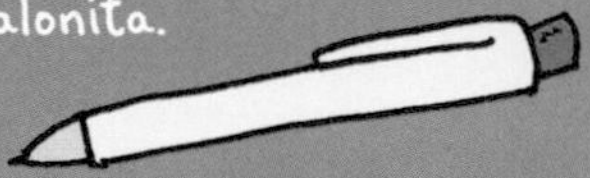